On S

Stephen-Paul Martin is North America's foremost master of the short story. His fiction probes center after elusive center, until we see that it's not just the subject that's changing, but also our sense of what it means for a story to have a subject.

Vernon Frazer, on *Changing the Subject*

Stephen-Paul Martin has got to be one of the finest and most interesting short fiction writers America has produced within the last few decades. He has been publishing in various modes of language-creation for years, and is a singular spark among conventional and lightless writing. Martin's stories are hilarious, philosophically rich, absorbing, and just plain fun. A selected stories volume from him would be an absolute killer. He is at the forefront of American storytellers.

Jefferson Hanson, *Rain Taxi*

Exceedingly clever and mesmerizing, Stephen-Paul Martin proves himself a master of both his own invented form and the flawless style with which he crafts it. How marvelous to see the story so reinvented and reinvigorated!

A.D. Jameson, review of *Changing the Subject* in *The Review of Contemporary Fiction*

Stephen-Paul Martin's stories are as 'true' as they are wildly comic and horrifying. They begin with ordinary situations and turn the natural on its head. Martin's seeming cool is actually a carefully channeled passion: a profoundly political writer, he plays on myth, legend, press release, and earlier fiction to show us what it is we really are.

Marjorie Perloff, on *Not Quite Fiction*

Martin's stories begin in safe, well-lighted rooms but by the end we find ourselves in strange darkened corridors. Such is the power of imagination on display in these texts that even for readers trained to expect the unexpected Martin's writing still manages to move in consistently surprising directions. Martin's stories wrench, or in some cases, completely upend, the form of the short story.

Matthew Kirkpatrick, *The American Book Review*

Martin's writing weaves a tight narrative with no room for error or escape. It's quick. It's sharp. It doesn't wait for you to catch up. It's dizzying with the constriction of air, and much like in erotic asphyxiation, you're turned on and want more. Moving from microcosm to macrocosm, Martin's prose questions the validity of storytelling.

Adrian Belmes, *Free-Form Review*

What an astonishing book! Beautiful, original, with delicious surprises lurking at the heart of sentences.

Eugene Lim, on *The Possibility of Music*, in *Goodreads*

The stories in *Changing the Subject* ask of the reader a commitment to uncertainty, an emphatic intelligence. They are as entertaining as they are gruelling, lifting shifting simulacra to the operational philsophies of junk food, animal rights, mass media, terrorism, and academia, all the while testing the vaulting of the language itself for unexpected seams. Though the stories make use of syntactical or symbolic repetitions, they are also powerfully digressive, hallucinatory. This book is up to more than literary parlor tricks. Its phenomenological exploits assemble a social commentary that eschews logical argument. It culls insight from annihilation; anti-authoritarian to the hilt and then some, its stories are strong enough to defy themselves. They ply the absurdity of the absurd. Saying no and saying it again, inviting us to reconsider history and possibility from a deep-zero perspective, from the blind eye of catastrophe.

Peter Moysaenko, *Bomb*

Marked by subversive wit and philosophical insight, Martin's prose is ultimately musical in construction, like a fugue for the ruin of time.

Andrew Joron, on *Changing the Subject*

It's fascinating to see how Stephen-Paul Martin moves from one fictional riff to another, playing fiction off history and history off fiction in one humorous, absurd, and serious tale after another. This is an ambitious and original effort.

Kirkus review of *The Ace of Lightning*

Entering Stephen-Paul Martin's witty contemporary monologues, the reader unravels great questions: does a person anticipate his or her own actions, as one word in a sentence anticipates the next? Or is an event an explosion of contingencies that arrive fully integrated?

Fanny Howe, on *The Possibility of Music*

Stephen-Paul Martin writes of a world where speculation and emotion, memory and duration, violence and tenderness fuse and split apart in the time it takes for a smile to change into a look of frozen terror. With only the reassurance of laughter to guide you, read Martin's fiction or risk discovering that a literary revolution is taking place, no one has told you, and your mind is the central character.

Nick Piombino, on *Fear & Philosophy*

Stephen-Paul Martin's stories reproduce the velocity with which we're hurtled through mystified public/private spaces, blindsided by the bizarre surplus of the marketed reality that bombards us; at the same time, the incongruous elements are turned into shock effects that interfere with the conventionally mediated flow of things, opening the high-speed narrative space to a critical meditation on repressed domains of culture and politics. Martin's work is a stunning invention of a hybrid genre capable of making our postmodern moment available to the senses and intelligence: an art that combines the pleasures of storytelling and the deconstructive Illuminations of discourse theory in a continuously surprising virtuoso performance.

Marc Kaminsky, on *The Gothic Twilight*

Other Books of Fiction by Stephen-Paul Martin

The Flood (1991)

The Gothic Twilight (1992)

Fear & Philosophy (1994)

Undeserved Reputations (1995)

Not Quite Fiction (1997)

Instead of Confusion (2002)

The Possibility of Music (2007)

Changing the Subject (2010)

The Ace of Lightning (2017)

TwentyTwenty

Stephen-Paul Martin

SPUYTEN DUYVIL
NEW YORK CITY

Acknowledgements

Some of these stories have appeared in *Antonym*, *Fiction International*, and *The Ground Up*. Thanks to the editors for supporting my work.

ISBN 978-1-959556-20-6 pbk
ISBN 978-1-959556-50-3 hdc.

Library of Congress Cataloging-in-Publication Data

Names: Martin, Stephen-Paul, author.
Title: Twentytwenty / Stephen-Paul Martin.
Description: New York : Spuyten Duyvil, [2023]
Identifiers: LCCN 2023000421 | ISBN 9781959556206 (paperback)
Subjects: LCGFT: Novels.
Classification: LCC PS3563.A7292 T94 2023 | DDC 813/.54--dc23/eng/20230113
LC record available at https://lccn.loc.gov/2023000421

CONTENTS

MOVIE

I met Colette in a microbiology class, then later in a phenomenology seminar. She was brilliant both times, even brighter than the professors, and intelligence like hers gets me really turned on. Since then we've had great conversations in coffee shops, and I get the feeling she thinks I'm a pretty smart guy. Now I want Colette to have sex with me, and I'm not sure how to move forward. I don't want to be too assertive and ruin the friendship we already have, but I'm also thinking she might be expecting me to make the first move. When we talk, it's so exciting that I want to rip off my clothes and get down to business. I'm pretty sure she does too. But what if I'm wrong? What if she gets offended?

I decide to play it safe and ask if she wants to go to a movie, where I'm hoping we can start touching each other by sharing a bucket of popcorn. She looks eager to go, says yes without hesitation. Fortunately, a great movie is opening later this week. Everyone wants to see it. It's understood that we won't get a seat if we're not there well in advance. We get there five hours before showtime, and the line is already ten blocks long. But since I'm with Colette, I'm not upset that we'll have a long wait. And besides, the city lights up and down the block are beautiful. There's a cool breeze. Large white clouds are moving in the night sky over the buildings.

I say: I'm glad we're here, even though I don't like crowds.

Colette nods: Me neither. I hate waiting in line for a movie. It's so stupid. You stand there like a moron wasting your time, then the movie sucks.

Right. But this time I think we're going to see something different, not the usual thing.

Let's hope so. I mean, I've seen so many movies where they say you're going to have an incredible experience. They highlight all the big-name stars. They spew all the lame superlatives. But then you finally get in and the movie starts and it's the same dumb thing you've seen a hundred times before. Annoying soundtrack music, formulaic plot, theatrical acting.

I nod and smile: But this time I'm pretty sure that things will be different. So different that we'll need a better word than different.

It's a good sign that no one seems to know what it's about.

There's no way to know what it's about. Reviewers

weren't allowed to see the movie in advance. No one even knows who the film maker is.

Colette laughs: Really? That's incredible! So the absence of reviews made everyone want to be here?

Apparently. But I've heard that at least one reviewer wrote about the film anyway.

He reviewed the absence of reviews?

Yeah. He was really hostile and dismissive. He said that the film's director told critics to fuck off, in no uncertain terms. So of course that got people interested, even though the critic urged people to stay away and called the whole thing a cheap publicity stunt.

Cheap or not, it worked. Look at all the people waiting!

And they all have no idea what the film is about. It could be anything!

Colette hesitates, then says: I hope I don't sound like a snob, but if you're like me, you don't care what a film is about.

I nod: What it's about isn't really what it's about.

So we'll also need a better word than about.

Like what?

She smiles and shrugs and puts her hand on my wrist and says: I wouldn't know where to begin.

I smile and shrug and say: Let's begin right here.

I pull Colette close to me and kiss her fiercely. She returns the kiss with equal intensity. It goes on for twenty minutes. Our teeth click and our tongues are dancing and wrestling. People in line start clapping and cheering and whistling.

When we finally stop Colette says: Wow, that was great!

It really was. I was planning to wait until we got inside, but when you said you didn't know where to begin, I knew I could say let's begin right here, and follow it with a kiss.

The timing was perfect.

I like the way she looks. She looks at me like she likes the way I look. Now she's pushing up against me, pushing me into the storefront behind me, a place that sells used books and vinyl records. For a second it's like she's about to push me right through the display window, and I'm thinking how cool it would be to be kissing and falling back through shattering glass, tumbling into the store with Colette on top of me, with all the people inside looking shocked and amused.

I've never had so much fun waiting in line before. I'm really glad I decided to ask Colette out. I like her more than ever now. She looks like she feels the same way.

I say: Wow! You really know how to kiss. You're so fucking good with your tongue!

She puts her mouth on my ear and says: I want you to lick my nipples.

We better wait until we're inside and it's dark and no one can see.

Yeah, if you lick my nipples out here we might get in trouble.

I wonder what the penalty is.

Colette shrugs: I'm not sure. But they'd probably put us in a car and take us somewhere and then we'd lose our place in line.

Would they use handcuffs?

Only if we fought back or told them to fuck off.

Maybe if we were nice and polite once they pulled out the cuffs, they'd let us keep them and we could use them on each other.

That would be awesome! I'm so glad you're into stuff like that!

Absolutely! I mean, you can buy handcuffs in those kinky sex equipment stores or order them online, but if we got the cuffs from the cops, we'd be using things that have probably used on actual killers!

Colette starts laughing: Would the pleasure would be more authentic?

I nod: Much more authentic, whatever that means.

The line for the movie keeps growing. People are checking their smartphones and saying that it's the longest movie line ever. I feel honored to be part of an unprecedented event. I can tell Colette feels the same way.

A cab pulls up and four people tumble out of the back seat. One of them asks: Where's the end of the line?

Someone says: It's got to be thirty blocks away by now, and it keeps getting longer.

Wow! That's incredible. We can't take the cab. It's a one-way street. I guess we better start walking.

Someone says: I'd run if I were you. It's pretty far.

Does anyone mind if we cut in line here?

There's sudden silence. The playful mood in the line disappears. Suddenly we're all looking at each other, not sure what to do. Finally Colette says: I'd like to yes. But it wouldn't be right. People who got here a long time ago would feel cheated.

I say: Exactly. I think you need to hustle back to the end of the line and wait your turn.

But then we might not get to see the film. We left early just like the rest of you. But the traffic was horrible. You guys just got lucky. You were close enough that you didn't need a cab like we did.

Colette says: Go home and get some booze and camping gear. Then come back and and pitch a tent and get drunk and spend the night in front of the ticket booth, so you'll be first in line tomorrow. You'll get the best seats in the house!

The people from the cab look stunned. They look at each other and clear their throats and stuff their hands in their pockets.

Colette says: Think about it. If you wait until tomorrow, you can read the reviews and find out if it's your kind of movie. Maybe it's not. There haven't been any advance reviews, so how would you know? Maybe it sucks, and if so, you'll be glad that you didn't waste your money. Right?

The people from the cab are nodding. One of them, a guy with a white bowtie and bowler hat, turns to me, points to Colette and says: Is this your girlfriend?

Yeah.

You're a lucky guy. She's brilliant!

I know. And she really turns me on.

He looks at Colette: Thanks for the suggestion. Things were just about to get nasty. But you really turned things around. You should run for president once you're old enough.

She frowns and says: I hate politics. I think it's all

bullshit! I think the president is a joke! And not just a joke, but a really bad joke, the kind that no one laughs at.

The people from the cab all nod and laugh. The bow-tie guy tips his bowler hat and bows. They all get back in the cab, which quickly disappears into the traffic.

Colette looks at me with bedroom eyes and says: I'm so glad you think I'm your girlfriend!

I say: You're fantastic. The way you turned that situation around really blew me away.

The rest of the line is cheering. Colette is their hero. They're telling me I'm the luckiest guy on the planet. I'm nodding and smiling.

A guy beside me says: You know what, buddy? I'd keep this woman around. Don't let her get away. She looks like the mother of your children.

The women beside the guy are eagerly nodding. One of them says: I hope you don't mind, but I've been catching fragments of your conversation. You're both so smart. Your children would be brilliant!

Colette smiles, but I can tell she feels weird. Once the people around us return to their own conversations, we give each other a look that says we're not quite ready for kids.

She says: Actually, I'm not sure I'll ever be ready for kids.

Me neither. It sounds too difficult.

Way too difficult. Not to mention expensive. And for me, because I'm a woman, and I'm almost thirty, it's hard to admit that I'm not desperate to have kids, but I'm totally not. I like my life the way it is.

Yeah, women really get a raw deal. They're brain-washed all their lives to think that they have to make babies, and it's going to be the greatest thing in the world. Then they have kids and find out that mother-hood is a pain in the ass.

Suddenly, I'm aware of a distant sound. I don't know what it is at first, but then I'm pretty sure that it's drumming of some kind, and maybe chanting. Then it's clear that it's kettle drums, a surging rhythmic pulse, and people chanting in unison—one, one, one, one, or maybe it's hum, hum, hum, hum, or maybe it's yum, yum, yum, yum, or sum, sum, sum, sum, or none, none, none, none, or fun, fun, fun, fun, or all of them at once. It sounds like a million footsteps approaching, feet on the pavement marching in time to the drumming and chanting.

I look at Colette: Do you hear that?

Yeah. At first I thought it was in my head, but—

What the fuck is it?

I don't know, but it's getting closer.

Over the next thirty minutes, it keeps getting closer and louder. Everyone looks puzzled, asking each other what's happening. The line keeps getting longer. The news reports from our phones say that the line is now backed up to the Lincoln Tunnel, blocking traffic, and backed up all the way across the George Washington Bridge, blocking traffic. Streets have been closed all over the city. There's talk of the mayor declaring a state of emergency.

The street is shaking. At the corner I can see soldiers, dressed like people in technicolor movies about ancient Rome, coming up the street, pounding drums and chanting fiercely. At first, I think it might be a re-enactment of some kind. But such a thing wouldn't make sense in midtown Manhattan, which doesn't look anything like ancient Rome and wouldn't work as a realistic setting.

Hundreds of Roman soldiers are moving toward us now. The drumming and chanting are deafening, shaking the street. I'm afraid that the shopfront windows are going to start shattering. Then behind the soldiers, a huge head appears, a woman's long black hair, her face and neck and shoulders, all gigantic, like her full body might be the size of an ocean liner. She's on her back, naked and chained to a giant pallet on wooden wheels, gagged and struggling fiercely. When the procession gets close, she gathers her strength, every huge muscle straining. She finally rips free, tears off her gag, stands ferociously, glaring around with disgust. The soldiers and start shouting and running in all directions.

Her voice is huge: You little fuckbrains! Now you'll pay for what you've done!

She bends and smashes groups of them into mush with her giant fists. There's screaming, the sounds of bones crunching. Someone in line shouts up at her: Why are you doing this? She leans down and spits in his face, knocking him back through a shopfront window. Her voice booms: Why am I doing this? Figure it out for yourselves!

She stomps down the avenue laughing loudly, squashing cars and kicking in shopfronts.

Soon she's out of sight. The streets are covered with dead Roman soldiers. Everyone is in shock. It occurs to me that they can't really be Roman soldiers, so I start to wonder what they are. Out of work Hollywood extras? But then where did they find this gigantic woman? How did they manage to get her tied up? I can only assume they secretly sedated her, but the drugs wore off too soon.

Colette says: She was really pissed off.

No shit.

I don't blame her. If someone tied me up like that, I'd be pissed off too.

Even if it was me?

Well, actually, I wouldn't mind at all if it was you.

I wouldn't either. You can tie me up and have a date, any old time.

That's like that song, which had a phone number for a title.

Finally the crowd begins to move. The line moves forward ten feet, stops, moves forward ten feet, stops, moves forward ten feet, stops, for more than an hour, then moves forward five feet, stops, moves five more feet, stops, moves five more feet, stops, for more than an hour, then moves forward three feet, stops, moves three feet more, stops, moves three feet more, stops, for more than an hour. Colette and I hardly notice how long it's taking. We're talking eagerly about psycholinguistic theory, doomsday bunkers, the weird apartments we've lived in, manatees in the Sargasso Sea, cognitive biology, our most embarrassing moments, the best dive bars in Brooklyn, the varieties of identity theft, the nasty profits made by detaining immigrants, the secret grove of redwoods in northern California, fractal patterns in baseball games, the Cuban Missile Crisis, kinky websites, cave paintings in southern France, our shared hatred of motorcycle noise, the weirdest micronations, the president's pathological self-absorption, the crazy jobs we've had, the tourist garbage in the Himalayas, the best unknown progressive rock albums, the Caspian Sea, Scriabin's piano sonatas, the endless replication of smiles in photo opportunities, the growing number of unaffordable cities, arctic rock formations, the subjects we don't like talking about, our favorite foods and books, but we're also using our mouths in other ways, sharing the longest kisses in the history of passion.

Someone checks the news on their phone, then loudly announces: That huge pissed-off woman—she's heading for Washington!

I pull out my phone and check my news feed. It says that she was just seen outside Baltimore, heading south.

I tell Colette: I'm amazed at how fast she's moving, getting from here to Baltimore in just three hours on foot. She sounds highly motivated. I'm figuring that in maybe thirty minutes, we'll get footage of her tearing down the Washington Monument, crushing the Lincoln Memorial. Or maybe she's got the White House in mind.

Colette says: She's probably going after the president. I'm glad that someone's got the balls to finally squash that mother fucker.

If they know she's on her way, they'll be prepared.

They'll probably nuke her.

They won't have much choice. She's clearly not in the mood for negotiation.

Finally, we can see the marquee, which says nothing except the word movie. Then we're past the robot in the ticket booth, a square metallic head and torso telling us to enjoy the show. The lobby is a blur of tightly packed bodies, no popcorn smell, no soda machine, no glass concession counter with overpriced candy. Then we're in what looks in the semi-dark like a massive place, vaguely resembling old pictures I've seen of opera houses in nineteenth-century Paris. It seems to get larger and larger as more and more people are squeezed inside. The seats are quickly filled on the ground floor, the second floor, the galleries, and the balconies. The aisles fill up, then we're crushed together, sitting on top of each other. No matter how large the theater seems to be getting, it's not enough to accommodate the masses of people surging in. Finally the doors are closed. We're stuffed like cattle in sardine cans, or sardines in cattle cars. The lights go out. But for the next hour, the screen remains blank. People start to panic, try to get out, but the doors are locked. Big guys form groups and try to smash their way out but the doors don't budge. People try their phones to call for help, but there's no reception.

Finally images form on the screen—no opening credits, no title or sound track music.

Colette looks at me, bewildered: Do you remember what this movie is called?

I say: I'm pretty sure it doesn't have a title. That's one of the things that made it so different, so different than different.

It's a film about a huge line of people waiting for a movie. The pace is extremely slow, exquisitely so. The camera pauses in front of each person or couple or group, providing detailed shots of each one, from a number of distances and angles, with ongoing changes in lighting and texture. Some scenes are in color, others in black and white, others are made of several scenes from other parts of the movie, and parts of scenes from other movies, juxtaposed or superimposed, running at different speeds, forward and backward. Soundtrack segments pop in and out, some of them specially composed for the movie we're watching, others taken from other movies cut up and recombined. All the dialogue segments last a long time, at least twenty minutes for each interaction. Nothing sounds scripted. Either the actors have mastered the art of sounding unscripted, or there's no script and the actors aren't really actors, just regular people. They don't have the screen personality look. They're not wearing any make-up.

Some of the conversations build to fierce levels of emotional intensity. Other conversations drift, going nowhere and taking a long time doing it, never going beyond small talk, or smaller talk, or even smaller talk. Other conversations are loaded with body language, some of it threatening, some of it playful, some of it crude or obscenely polite. Other conversations have no body language at all, the people never moving even slightly. Other conversations seem to have come from another language, with English dubbed in awkwardly, absurdly out of synch. Other conversations condemn the President. Other conversations avoid politics and the weather. Other conversations develop as if the world came to a ludricrous end a few days, months, or years ago, without anyone knowing it. Other conversations make the end of the world sound like parlor talk or pillow talk. Other conversations go back and forth like ping pong. Other conversations rage like a mastodon trapped in a tar pit. Other conversations turn philosophy into philately into philology into philogeny. Other conversations are microscopic or telescopic, making the difference between them seem unimportant. Other conversations move like trains making dangerous turns on snowy mountains, or surfers cutting back and forth on mountainous waves. Other conversations contain all other conversations. Other conversations acknowledge that something is always missing. Other conversations conclude that nothing is ever missing. Other conversations are interrupted by people cutting in line, or failing to cut in line and feeling like shit for even trying. Other conversations focus on shirts. Other conversations focus on weapons. Other conversations focus on sex, or make it seem that no one has ever had sex, or even thought about sex. Other conversations turn mammals into plants, or plant microphones in flowers. Other conversations make botany sound like astronomy, or make Austria sound like Australia, or make it sound like germs all come from Germany, all perfume from Peru, all fire from Tierra del Fuego. Other conversations can't get started. Other conversations echo other conversations. Other conversations make no difference, while seeming to make all the difference in the world, making it clear that words like difference need to be more than different.

Then silence—five four three two one—then it's all

conversation again, then silence, then a stormy background scene, a gigantic woman smashing the White House, lifting the President into a flashing sky, taking obvious pleasure in watching the President squirm and beg, then biting his head off, spitting it out, wiping her mouth with the back of her hand, laughing savagely, stomping into a thundering distance, then silence—five four three two one—then it's all conversation again, camera work so carefully designed that each moment is worth years of close observation.

I'm packed so close to Colette that I'm feeling orgasmic pleasure in every cell of my body. I say, "Are you feeling orgasmic pleasure in every cell of your body?"

She says, "Yeah. I'm feeling orgasmic pleasure in every cell of my body. It's fun to watch a movie this way. It makes everything on the screen much more exciting."

"It's like listening to music on acid."

"Or like a joke that keeps getting better."

"My dick feels hard enough to fuck the Grand Canyon."

"My cunt feels wet enough to flood the Grand Canyon."

The line in the movie keeps getting longer, caught between parallel lines of receding street lights. The buildings around them are dark and distorted by moonlight. Half of them are empty; the other half might as well be. The longer the film goes on, the more the conversations keep changing. With so much time set aside for each dialogue segment, everyone here will die of old age before the movie is over.

PHOTO OP

I've never seen a Reality TV show. My partner Jane Tambourine has seen a few, and thinks they're stupid. But her closest friends are throwing a Reality TV party, and they went to the trouble of sending her a formal invitation. She decided to be diplomatic and accepted, but she asked me to come along to help her tolerate the picture tube.

The party is in a converted loft in the warehouse district. Floor to ceiling windows open onto the roof of the building, so it's almost like being outdoors, which greatly reduces the danger of Covid-19 transmission. There's an unobstructed view of the Brooklyn Bridge. I'm not a party person, but now I'm liking what other guests are talking about. I join a group where everyone has been north of the Arctic Circle, then a group where everyone has spent a night in a haunted house, then a group where everyone has at least one aquarium filled with tropical fish.

Now I'm at the food table, stuffing myself, eavesdropping on two young women sitting in a corner. One of them is wearing a long iridescent gown. Her hair is curly black and she's deeply tanned. Something about her makes me think of waterfalls in the tropics, though I've never been to a waterfall in the tropics. She says: So anyway, Jackie, that's how it works. All you have to do is get him to say his name backwards. Then he'll vanish into the Phantom Zone.

Jackie shakes her head: That's it? Really?

Yeah, that's all it takes. It doesn't have to be his exact name, letter by letter. Even if it just sounds like his name backwards, it'll send him into the Phantom Zone.

Jackie looks puzzled. She's blond with a shoulder-length bob and a sleeveless hoodie. Something about her makes me think of coffee shops in Seattle, though I've never been to a coffee shop in Seattle. She slowly says: So, let's say his name is Rat. Tar is rat backwards. So if I get him to say guitar, he'll vanish into the Phantom Zone?

Yeah. Or even a word like alarm would work.

Sorry, Nancy. I don't get it. Alarm and guitar are common words and he's probably said them many times. So why hasn't he already disappeared?

I was confused about that too, at first. But my brother explained it to me, and the answer is simple. It's the act of *getting* him to say it, *tricking* him into saying it, that makes him disappear.

Jackie sounds impatient: I still don't get it.

It's not about getting it. We're talking about magic, not logic. The Phantom Zone isn't part of our scientific universe.

Then what is it?

It's whatever doesn't exist anymore, or never did or never will.

He'll disappear and never come back?

Nancy nods. When they see me looking in their direction, they smile politely and stop talking, focusing on the paper plates of food in their laps, taking sips from plastic cups of wine.

Jane Tambourine has been talking to friends on the other side of the room. Now she sneaks up behind me, taps me on the shoulder and says: Having fun?

Yeah. I've heard some great conversations tonight.

I start to tell her about the aquarium discussion, the politics of tropical fish, but theme music starts to play from a wall TV on the other side of the room. Guests are slowly moving toward a semi-circle of couches and chairs, arranged so that everyone has a ringside seat.

Jane Tambourine smiles sarcastically and says: The main event is about to begin.

What's it called?

Photo Op. In every episode, a famous person shows

up somewhere to get their picture taken. Today it's set in the White House.

Really? A stage set or the actual White House?

The actual White House. Which isn't really much different from a stage set.

I nod: So it's questionable to call it a Reality TV show?

Sure. But you've heard that on Twitter they're calling the president Bunker Bitch, right?

I laugh: Is that because he got freaked out by the Black Lives Matter protests a few days ago, and spent the night in a White House bunker?

Yeah, and he claimed he was there to perform an inspection, but his aides knew the truth, and now he's the laughing stock of the Twitter nation.

I keep laughing: So on the show he'll be trying to reconstruct his manhood? Or his public image?

Something like that. After all, you can't be the leader of a nuclear superpower and have people calling you Bunker Bitch!

A guy in tennis shorts and a light blue blazer waves to Jane Tambourine from across the room. She nods in his direction and says to me: That's Fred. Remember him?

I nod: Isn't he the guy who worked for Liberty Mutual? The one who quit because he didn't like the way ostriches kept showing up in their commercials?

Yeah. But they were emus, not ostriches.

What's the difference?

Emus are smaller and not as combative. Ostriches will eat anything, while Emus are vegetarians. Anyway, I should talk to Fred for a minute. I'll be right back. Save me a seat.

She walks across the room. Nancy and Jackie are talking again.

Jackie says: I hate to say it, but the Phantom Zone sounds like something from DC comics.

Nancy says: Never mind what it sounds like. You want to get rid of him, right? I mean, you've been living with him for years, and he's the worst boyfriend ever.

That's for sure. But he won't let me break up with him. You remember how violent he got the last time I tried to leave.

So what have you got to lose? Give it a try. Get him to say his name backwards. His name is Lee, isn't it? That should be simple. Just get him to say common words like steal, feel, real, or kneel. If Lee were the president, you could get him to start promoting his ghost-written book, *The Art of the Deal.*

Jackie's about to say something else, but now the

show has begun, an exterior view of the White House, protesters holding up angry signs on the North Lawn facing a fountain. I sit on a small green sofa. Jane Tambourine returns and sits beside me. Now we've got an interior view of the presidential mansion. U.S. President Barry Trap is standing beside the Resolute Desk in the Oval Office, making stern eye contact with the camera, the TV nation, trying to look forceful and decisive, in charge of the situation.

I whisper to Jane: That's look he's giving us—it's so clearly planned. I thought Reality TV shows were supposed to be spontaneous.

Jane nods but keeps her eyes on the screen, as if she were trying to stare the president down, get him to admit that he's a wimp, a Bunker Bitch, even though he's supposed to be the most powerful man in the world.

A voice-over says: June 1, 2020. The 45th president of the United States of America is facing an unprecedented crisis. The nation has erupted in protests, outraged by the violent death of a black man named Jeff Toy, whose neck was fatally crushed in Minneapolis by Officer Dirk Bender, while Mr. Toy pleaded for mercy and bystanders warned Officer Bender that he was going too far. Now the Black Lives Matter demonstrations have reached the nation's capital. Thousands of angry citizens are camped outside the White House lawn. The president can hear them calling for justice. He can see them from the Oval Office windows behind his desk. Will he take decisive action? Behind him in the Oval Office right now is Marv Expire, the Secretary of Defense. Bill Barf, the Attorney General, is due to arrive in a minute or two. We've reached a turning point in American history. Let's see what happens!

I turn to Jane Tambourine and say: It's weird to be watching TV. I haven't watched a TV show in decades. Will this one have commercials? I can't stand commercials. Someone told me that TV ads today are works of art. I don't believe it.

She gives me a whispered shhhh with a finger on her lips.

I nod and turn back to the screen, where Barry Trap looks tense and angry. He's pacing up and down in the Oval Office, wolfing down a party-size pack of double stuff golden Oreos. He turns to Marv Expire and says: We need to get federal troops here now! That mob outside might torch the White House. It's a goddamn election year. If the White House gets burned down, think of all the votes I might lose.

Marv Expire gives him a strange look and says: Mr

President, we're doing just fine with the protesters. They're actually rather peaceful and—

Rioters, not protesters. They're rioters, they're a dangerous mob. We need 10,000 troops and we need them now!

Mr. President, is that really the best way—

You hard of hearing? I said we need ten thousand troops, right now! Look at those crazy people out there! We can't let things get out of hand. Democracy is in danger!

Sure, Mr. President, but—

Ten thousand troops! Right now! Not 9,999 troops tomorrow. 10 fucking thousand! Right fucking now! Do I make myself clear?

There's a close-up of Marv Expire, who's acting like he doesn't mind being spoken to like he's an idiot. He tries to lighten things up. He looks at the rapidly dwindling pack of Oreos on the President's desk, winks and says: Those Oreos are my favorite kind. The golden ones are so much better than the black ones! Can I have a couple? I didn't have a chance to get breakfast this morning.

The president says: You should have brought your own cookies. I don't share food!

A door opens and Bill Barf walks in, looking pooped

out and annoyed, like a baked potato with glasses, just as the President says: We need to invoke the Insurrection Act. Someone told me that it worked wonders back in 1831, when Andy Jackson used it to squash Nat Turner's Revolt. If it was good enough for Andy Jackson, it's good enough for me. After all, Andy's face is on every twenty dollar bill that's ever been spent, real or counterfeit.

Bill Barf tries to smile: Mr. President, the two situations aren't exactly the same. Nat Turner's revolt was a slave rebellion. The protesters—

Rioters. Call them rioters. They're a dangerous mob.

Bill Barf looks annoyed and says: Dangerous? Really? They're disturbed and they're letting us know about it. They have a right to be angry, and a constitutional right to express that anger.

Marv Expire says: The so-called chaos outside isn't nearly extreme enough to call in federal troops. I think that would be a huge mistake, Mr. President. It would—

Are you telling me how to do my job again, Marv? You can fuck off! That dangerous mob outside is filled with antichrists, foreign agitators—

Bill Barf looks concerned: Antichrists, Mr. President? I think you mean anarchists.

What's the difference?

Anarchists want chaos. They think governments restrict freedom. Antichrists are mythic beings who disrupt the mission of Jesus. They—

So they're basically the same thing. Except one group is focused on Jesus and the other one isn't. What difference does it make?

Bill Barf clears his throat: The Antichrist has the number 666 tattooed on his forehead.

Anarchists don't have tattoos? Marv told me that lots of anarchists have tattoos.

But they don't have the number 666 carved into their foreheads.

Why should I care about the number 666?

It has special symbolic significance. We should probably consult a numerologist.

Is that some kind of doctor? I can't afford to consult a doctor now. It might make me look like a wimp, like a kid who gets a medical note at school so he can leave early. Or going to a doctor might make it seem like I have the covid virus. It looks weak, and we can't look weak at this point. We've got to show them who's boss. A show of force is the only thing that people respect. Look what happened in Minneapolis. They're a blue state, a bunch of limp-dick liberals, and now the city is burning, just because some cop got rough with a black guy. We can't let that happen here. We need to clear the rioters out. Right now! They're in the way!

Marv Expire asks: What are they in the way of?

You'll see.

Marv Expire says: But they're exercising a fundamental right, a constutitional right, Mr President. There's no reason to clear them out. Let them make their noise. Eventually they'll get sick of it and go away, and a month from now, no one will remember they were here. No one will even remember Jeff Toy's name. Besides, Mr. President, you can't use federal troops for domestic law enforcement.

Bill Barf says: If that mob were being controlled by foreign agitators, then it might make sense to consider the Insurrection Act. But there's no evidence—

The Presidentshakes his head fiercely and says: I want them out. I want all of them out, the antichrist and the anarchists and the foreign agitators. Get rid of them! I need to walk outside, in broad daylight, show people I'm not afraid, and the mob out there is in my way! I need a clear path to make a proper entrance. And I need more double stuff golden Oreos. Send someone out for them now! On the double!

Marv Expire sends two aides out for the Oreos, telling them to be quick about it, to use the White House limousine if they can't find a cab right away.

Bill Barf looks confused and says: You want to take a walk now, Mr. President? With all those crazy people out there, you want to go out for a walk? Really?

Yeah, but first I need to make a speech. Where's Dick? Where's my Fool? I mean, my Tweeter.

Someone sends a text, and within a few minutes the door swings open. The Director of Social Media walks in, looking like a constipated bear: Yes, Mr. President?

About time you got here Dick! Sleeping on the job again?

No, Mr. President, I—

Shut the fuck up, Dickie boy! I need a speech and I need it now. It needs to sound tough and it needs a good last line, a good sound bite, something for the history books of the future.

Ummm...okay. What's the topic?

The need for law and order and stuff like that. Mention Black Lives Matter, the black guy who got killed by a cop for using a counterfeit bill. George Void, or something like that.

Jeff Toy?

Yeah, George Toy. What a fucking weird name! He

sounds like something for toddlers to play with and break. He really lets people call him George Toy?

It's Jeff Toy, Mr. President. And he's dead.

Whatever.

The Director of Social Media, former Director of the Winter White House Golf Club, former Chief of Coca Cola's Public Relations Department, pulls a laptop out of his briefcase and starts writing a tweet-speech, a form he's mastered so well that he hasn't been fired yet, unlike everyone else.

Bill Barf looks at the painting of Thomas Jefferson on the wall. There's a reverential silence as Dick the Tweeter taps on his laptop. The mood in the Oval Office now might be compared to the somber silence Jefferson insisted on as he wrote the Declaration of Independence, getting annoyed when Ben Franklin and John Jay made suggestions, even though he'd asked them to be there in Declaration Hall to make suggestions, some of which led to revisions that appeared in the final version. The Attorney General strokes his chin, like someone trying a little too hard to seem pensive, maybe thinking of the silence Jefferson insisted on from his mistress, when he didn't want his wife to know that a slave was sitting on his face in a Monticello stable, pleasured by the very same mouth he used in making presidential speeches.

I whisper in Jane's ear: It's weird that no one's talking right now. In the shows I remember watching when I was a kid, there weren't any gaps. Someone was always talking. Or there was music.

She quickly whispers: It's unscripted. Remember? Reality TV?

I nod and look back at the screen, where Dick is still typing, and Bill Barf is still staring into the framed and famous face that appears on two-dollar bills, real or counterfeit, the man who made the Louisiana Purchase, setting the stage for the Manifest Destiny era.

A few minutes later Dick looks up and smiles, taps a button on his keyboard, and a printer across the room starts making noise. An aide retrieves the pages and starts marking them up, correcting the grammar, changing words and phrases, then hands them to another aide, who makes further changes, struggling to keep a straight face, then hands the speech to another aide, who scans the text into her phone, then says it's pretty much ready for the teleprompters, where she says that final corrections can be made. She asks the president if he wants to take a quick look.

Why would I want to do that? I can read the goddamn thing from the teleprompters.

I don't know, sir. I thought you might want to make a few last-minute changes.

I can do that while I'm talking, right? I mean, it's not like I'm an actor reading a script. If stuff comes into my head, it comes out of my mouth, uncensored. I'm the nation's greatest master of impersonation.

I think you mean improvisation, Mr. President.

Whatever.

She nods and shows the text to another aide. They turn their backs to the camera, talk quietly in the background, trying to keep what sounds like laughter in check.

The President turns to Marv Expire and yanks his tie and says: Now get those Black Lives Matter motherfuckers out of the way. We need to own the situation, show those jerks outside who's really in charge.

Marv puts his tie back in place, starts punching buttons on his phone, no doubt using secret codes to get around the automated systems.

The president says: What the fuck is taking so long?

Marv snaps: I'm typing as fast as I can! If you can do it faster, then be my guest.

He holds up his phone to the president. For a second it looks like Marv Expire might have a secret identity, like there might be a demonic smirk behind his blank professional face.

The president tries to look like an angry turtle, but his voice cracks when he says: Just keep typing!

I whisper in Jane's ear: For a second there, I thought Marv Expire was channeling Anthony Perkins.

She smiles, but puts her finger on her lips again, grabs my hand and squeezes. I get the message. It's time for me to shut up. The other people here don't want interruptions. They're scared that something sinister might happen on the screen.

A few minutes later, right outside the three tall windows behind the President's desk, chaos explodes. The TV cameras bring the scene to life. Tear gas and flash-bangs and truncheons and mirroring shields, chemical grenades, pepper bombs, deadly cannisters. People are choking and stumbling away. Cops on horses parade down the street, swinging billy clubs. Skulls and shins get cracked. People are bleeding and passing out. I don't see the number 666 engraved on anyone's forehead, though it might be tattooed on their private parts, secretly promoting diabolical agendas.

The scene shifts to the Rose Garden podium, flanked by teleprompters, four American flags in the background, and the president slouching toward the microphone. Selected members of the press are eagerly waiting, apparently having received a melodramatic last-minute summons. The sounds of battle can still be heard in the background. The president begins by quickly mentioning the Jeff Toy incident, then changes the subject, brags about the electoral votes he received in the last election, brags about how great his response to the Covid pandemic has been, refers to Andy Jackson squashing Nat Turner's revolt with federal troops, calls himself a great ally of peaceful demonstrations, then says: If a city or state refuses to take actions necessary to defend the life and property of their residents, then I will deploy the U.S. military and solve the problem for them.

He pauses to let the threat sink in. He puts a mean look on his face, like he just kicked a bully's ass in a schoolyard fight. Then he makes the decisive statement, the sound bite of all sound bites: I am your President of law and order!

He dusts off his hands, clearly likes the way it makes him feel and dusts off his hands again. He grins like he's eager to show off his teeth, eager to show that he feels no need to wear a covid mask. If he's not afraid of the virus, he's not afraid of anything. He walks from the podium back to the Oval Office, waving goodbye to the press like someone swatting at a mosquito.

An ad begins. There's a guy in a yellow shirt. He's facing the camera focusing his own camera, apparently taking pictures of anyone watching the commercial. He talks like he doesn't have enough time, claiming that Liberty Mutual customizes car insurance, so that you only pay for what you need. Then it's clear that he's at a wedding reception, taking pictures of emus who just got married, wearing shades and wedding gowns beside a yellow three-tiered cake. Suddenly the room is filled with emus attacking the cake, squawking and pecking and chewing like nothing else matters. The photographer freaks out and runs away. High-pitched voices end the scene with Libertyliberty Li-ber-ty.

I hear Fred cursing under his breath: That's disgusting. Emus don't eat cake!

Someone laughs: Disgusting? I think it's really clever. The extra emus *crashed* the reception, just like Liberty Mutual insures us if we *crash* our cars. It's a brilliant pun.

Fred's loud this time: I didn't say they're not clever. Obviously, the Liberty ads are terribly terribly clever. But they're asking us to believe that shy desert birds like emus have junk food cravings and don't mind forcing their way into human events. The truth is, they'd never go anywhere near the noise of a wedding.

The other guy laughs again: Seriously, dude, lighten up!

I pull off one of my loafers and start to throw it at the commercial, but Jane Tambourine yanks the shoe out of my hand, puts a finger on her lips, then points at the screen. We're back in the Oval Office again, with Barry Trap, Bill Barf, Marv Expire, and two aides, having returned with shopping bags full of double stuff golden Oreos. They spray the bags with disinfectant. Then the Chief Executive tears open a package and starts wolfing the cookies down. A door opens and his daughter walks in, dressed like a runway model in mourning. Right behind her, there's a gray-haired five-star general, decked out in battle fatigues.

I hear Jackie's voice: Who's the army guy?

Someone says: That's Mark Milestone, the chairman of the joint chiefs of staff.

Nancy laughs: That's a mouthful! They couldn't give the guy a less cumbersome title?

Jackie says: What's the joint chiefs of staff? Does that even mean anything?

Someone says: Will everyone please shut up! We're here to watch the show, aren't we?

The room gets quiet, but there's noise outside, as a yellow helicopter hovers over the Brooklyn Bridge.

On screen, the president is still wolfing down the double stuff golden Oreos, spilling crumbs on his desk. An aide rushes up with a whisk broom and miniature dustpan. Everyone looks confused, not sure what they're supposed to say, like they wish they had a script, roles to play and lines to deliver. Bill Barf clears his throat. Mark Milestone snorts. A door crashes open, and a huge English Mastiff bursts into the room, jumps up and down in playful ecstasy, bounds across the royal blue carpeting, leaps up onto the president's chest, slobbering all over his crisp white shirt and sky-blue necktie, knocking him onto his back, licking his face in sheer delight. Someone shouts off camera, "Bozo! Come!" and the Mastiff freezes in place, then turns and bounces back out into the corridor. An aide quickly slams the door shut and locks it twice. The president slowly gets to his feet, straightens out his suit, pulls an orange handkerchief out of his suit coat pocket, wipes the slobber off his face and lapels, tosses the handkerchief onto the carpet, watching as it lands on the Seal of the President, just above the phrase E PLURIBUS UNUM, unfurling on a scroll from an eagle's beak. Everyone stands in silence watching the president, who turns to his desk and rips open another pack of golden Oreos, without even waiting for one of his aides to spray the disinfectant again.

Everyone at the party looks like they're waiting for a commercial. Then a guy starts laughing and everyone else starts laughing.

Everyone starts talking at once:

What kind of dog was that?

An English Mastiff.

So fucking big! Like a cross between a buffalo and a bull dog.

It's my favorite breed. I've had several of my own.

Are they dangerous?

Mostly no. They're gentle giants. But if they're provoked, watch out!

He looked friendly. But his mouth was only an inch from Barry Trap's neck.

One false move, and he might have bitten the president's head off.

That would've looked really weird—the president's head rolling in its own blood across the Seal of the President.

Gross!

The dog would have been in deep shit. He would've been euthanized.

Why do we keep assuming that the dog was male? Was anyone watching its genitals closely enough to know for sure?

No but—

Then shut the fuck up! The dog was probably a bitch.

Yeah, seriously. No way the dog was male. Everyone knows that the President only does women. Even if they call him Bunker Bitch, there's no fucking way that he's secretly gay.

What difference does it make? Gay or straight, he's a gutless moron. J. Edgar Hoover was gay, but he was tough enough to get millions of people killed, including JFK.

You believe that stupid theory?

It's more than a theory. It's documented—

A woman from the Arctic Circle discussion firmly cuts him off: Documented or not, can we all agree to shut the fuck up? We're not here to figure out who fired the magic bullet!

Everyone turns back to the screen, where Marv Expire finally says: You okay, Mr. President?

The president snorts.

Marv Expire clears his throat in reply, then nods to Mark Milestone and says: Thanks for coming, Mark. I'm glad you listened to what I said on the phone.

You mean about coming here in camo? I feel like an idiot. Why am I here dressed for battle?

Bill Barf says: Relax, Mark. You're the visible symbol of the U.S. war machine.

The president says: Those anarchists and terrorists need to see that we won't put up with any shit! We can nuke them any time we want!

Mark Milestone looks annoyed: Terrosts? Anarchists? As far as I can tell, they're just regular people peacefully demonstrating, exercising a constitutional right.

The president says: Look again! Some of them have the mark of the beast on their foreheads!

Mark Milestone stares out the windows and mutters: The mark of the beast? What the fuck—

The president's daughter quickly says: Okay dad, what's next? You gave a magnificent speech. The final line was awesome!

Mark Milestone turns away. He stares up into the eyes of the nation's number one founding father, George Washington in Gilbert Stuart's portrait, presiding over the room from a frame on the wall, the face that everyone sees on one-dollar bills, and also on at least a hundred million counterfeit one-dollar bills, currently getting spent throughout the nation.

The camera zooms in on Mark Milestone's puzzled face. In profile, he looks like the quintessential warrior, a cross between George C. Scott and an English Mastiff. But he's slowly shaking his head and stroking his chin, as if he were noticing something new in Washington's eyes, which look judgemental, like he might be the kind of guy that can't take a joke and doesn't mind being a prick. Two of Washington's slave girls found this out the hard way, when as a prank they stole his clothes while he was swimming in the Potomac. The girls were later severely whipped for messing with their master. Both had trouble sitting down for the rest of their lives. I can't imagine how painful it must have been. Still, it would have been amusing to see the same guy who crossed the Delaware, looking fierce and resolute, now standing naked and blushing in the Potomac, shivering pale arms wrapped around his chest, losing his cool yet still getting cold in the late November water, while the girls were hiding in shoreline bushes laughing their heads off. But the warning in Washington's dollar bill face can't be ignored. It says that you'll pay a high price if you try to be funny.

Washington isn't showing his teeth in the painting. No one showed their teeth in pictures back then. The reason may have been that they didn't have teeth, or if they still had a few they were in bad shape. Dentistry back then wasn't what it became after World War II. But Washington got teeth from the slaves he owned. He had their teeth pulled, since he badly wanted a functional set of dentures. So it's possible that he could have flashed a big smile. But back then, such an expression would have seemed sinister, especially if people figured out where he got the teeth.

It's obvious that General Milestone doesn't feel like showing his teeth. His lips are tense. He's not exactly a photo-op kind of guy. He finally turns away from the painting and says: Mr President, what am I doing here?

The President stares out the three tall windows behind his desk. He says: We're all going out for a walk. We're going to church.

On a Thursday, Mr President?

Yeah. You got a problem with that? I go to church whenever I feel like going to church. Like, you know, when I need to talk to God and stuff like that.

You can't talk to God in the White House, Mr. President?

I'm the one in the White House, God is the one in church. We've got two different jobs, in case you haven't noticed. Now why the fuck are you asking me all these questions?

Sorry, Mr. President. I didn't know it was a problem.

If I say it's a problem, it's a problem. If I say it's not a problem, it's not a problem. If I say it's not a problem, and it turns out it's really a problem, then it's either a problem or it's not. If it's either a problem or it's not, then it's a problem, unless I say it's not. Got it?

He faces the camera, which zooms in for a close-up, trying to make it seem that his face has come right through the screen, dominating every living room in the TV nation. He dusts off his hands and shows his teeth and says: Got it?

Most of the people here in the loft are nodding. They get it.

There's another commercial. It's set in a yellow chopper circling the Brooklyn Bridge. There's an emu with air force goggles beside the pilot. They're both wearing yellow aviation helmets which boldly display the Liberty Mutual logo. The guy is talking about car insurance, setting the copter's sights on a car driving over the bridge. The pilot shouts to his emu navigator, "let's see what this bird can do!" descending on the car. The scene changes. The pilot and the emu are in a professional office. The pilot is holding a toy chopper, shouting "let's see what this bird can do," as if the initial scene was all in his head. The emu looks annoyed, like he might start pecking and biting and squawking. A well-dressed woman, apparently the pilot's boss, sits behind a big desk, shuffling papers. She shakes her head and firmly says, "We are NOT getting you a copter." The pilot turns to the emu and says, "Looks like we're walking, kid!" The high-pitched voices return with Libertyliberty Li-ber-ty, then a deep male voice declares that you only pay for what you need.

Jackie stands up and shakes her fist and shouts: Fuck those ostrich commercials!

Nancy stands up and shouts: Who decides that we have to watch those dipshit insurance ads a hundred times every day? I'll bet even the president doesn't have that kind of power!

Someone I remember from the haunted house conversation says: It's an emu, not an ostrich. But I think it's cool that the ad shows a black woman telling a white guy what he can't have. Historically, it would have been the other way around.

Jane Tambourine says: That's probably why the ad showed up right now, since we're watching a show that includes a Black Lives Matter demonstration.

Jackie says: Fuck that! They were just staging a pseudo-progressive situation to get our attention and sell a product.

Nancy is nodding fiercely, hands on hips: And it's not just that! My brother is down in Washington right now, risking his life to participate in the Black Lives Matter protests. It's deeply offensive that a historic and risky political action is being used to sell car insurance!

I decide to put my two cents in: And what about Barry Trap's comment on Jeff Toy's name? I don't think he knew what he was saying, but he was right by accident, wasn't he? The name is a good description of the shit black people have to put up with. They get played with by overgrown toddlers, then thrown out when they get broken.

Someone from the haunted house conversation says: And we all act like we don't see what's happening. Like ostriches, we're hiding our heads in the sand, and—

It's an emu, not an ostrich!

What the fuck difference does it make? Columbus thought he saw mermaids in the Devil's Triangle. Now we know that he probably saw manatees, not mermaids. But the truth is, they really might have been dugongs, not manatees, since dugongs like to spend time in the Devil's Triangle and manatees don't. But who really cares? Dugong or manatee, emu or ostrich? Does it really make any difference?

It makes a huge difference, dude! Emus don't hide their heads in the sand!

Jane Tambourine's client, Fred, stands up says: Would all of you shut the fuck up! The fate of our nation is playing out in real time, right here on the screen, and we all came here to see it happen. Didn't we? Why are we wasting our time discussing stupid commercials? We've already given them far more attention than they deserve!

Everyone nods and turns back to the screen. Jackie and Nancy look at each other and shrug and sit back down.

The President and his entourage have left the White House.They're walking toward St. John's Church, across Lafayette Park, protected by U.S. Police wearing football helmets, surplus gear they got from an abandoned Washington Redskins training camp. The team itself is quarantined in other parts of the city. The team's name is due to be changed, but so far no one can think of anything new that doesn't sound stupid or offensive. Most of the really cool names have already been taken by other teams. The President wants to call them the Washington Pigskins, but something about the short version, the Washington Pigs, gets on his nerves, even though he likes pigs—or rather, bacon, especially uncooked bacon at three in the morning, when he's secretly watching the porn they won't let him watch during business hours.

The President turns to his daughter: OK now, figure things out in a hurry. You're on the payroll as a senior advisor. So start advising. Why are we doing this? Why are we going to church?

She's remembered to stash a Bible in her $2000 handbag. Now she looks at him with a counterfeit smile: I don't know, dad. It was your idea. Something about doing what all other Presidents have done? And I think you want to make sure all the white trash evangelicals vote for you again, so posing in front of a famous church makes good sense. They know all about the Antichrist and the number 666. But when we get to the church, I think we need some keywords, like maybe compassion and freedom and sacrifice or—

Compassion? What the fuck are you talking about?

Compassion, you know, like—

Like when you get horny and want to fuck?

No, dad, that's passion.

Compassion?

Like feeling sorry for someone. More or less.

No way! Feeling sorry for people is a waste of time. What they really need is a good kick in the ass. They live in the land of the free. They can do whatever they want here. There's nothing to stop anyone here from rising to the top. You can go as far as you want to go, make as much money as you want to make. Compassion just makes people soft. It's a word for losers. That's the last thing we need! So—

Wait! I know! Forget about compassion. We can say you're inspecting the damage done to the church by anarchists and foreign agitators. Someone told me there was vandalism there a few days ago. Churchill did the same thing, I think, inspecting damaged buildings during the Blitz.

If it was good enough for Churchill, it's good enough for me.

The President pumps his fist as he walks past the riot police, trying to look like a Pigskins coach preparing his team for the Superbowl. The trees in Lafayette Park are swaying gracefully in the summer breeze, filling the space with beautiful patterns of shadow. But the president and his entourage look fierce, like they don't have time for relaxing background imagery.

Marv Expire asks: Mr President, what are we doing? In case anyone asks me.

Inspecting the damage.

Damage?

To the Church. The Church of the Presidents.

There's damage?

There better be, the President's daughter says. There's got to be a problem we need to confront. Let's just say that the church has been desecrated. Some anarchist tagged a toilet stall in the church bathroom with the number 666, and we need to inspect it.

Inspect it?

Yeah. Find out what it means. Someone told me it's dangerous. The number all by itself has the power to mess things up.

Mark Milestone looks puzzled and says: Will the cameras follow us inside and watch us inspecting the mark of the beast? Will we have to wear surgical gloves and use sterilized instruments to perform the inspection?

Fuck no, the President says, we'll just go inside for a while and pretend to inspect it. The cameras can stay outside. Then we'll come back out and look like we've accomplished something. I'll dust off my hands and show my teeth.

Mark Milestone takes the President's daughter aside and says: I had a roommate in prep school who was into shit like that. He wrote a paper for an English class, and the teacher wouldn't read it because it contained the number 666, which apparently would have gotten him fired.

Just because he read it in a student paper?

That's what my roommate said. Just the number itself, as a visual sign, would transmit sinister energies and make people do bad things. So he wrote another paper instead, a last minute thing based on a popular song.

What song?

Something called Itsy-Bitsy Teenie-Weenie Yellow Polka Dot Bikini. It was popular back in the fifties.

A paper with the number 666 was rejected, but a paper about a bikini was ok?

It wasn't really about the bikini. It was about morality. In the song, the girl a wears a revealing bikini to the beach, goes swimming, but then she's afraid to come out of the water because the bikini makes her look like a slut.

He wrote a paper on that?

Yeah, and he got an A too. He claimed that the song was meant to warn and shame loose women who wear bikinis and show off their bodies. The song makes it seem that girls who do it deserve to get ridiculed and humiliated, since the song says the girl was so embarrassed she couldn't come out of the water.

She wasn't embarrassed before that? I mean, she was wearing the bikini *before* she went into the water, right?

I guess when the bikini got wet it clung to her body and showed her tits and her ass much more than she thought it would.

Your roommate sounds pretty fucked up.

He was always pretending to read the Bible, but his Bible was hollowed out and he had porn stashed inside it. When I told him it was a counterfeit Bible, he said he bought it with counterfeit money.

Like Jeff Toy buying cigarettes with a fake twenty.

They don't really know if it was fake. And besides, people spend fake money all the time, without even knowing it. You look like you've spent a lot of money over the years. Are you absolutely sure that none of it was counterfeit?

I never really thought about it.

But if at some point you spent a fake twenty dollar bill, and a cashier figured out that it was countefeit, do you think there would be a problem?

No. The cashier wouldn't even mention it. Or if he did, he'd be extremely polite and nothing would come of it.

Mark Milestone looks amused and says: Exactly. Now, can you ask your father how long I'm supposed to walk around in my battle fatigues? It's really embarrassing. I feel like that girl in the song.

She laughs: Dude, you've got to look like you're in a war zone. Otherwise people might wonder why we're doing this.

They *should* be wondering why we're doing this. And with me here, it makes it look like the President has military support in forcing out these protesters, who aren't doing anything wrong. I shouldn't be here. Your father is making political use of the U.S. Army, when in fact the U.S. army has nothing to do with politics. Besides, I saw the Jeff Toy videos, and I was horrified. There's no way the U.S. military supports behavior like that.

Not even in places like Iraq and Afghanistan?

That's different.

I'm sure it is. But just stop being a dick, okay? Just look like you're deeply committed to what your commander in chief tells you to do.

Commander in chief?

My father.

I've been a soldier all my life. I'm supposed to take orders from a guy who's never even been in boot camp? A guy who used his money and connections to avoid military service? I'm supposed to take a guy like that seriously?

Yeah.

And I have to keep a scowl on my face, like I'm just about to kick ass, like I'm ready to make decisions that destroy whole nations in a matter of minutes?

Yeah. You're supposed to look tough, ready for anything.

This is the most ridiculous thing I've ever done. I feel like I'm dressed up to go on stage and play a part, but there's no script.

Do you really need a script? Just get into the role. How difficult can it be?

Reporters are jogging beside them with their phones, getting pictures. Soon the president's task force reaches the church patio, where a St. John's minister is working with a Black Lives Matter team, offering water and sandwiches to homeless people. The police in their riot gear quickly take over the space with flash-bangs and billy clubs. Sirens fill the air. The President stares at the homeless people hobbling away, some of them injured. He pats his paunch and smiles, apparently pleased that the anarchists have been subdued. His daughter slips him her Bible and the President holds it up for photographers to see, as if he were swearing to tell the whole truth and nothing but the truth. He looks like he's never touched a book before, or like he's planning to swat a fly with it. He gives the victory sign. He gives the white supremacy sign.

Squads of cell phone photographers are finding the best angles, bending and kneeling and squinting and creasing their foreheads, knowing that the best picture might go viral and make them famous.

Marv Expire tries to get the President's attention, noticing that the Bible is upside down, as if it were meant to be read by someone standing on his head.

His daughter whispers: Dad, I think you should pray or something. You know, offer words of condolence, compassion for those who are suffering.

Who's suffering?

The whole nation, but especially Jeff Toy's family.

Who?

Jeff Toy, the guy who was was recently killed when a cop—

Him again? Fuck that! I already said I was deeply sorry back in the Rose Garden. And I didn't really do anything wrong, but still I apologized for it. I'll bet Andy Jackson never did anything like that!

Marv Expire looks confused: I'm sure you're right, Mr President. But you've got your pictures now, right?

No one will suspect that you've never been to this church before. The picture can be photoshopped, so it doesn't look like the Good Book is upside down. No one will remember that you were hiding out in a bunker. They won't call you Bunker Bitch anymore. Everyone will think you're really tough and you believe in God.

Damn right!

Mark Milestone looks at the President with disgust and says: Can we go now, Mr. President? There's stuff Marv and I need to get done today with the FBI and—

Fuck the FBI! Did you know that J. Edgar Hoover was a fag? He used to go to strip clubs dressed as a woman.

He's dead, Mr. President. And besides, who cares what he did when he wasn't on the job? Don't you have stuff you like to do when you're not on camera? I mean, aside from playing golf.

Yeah, but—

Anyway, I think we've done what you wanted, haven't we? You look like the toughest guy in the Western Hemisphere.

Hell yeah! And I'll feel a hundred times better if they've still got those Oreos back in the Oval Office. I mean, seriously, why wasn't there another full pack waiting for me when I finished the first one an hour ago?

Marv Expire says: But wait, Mr. President, aren't we supposed to go inside and inspect the mark of the beast?

Fuck the mark of the beast! I need a snack. And the Oreos better be there. If those aides ate them all while I was out here, they're in deep shit. I really needed them before. I can't believe we had to send out for more! That better not happen again!

The cameras keep clicking and clicking, as if physical space were just an excuse for photographic space, inflating Barry Trap like he's being photoshopped into a giant. Soon he reaches the point where his body can't expand any further. A hundred cameras click in the next five seconds. A hundred more cameras click in the next four seconds. A hundred more cameras click in the next three seconds. A hundred more cameras click in the next two seconds. A hunded more cameras click in a second, then in less than a second. It's like they've reached the point where pictures can't stop being taken. They're making the president larger than life, even larger than larger than life, turning him into the largest blow up doll in sex toy history.

A loud voice comes from a space outside the frame of the TV screen, apparently a protester with a question: Mr. President, what part of this sentence am I leaving out?

The president stares, blinks a few times, then says: The second part comes before the first, but the second part doesn't exist yet.

He trembles for a second, then pops loudly out of existence, as if he were made of a billion microscopic party balloons. There's nothing left but a limp white shirt with a sky-blue necktie, a folded piece of scotch tape connecting the shirt to the tie, and a smoking heap of orange dust on the sacred pavement.

The scene is replaced by a Liberty Mutual ad, the emu and the pilot from the previous ad, but before the guy can say that you only pay or pray for what you need, the TV screen goes blank. Everyone stares in shock and silence, then everyone says what the fuck, staring at the Brooklyn Bridge as if it might explode. The chopper turns and disappears in flashing sunlight.

I turn to Jane Tambourine and say: That really happened, right? I mean, it's Reality TV.

She smiles and says: That right: Reality TV. None of it's fiction.

I scan the room and see Nancy laughing softly: I'm pretty sure that was my brother's voice. He's down in DC, remember?

Jackie nods, looking puzzled.

Nancy says: And you heard Barry Trap's last words, right? He said the word **part** two times. You heard that, right?

Jackie says: Yeah, something like: the second part comes before the first, but the second part doesn't exist yet.

Nancy says: That's what I heard too, word for word.

Jackie says: So?

Nancy: Remember what I told you before? He said the word part, and he even said it twice. What's part spelled backwards?

I look at Jackie, watching the answer make her face turn red. She finally says: You've gotta be fucking kidding me!

GOING VIRAL

It's not a fancy place, but Chip doesn't mind. Any place looks good if Doreen is there and they're making love. Her apartment is in a complex that looks like an old two-story motel. All the units face a central pool, with plastic folding chairs and deck umbrellas. The place is gated, secure. Visitors have to identify themselves and get buzzed in. The intercom doesn't work, so most people text or phone when they reach the gate. Some of the tenants have shared their security codes with selected people, but not Doreen. Even the two men in her life have to text and wait for the buzzer. Frank, her fiancé, lives in Los Angeles, more than a hundred miles north. They get together only on weekends and holidays. This leaves Chip and Doreen lots of time to fuck. That's what they're doing right now.

The pool is old and trashy. Most of the tenants pretend it's not there. But it opened things up for Chip and Doreen in surprising ways. On their first night together, they went up onto the roof of the building. After kissing him fiercely, getting him hot and hard, she turned and hurled herself into the darkness, did a flawless double somersault in mid-air, plunging thirty feet into the pool. Chip was stunned. He moved cautiously to the edge of the roof and looked down. She was laughing and beckoning, wet with moonlight. Though he'd always been afraid to dive, even from a normal height, he jumped feet first off the roof and splashed down awkwardly beside her. They made noisy love in the water. Somehow none of the neighbors complained.

Chip and Doreen have been feasting on each other ever since. This afternoon is no different. They've been doing all sorts of exciting stuff in bed and they're dizzy with passion. But now there's a beep and a text on her phone from her fiance. He's at the gate. She jumps out of bed, puts her hands on her mouth, takes two steps forward, two steps back. Chip doesn't understand. He's still in a post-orgasmic daze.

She can't believe that Frank is here. She told him she was sick, staying in bed, just wanted to sleep all day, and now he's shouting her name from the gate, telling her that he's got a pot of chicken soup that he made himself, the best thing in the world for the common cold. He's a nurturing guy who wants to spend the rest of his life with Doreen. If he had his way, they'd be married now, making babies. Yet here she is with Chip, who's clear that he doesn't want anything long-term.

But he wants Doreen, who knows how to be what he wants in bed, and vice versa.

Frank shouts her name again from the gate, one floor below. She knows it's strange to not buzz him in right away, like she's always done in the past. Though her front door isn't visible from the gate, she can peek through the kitchen window blinds and see confusion distorting his face. She gets another text: Buzz me in! I'm here with soup! She sits beside Chip on the bed and whispers a tense explanation.

Chip shrugs and says: Look, it's no big deal. We can get dressed and say that I'm your accountant. We're going over your tax returns.

Frank won't buy it. We don't have documents. He'll know there have to be documents if we're figuring out my taxes.

Then tell him I'm a handyman, fixing your plumbing, so to speak.

He'll know you're not fixing anything. You don't have tools.

Okay, so you can just say I'm a family friend who stopped by.

He knows my family doesn't have friends in southern California.

So tell him I just stopped in from northern California. I'm on my way south toward Mexico, where I'm going to study the migratory patterns of Monarch butterflies.

Frank knows a lot about butterflies. He'll know that Monarchs don't migrate into Mexico in March.

Okay, so we can say I'm a freelance journalist, an old friend of yours stopping by on my way to study the detention centers on the Rio Grande, since I've heard that refugee children are still being separated from their parents, and I'm going to write an article for *The Nation*, condemning the president's continuing inhumane treatment of people desperate to escape cartel violence in their own countries, people forced to choose between death and starvation.

He subscribes to *The Nation*. He has friends on their editorial board.

So we can say I'm doing the article for *Harper's*.

He knows too much about the refugee situation. He'll mention things about gang violence in Honduras and El Salvador, and when you look puzzled he'll see that you don't know what you're talking about. Frank likes to find out that people don't know what they're talking about.

Okay. So we can say I'm a Jehovah's Witness and I'm trying to bring you—

They always have pamphlets. You don't have pamphlets.

So why don't you just buzz him in and leave your door unlocked and we can start fucking again and let him catch us doing it? I've always wondered what it's like to be caught red handed. Especially by a guy with a pot of chicken soup in his hands.

I don't want to hurt his feelings.

Then why are you seeing me? You know that he might find out and get his feelings hurt.

Because he won't give me what I want in bed. Frank always has to be dominant, and you know I like to be dominant.

So he's getting what he deserves.

He doesn't deserve to get cheated on.

You should have left him, or told him you needed two lovers because he wasn't willing to compromise in bed.

He wouldn't have been okay with it, especially since it would have been clear that I wanted you more than I wanted him.

But it might have forced him to change and give you more of what you wanted. He might have learned something new about how to make love.

I doubt it. He didn't see any reason to change, and

besides, I don't think your sexual personality is something you can change.

Of course it is. Most people who like the kind of kinky stuff we like start out as vanilla lovers. Then they figure out what they really like and make adjustments. At least, that's how it worked for me.

Frank shouts her name again. He wants to know why she's not buzzing him in. He was friendly at first, pleased to be surprising her with soup, but now there's an edge in his voice, like he might be figuring out what's going on. The panic on Doreen's face increases.

She whispers: What the fuck am I going to do? I can't just leave him there. He drove all the way down here from L.A., over a hundred miles—

I can just leave, can't I? Your door isn't visible from the gate. He won't see me walking out of your apartment. He won't see me until I'm half-way across the complex. He won't know I was here. He'll just see some guy on the second floor walkway.

She nods and says: Okay, get your clothes on and go. I'll hang out with him for a few hours, then call you and you can come back.

Or you can let him stay overnight and we can hook up again tomorrow. After all, he came all this way.

Right.

Chip gets dressed and quietly opens the door and walks along the upper walkway of the complex. He acts like he doesn't know that Frank is there. He goes down the stairs to the first floor, on the opposite side of the pool from the front gate, and he's just about to go out through the exit by the garbage bins when he decides he wants to check Frank out, see what he looks like, maybe chat with him for a minute or two. After all, Chip is curious. He's heard a lot about Frank.

Chip turns and walks around the pool toward the front gate, where Frank is waiting. Chip opens the gate and Frank says thanks. Chip likes the way Frank looks, tall and trim with short blond hair and wire rim glasses, roughly the same thing Chip sees when he looks at himself in the mirror. From the pleasant look Frank has offered him, Chip assumes that Frank has no idea. Frank walks toward the stairs leading up to Doreen's apartment.

Chip says: That soup smells great! Did you make it yourself?

Yeah. It's my mother's chicken soup recipe.

Chicken soup for the soul! Filled with wonderful things for the mind and body!

Frank smiles and Chip thinks he's probably a good guy. Doreen always says he's really terrific—helpful, funny, devoted. It's just that she wants Chip more, mainly because of the sexual thing.

Frank says: It's the greatest! My mother knew how to make it better than anyone.

And now you probably make it better than anyone.

My girlfriend always says so. In fact, I'm bringing this to her right now. Why don't you join us? I mean, she said she had a sore throat, but it's not every day that you get to taste the greatest soup in the world.

I don't see how I can say no to a great offer like that! By the way, I'm Chip.

Frank.

They shake hands warmly. Chip likes the way Frank shakes his hand. Chip always judges people by the way they shake hands. One of the best things about Doreen, when he first met her six months ago at a party, was her powerful handshake, which matched up well with the forceful way that she spoke.

They walk up the stairs to the door and knock. Doreen opens it and stares in disbelief, confused that both men are standing there smiling.

Frank pats Chip on the back and says: Doreen, meet Chip. He's going to share some chicken soup with us.

Chip likes the way that Doreen tries to conceal her

shock and fear, the way she makes herself smile and say: Hi Chip. Come on in.

Chip's amazed at how quickly she fixed up her place. Three minutes ago, it looked like a five-year-old's room after a pillow fight. Now it looks like a tasteful homemaker lives here.

Frank laughs: Wow honey! I don't think I've ever seen this place so nice and tidy!

She laughs, but it's clear that she isn't sure how to respond. She finally says: If I'd known you were coming, I would have left it a mess. But every once in a while, I get guilty and need to fix things up. It helps me when I'm not feeling well. Plus now I can make a good first impression on Chip.

Chip smiles. Of course he already knows how messy Doreen's apartment usually is. It's almost endearing that she's such a slob, especially since she dresses like a runway model, and in public gives the impression of being well-groomed and professional. The men sit facing each other at her small circular table. She pours the soup into bowls and gives them to Frank and Chip, who beam with anticipation.

She gets a bowl for herself, then sits and changes the subject: I saw something on my news feed a few minutes ago. Did you guys see it? The President got abducted.

Frank says: Yeah, I heard something about that on the radio right before I left to come down here. It happened this morning, didn't it?

Doreen nods: About six hours ago. Apparently, his body guards this morning were secretly members of a left-wing activist group, and one of them knocked him down, pretending it was an accident, while the others circled around him, pretending to be concerned, and a fake ambulence arrived and took him somewhere, no one knows where.

Chip says: Wow! Really? Very clever. I was hoping someone would get him. I'm surprised it took so long. Remember that song? "America, where are you now, we can't fight alone against the monster." But the monster today is America. The monster lives in the White House.

Frank nods: In the Pentagon and on Wall Street too, and in Silicon Valley.

Doreen holds up her phone and plays a one minute youtube clip of the abduction. Four men in dark blue suits are walking across the White House lawn, guarding the chief executive. There's a woman in a red jumpsuit beside him, showing him something in a folder, talking steadily. She lurches into him, knocking him down, then bends down beside him. The four men form a circle around the woman and the President. Two of them kneel and look concerned; the other two have pulled out walkie talkies. Fifteen seconds later an ambulence comes, so quickly that it must have been summoned before the accident took place. The four men lift the President onto his feet, walk him into the ambulence, and strap him to a gurney. The woman jumps in beside him. The doors close and the ambulence speeds away, red lights flashing. The video ends with sirens in the distance. A voice-over says that no one currently knows where the President is. But the President's real bodyguards have been found tied up in a White House basement closet. They all said the same thing: they weren't sure how they got there. Apparently they'd been drugged and passed out, replaced by a team of secret agents.

Frank looks at his phone and says: That clip has already gone viral.

Frank, Chip, and Doreen stare at their phones, reading the responses below the video. Almost all of them are smiley face emojis or abbreviations like OMG, LOL, and WTF, but one of them is longer: "That orange motherfucker deserves it! I hope they torture him! They should use an electric prod on his genitals, or pull out his teeth and fingernails one by one." Another one says:

That chick is hot! Anyone recognize her?

Wasn't it Beth Barton?

No way! Why would a well-known anchorwoman be involved in something sinister like this?

Looked just like her.

I've heard she's a closet left-wing radical.

I've heard she's a closet Republican.

She sleeps with women, doesn't she? Ewww!

You got a problem with that? Why do you care what she does BCD?

BCD?

Behind closed doors, duh!

Lol!

I fucking hate all these dumbass abbreviations.

What century are you living in? Lol!

Chip asks if he can have more chicken soup, smiling at Frank. Doreen takes Chip's bowl and goes to the kitchen, where the pot is on the stove, simmering. She fills the bowl and returns. Chip says thanks, then holds up his phone and says: Check this out!

It's another youtube clip of the abduction, but in this one there's a clown in the ambulence. He takes out a knife, holds it up so everyone can see it, flashes a broad theatrical smile, then reaches into the President's crotch and unzips him, pulling out his dick. The ambulence doors get shut, so no one gets to see the full castration.

Frank shakes his head and says: I think that's going too far.

Chip says: Too far? Too far for what?

Frank says: I mean, sure, after all the bullshit things he's done over the past three years, he deserves to get his ass kicked. But—

Doreen says: Was the clown even real?

Chip shrugs: The whole thing was probably photoshopped.

Doreen says: Let's check the network news.

She turns her TV on. A commercial is in progress, a shot of New York Harbor, the Statue of Liberty in the background. A guy with his face blurred out says he's in a witness protection program, then talks about insurance. Someone shoots his picture, the flash reveals his face, and someone else calls him by name. Now the sinister people he's helping to convict will know who he is. They can easily track him down. If anyone ever needed life insurance, he's the guy. He freaks out and jumps over a fence and splashes loudly into simulated water. High pitched voices sing: Liberty liberty liberty.

Then the Cable News logo appears, dissolving into Beth Barton's face. She's in a room with old brick walls, wearing nothing. She begins what sounds like a carefully prepared speech: Language is a battlefield. It's a fundamental human technology, a crucial part of our evolutionary toolkit, one of the major factors that's made our species what it is today, not just bipedal hominids, but apex predators, indeed the greatest apex predators our world has ever known. Yet millions of people all over the USA want portions of language banned from public use. For such people, the word BLIP should never be said, yet copulate is fine; the word BLIP should never be said, yet excrement is fine; the word BLIP should never be said, yet vagina is fine; the word BLIP should never be said, yet penis is fine. In each case, the unacceptable word means exactly the same thing as the acceptable word. Yet somehow words like BEEP and BEEP and BEEP and BEEP disturb millions of people greatly. In fact, it goes beyond disturbance. Such people are convinced that these words are evil, and can do great damage if they circulate freely through public space. Of course, they *do* circulate freely through public space, and millions of people enjoy saying them, precisely because they're considered naughty and wrong, tools of Satan. Right now, as I speak to the nation, much of what I'm saying is being deleted, obscured by an infantile noise, a beep or blip that tells people that an evil word has been suppressed, that Cable News, like all other commercial news networks, is protecting public space from the sinister influence of Satanic words. Yet nothing protects anyone from the truly dangerous language. Public space is filled with ads and political speeches, sound bites and and top-forty lyrics, deceptive and invasive images and messages, generating stupidity and confusion. No one questions this. No one thinks of protecting us from bullshit. I myself am a powerful part of this bullshit. I'm an image that sells a carefully edited version of the world. It's made me rich enough to buy almost anything I want. I can even shop at Whole Foods without going broke. But I'm here today to announce that from this point on—

The picture tube blanks out. Doreen says: What the fuck! She slaps the side of the set three times, then shrugs and says: Oh well. No big deal. The rest was probably bullshit.

Chip smiles: The voice and face of sexy news just called herself a consumer product. And they forgot to beep her out when she said the word bullshit. She got to say it twice!

Frank says: She's awesome!

Doreen says: Awesome? Really? Fuck you! My body is better than hers.

Chip says: Much better.

Frank looks at Chip and says: How would you know?

Chip shrugs: Just by looking at her.

Frank narrows his eyes: Really?

Chip says: You're a lucky man, Frank. Your girlfriend looks better with her clothes on than most women look with their clothes off.

Doreen looks annoyed: Are you saying I look better with my clothes on?

Chip shrugs again: I wouldn't know. I'm just saying you look great, even better than the sexiest journalist in the world.

Frank laughs: You're calling Beth Barton a journalist?

Chip smiles: That's probably what it would say on her resume. And I think she's won awards of some kind for journalism. So that makes it official. Even if the awards are bullshit, and she didn't deserve them.

The TV pops back on. Beth Barton stares at the nation from the screen, as if daring anyone to object to her naked body, maybe suggesting that viewers have been undressing her for years, fantasizing about her in their bedrooms. Then suddenly she's replaced by the

Liberty Mutual ad, the opening fifteen seconds, which they missed a few minutes ago. The witness protection guy is there with his face obscured and his voice distorted. He says: I can't tell you anything about myself. I'm not your average consumer.

Doreen turns off the set. No one says anything. It's as if the ad has taught them something they didn't know before, that if they're being honest, they can't tell anyone anything about themselves, that anything they said would be at best a half-truth, a distortion, a fabrication. The average consumer doesn't know this. The average consumer assumes that self disclosure is an unproblematic aspect of daily life. The average consumer feels no need for witness protection. Consumers, at least in America, witness themselves and speak freely, without hesitation. Yet when people suddenly see who they are, suicide is the only option. They jump the fence like the witness protection guy in the Liberty Mutual ad. Though the ocean may be nothing more than a visual simulation, it signifies death, and as the high-pitched voices sing of liberty, it's clear that the only liberation is the final release from the burden of self-disclosure.

Doreen says: Every time I see that fucking commercial, I want to kill the people who make sure that it's shown a hundred times a day.

Chip laughs and says: My wife works in advertising, and she knows the team that came up with those Liberty Mutual commercials, and they're brilliant people. A graduate student at Columbia did a PhD dissertation exploring the semiotic elements in those ads and—

Doreen looks shocked: Your wife? Your fucking wife?! You're married?

Chip looks guilty, looks at his hands.

Doreen says: You never told me you were married!

Frank says: You know this guy?

She says: Yeah. I mean, no, not really. I met him at a party last week.

Then why did you act like strangers a few minutes ago, when I introduced you?

I didn't recognize him at first.

And now you do?

Yeah. It was like in that commercial, when the witness protection guy is exposed, and gets recognized, and now the wrong people know his name and what he looks like.

Chip says: The truth is, I'm not really married, not anymore. My wife left me a few months ago. I should have said ex-wife.

Frank stares at Chip and Doreen. Noise comes through the window. There's a helicopter approaching.

Soon the sound is almost deafening. Above Doreen's bed, beside the window, there's a framed cover of an old Life magazine: Tenzing and Hillary on Mount Everest, having reached the roof of the world. Tenzing is smiling at Hillary, who looks down, like he doesn't want his picture taken, especially when he's exhausted and low on oxygen.

Frank finally says: What's really going on here?

Chip says: That chopper is really obnoxious. Why is it legal to use machines that generate so much noise? I wish I could lean out the window and shoot it down.

Doreen: There ought to be noise regulations.

Chip says: No chance of that. Our president strongly believes in deregulation.

Frank says: No, seriously: What's really going on here?

Doreen nods at the picture: I just realized something. I've had that picture for five years now, and I've never noticed the weirdest thing. Those two guys have just reached the top of Mount Everest, right? They're the first ones ever to do that. So who was up there waiting to take that picture? Why doesn't he get credit for being the first person to reach the top of the world?

Chip says: The shot was actually taken hours before they reached the top, at their base camp, by one of the other guys on the expedition. Yet almost everyone assumes that they're on the roof of the world, which is what the magazine's editors were expecting, and what they were hoping for, since it makes the picture more dramatic, more likely to sell magazines. It's interesting that Hillary is looking away, clearly uncomfortable, even though he grew up around cameras. But the other guy, the sherpa Tenzing Norgay, looks happy and relaxed, and he's got the kind of smile you expect from people who don't mind having their picture taken. Yet someone told me that Tenzing had never had his picture taken before, and didn't even know how to use a camera.

Frank says: Would one of you two please answer my question: What's really going on here? What the fuck is really going on here?

Chip says: Think about it: In 1953, when Everest was first conquered, there were people in the world who'd never had their pictures taken or taken pictures of anyone else. Yet now Mount Everest is crowded with people whose main goal is to get pictures of themselves at the top of the world. They climb all that way just to get the pictures.

Frank says: I'll count to three. At the count of three,

I want to know what's going on here. If I don't get a real answer, I'll pour hot soup on your heads.

Doreen says: You'd really do that?

Frank says: One!

You'd really do that?

Two!

I can't believe you'd really do that.

Three!

There's a garbled electronic message from the chopper repeating over and over again, something about the President being abducted.

Doreen narrows her eyes: Am I hearing that right? The President's been abducted, and they can't find him, so they're sending helicopters out with messages that say: If anyone knows where the President is, please call 911. This is too too funny!

Frank says: Time's up. I want to know what's really going on here!

Doreen says: Give us another chance. Count to three again.

Okay. One more chance, starting now. One!

Chip shakes his head: It's so fucking stupid. They want us to hear the announcement about the president, but the noise of the chopper drowns out most of the message.

Frank says: Two!

Doreen takes Frank's hand and starts massaging it, like she's comforting a scared guinea pig. She reaches between Frank's legs and starts to unzip him. She says: If you'll stop asking what's really going on here, I'll give you a blow job.

Frank says: Really? Right now?

Yeah. And Chip will get to watch.

Really? Chip, you don't mind watching?

Chip smiles: I like to watch. It's one of my favorite things, like in that song.

Really? Okay, honey. Wow! I'm starting to get hard!

Frank leans back in his chair and stares at Mount Everest in the poster. His dick is getting bigger. Doreen starts to blow him. She makes incredible slurping sounds to make what she's doing seem more intense.

Chip says: You really know what you're doing, don't you?

Doreen stops and turns to Chip and says: You better believe it!

Frank says: Don't stop, Doreen! Chip, shut the fuck up. Seriously!

Chip says: Okay, but after she's done with you, I want a blow job too. Deal?

Frank says: Yeah, yeah, deal! No problem, dude!

Doreen puts Frank's dick back in her mouth, then makes the slurping noises again. They drive Frank crazy. He's moving his hips up and down. Chip unzips himself and starts jerking off, getting himself big and hard so he'll be prepared when Doreen's done with Frank. The chopper is moving farther away, but another one is approaching. Soon the second one sounds like it's right overhead, hovering. The noise is brutal.

Chip says: I'm ready, Doreen! Do us both at once!

She and Frank look at Chip like he's out of his mind.

Doreen says: Both at once? How the fuck would I do that?

Chip says: My wife could do it.

Frank says: She must have been really good!

Chip says: This cop was at our door. We got complaints because we were doing acid and playing the first Led Zeppelin album really loud at three in the morning. This cop looked super mean. He had handcuffs and a gun and he wore mirror shades at three in the morning. What kind of asshole wears mirror shades when it's dark out? So she told the cop she'd blow him if he left us alone. I thought he was just going to say something like *That won't be necessary ma'am* and look even meaner, but instead he had his dick out in a second. She started working him so skillfully that he collapsed against the wall. It was totally cool. I pulled my dick out and got myself hard and begged her to do both of us at once. She did him for ten seconds, did me for ten seconds, did him for ten seconds, did me for ten seconds, and we came at the same time. Then she pulled down her pants and got herself off while the cop and I played with her nipples.

Frank says: That's way cool, dude! But—

Doreen says: Totally! I can see why you're sad that she left you. She sounds like she must have good in bed.

She was. I wasn't.

Frank stares at Chip, then shakes his head and says: That's amazing. That's the first time I've ever heard a guy admit that he's not good in bed.

Doreen pats Chip on the back and says: Oh come on! I'm sure you'd be good with the right person.

Chip says: I've never been good in bed. Women always complain that I'm selfish and I don't know what I'm doing. There's only one woman who ever seemed to like me in bed, and she was with another guy, so I had to see her in secret and—

Frank points to his dick and says: Can you finish me?

She says: Oh yeah, sure.

She gets him off in ten seconds. Chip gets himself

off in ten seconds. Then she gets herself off while Chip and Frank tell her all sorts of filthy things in bedroom voices. She screams when she comes, then worries that she might have pissed off the neighbors.

Chip says: Don't worry. If they call the cops, we'll know what to do when they get here.

Frank says: Right. But finish your story: What did that cop do after your wife got him off?

Ex wife, remember?

Yeah, sorry.

He lay there in the open doorway smiling like he was stoned. He told us he liked the second Zeppelin album better. Then he left without saying anything else.

The noise from the second chopper fades, but the noise from the first one returns, and the garbled message repeats and repeats and repeats: If anyone knows where the President is, call 911 immediately.

By now, the message sounds to Chip like noise pollution. In his alternative version of the present moment, the chopper crashes into the pool and sinks and disappears and no one notices.

In Doreen's alternative version of the present moment, the chopper appears in a commercial, circling the Brooklyn Bridge, but the actors all talk trash and the ad gets cancelled and fines are imposed.

In Frank's alternative version of the present moment, the chopper is caught in the flames of the opening scene of *Apocalypse Now*, and the spooky voice of Jim Morrison sings that the end is our only friend.

No one says anything for fifteen seconds. Then Doreen takes a deep breath and says: So where do you think he is?

Frank says: No idea. But maybe we should go outside and look around.

Chip and Doreen look at Frank like he's an idiot, or like they're wondering if he'll remember his ultimatum and pour hot soup on their heads.

Chip says: Look around?

Yeah. You know, look for the President.

You really think we can find him? How? Going door to door, looking in everyone's closets? Where do you hide one of the biggest assholes in Western history? We're more than three thousand miles away from the capital. Why would someone be hiding him around here?

The noise of the first chopper finally fades out entirely, but the noise of the second chopper comes back, as if it's forgotten something. Soon it's hovering right above the apartment shaking like it might be taking a shit. There's noise from the downstairs apartment, voices and laughter, a slamming door, then a loud splash in the pool.

Doreen says: What was that? Someone's in the pool? That's weird. I thought I was the only one crazy enough to dive into that pool.

Frank says: You dove into the pool? When was this? You always said you were afraid of what might be in the water, like it might be filled with viruses or amoebas. And now we keep hearing things about that deadly virus from China. We might all have to wear masks. You really dove into that filthy pool?

Chip quickly changes the subject: There's something going on downstairs. It sounded like Karla's voice.

Frank says: Karla? The downstairs neighbor? That's odd, Chip. How do you know who Karla is? I mean, if you've never been here before?

There's a knock on the door. It's Karla, dressed like a farmer's wife in a pornographic movie, tight overalls with nothing underneath. She clears her throat and says: Could the three of you come downstairs for a minute. I've got something I need to show you. And bring your phones. The camera on mine doesn't work, and I want to make a video.

They hurry outside and hear commotion in the

pool, someone splashing frantically, shouting for help. As they get closer, they can see that it's a guy in a suit.

Doreen starts laughing: Oh my god! It's the president!

Frank says: You're right. But what's he doing here?

Karla says: I'm sure you've heard that he was abducted this morning. My cousin was involved in the action. He bought a special clown suit for the occasion. Their plan was to drop him off here.

Doreen can't stop laughing: Why here?

Karla says: Because my cousin knew I wouldn't rat him out. He knows I hate the president even more than he does. The plan was to tie him up and hold him for ransom.

I say: So they dropped him in the pool?

Karla says: Right. But they never found out if he knows how to swim. Apparently not. I got a text from my cousin a minute ago. He said they were planning to lower the chopper about twenty feet above the pool. But the president was struggling so much that he fell out before they descended, and he dropped at least two hundred feet. The impact probably stunned him.

Frank says: So we should save him, right?

Karla says: No way! Would we save Hitler or Genghis Khan if they were drowning? This is the same guy who treats refugees along the border like they're all prostitutes and drug dealers, when in fact these people are seeking asylum here because drug cartels are making life in their own countries unsafe. A close friend of mine used to work in a detention center. She quit because she couldn't stand it any longer. She heard those refugee children crying for their parents. The president is the one who put them there. He doesn't get compassion from me, and he doesn't deserve it from anyone else. I just want a video as he goes under. He's always described himself as a "sink or swim" president. Let's let him find out what sinking is all about.

Chip and Doreen raise their phones and start filming. Other tennants are watching from their doorways, but they don't seem to know what's going on.

Frank looks around, starts to panic: Other people can see what's happening. Won't we get in trouble if we don't fish him out?

Karla says: We can just say that we weren't sure what to do, like we didn't know who he was and we don't know how to swim.

The president stops thrashing, floats face-down for a few seconds, then sinks like a gigantic bag of dogfood. Soon he's resting on the bottom.

Karla says: Did you guys get some good footage?

Doreen studies her phone, then says: Yeah, mine is awesome. Should I post it right now?

Karla nods: No reason to wait. Within a few minutes, the thing will go viral. Some people will assume it's been photoshopped, or it's some kind of joke. But so what? It's sure to be the biggest hit in virtual history!

IDENTITY THEFT

I answered the phone. The man on the other end sounded rough, unprofessional. He didn't have the blandly scripted voice of the government bureaucrat he was pretending go be. He said that the IRS had filed a law suit against me, that someone who'd gotten my credit card numbers was using them in drug-related activities. He said he was part of the IRS fraud department, provided a badge number, and claimed that my bank accounts were about to be frozen. The only way to prevent this was to give him my credit card number. I was nervous. Something about it sounded wrong, but I didn't want the IRS seizing my assets. I pulled out my card, stared at the numbers, got ready to speak them into the phone. Then I remembered that in the past the IRS had always contacted me by mail, on official IRS letterhead. The guy on the phone didn't have a letterhead voice. His manner of speaking was clumsy, his grammar suspect. I hung up.

I entered "IRS phishing identity theft" into my search bar, and got over half a million results in less than a second. I took the time to read three. They all said the same thing, describing my experience exactly. I also found out that even though this phishing technique is inept, obviously fraudulent, it works. Thousands of people fall for it every day. I'd almost fallen for it. And I'm not in a position to fall for anything. I haven't had a job in almost a year. There aren't many openings in the field I'm trained for, so I haven't really been looking too hard. Besides, I think all jobs are stupid. No matter what the work situation is, I always end up feeling that there have to be better ways to spend my time. But I don't have much choice at this point. The heap of unpaid bills on my desk gets larger every day. If it wasn't for the online work my wife does, we'd be in serious trouble.

But this morning I saw something promising in the Help Wanted section of the paper. It offered high pay for someone with brains and a good phone voice. I've been told many times that my voice on the phone sounds good. I've got a PhD, so I guess I have brains.

I made a call, made an appointment, and now it's two days later. I'm here at the address in the paper, knowing I need to convince the guy I'll be talking to that I'm the best person for the job, no matter what it turns out to be. It's a brownstone on a tree-lined street, a block away from site of the cottage where Poe wrote "The Raven."

I've always thought the poem was over-rated, a tedious display of death-obsessed rhyming. But I like the image of Poe at his desk in his dumpy cottage, quill pen scratching its way across the page, writing in bursts, pausing and staring into space, then scratching out words and adding others, playing with verbal sounds, counting syllables, not producing great poetry, but briefly releasing himself from his daily anxieties. Like me right now, Poe was in this location because of money problems. But the neighborhood has changed. Poe's cottage was falling apart and cost him almost nothing. Brownstones here now sell for ten million dollars.

I go up ten flights of stairs to the fifth floor, even though from the outside it looked like a three-story building. I knock on a carved oak door and a voice tells me to come in. Inside, there's a guy with a bowtie and suspenders sitting at a huge wooden desk. It looks old enough to have been the desk Poe used when he wrote "The Raven."

I say: Hi. I'm Pete. We talked on the phone two days ago.

He stands and smiles and shakes my hand and says: Hi Pete. I'm Pete too.

Really? What a coincidence! How often do you meet a guy whose name is the same as yours.

Not often. But whenever it happens, it's a pretty cool feeling.

It sure is.

We stand there in silence for more than a minute. It's amazing how long a minute feels when you're facing someone and you've both got stupid smiles and you don't say anything.

Pete's head looks like a pencil, much too long and thin for the rest of his body. He reaches up to press the knot in his bowtie, which spins three times and squirts me in the face. We both laugh. The laughing makes us laugh even harder, which makes us laugh even harder, which makes us laugh even harder. Finally we make ourselves stop.

He says: It sure feels great to laugh, doesn't it?

It's the greatest feeling in the world, even better than sex.

It sure is.

We start another pause with stupid smiles, but then his face tenses up, like he just remembered something. He says: Okay. You need a job, right?

Yeah. I'm broke.

Great. You're hired.

The interview's over? I made a good impression?

Yeah. I can tell you've got a good sense of humor.

That's the main thing I look for when I'm interviewing someone. You passed the bowtie test. And now you're about to commit identity theft.

Really? Someone tried that on me just a few days ago. I almost fell for it. But—

Thousands of people fall for it each day. It's a billion dollar business.

And now it's my job?

Now it's your job.

How do I do it? I've never done it before.

You make random calls. You mostly get voice mail and leave threatening messages, but even when a person really answers, you say the same thing.

What do I say?

You say that one of their credit cards has apparently been stolen, and it's been used in a series of cocaine deals, and now the CIA is planning to freeze their bank accounts—or no, not the CIA, it's the FBI; or no, not the FBI, it's the NSA; or no, not the NSA, it's the IRS.

Do I use those exact words? Do I have to say *or no* five times.

I said it three times.

Okay. Do I have to say it three times?

Yeah.

Why three times and not five?

If you say it three times, it adds to the authenticity of the experience. If you say it five times, it sounds like you don't know what you're doing.

What if I say it four times?

That's an even number.

Oh, okay. So then what?

You tell them to give you their credit card number, their social security number, and their bank account number.

What if they won't?

You tell them if they won't, you'll take all their money.

What do I do when I've got all their numbers.

You take all their money.

This sounds like a really great job.

It's totally great. Before too long, you'll be worth millions.

I'll be able to buy this house.

You'll be able to buy the White House.

When do I start?

You've already started.

I have? There's no paperwork?

Paperwork is for losers. Think of all the time that gets wasted on paperwork.

You sound like you know what you're talking about.

It's always better to work for someone who knows how to sound like he knows what he's talking about.

What's the alternative?

You work for someone who doesn't know how to sound like he knows what he's talking about, even though he knows what he's talking about, or you work for someone who doesn't know what he's talking about, but knows how to sound like he knows what he's talking about, or you work for someone who doesn't know what he's talking about, and doesn't know how to sound like he knows what he's talking about.

Options two and three would totally suck.

Which would be worse?

Option two: the guy would sound convincing while he was fucking everything up. The option three guy would clearly be inept, and you wouldn't have to take him seriously.

Actually, you might. Think of the current U.S. president.

I don't take him seriously.

But if you worked for him, you'd have to.

I'd have to pretend to.

And the president is just the most toxic example. More subtle versions of the same thing are everywhere.

I was just about to say the same thing.

So we're on the same page. I can already see that we're going to work well together.

You tell me what to do, and I do it. You make ten times as much as I do, and you just sit there giving orders. I do all the work and I don't mind doing it. I'm glad I'm making money and I don't care that you're making ten times more and just sitting there giving orders.

Exactly.

But you act as if you're not giving orders, and you do it so well that I act like you're not giving orders, and things get done your way, though it feels like my way.

Exactly.

Suddenly, we're shaking hands and smiling. It always feels great when you're shaking hands and smiling.

I decide it's time to leave. Timing is everything. If I don't leave right away, I might say something stupid and fuck things up. Pete might think I'm an idiot and fire me, even though the job hasn't started yet. Then I remember that the job has already started, so maybe it's not the right time to leave. So much depends on timing. The same thing isn't the same thing if the time is right or the time is wrong. But this thought is quickly replaced by something that doesn't mean the same thing. It's replaced by the thought that the brownstone we're currently standing in is taller outside than it is inside, five floors instead of three, and it might be dangerous to accept a job in a building that's not the same thing inside and out. It suggests that you're not really where you seem to be, which isn't a good foundation for mental health. This reminds me that there's no name on the door to Pete's office, which is weird because if you're running a business it probably has a name, which typically appears on the building owned or rented by the business, or at least on the door of the room or floor where the business does what it does. But if Pete is doing identity theft, he might not want what he does to be called anything, like Pete's Identity Theft, or New York Identity Theft, or U.S. Identity Theft, or Global Identity Theft, or Cosmic Identity Theft, or Deluxe Identity Theft. But if I'm working now for a company that doesn't have a name, what am I going to put on my resume? I know people often put fake stuff on their resumes, so maybe I could call my current job something like New World Finance or East Coast Transactions or maybe Lizard Bay Transitions, since I heard at a party recently that New York was once called Lizard Bay, but when I looked it up later I found no evidence that New York was ever called Lizard Bay, though of course it's been called all sorts of things over the years, like the Big Apple, which has never made any sense to me. I keep smiling at Pete and shaking his hand. He does the same thing. I'm thinking we've been smiling and shaking hands for almost a minute now, which is far too long to shake hands. I remember that right now I might be standing in the very same spot where Poe wrote "The Raven," only I'm five floors up while Poe was on the first floor. I'm higher than he was. People say that being high is good for your poetry. I try to picture Poe at the writing desk five floors below me. I see flat black hair, a huge white forehead, fiercely wrinkled, a tense mouth spitting out syllables, troubled eyes glaring at the result. A famous portrait comes to mind, a daguerrotype in which Poe looks like he just got punched in the face but he's trying hard to look like it didn't hurt. His tie looks like a dead butterfly and his moustache is longer on one side than the other. He's wearing a cloak of some kind, but it's buttoned up wrong, like he slept in it, got up in a hurry and couldn't find a mirror. I wonder how our sense of Poe's writing would change if we had daguerrotypes that showed him smiling and laughing. Is it possible that he spent lots of time in playful, goofy moods? What if he was nothing like the Edgar Allan Poe described in the biography written right after his death by one of his arch enemies? What if the biographer committed a kind of identity theft, deliberately making Poe look more depressed and insane than he really was? I decide that if I ever have enough money, I'll make a movie featuring Poe, and he'll be happy all the time. Or would this also be a form of identity theft? Pete and I are still smiling and shaking hands and now it's almost been two minutes. I'm thinking back to the news last night, a political rally, the President saying offensive things while the crowd went wild, chanting *send them home, send them home, send them home, send them home*, referring to the Squad, four non-white congresswomen, all of them U.S. citizens, all of them home already, with no other home to be sent to. It looked to me like the President was promoting racism, hatred, and violence, or committing another kind of identity theft, making the Squad women look like they don't belong here. I'm about to say this to Pete, but for all I know he might think the President is a great guy, even though a few minutes ago he called him a toxic asshole, but who knows whether he meant it or not, or if he was just trying to see who I really am, and not who I pretend to be, so I keep my mouth shut. For years, I've been trying to learn how to keep my mouth shut. It hasn't been easy, even after many embarrassing moments. Pete and I are still smiling and shaking hands and now it's almost been three minutes. I can't tell if Pete thinks there's anything weird about it, since I can't see beyond his eager facial expression, but it feels like we're both in a trance, like the state of mind my wife can induce with a few well-chosen words and compelling images. She makes a good living online as a hypnotist, and on our first date, five years ago, I asked her to hypnotize me. I was hoping she would lead us both into a sexual dream, but instead I felt like I was drifting toward the bottom of the sea, except that I was sitting at my kitchen table, fully aware of the pots and pans on the stove, the black microwave on the counter, the faint humming of the old white fridge beside the bathroom door, flies buzzing and darting and circling above the dishes in the sink. I heard her voice telling me that I was drifting over sacrificial stones in the public squares of Machu Pichu, gliding over the fleets of reed boats moored on the shores of Lake Titicaca, circling over the coast of Tierra del Fuego, a labyrinth of prismatic mist, which looked like a gigantic scheming octopus, camouflaging itself by changing colors. I was pleasantly confused. I was where she said I was and also where I knew I was. I felt like a bowl of ice cream slowly melting. Then I heard her snap her fingers, and I knew I would never want to watch TV again. Instead I would surround myself with the silence and grace of tropical fish, designing tranquil aquariums for every room in the house. And I knew right away that she and I would be together forever, or what passed for together forever in the twenty-first century, even though at that point I didn't know who she was, beyond our initial attraction to each other. I felt like the person I was had been replaced by something better, yet it's taken me a long time to figure out what words like better mean. It's the kind of identity theft I've learned to enjoy, though it's been loaded with uncertainties, just like what I'm feeling now, shaking hands with Pete, someone I've never seen before. We're still smiling and shaking hands and now it's almost been four minutes. Maybe one of my new duties will be to smile and shake hands for extended periods of time. So it's a good thing Pete is a good guy. I wouldn't want to be shaking hands with an asshole all the time. But of course there's no telling who else I might have to shake hands with. There might be people who try to prove how strong they are when they shake your hand, or people who barely grip your hand at all, making it seem that they're not really pleased to meet you, unless the limp hand is a way of suggesting that there's no need to worry, that they won't ever try to be in charge, at least not in obvious ways. I remember reading a book about shaking hands, filled with pictures and personal stories, comments from celebrities, atheletes, politicians, and business people. My guidance counselor in high school told me to read it. He gave me a test on it, which I didn't pass. He made everyone in the school practice shaking hands with him on a regular basis, and he offered suggestions, corrections, over and over again, until most of us wanted nothing more than to cut his hand off. But Pete and I gripped each other's hands in a forthright way, made firm and friendly eye contact when we first met a few minutes ago, which told me that we're probably compatible. Or com-pete-ible, a word that might mean equally competetive, if it really existed. But now the fact that our shared name is Pete reminds me of peat, the peat that's making the Arctic burn. I was reading about it last night, and somehow my thoughts about the weird phone call I'd gotten the day before got superimposed on the melting ice caps, and I thought of climate change as a kind of worldwide identity theft. Peat is the heavyweight champion of carbon emissions, the muck from which our ecosystem sprouts in wild variety. It's ninety-five percent water, but now because of global warming it's dry, condensing into the world's most flammable substance. With the Arctic permafrost melting, far more peat is exposed than ever before, drying relentlessly, turning the world's coldest region into a conflagration waiting to happen. When lightning strikes the peat smolders like a lit cigarette, burning downward into the earth and sideways across the tundras of northern Siberia. So it's no accident that our shared name is catching fire in my head, reminding me that my new boss is such an amazing guy, so easy to please. But I don't want to assume too much. A friend told me once about a former boss who acted nice all the time for the first three weeks, then acted nice only half the time for the next three weeks, then acted mean all the time for the next three weeks, and after that the job was impossible. Even the boss couldn't stand it. He hated acting mean, but apparently felt it was part of the job. The boss he thought he was supposed to be replaced the person he wanted to be. Still, with Pete making ten times more than I do for doing nothing, he might think that he's got to be nice all the time, for as long as I'm working here. Then I remember that I've got to be nice all the time too. Otherwise, I might get fired. It's one thing to get fired from a shitty job. It's another thing to get fired from an easy job. Getting hired and getting fired are only one letter apart, suggesting the instability of twenty-first century work for almost everyone. I catch myself assuming that Pete would never get rid of someone who had the same name, but it could also be a source of disturbance if he didn't like sharing a fundamental part of his identity. Again, I'm thinking of Poe, who wrote a story called "William Wilson," where the narrator keeps running into his double, and eventually kills him, only to realize that he's murdered an essential part of himself. Is Pete an essential part of me, the part that knows how to get what he wants and ends up as a boss and not just a worker? If I follow Poe's story and kill Pete instead of doing what he says, will I be killing off the clever, ambitious part of me that could end up making lots of money and not taking orders from anyone? I know I've never liked doing jobs where someone I don't respect can yell at me whenever they want and I have to put up with it, jobs where someone can fire me and mess up my resume and my credit rating, and I can't take the kind of revenge I want without making things worse. But maybe none of it matters because Pete isn't really a double, and doesn't look anything like me, as far as I can tell, and he doesn't seem to be the kind of jerk that likes to yell and threaten. He probably knows how to get results without getting tough about it, and indeed his demeanor seems almost insanely pleasant, like he really belongs on his back in a meadow enchanted by the shapes of passing clouds, though his facial expression also reminds me of Vincent Costco, the very sweet guy who's painted American flags on his van and named it after the President, religiously attending all his rallies, no matter how far he has to travel. The QAnon people think he's secretly JFK Junior, who supposedly faked his death twenty years ago to avoid the murderous wrath of Hillary Clinton, but has now come out of hiding in disguise, uniting with the President to help him squash the liberal conspiracy that's supposed to be ruining our country by promising universal health care and free education. It's disturbing that millions of people believe this, especially since Vincent Costco is five inches shorter than JFK Junior was and looks nothing like him. Even more disturbing is their claim that Vincent Costco has a double, suggesting that JFK Junior also had a double, so that two sets of doubles are now prepared in disguise to help the President, even though JFK Junior's political views were nothing like the President's. The whole thing makes me want to laugh, but it's not really funny, since all of these QAnon weirdos will vote for the President later this year, and besides, I'm not sure Pete would understand my laughter, since there's no apparent reason for it in our current situation, and I don't want Pete thinking that sometimes I just break out laughing for no reason. It might seem unprofessional. I've always hated words like professional. They're so formulaic. They suggest an image that you need to maintain if you want to make money. They tell you to be serious and tell you how to look serious, as if there was only one way to look serious. They tell you laughing is only okay if someone tells a joke, that laughing at the wrong time will make it seem like you're getting nervous. They tell you that jokes work best at parties, but only certain kinds of jokes at certain kinds of parties. I'm hoping Pete won't ask me to go to parties, especially parties where people are practicing forms of identity theft. I wouldn't want to be drunk at a party where people are trying to get you to say your social security number, recording it on their phones, opening fake bank accounts in your name while your back is turned or you're upstairs using the bathroom. But I don't think Pete's the party type, and I'm guessing he can tell that I'm not either. The handshake is making me think that I can assume all sorts of things about Pete, and vice versa. In fact, our hands are so firmly connected that I'm starting to think I can read the lines in his palm without even seeing them. I'm not interested in fortune tellers, but a friend of mine went to an Internet psychic last year for a virtual palm reading and was told he'd be dead within six months, a victim of a new and deadly virus that no one would be concerned about until it was too late, and now this friend is dead after spending a month in China, delivering lectures on microbiotic mutations, and still no one here in the States is paying attention, probably because the President has other priorities, like making sure that the next luxury suite he checks into will be well stocked with double stuff golden Oreos, which leads me to wonder what Pete's food obsessions might be. I've had food obsessions all my life, and I don't understand people who don't want to stuff themselves with unhealthy food, so I'm sure Pete likes Cheetos or Big Macs or thickly buttered popcorn, and I'd feel betrayed if he was on a carefully maintained microbiotic diet or protein diet and never at any point in his life had even the slightest concern about getting fat. I'm not fat enough to be called fat, though of course the deadly new term is obese, and apparently almost ninety percent of all Americans are obsese, which is one of those alarming statistics which can't be true, since most of the people I see on the streets aren't even overweight, let alone obese, though most of them are flabby, even skinny ones like me. But apparently Pete isn't all that concerned with how physically fit I might be, since after all you can excel in the field of identity theft without a gym membership. I'm not getting health food fanatic vibes from Pete's warmly professional eyes or body language, and by now, after six minutes of shaking hands, I think it's fair to say that I would have picked up warning signals, but I'm more concerned at this point that we're still shaking hands after three hundred seconds, with no sign of ending. Once something takes much longer than it should, you start to think about time in a different way. You start to suspect that it's not the best way to keep track of what you're doing, since five minutes of smiling and shaking hands probably feels quite different than five minutes of writing a poem like "The Raven." I imagine Poe five floors below me getting annoyed by the rapping at his chamber door, getting so distracted that he can't maintain the precision the poem requires, just when he was almost convinced that the words were taking him somewhere, a place that was strange in all the right ways, a place he might almost enjoy. I like words like almost. I wish all words were like almost. It feels precise in a way that other words don't, though maybe not as precise as words like maybe. Maybe there's nothing more precise than maybe. Suddenly maybe feels like the safest word in the English language. Maybe it's safe to stop smiling and shaking hands.

Pete drops my hand and says: This won't just be a job. It will also be similar to a job, similar in ways that make words like similar obsolete, obsolete in ways that make words like obsolete obsolete.

I drop his hand and say: I like the way that sounds.

If it sounds good now, it will sound even better next week, and the week after that. You're about to become the most powerful man in the world.

I smile at Pete and say: Except for you.

That's right, Pete, Pete says, except for me.

I hear faint cursing and laughter, a voice that sounds like it's coming from five floors below. For a second, I think it's Poe, glaring at his pen like it's making fun of him, tearing the page in half and then in half again, again and again, tired of ravens, tired of rhymes, finally convinced that there have to be better ways to spend his time.

ALMOST FAMOUS

Clark is in his bedroom jerking off when his iPhone rings. It's flashing and vibrating on the nightstand, like it might explode, so he answers. There's no one there, just a link on the screen. He stares at the seemingly random combination of numbers and letters, then shrugs and clicks. There's a flash on his screen, a clip of someone jerking off in a bedroom. Clark thinks it might be a picture of himself right before the phone rang, but the image is gone before he can see it clearly.

He's not sure what's going on, but when he tries to start masturbating again, it doesn't work. The spell has been broken. It's the fifteenth robocall he's gotten since breakfast. He knows that over the course of the day, he'll get at least fifteen more. Friends have told him that the calls can be blocked, but he doesn't think he should have to get an extra app to protect himself. It's as if the true purpose of the phone is not to help him keep in touch with the people in his life, but to make him an easy target, to put him on a leash that can be jerked at any moment, reminding him of all the overpriced bullshit he can buy, all the irrelevant things he needs to consider, making sure that he can't relax, that he's never too far from the next interruption.

He wolfs down a late lunch and takes a train to his favorite park, where people are eating and jogging and playing music and throwing frisbies. Clark likes the park better when it's empty, but he finds a quiet place in a wooded area near a waterfall, sits on a bench and watches the light and shade and starts to feel better.

A few minutes later a woman comes and sits beside him on the bench. She's tall and tan with a baseball hat. Her long white curly hair leads Clark to assume that she's over sixty, but her skin is so moist and smooth that Clark assumes that she's under thirty. He doesn't want her to see him checking her out, so he puts on a dreamy look and watches the motion of light and shade in the trees. Two minutes pass, then she moves a few inches closer. Her bare left arm is almost touching his right arm. He thinks he can feel her eyes moving over his body. He wants to say something to her, make her laugh, act like a really cool guy. But he's not a really cool guy. So he keeps his eyes on the light and shade in the trees. They sit a few minutes longer. Then she hands him her phone and asks him to take her picture beside the waterfall. He stares at the phone like he doesn't understand it, so she laughs and leans up against him and shows him how to frame a shot and push the right buttons.

He says: I almost never use my phone as a camera. I don't like pictures.

She laughs: You'll like taking pictures of me. People tell me I look fantastic in pictures.

He wants to tell her she looks fantastic now, but she's off the bench and posing in front of the waterfall, assuming what looks like a yoga position. He takes five shots, from different angles. Then she snuggles beside him to look at the pictures. They agree that she looks terrific, especially in the final shot, where she's holding a Scorpion Handstand pose, difficult enough to do with both hands, but she's only using one.

She moves her lips close to his ear and softly says, I really want to use that final shot on my next album cover.

You're a musician? What do you play?

Guitar.

What do you sound like?

It's hard to describe.

Rock? Folk? Jazz? Blues?

All of them put together, a whole new genre.

You have a band?

Yeah. I do the vocals, and I play guitar like a more

versatile Jimi Hendrix. I've got a great rhythm section and a killer keyboard guy.

So you've got a new album coming out?

Yeah. It's called *Kill the President.*

Good title!

I thought you'd like it.

You did? How could you tell? You don't really know me.

I know you better than you think.

What's that supposed to mean?

Check this out.

She pushes buttons on her phone, tells him to read the writing on the screen: "It's as if the true purpose of the phone is not to help him keep in touch with people he cares about, but to make him an easy target, to put him on a leash that can be jerked at any moment, reminding him of all the overpriced bullshit he can buy, all the irrelevant things he needs to consider, making sure that he can't relax, that he's never too far from the next interruption."

He says: What's this?

You don't recognize it?

I was thinking something like this two hours ago. In fact, I'm pretty sure it's exactly what I was thinking, word for word. But why is it on your phone?

Because you were thinking it.

Right, but I didn't say it to you on the phone.

You didn't need to.

He stops and looks for a hint of laughter in her eyes, but there's nothing. She's deadly serious.

I didn't need to?

Earlier there was a link on your phone. You clicked on it. Remember?

Yeah.

Do you know what that link really was?

He stops and looks around. Three big guys with mirror shades are approaching. She nods in their direction.

Do you know what that link really was?

No. What was it?

Spyware. It instantly installed a face recognition program on your phone.

But I wasn't looking at my phone for more than a few seconds.

That was enough. The program can tell what you're thinking just as you're thinking it, based on the look on your face right before and after you click on the link. One thought leads to another. The spyware instantly calculates all the possible progressions and permutations of your thinking, with degrees of precision the brain can't even approximate.

Clark can't believe it. But the proof is there on her phone, word for word, exactly what he'd been thinking, except that the writing isn't in first person, like the voice in his head would normally be. It's as if someone else were telling his story, narrating from a third-person point of view, a term he remembers from an English class he took a long time ago, when he first came to the city. He did badly in the class. There were too many technical terms he failed to memorize.

She smiles and says: Confused?

I guess so, yeah. This is really weird. What else do you know about me?

All sorts of stuff you wouldn't believe.

Like what?

I know that your favorite thing isn't hiking or tennis or meeting new people, or any of the other shit that might end up on a Facebook profile. Your favorite thing is falling asleep during movies, waking from time to time and catching brief segments, then drifting back to sleep. You've never seen even one movie from start to finish, but your mind is loaded with cinematic fragments, and thinking about them gives you tremendous pleasure, especially late at night, when you're sitting on your balcony half-asleep, and the trees are filled with wind up and down the street, and pools from an afternoon thunderstorm ripple with moonlight.

You're not just reading me like a book; you're reading me like a book I wish I'd written. But I'm not a good writer. What else do you know?

Ten years ago, when you were 22 years old, you were in Wyoming, hiking through the Wind River Mountains, pleased that the place wasn't filled with noisy tourists. In fact, in the five days you were there, you didn't see anyone. You had the place to yourself. You felt like you were in paradise.Then you got attacked by a black bear, who knocked you down, mounted your chest, and was just a few seconds away from biting into your throat, slashing your wind pipe, hacking through the vertebrae in your neck, separating your head from the rest of your body. You made eye contact with him for a few seconds. You got the impression that he could see that you posed no threat, that you weren't the kind of guy who hunts and kills animals. He got up and wandered away, disappearing into the forest, leaving you with only a few slight wounds on your neck, chest, and shoulders.

I never told anyone about that, not a single person. It left me terrified and confused. I didn't completely believe that it really happened. I still don't.

It did, and you've never been the same, though you can't remember who you were before you became what you are now.

Can you? Since you seem to know everything? Can you tell me who I was?

Maybe later. Right now we've got important things to do.

She pushes her chest up against his chest, straddles him and grips his wrists. He struggles but he can't move.

Answer truthfully. I'll know right away if you're lying. Why haven't you tried to fuck me?

I haven't had time. We've only been here for ten or fifteen minutes.

Most guys start putting the moves on me right away. They're in love with my long white hair, the way it makes my tan look smooth and moist, instead of making me look like I'm over sixty.

But we haven't even had a chance to find out if we like each other.

I could tell you liked my body as soon as you saw me.

Yeah, but I don't try to fuck every hot woman I meet.

I'm not hot enough for you? Most men can't control themselves. They want me, especially when I snuggle up to them and hand them my camera.

It's not that I don't want you. But I'm too insecure. I don't assume women want me. I don't want to get rejected if I approach them.

But now that I've got you pinned against the bench, and my mouth is only an inch away from your mouth, and my tanned and supple arms and shoulders are gleaming with sunlight, and my nipples are fully erect and touching your nipples, you can't respond?

You're out of my league.

No shit. But how often do you get to fuck someone who's out of your league? If I were you, I'd strike while the iron is hot. You might never get a chance like this again.

Can't we just talk for a while? It works better for me that way.

She leans back with a puzzled expression, like she might be remembering something important. Clark wants to know what it is, but he's never been good at reading minds. He finally says: It's really okay to make love to you? Even though you know you're out of my league?

She studies him with an even more baffled expression, smiling and shaking her head, like she's looking at a rare and exotic animal, something no one has ever seen before and might not even exist.

Clark looks at the three big guys. They're getting closer. They don't seem friendly. She turns and nods in their direction.

See those guys?

They're friends of yours, right?

Not friends, but they'll do what I tell them to do.

That doesn't sound good.

It all depends.

On what?

On how you handle yourself.

Care to explain?

You remember that Twilight Zone episode where a guy is declared obsolete? Well you've been declared irreversibly problematic.

You've got paperwork on that?

Yeah.

Who decided?

A panel of serious guys in coats and ties.

Irreversibly problematic? What does that mean?

You've gone past the point where your mind has selection value. It might be time to remove you from normal society, take you to a place where you can be trained, made less problematic.

What the fuck? I don't need training. I—

You claim that you don't like being on a leash. Then

why do you keep your phone with you at all times? Could you function without it? I don't think so. Then why resist it? You think it makes you a target? You think evil people are trying to make you buy things? You're right: people want you to buy things. But there's nothing evil about it. If you didn't spend more money than you've got, the economy would collapse, and then where would we be?

I don't know. Where would we be?

Don't be stupid. You know damn well where we'd be, and you wouldn't like it.

How do you know? Have you ever gone off the grid? It might be awesome.

It would totally suck. Do you really want to take shits in the woods and wipe your ass with dead leaves crawling with insects? Do you really want to hunt with a flat stone and a makeshift wooden spear, confronting animals that might kill you, assuming you can find them? The next bear you meet might not be so nice. Don't act like you can live in harmony with nature, whatever the fuck that means. You need the grid you hate so much. It's made you what you are, and you don't know how to be anything else.

What are you? Some kind of bounty hunter?

Not exactly. It's called something else. I'm a Damage Control Technician—DCT, for short.

What's that?

It's whatever the fuck I want it to be.

He knows he has to get away fast. It's clear that the DCT works for the FBI or the NSA or the CIA, or maybe Google, Microsoft, Amazon, or Apple, or some other corporate giant with its own surveillance team and secret police force. Whoever they are, he knows they have ways of dealing with people like him. They wouldn't think twice about locking him up and doing horrible things to him, putting him in a labor camp with cutting edge torture devices, denying him the legal protection he couldn't afford to begin with. They won't put up with anyone who doesn't want to buy things. They apprehend people who don't like wearing a leash.

He looks at the sky, pretends that he sees a UFO approaching, looks terrified, and starts yelling: Oh my God! Oh no! They're really here! We're all going to die!

The DCT looks at the sky. The three guys look at the sky. He shoves her off and darts away, moving quickly toward the top of the waterfall. He ducks behind a large rock, then between two more large rocks, stops to catch his breath, then darts behind another large rock. He climbs a tree, jumps to another tree, drops down behind a bush, then scampers behind another large rock. He knows he's not really safe, but it's the best he can do right now. He's always hated action movies, where tough guys say clever things and punch people out. But right now he'd like to be one of them, doing astonishing martial arts moves, ducking into secret passageways that lead to underground mazes no one can solve. Instead, he can only hope they'll think he ran in the other direction, toward the base of the waterfall and the open spaces of the park, where lots of other people can see what's happening, and the DCT and her thugs will have to think twice about roughing him up, since someone might call the police.

But five seconds later, two big guys come rushing from opposite sides of the rock. He steps aside and they collide head first, knocking each other out. Their bodies flop down like giant sacks of dog food. The other thug shows up and grabs Clark by the lapels and calls him a dirty little shit, but the DCT shows up and jabs her fingers into the nape of the big guy's neck. He goes limp and collapses, twitching on the ground for a second or two, then falling asleep.

She turns and smiles at Clark and says: Pretty cool, right?

He says: What the fuck!

She studies the guy on the ground, shakes her head in disgust and says: Look at this guy! What a fucking slob! He's got pizza all over his face. What kind of asshole comes to work with pizza all over his face?

I hate pizza!

Really?

There's only one thing I hate more than all the robocalls I get every day, and that's pizza.

She looks at him in shock: Are you kidding me? You really don't like pizza?

I can't stand it. I hate the way it burns your mouth and the cheese runs down your chin and gets on your shirt and makes you look stupid. And I hate the way everyone simply assumes that everyone likes it, so it's always at parties and other places where people are having fun. You can't escape it. When I was growing up and my father took me to baseball games, the food was always hot dogs, cracker jacks, and shelled peanuts. No pizza. Now everyone at the stadium is pigging out on pizza. It doesn't feel like baseball any longer.

Her look of shock turns into recognition, as if something is falling into place and she can't believe it.

He says: You look really weird. Is something wrong?

She shakes her head: I hate pizza too, but for different reasons. Back in high school, I was a finalist in a spelling bee. My parents were putting huge pressure on me to win. They even placed bets on it. On the big day the school auditorium was full, and the Principal made an impassioned speech about spelling, how important it was, how the world would be a better place if everyone knew how to spell. My parents were in the front row. I could see they were tense with expectation. The final word I had to spell was piazza. It's not a common word but I knew how to spell it. But somehow when it mattered most I spelled the word pizza: p-i-z-z-a. First there was silence, then scattered giggling, then everyone was laughing. Even the Principal was laughing. My parents were enraged. They were hiding their faces in their hands. In the days and weeks that followed, my life fell apart. I was afraid to show my face anywhere. I started getting bad grades and my friends wouldn't talk to me. Within a few months, my hair turned totally white. I was horrified at first, but over time I got used to it, and now I see it as an asset. But ever since then I've hated pizza. I look the other way whenever I'm near a pizza place. And now this guy shows up for work with pizza on his face!

Clark says: That's pretty fucked up! I'm sorry that happened to you. I've never been good at spelling.

She looks at him with even more amazement. She grabs him and kisses him fiercely, giving him a stiffy.

He says: Wow! But wait a minute. Just a few minutes ago, you said I'd been declared irreversibly defective.

She nods: Irreversibly problematic.

So why did you zap your friend? Was it just the pizza on his face?

I don't like him.

Really?

And I like the guys he works for even less.

Clark looks puzzled.

And I like the guys that those guys work for even less than even less.

Clark wants to ask her to be more specific, but he doesn't want to get himself in trouble, as if anything he might say could be used against him. He feels like he's back in school, where he was always afraid to raise his hand, knowing that he might get a bad grade if he gave a stupid answer, knowing he might get a bad grade if he didn't raise his hand.

She says: And I like the guys that those guys work for even less than even less than even less. Should I continue?

Clark finally says: No, I get it.

The guy the other guys work for works for guys who

work for guys who work for the guy in the Oval Office. He's a total shit, and he gets worse every day.

You hate the President?

Totally. Don't you?

Yeah. Totally. So you're deflecting?

Defecting.

You're sick of working for assholes?

Yeah.

So why are you still doing this job? You sound confused.

I'm never confused.

Never?

Never.

That's weird. I mean, it's pretty scary. I thought everyone was confused most of the time.

They are. But not me.

You must be the world's coolest person.

I'm in the top five.

So are you still going to take me to the place where apprehended people go. Some kind of gulag or detention camp?

Not unless I have to. They're overcrowded already, and new people get taken there every day. It's not a good option. But it all depends.

On what?

How well you make love to me.

That's it? That's all I have to do?

That's all you have to do. But you have to be good. So good that I feel like I've really been fucked.

How will I know if I'm doing it right?

I'll make all the right noises and facial expressions.

What happens if I don't get it right the first time? Do I get a second chance?

No one ever gets a second chance with me.

I don't perform well under pressure.

This time you better.

Why are you doing this?

Doing what?

Fucking me and arresting me.

I like sex and I like doing well at my job. The more good sex I have the better I feel. The more people I apprehend the more I get paid.

You work on commission?

Something like that.

You don't mind using spyware programs to fuck people up?

It's better than having people fuck me up with spyware programs.

You've got everything figured out.

It's better that way.

But you work with guys who work for guys who work for guys who work for guys who work for someone you hate. So you don't have everything figured out.

I do now—now that I've found the man I need.

Me?

You.

How can someone as cool as you need someone defective like me?

You're just the right kind of defective. I had a dream a few years ago, something about a huge pair of pants on the shore of an Arctic island. They were more than 200 feet tall. My therapist at the time was big on dream interpretation. After weeks of discussing the imagery, we concluded that I had an important mission, a challenge I was destined to confront, where I would perform an important service to the nation, but only after certain conditions were met. I'd know the time was right after fucking a really dumb guy who didn't like pizza.

So that's me? I'm the really dumb guy?

That's you. You're really dumb and you don't like pizza.

But how do you know it's me? Aren't there other really dumb guys out there? Couldn't one of those guys be the one you're really looking for?

I don't think so. I can tell you're the one.

You're absolutely sure?

You asked for permission to kiss me. No guy has ever done that before. Most guys can't resist me for even a minute. They've got their hands on me right away. They're wild that my hair is so white and my skin is so moist and tan and young. I don't hesitate to put them in their place, even when their faces aren't covered with pizza. But you're different.

Sure. But asking for permission wasn't part of the deal, was it? Your therapist didn't say anything about permission.

No. But remember: It wasn't his dream.

Okay. Good point.

But he and I came to a clear conclusion: I would be the best person I could possibly be and do the best thing I could possibly do if I fucked a really dumb guy with a subprime credit score who didn't like pizza.

You checked my credit score?

I didn't have to. It's already clear that you don't know how to spend money. You might know how to save it, but you don't know how to spend it. Besides, you liked the name of the fake band I told you about.

Clark stares at the flashing water cascading beside them. There's clearly something wrong with the situation, something he's not quite getting, though he's guessing that smarter guys would understand it. They might connect what's happening to one of those classical stories he had to read in college, where characters had to do extreme things that didn't make sense and had to follow bizarre instructions perfectly or face horrible punishments designed by obsessive-compulsive deities. If the software she put on his phone has somehow made him part of an ancient narrative, he might have to start thinking more carefully than he normally does. But he's always told himself to keep things simple, to avoid complications he can't sort out.

He finally says: I feel like if I say the wrong thing there might be consequences I can't recover from, no matter what I do. But I'm stunned that I've got a chance to fuck someone like you. I mean—Okay, I'm glad I passed the test. Back in school, I always used to flunk. One time I actually had to wear a dunce cap and sit on a stool in a corner saying I'm a dunce and that ain't good until the teacher got sick of it.

The test you've just passed did more than measure your skill with numbers or metaphors. This one will make a huge difference in how the world functions.

That's hard to believe. Something about this isn't quite adding up. Something is missing.

Something is always missing.

Always?

Always. Trust me. Now let's get started.

We're doing it right here in the park?

Yeah.

But we're in a public place. And with everything that's just happened, people here have probably noticed us, and they're wondering what's going on.

He looks around and notices people noticing, some of them trying to look like they're not noticing, others not even trying to look like everything is normal.

She looks at them briefly, waves and smiles, then shrugs and says: Fuck them! They're just looking for excitement. Let's give it to them.

No, really. What if there's trouble? What if someone calls the police? Do you have some kind of badge you can flash that makes the cops nod and smile and leave you alone?

I look good when I'm fucking. The people who see us will like what they see. They'll want to take pictures, videos they can post on their Facebook pages.

Two of the big mean guys are waking up, blinking and rubbing their heads. When they see her only twenty feet away, they look scared and try to get up, as if they might get accused of sleeping on the job. She smiles and snaps her fingers. Suddenly it's like they've got powerful magnets in their heads, and when they try to stand they're yanked violently toward each other. Their heads clang together loudly, like hammers on an anvil. They pass out again.

He says: Wow! That must have been painful.

She shrugs and says: No shit! Now stop acting like you don't want me. It's pissing me off. Fuck me like I'm just about the change the world in major ways, like I'm just about to become a big name in future history textbooks.

She throws him down and gets on top and puts him inside her. Apparently, she's a master of sexual yoga. She's strong and graceful and knows how to guide his body, making him perform much better than he normally does. The people watching earlier have come closer, forming a circle. They're all worked up like they're watching a fight, jumping up and down, shouting words of encouragement. When the sex is over, there's wild applause. Everyone nods in firm agreement. It's the hottest fucking thing they've ever seen. It's clear that they want to go home and jerk off. They disappear quickly, leaving the park.

She stands and pulls Clark up to her mouth and gives him the hardest kiss in the history of passion.

He says: So everything is okay? I don't have to go to Guantanamo?

Everything is okay. You're exactly what I was hoping for. Now I feel ready to do what needs to be done.

So maybe we should go out for coffee or something?

I'd love to. But I've got important plans for the night.

So maybe tomorrow? Can I call you up or shoot you an email or a text?

I'll call you. Remember? I've got your number.

She starts to walk away. He watches the way her body moves and loves it. Even though he's just had the best intercourse of his life, he still wants to go home and play with himself. She turns and sees that he's watching, pulls a small pistol out from between her breasts. Before he can react, she points it at her ear and pulls the trigger. It squirts water. She dries her ear with her finger, laughs and waves and disappears into the twilight.

He leaves the park and gets on the subway. Every cell in his body feels excited. The people on the train look like they're vibrating with pleasure. When he gets home he turns off his phone and spends hours gazing at the fish in his large aquarium. They move like music made for relaxation. When he finally goes to bed he gets himself off, still feeling the woman's flesh against his body, the sound of the waterfall rushing in the background.

He sleeps like he's on a small raft a thousand miles from nowhere, riding massive swells that lift him into the stars and slide him gracefully down to the ocean floor. When he wakes up he's never felt better.

He gets the morning paper from his doorstep. He takes it inside and sits and prepares to skim the pages quickly, but the headline story makes him stop. He reads the first three paragraphs three times. The President and the Vice President were shot and killed the night before. They were standing beside each other and the same bullet killed both of them, passing in one ear and out the other twice. Riots and celebrations are taking place all over the nation. There's a picture of the assassin smiling, making the peace and victory sign with her fingers. Clark stares in disbelief but there's no doubt about it. It's her—the woman who fucked him in the park, the rogue Damage Control Technician. Her long white hair and deep tan look delicious in the picture. He thinks about what she said right before they made love. She wasn't kidding. Her name will appear in history books. He feels like he's almost famous.

SONG FOR OUR ANCESTORS

I've just been thrown out of my house. The fight with my wife got so bad that I didn't even try to get back inside, either by sneaking in through a window or by shouting at the locked back door. So now I'm slumped in a chair on the back porch, warming myself with an old blanket, and I close my eyes, somehow drifting off to sleep in the chill of the city's thick fog. Then I'm wandering through the late night streets, looking at old houses and stores as if they were great works of art, fascinated by dormers, porticos, cupolas, gables, columns, transoms, bay windows and oriel windows, and other architectural structures I don't know the names of. I walk for hours with no destination, finally reaching parts of the city I've never seen before, streets with vacant lots filled with garbage, old brick warehouses with shattered and boarded up windows, silhouettes of factory smokestacks looming in the distance.

I reach the place where the streetlights come to an end, but the street keeps going. I keep walking. Soon I come to a free-standing door, apparently propped up by the fog alone, no evidence of a building having been there. It's made of light blue paneled wood, and I like it so much I can't keep myself from knocking. A voice invites me in, so I open the door into what looks like a recording studio. There are microphones, keyboard instruments, drum kits, guitars propped on stools and chairs, a mixing board against the far wall, beneath a clock that reads 3:15, and on a folding chair near the door a newspaper dated December 29, 1968.

I'm tired so I sit on the concrete floor, my back against the wall. I hear laughter and voices approaching, young men with long hair and thrift shop clothing. They don't seem to notice me. A guy with mirror shades starts playing with the mixing board, and slowly the room is filled with harbor sounds: seagulls, lapping waves, foghorns, ship's bells and buoy bells. A guy with a vest and an ascot settles in behind the keyboards, adding soft washes of symphonic sound that seem to go on for hours. I drift into sleep, wake briefly, see from the clock it's 4:45, hear the keyboard symphony swelling and surging, laced with gently distorted guitars and barely audible drumming. I fade back to sleep again, wake briefly, see that it's 5:35, hear the keyboard symphony surging and swelling, softly distorted guitars and subliminal drumming, glide back to sleep again, wake to a waterfront morning dense with fog.

I'm sitting up against a metal warehouse door. Everything is slightly blurred, but I let myself fully breathe in the moist air, and before too long I'm clear and refreshed. I get up and walk without knowing or caring where I'm going, but soon I'm home and Corina looks great, smiling at the breakfast table, telling me how worried she's been, asking me where I've been.

I say: That fight we were having last night was so stupid, I couldn't see any reason to come back inside and start arguing again.

She laughs: Sometimes you're the biggest asshole in the universe.

But I was trying to be nice.

If you have to *try* to be nice, something is wrong.

I always try to be nice.

It's not convincing. I can always tell what you're really feeling. You might as well just be honest.

Honest? Really? What if I don't like being honest? What if I think honesty is over-rated? What if I think I'm better off not being honest?

You've got a black belt in passive aggression.

At least I'm good at it. Anyway, I sure don't want to spend another night on the street. But actually it wasn't bad. It was like being in a dark museum.

A dark museum? How would I know what it's like to be in a dark museum?

Picture yourself in a museum with all the lights off. You know the paintings are there on the walls, but you can only make out vague frames and forms and muted colors, and there's no one else there.

Why would I do that? I like looking at paintings. Why would I bother looking if I couldn't see them clearly. They weren't made to be seen in the dark.

It's like being in a haunted house but there aren't any ghosts, so there's nothing to be afraid of, and you can just enjoy how weird the house looks in the dark.

Whatever. So where did you stay last night? An all-night fast food place? A Motel 6?

Nowhere. I just went. I didn't know where I was going. I just walked until I was back here again. It was like I was walking in my sleep, but I know I wasn't dreaming.

She gives me a funny look. But an hour later she's acting like everything's great. She's doesn't mind bad arguments because she's clever when she fights and doesn't hold on to shitty feelings once the conflict is over. I'm the type who feels disturbed after a fight and holds on to the feelings for hours, and sometimes for days, until I find some way way to distract myself, often by doing what I'm choosing to do now, sitting down at my computer and doing my freelance job, designing virtual environments for computer game companies. I'm working on one right now that includes a subterranean cave, walls filled with images that glow in the dark.

After dinner Corina wants to make love and as usual she's terrific in bed, strong and supple and skilled, so afterwards I'm convinced that our problems aren't as bad as they often seem to be. Then she's amusing me with her opinions about the President's latest absurd proclamation, how he thinks there's no such thing as global warming and how it's better not to regulate big corporations because then they get richer and give people jobs and the people have more money to spend, the ongoing capitalist bullshit that sounds especially misguided coming out of the President's big mouth.

But now she and I are falling asleep in each other's arms, something we've always done beautifully, probably the best thing about our marriage. Then it feels like something is easing me out of sleep and the clock says it's two hours later, 2:25. I see that she's sound asleep so I get up and go downstairs and think about making a snack. But then I'm focused on the street lights out the kitchen window, and something about the way they're receding into a mysterious distance makes me want to go out and start walking. I don't know where I'm going or why I'm going there. But something happened last night that I can't quite remember, a gap in time that I want to recover, assuming that gaps in time can be recovered. Or maybe they can only be reinvented, like dreams that change from poetry into prose when you try to talk about them later. Somehow it feels important not to know where I'm going, so I turn randomly down cross streets onto side streets, from side streets back to main streets back to cross streets back to side streets, all of them lined with brownstones and old brick buildings with gables and cupolas, until I reach the warehouse district, where the silhouettes of water towers and smokestacks tell me I'm where I was before. I recognize the stand-alone blue door in the foggy darkness. I open it quickly. I knocked the night before but this time I don't and this time there's nothing. Not even nothing. It's whatever makes nothing nothing. Not the word for nothing used in a sentence, but the nothing that makes the sentence itself impossible. I step back and turn. There's no safe way to keep looking.

I walk ten blocks to an old café, half-way below the sidewalk. I sit at a small circular table. There's a *Chronicle* on one of the chairs from December 29, 1968. There's a faded black and white picture of the Fillmore West on page 44, the Steve Miller Band on stage, performing what the reviewer calls a sound montage, a term I like, though I'm not sure what it means. I stare at the date. The paper was published more than half a century ago, the same day I took my first tab of acid. A friend had given it to me as a birthday present.

Footsteps approach and a woman sits at my table. She's got long red hair, torn black jeans, and a powder blue cowboy shirt. She pulls out a joint, lights it and takes a long hit, and hands it across the table. I take a brief hit and smile my thanks and hand the joint back.

She looks at me carefully, then says: You don't remember me, do you?

Actually, your voice sounds familiar.

Remember that trip we took to Timbuktu?

Sort of. I remember taking a trip there with someone named Elaine. I guess that's you? Sometimes I'm not even sure that really happened.

Trust me. It really happened. And my mother was your boss a few years before that. You must remember—

At the pet store? That really cool spaced-out woman was your mother?

Of course! What's happened to your memory? Too much acid?

That's one way of putting it.

You were quote unquote working at her pet store near the Fillmore, a year before it closed. She introduced us. I was getting my PhD in anthropology.

Oh yeah, that's right. And we went to Timbuktu because you wanted to study those manuscripts, and I had a strange meeting with a musician in a club on the edge of town.

You never told me much about it.

Things got weird. I think at some point I was lost in the desert.

I remember a call from a Red Cross mobile unit. I got you on a flight back home. You weren't the same after that. You got more serious. You stopped returning my calls. I remember you moved to New York to study computers. What are you doing now? Still into computers?

Kind of. I do virtual environments. Right now I'm doing one that has Stone Age cave painting imagery. But what are you doing here?

It's my favorite place. I get up at two every morning, since I do my best work in the middle of the night. For some reason, I can't get myself to work at home. But here, I can really get things done. I love the coffee. They've got their own special blend. You should try it!

Anyway, when I saw you come in, I said to myself: Hey! I know that guy! And then it all came back to me.

It's been decades, hasn't it?

It feels like another lifetime.

What are you working on?

I'm translating a pre-Islamic mathmatical treatise. I found it in someone's basement in Timbuktu. The guy who had it told me it was dangerous. He was keeping it in a locked room to keep people from having any contact with it.

That's weird. How can math be dangerous?

I think it was a religious thing: pre-Islamic math instead of Islamic math. Math that the Prophet would have condemned, instead of what passes today for math in mainstream schools.

Sacreligious math, not officially sanctioned? Math for dreamers? Is the treatise any good?

I've been working on it for decades. It's fucking amazing!

I've never been good in math.

Me neither. But the math in this treatise really gets inside your body. It's not just a mental thing. It's more like music. It takes you to places that don't even need to exist.

Sounds like my kind of math!

She hands me the joint and I take a long hit and lean back and close my eyes. When I open my eyes to pass the joint back, she's gone. I search the room. There's nothing but faint light coming from scented candles on the tables. The guy at the cash register is snoring into folded arms. I like how relaxed he looks, so I let him sleep. I step outside and look both ways but she's not there walking away. The only reason I know she was really here is the joint I'm holding. It's still smoking. I take a final toke, then snub it out on my jeans and put the roach in my back pocket. I feel so calm just standing here in the fog. Maybe if I never move again I'll go to heaven, even if there's no such thing. But the emptiness of the streets, so enticingly defined by the streetlights receding into the darkness, tells me that I need to start walking, and soon I'm standing again in front of the blue free-standing door. This time I know what to do. I knock, like I did last night. A quiet voice tells me to come in.

I open the door into what looks like a recording studio: keyboard instruments, drum kits, guitars propped on stools and chairs, microphones everywhere, a mixing board against the far wall, beneath a clock that says it's 3:15, and on a folding chair near the door a newspaper dated December 29, 1968. I'm not sure what to make of the date. I was born on December 29th, and the paper is more than fifty years old. Why is it here? Why isn't it in a library or a museum? Why does the paper itself look fresh, like it's hot off the press? The headline mentions troops confronting rioters. I think of the Vietnam War. I might have been one of those rioters.

I'm tired so I sit on the floor. I hear laughter and voices approaching, young men with long hair and thrift shop clothing. They don't seem to notice me. A guy with mirror shades starts playing with the mixing board, and slowly the room is filled with harbor sounds: seagulls, lapping waves, foghorns and ship's bells and buoy bells. A guy with a vest and an ascot settles in behind the keyboards, softly replacing the foghorns with washes of symphonic sound that seem to go on for hours. I drift into sleep, wake briefly, see from the clock it's 4:45, hear the keyboard symphony swelling and surging, laced with calmly distorted guitars and barely audible drumming.

Someone sits down beside me and stares at the ceiling. I'm not sure what to say so I don't say anything. He finally says: This music is really awesome.

I say: I remember it from a long time ago, I think at the Fillmore West, but it sounds even more amazing now than it did back then. There's something psychedelic about it, but in a quiet way, not blowing your mind but gently taking it places, maybe to the border of silence, where conscious thought is still possible, but just barely.

He says: Psychedelic. I haven't heard that word in a while. But I can tell you about psychedelic, no question about it. I mean, I was wasting my life, becoming a total couch potato. The only thing I read was TV Guide. Then I answered an ad. At UC Berkeley they wanted volunteers, people to take psychedelic drugs and then get observed by bearded guys with flannel shirts and clipboards.

He takes an envelope out of his inner coat pocket, pulls out a page of perforated squares, and says: Ever try one of these?

I laugh and say: It looks like blotter acid. I haven't seen stuff like that in a long time.

The first time I sucked on one of the squares, I felt like I was back in the Stone Age, like I was in a subterranean cave, with strange equations painted on the walls.

Were they doing math back in the Stone Age?

I didn't say it was math. Just things that looked like numbers in patterns that looked like equations. Not the stuff they used to make us do in school.

Equations without math?

Sure. Why not? It was back in the Stone Age. Who the hell knows what they were doing back then? Who knows what would have made sense to them, assuming that they cared about making sense?

He looks at me like I'm supposed to know what to say to that, but I'm barely awake and can't think of anything, so he nods and smiles and says: Everything starts right here, man, right here and right now.

It feels like I'm at the job I had a long time ago, surrounded by fish in beautifully designed fishtanks, parakeets and canaries chirping and singing, puppies and kittens playing and wandering freely, keeping everyone company, a store where people come and go without being pressured to pay for anything. They just sit and relax and talk pleasantly about things that seem to matter.

I close my eyes and the music is taking me back there, the bubbling of large aquariums in dim blue light. I slide into sleep again, wake briefly, see that it's 5:35, hear the keyboard symphony surging and swelling, softly distorted guitars and subliminal drumming, drop off to sleep again, wake to a waterfront morning dense with fog.

I remember waking up like this yesterday morning, after a night of wandering the streets in the warehouse district. Now I'm puzzled by the memory of a basement café, a *San Francisco Chronicle* from 1968, an article about the Fillmore West, which was closed on Independence Day in 1971, a place where I spent my seventeenth birthday, a memory enhanced by the blotter acid I'd been given by a friend. It's all blurring, like images in a dream before they get sorted out when you talk about them later. Was I in that basement café last night, and if so, why was I there? And why do I remember someone talking about equations in a subterranean cave? And what's my partner thinking now, since I've been out all night two nights in a row?

I get lucky. She's still asleep when I get home, and when I wake her up with my mouth between her thighs, she couldn't be more excited. She comes twice, then again when I penetrate her, thrusting fiercely to build a savage climax.

Resting beside each other as the dense fog presses on the windows, it's like we're in love again, though we both know the feeling won't last.

She laughs lightly: I like you so much more when you're fucking me.

I like me so much more when I'm fucking you.

I can tell. You're not such a passive aggressive creep.

I smile and stand beside the bed. If she knows I was gone the night before, she's showing no sign of it. We go downstairs for breakfast, open our laptop youtube account, and catch footage of a detention center on the Rio Grande, desperate faces pressed up against chain link fences. Then footage of the President bellowing about national security, drug dealers and prostitutes from degenerate nations flooding our country, stealing jobs.

I look at Corina: Drug dealers and prostitutes from degenerate nations? Does the man have any idea how stupid he sounds? Those people aren't in sinister gangs dealing drugs. They're trying to save themselves from gangs dealing drugs! And families are still being separated, two years after a federal judge declared the Zero Tolerance policy unconstitutional. What the fuck!

Corina says: He's such an offensive shit! And I'm never sure if he's just totally ignorant, or if he's playing dumb to manipulate public awareness. How long do we let this motherfucker survive?

We've waited too long already.

Where are today's great assassins when we need them? How long would Gavrilo Princip have tolerated someone like this.

Princip thought he had nothing to lose. He was dying of consumption, starving, living in borrowed rooms or on the streets.

But people like us have got too much to lose, right? We like our bourgeois comforts too much to do what needs to be done.

I take my laptop upstairs to the small room I use as an office. The fog is so thick at the windows it feels like it's in the room, making everything chilly and vague. I see the term "night terrors" on my newsfeed, and I click to the article, but get distracted by a distant memory, triggered by the woman I met last night in a basement café. I haven't thought about her in years, but now a strange trip we took is coming back to me in fragments. I'd first met her in the late sixties, at the pet store where I had a part-time job. She was getting her PhD at UC Berkeley. A strong attraction quickly developed, and soon we were thinking of moving in together. Then she told me she had travel plans that she didn't want to change, a trip to Timbuktu, a place that had once been one of the world's great centers of commerce and learning. I convinced her to take me along. I'd always thought the city had a cool name, but I knew from reading I'd done that the place was falling apart, fading into the desert, despite its fabled past. Elaine wasn't there for the fables. She was trying to get her anthropology dissertation started, and she wanted to see the hundreds of thousands of ancient manuscripts there, all kept in private homes in secret places, commentaries on every conceivable subject, so many things that people don't know anymore.

Things went well at first. The people were friendly, seemed eager to help, and we soon found a pre-Islamic text about sexual pleasure, positions and techniques we tried and enjoyed. But Elaine wasn't there for sex, and soon she was so caught up in her work that she didn't have time for anything else. We had several bad fights, which made it clear that we didn't have much in common. We said goodbye and I moved to a different hotel. I was left to explore Timbuktu by myself. But the place was way too hot, and aside from the ancient books, there wasn't much to explore. There were scorching winds, dunes closing in on all sides, streets that were buried in sand.

I spent most of my time in my air conditioned hotel room watching pornography. I ate cheeseburgers and French fries every day in the hotel café. I felt stupid. Here I was in a town that was once considered the African version of El Dorado, and all I wanted to do was play with myself. So a few nights before my departing flight, I walked through the older section of the city, patting myself on the back for not completely wasting the trip. But I quickly got lost on narrow unlit streets that all looked the same. The sand was so deep that the doors of the buildings were half way below street level. If I'd wanted to go inside I would have been forced down onto my knees to dig my way in.

I finally found normal access into a small cafe on the outskirts of town. The place was falling apart but they had live performers, two young women making music I found a bit strange at first, but the sound became intoxicating once I adjusted to it. Flute sounds were quietly mixed with subliminal drumming, gliding through the room like tropical fish in a huge aquarium, drifting out the open doors into thousands of miles of sand and wind and stars and nothing else. At times it felt like I wasn't wearing anything, or hearing anything for that matter, or like the music was coming from me, as if by listening to the sound I was creating it.

At some point there was a pause, though I wasn't aware at first that the music had stopped. It was moving through my veins. It was on my skin. It was in my breathing. I sat on a bench in the corner watching shadows move on the walls. It felt like if I watched them long enough I would understand everything, all the arcane wisdom in the books of Timbuktu, though none of them contained a word of English. Then the drummer came to my table, took my hands with bedroom eyes, told me in graceful English to buy her a drink, then asked me about myself in a way that sounded like she cared. Our talking was playful and somehow familiar. We seemed to know exactly what to say to each other. Our legs were touching under the table. I sat eagerly through her second set, which made what she and her partner played before sound elementary, like a prelude to something developing into a prelude to something else.

Then we hurried down dark streets to her house, a place like nothing I'd ever seen before. It was all one room, lit by scented candles. The walls and floor were dried mud harder than rock, all faded blue. The windows were circular openings without glass. The ceiling was ten feet high made of branches and palm fronds woven together, stitched tightly enough to keep out the almost non-existent rain. She said the place had been in her family for countless generations, going back more than a thousand years, back to pre-Islamic times, when the town was nothing more than a seasonal settlement. She told me the music she and her partner played each night was sacred, something their ancestors needed to hear, an ongoing improvisation keeping the living in touch with the dead.

She knew from memory everything that was in the sexual text. I'd never gone to bed with anyone even half as good as she was, which surprised me because I'd assumed that Timbuktu was a religious place, too steeped in Islamic tradition to encourage erotic performance. But her big soft body moved with athletic power. I felt like I was wrestling with the ocean. I felt I'd been making love to her all my life and everything still felt new. We came together several times in different positions. The candles were making the walls come alive, as if their faded blue were like the sky, concealing a darkness filled with stars, constellations telling ancient stories.

At some point we passed out in each other's arms. I woke at four in the morning, ready for more of the best sex ever. But she wasn't there. The house wasn't there. The streets weren't there. Timbuktu wasn't there. I was in a small shed with a broken roof. The temperature had dropped at least fifty degrees and the wind was strong. The shed was falling apart and empty except for one crucial thing, a garment large and heavy enough to function as a blanket. It was smelly and torn but it kept me warm enough until the sun came up. Without it, I would have been frantically pacing, hugging myself to fight off the cold, right after spending four of the most ecstatic hours of my life. In the light of day, I saw that I was nowhere. I was lost and the desert was empty in all directions. At first I didn't care. Every cell in my body felt beautifully fucked. I snuggled back into the garment and let myself rest in the ripples of pleasure. I don't know how long I was there. At some point I was dreaming of a sinking ship, dolphins leaping and splashing in an ocean filled with ice. But finally something like hunger told me I couldn't stay there forever.

I wasn't sure what to do so I started walking. I turned around five minutes later, thinking I might need the garment again at night. But the shed wasn't there. I looked in all directions, blinking and rubbing my eyes. I knew the place wasn't a fantasy. The shelter and warmth had kept me alive. But even though I retraced my footprints carefully, back to where they began, there was no sign that a shelter had ever been there, no torn and smelly garment, only wind getting hotter by the second.

I walked for maybe an hour before I passed out. I woke in a room surrounded by concerned faces, needles in my arms, IV poles and monitors, nurses and doctors asking me questions, a Red Cross mobile unit. I wasn't making much sense, but I told them how to contact Elaine, and she figured out how to get me on a flight back home the next day. Back in the States, I was glad to be alive, knowing how close I'd come to being dead. I didn't understand what had happened, how much of it was real. But I didn't care. I was so relieved to be back in my normal life that I didn't even try to get in touch with Elaine and discuss what happened.

Now I'm staring at my newsfeed, a scientific article explaining the term "night terrors," and I'm thinking about Elaine, the pre-Islamic math that she's been studying. Somehow the two things are connected, but I'm not sure how. Sometimes I wish I'd become a cognitive scientist, doing research on the architectures of consciousness, or maybe trying to identify the general activity, common throughout the universe, that human thinking is one specific example of. But I'm not sure thinking can be defined in architectural terms. Maybe it's more like a fishtank with boundaries that reshape themselves in response to what they're containing, an aquarium like a transparent water balloon.

For the next few days, my cave painting video project takes most of my attention. But Corina seems agitated, a bad sign. When she's in difficult moods, she takes them out on me. I try to fuck her into relaxation, but in bed she's ferocious, no tenderness at all, insisting on strap-on sex, taking me up the ass as roughly as possible. Then she flips out when she sees the President's face on our morning laptop, another molestation story, this one involving a teenage girl he supposedly called Lolita, though he seemed sincere when he claimed that he'd never heard of the book or its author.

Corina's spits on his meaty self-satisfied smile on the dusty screen. Speaking in her loudest, most powerful voice, she points at me and says: If you were caught fucking a teenage girl, you'd be behind bars in a second, no questions asked. But the president? If he even gets charged with anything, nothing will happen.

And he's claiming *she* seduced *him*. Can you believe it?

You men are disgusting. It creeps me out to think I'm not a dyke any longer. I'm sleeping with the enemy.

I'm the enemy?

You know what I mean. Oh, I meant to ask you: Who's Elaine?

Elaine?

Yeah, the one who texted you.

Texted me? What are you talking about?

She picks up my phone from the kitchen table and pulls up a text and reads it out loud: Great being with you last nite! Good to see you're aging so well! CU soon! –Elaine.

I don't remember giving her my number, but she got it somehow and now I'm fucked. There's no way to make what really happened seem plausible. I quickly say: When you threw me out I didn't know what to do, so I just started walking, stopped in a café, and ran into someone I used to know.

At three in the morning? Really? You're so full of shit. You're just as bad as the asshole in the White House.

That's hitting below the belt.

So to speak.

I can see that she's just about to blow up. Her fists are clenched and her face is red. I don't want to get slapped. I'm afraid I might hit back. So I grab my coat and go out the back door without saying a word.

I take a room in a small hotel three blocks away. It's a nice little place but the bed feels wrong and I toss and turn for hours. I keep thinking about the night terrors article, a term the author kept using: "the alternative past," memories based on things that really happened, but available to us now only in reconstructed form, as partial events overshadowed by vivid images, which initially were just background details, though now they've taken center stage and we can't get them out of our minds. I can't remember the author's discussion clearly. It's like I'm getting more and also less than she intended, like I'm telling someone about a dream but I know I'm getting it wrong, making it sound more coherent than it really was. Finally I fall asleep but then I'm awake, moving quickly out through the lobby into the street, rushing past the desk clerk sleeping on the job, face down on a newspaper crossword puzzle.

I'm feeling unhinged, but the fog calms me down, and soon I'm caught in the rhythm my footsteps make. If I had to state a religious preference, I'd say I believe in walking. There's almost nothing better, especially when you don't know where you're going and don't want to. The old brick buildings make the fog seem fluidly sculptured. The fog makes the buildings drift, makes them seem closer and farther away. Time is nothing more than the sound of my shoes against the pavement.

When I see the blue panel door, I think at first that it must be part of a building. But then I see that there's nothing but the door, floating in fog. I know I've been here before, but the only thing that comes to mind is the back door of the Fillmore West, July 5, 1971, the night my friends and I tried to break in after the place was closed for good. We couldn't believe it would soon be a used car dealership. We were stoned and wanted to spend the night on the stage where our favorite groups had played. I remembered the Steve Miller Band, their sound montage that lasted all night, the amazing transformations in the way the guitars and keyboards sounded, something more than music, or maybe I was just on some really great acid. When I think about the lame big hits that later made Steve Miller and Boz Scaggs rich and famous, I want to put my fist through the door. But instead I just knock. I think I hear a voice telling me to come in.

I open the door into what looks like a recording studio. There are keyboard instruments, drum kits, guitars propped on stools and chairs, microphones everywhere, a mixing board against the far wall, beneath a clock that says 3:15, and on a folding chair near the door a newspaper dated December 29, 1968. I'm tired so I sit on the floor. I hear laughter and voices approaching, young men with long hair and thrift shop clothing. They don't seem to notice me. A guy with mirror shades starts playing with the mixing board, and slowly the room is filled with harbor sounds, lapping waves and seagulls, ship's bells and buoy bells and foghorns. A guy with a vest and an ascot settles in behind the keyboards, softly adding washes of symphonic sound that seem to go on for hours.

I feel myself drifting off. Then someone's beside me, long red hair and a cowboy shirt and sandals. She's in the lotus position, which doesn't seem right for the way she's dressed. The music swells and slides from side to side like I'm on the deck of a ship, or like I'm in a cave surrounded by images in torchlight. She pulls out a joint, takes a long hit, and slides it into my hand. I take a brief hit and smile my thanks and hand the joint back.

She says: Nice to see you again.

How did you get my number?

I just tried the one you had thirty years ago, when we took that horrible trip. It's weird that you've still got the number you had before. How did you manage that?

It wasn't easy. But what are you doing here?

What are *you* doing here?

How did you know where to find me? I wasn't planning to come here. I'm not even sure where we are. My wife saw your text and got mad. I had to get out.

I'm not surprised. The last time we saw each other back in Timbuktu, we had a bad fight. Do you always fight with the women you're with?

I shake my head, laughing: It's really weird. In principle, I refuse to approach any situation that's likely to produce a disagreement, especially an intense disagreement, and I resent it when people try to create tense situations. Yet I seem to choose such people as romantic partners.

Why?

I'm an idiot.

It sounds like you should write a book about how to avoid relationships. There are so many books about how to find the right person. You should write about how it's better to live on your own.

I'm sure someone's already written a book like that. In fact, if I did a quick Internet search, I'd probably find at least five books on the subject. Besides, I don't have enough experience to write such a book. I always end up in relationships, even though I know they suck. Like right now, I'm liking the way you look, and I'm thinking I might want to get you in bed, even though I know how bad things were before, when you threw me out of our Timbuktu hotel room. It's like I don't learn from experience. How can you write a book when you haven't learned anything?

She pats my back and says: I don't go to bed with men anyway, not anymore. So don't worry about it. Just listen to the music.

Her face slowly blurs into something I think I recognize, a face that takes the form of all the faces I've forgotten. I drift into sleep, wake briefly, see from the clock it's 4:45, hear the keyboard symphony swelling and surging, laced with gently distorted guitars and barely audible drumming, then glide off to sleep again, wake briefly, see that it's 5:35, hear the keyboard symphony surging and swelling, softly distorted guitars and subliminal drumming, fall off to sleep again, wake to a waterfront morning dense with fog.

When I get home, Corina's sleeping on the couch with the TV on. The TV's never on, except to watch movies, which we only do once a month, if that. Sometimes I think we should just get rid of it, since we can watch movies on our laptops. Corina used to watch Cable News because she had a crush on Beth Barton, the glamorous picture tube journalist, or at least that's what Corina repeatedly told me, trying to make me jealous, and when I agreed with her that Beth Barton was hot, Corina got nasty, claiming I was imagining Beth Barton during sex. That was the end of TV news for both of us, and I don't miss it at all, especially not the commercials. But now the set is back on, though at least the sound is off.

I take a closer look. Instead of morning news, the

tube looks like it's become an aquarium. It's filled with the graceful motions of tropical fish. The only sound is the bubbling of the filter, which reminds me of the pet store I worked in back in my late teens, a small shop near the Fillmore West. It wasn't just a place that sold animals. In fact, few animals were ever sold. It was more of a place to hang out surrounded by dogs and cats and birds and large aquariums of tropical fish. I remember sitting on the floor with friends and complete strangers having stoned conversations about *The Politics of Experience, One Dimensional Man, The Joyous Cosmology,* and *The Doors of Perception*, books we only vaguely understood but enjoyed talking about at great length, discussions filled with laughter and confusion, playful arguments that didn't go anywhere and didn't need to, people pausing half-way through their sentences to watch the fish in their tanks, thirty minutes later picking up right where they left off. No one was entirely sure who the owner was, but a woman who liked wearing cowboy shirts was there all the time and seemed to be in charge, though she was never bossy. We were all half in love with her, but everyone somehow knew that it would have been wrong to say it out loud. It was just that she had such a range of relaxing facial expressions, such cheerful and generous body language, that no matter who you were, you would want her to care for you for the rest of your life. She never said much about herself, but she was fond of mentioning that her ex-husband had supported himself in college by volunteering for tests in which he dropped acid and then got observed by men with clipboards. She didn't seem to be managing much of anything, but she always played the most relaxing music, something that began with harbor sounds, slowly replaced by symphonic keyboard atmospheres of various kinds, mellow jazz guitars and soft drumming, the same music I heard that night at the Fillmore, that sound montage by the Steve Miller Band, years before they sold out. It's weird to think that she was Elaine's mother and the blotter guy was Elaine's father. She might have been born with "Song for Our Ancestors" playing softly in the background, ambient music before the term become popular.

Now I'm watching the fish while Corina sleeps, not sure why the pet store memory seems so important, like a dream I can't quite get myself to interpret, knowing how different the interpretation would be than the dream itself. Something happened last night, and the night before that and the night before that, something about a door in the fog, a group of young men playing music. I'm glad that the picture tube is filled with fish.

I'm glad there won't be any more news or commercials. The world has been sold and sold and sold and sold, and now it's not worth much anymore. But music remains, and it's nice to think that we don't need anything else.

THE RIGHT THING

I wait until he's finished loading his tools into his truck. When he gets behind the wheel and turns the ignition, I slip into the passenger seat, point a small pistol at his crotch, and tell him to drive.

Don't panic. Do everything I say, and there won't be a problem.

Okay.

I point to the mansion we're driving away from and say: You work for this rich motherfucker, right?

Yeah. Or no, I work for the maintenance guy, who works for the rich motherfucker.

Right. And you know he pays you below minimum wage to do hard work, while he himself makes millions a day doing nothing.

Yeah. So?

I tell the guy to pull off the local road onto the freeway. Soon we're going eighty miles an hour, whizzing past billboards and fast food places.

So right now, he's having a doomsday bunker built somewhere near here.

What's that?

A doomsday bunker is an underground mansion designed to last beyond the end of the world. While the planet becomes a waste land, rich people will be surviving in subterranean mansions, with all the luxuries they're accustomed to.

Where will they get food?

Hydroponic farms underground.

They'll be indoors all the time?

Yeah. But they'll have simulated outdoor pleasures, VR devices that allow them to think they've just come back from a luxury safari, or a cozy and charming ski resort in the Alps, or a party with rich celebrities on a patio facing the sea.

So what's this got to do with me?

I need to know where the bunker is. You need to find out and tell me.

I need to find out?

Right.

I tell him to take the next exit off the freeway. Soon we're on a local road leading past a subdivision into the foothills of a mountain range.

He looks puzzled and says: You're talking to the wrong guy. It's not like the great man talks to me. I've never said a word to him. I've only seen him from a distance. I've never been inside his house. How would I know where the bunker is?

But the guy you work for probably has occasional contact with him. He might know where the bunker is. Or he might know someone who does. You need to find out.

What if I can't?

I move the gun closer to his crotch and say: You can.

I tell the guy to pull off onto a dirt road leading back several miles through a dense forest to a small cottage in a clearing. Two friends come out and tie him up and take him inside. I wait by the truck. Once we know where the doomsday bunkers are, we can start destroying them one by one, preventing rich people from escaping the devastation their greed is creating.

Thirty minutes later my friends bring the guy back out, having inserted a nanoscopic tracking chip through the back of his neck. Now we'll be able to see and hear everything he does. If he tries to tell anyone what we're up to, we can shut him down with the push of a button.

I explain this to him. He nods. I tell him to get in his truck and start driving again. He seems fully alert, showing no outward signs of having just undergone a surgical procedure. I ask him if he's dizzy or sleepy. He says he's fine, but wants to know what we expect him to do.

I say: We'll see and hear everything through your eyes and ears. You'll be our tracking system. You'll do your normal job, the things you always do, except that you'll be finding out where the guy's doomsday bunker is, and how to get inside. We'll give you a month to find out what we need to know. We'll have full access to everything you learn, and we'll send you updates through the chip. You'll suddenly hear a voice in your head, giving you new instructions. Once we get the information we need, we'll neutralize the chip through remote control, and you'll have no recollection of anything we've made you do. You'll be back in your normal life without knowing what's happened. You won't remember this conversation. If you see me on the street at some point, I'll be a perfect stranger.

He looks at my gun and nods and says: No problem.

I tell him to turn onto a small road through the mountains. I don't want to take him back the same way we came. If the chip doesn't work as well as it's supposed to, I don't want him to remember how we got here. I could have done the driving myself and made him wear a blindfold, but the situation was already weird enough, and the blindfold would have made it even worse. I feel bad about what I've done to him. It's the kind of thing they do in the so-called intelligence community, in dictatorships, or in sci-fi movies. But I've never thought of myself as the kind of person who would do such a thing. It feels wrong.

It also feels right. My partners and I have important goals. Fucked up things have been fucked up far too long. They need to stop now. There's no use working through the so-called system to make vanilla changes that take forever and accomplish nothing.

The road goes up through towering peaks. Soon we're over 10,000 feet high, nothing but snow-covered mountains in every direction. I think we're feeling the same thing, that the views are so expansive that words would be meaningless and intrusive. Finally the guy says: I've never been this high before. I feel like a different person.

I spend as much time up here as I can. It makes everything better.

You don't have to work?

I got lucky and sold a screenplay twenty years ago. I didn't get rich but I still get royalty checks that keep me going. I don't have expensive tastes and I've got a rent-controlled apartment. And best of all, I've learned how to sleep like a dog.

Sounds nice. I've always liked the way dogs sleep. They don't mind sleeping all day. They're not conflicted about it.

That's right. Nothing tells them they ought to be getting things done.

What's your screenplay about?

People who have to work all the time to pay off student loans.

I know so many people in that position. They tried to get an education, and now they're paying the price for the rest of their lives. I saw the writing on the wall, and dropped out after my freshman year. But now I'm stuck doing meaningless work for almost nothing, one deadening part-time job after another. I can't even remember most of them.

I'm not sure what to say. I look outside, watching clouds passing over the mountains. I feel like a jerk. I'm intruding on a person's life, changing it in substantial ways, and he seems like a decent guy. I wouldn't mind so much if he was an asshole, like the current U.S. president. I wouldn't mind messing with Barry Trap's mind. I'm sure he's got doomsday bunkers all over the world. But the guy at the wheel hasn't done anything wrong. I admire him for backing away from a lifetime of student debt. But of course the alternative hasn't been easy. I know first-hand how depressing such situations can be. For years, I did the same thing. My masters degree in nineteenth-century history led nowhere. My thesis on Marx and Bakunin got me nothing. But five years ago, something happened that changed me forever.

My girlfriend at the time was an anthropologist. She was doing field work near the Great Bear Lake in northern Canada, interviewing the Bear Lake People about a class action suit they'd filed against the U.S. government, claiming that their high incidence of cancer over the past fifty years was caused by uranium mining the U.S. had done near the lake in the 1940s, when they were developing the first atomic bomb. I'd gone there with her because she thought it might be dangerous to travel to such a remote place by herself. In conducting her interviews, she got close to the tribal shaman, who showed us a sacred place, a cave leading down to a subterranean gallery. Nancy was eager to make the descent, but the shaman refused because tribal custom dictated that only men were allowed to see the magic images below. He said I could take the trip and tell her what I saw. Nancy had been trained to respect the values of the cultures she studied, even when they seemed misguided. So she agreed to let me take the trip in her place. I was terrified, but I wanted to do the right thing, so I traveled with the shaman far below the surface of the earth, where I saw the first cave paintings ever discovered north of the Arctic Circle.

Of course, Nancy and I were clear that we hadn't "discovered" the cave. It had been known to the shaman and his ancestors long before Nancy published a controversial article about it in an anthropology journal. Her discussion was based on the account I gave her when Jack and I came back to the surface. Jack wasn't the shaman's real name, but his tribal name was difficult to pronounce for people like Nancy and me, so he told us to call him Jack, though he could say our names correctly with no problem.

The entrance to the cave was small, and the cave got smaller and smaller the deeper we went, until it was finally nothing more than a claustrophobic tunnel. We had to crawl on our bellies for hours in total darkness, the kind of darkness most modern people can't comprehend. We're accustomed to bright lights, especially in cities, but even in the darkest places, on lonely roads in the middle of nowhere, our minds and bodies are filled with memories of illuminated places, and by the expectation of being in one of them soon. The light is in our bodies, in every neuron, in the flow of our blood. But in that tunnel the light wasn't anywhere. I could barely remember what it was. I was nowhere. I was crunched in on all sides by the darkness of dirt and stone. I didn't know where we were going. It was terrifying on a level I'd never known before.

There was no turning back. We couldn't crawl in reverse. The incline of our descent had gotten too steep. We were being pulled down. When we finally came to the chamber of images, it was still pitch dark and I was dizzy, terrified that we'd never get out. It was like being buried alive. Jack told me I would have to learn the darkness, get used to it, stop resisting it. At first it felt stark and tense, but slowly I started to like the absence of sight. Finally after an hour he lit a torch. It flickered over the walls. They were filled with colorful shapes and patterns. I wasn't sure what I was looking at, but it was like some kind of psychedelic math, unlike anything I'd seen in pictures of other Stone Age caves. I knew my impressions were absurd—psychedelic math—but I couldn't think of a better way to describe it. For Jack, it might have been musical notation, a song for his ancestors, but for me it looked like a group of complex equations, or the computations you make when you try to solve the equations, never quite sure if you're on the right track, if you're moving toward a false result, something you settle for because you want an answer of some kind, and anything is better than nothing.

I wanted to use my phone to get pictures, but Jack had made me leave my phone back in the camp. He knew I'd want photographic documentation, and he wouldn't allow it. He said pictures would create a false impression, and in retrospect I think he was right. No video or photo could have captured the way the images looked in the flickering light, darting and jumping as if the numbers were alive. I say numbers, but that's probably not what they really were. I'm just using that word because I didn't know what else to call them, because I saw them as parts of a group of equations. But thinking back on it later, I remembered pyramids and whirlpools and lightning bolts, cyclones and waterspouts, millipedes, butterflies, and spiderwebs, multi-colored moire patterns, things that looked like neurons and amoebas, other things that might have been squids and manta rays and flatworms, all of them throbbing and falling apart and coming back together, changing into each other, moving above and beneath each other, yet also combined like there should have been an equals sign at the end, like they should have been coming together to make something else. I tried to say this to Jack but he shook his head. He said it was visual music.

But not the kind you could listen to. You just had to let it happen. And it was happening. Everything was in motion, animated by torchlight. I don't know how long we were there. The images were surrounding us, on all the walls, the floor and the ceiling. I felt like we were inside a globe, and it was moving wildly, not spinning in a regular way like a planet. Few people know what it's like to have a light show beneath their feet, not just above them. It felt like I was standing on nothing, nothing solid, and all I could do was laugh and laugh, and then I was vomitting, like I'd taken mushrooms. But I hadn't taken anything. I was losing my mind and finding it again, though I only found part of it. The rest remained in those images. They shook me out of the mental state I'd lived with all my life. When Jack and I finally came back to the surface, I knew I could never go back to my normal existence.

Nancy wrote a great article based on what I told her. Her text wasn't scholarly, but coherent as an impressionistic response to a paranormal situation. I was impressed by her verbal abilities. She'd never written anything literary before, just professional ethnographic reports. Of course, it probably belonged in a cutting edge arts magazine. It was amazing that it got published in an academic journal. The journal's editor hesitated at first. But he had to publish it. He owed Nancy too many favors, and besides, he wanted her body. He begged her to make changes, to make it more suitable for scholars, to add citations and get rid of all the weird imagery, or at least tone it down. But she wouldn't change anything.

The reviewers roasted us. One of them even claimed she was making the whole thing up. But the editor got what he wanted. His reputation took a beating, but within a few weeks he and Nancy were lovers. I was left with all the weird images the editor wanted Nancy to edit out.

I was bitter at first. I haven't said a word to Nancy since then. But I know now that the images were worth it. As time goes by, they seem to be teaching me a new way to read, not as a mathmatician solving equations, not as a linguist making a translation, but as a viewer in a four-dimensional gallery, as if my mind has become its own aquarium. Back in the sixties, we were told to turn on, tune in, and drop out. Of course, it was easier said than done, as so many counter-cultural friends harshly discovered. But since I've come back from the center of the earth, I've been dropping out without trying to, and I've made new friends, a network of people I like and respect. I've learned a lot from all the things we've shared. Can history be knocked off course, taken out of the hands of those who control the means of image production? My friends and I have plans. The doomsday bunkers are just the beginning.

I tell the guy at the wheel to take a left, and soon we're descending. We reach a point where we've got a great view of the ocean a thousand feet below. We drive by three mansions near the cliff, surrounded by huge landscaped yards filled with palm trees and koi ponds. They look like expensive resorts, like they might have golf courses and private airstrips. They seem uninhabited.

I say: When you see places like this, don't you hate rich people? Don't you hate that they can live here part-time and also live in mansions in other parts of the world, glamorous locations people like us can only dream about?

I try not to feel bitter. It won't do me any good to get worked up about it.

Even though you probably live in a trashy apartment in a dangerous neighborhood?

I'm just glad I've got a place, even though the rent is way too high. But listen, sorry to change the subject, but do you mind if I ask you a question?

Depends on the question.

What's your name? I mean, you can tell me, right? I can't afford to tell anyone, right?

Right. I'm Rip Van Winkle.

He looks puzzled: The guy in that story?

Yeah, that guy.

That's really your name?

It is now. I used to be someone else, but I had my name and social security number changed about ten years ago, so the student loan people can't track me down. I owe them at least a hundred thousand dollars.

Were the identity changes expensive?

Yeah but it was worth it. I paid an identity specialist five thousand dollars, which was nothing compared to what I owed. So what's your name?

Stu Vortex.

That's really your name?

Just as real as yours.

He's looking toward the ocean, as if it might be telling him something. Somehow his name seems right, like a description and not just random sounds. He's tall and thin with messy brown hair and a goatee, like he should be playing upright bass in a hard-bop jazz ensemble, performing in small cafes at three in the morning.

He finally says: So how did you end up hating the

rich so much? I mean, sure, lots of people hate them, and most of them deserve it, but not everyone would go to the extremes you're going to.

I say: That guy who founded Amazon, Jack Bozo, makes more money in the time it takes to watch a TV commercial than you and I will make for the rest of our lives. That's not okay. And we all just assume that nothing will ever change, that we'll always have guys who want more than anyone else and know how to get it. We're resigned to it. We think it's part of the human condition. That's even worse than not okay.

Stu Vortex nods: Right. It's even worse than not okay. I just wish you'd asked me before you put that thing in my head. Did your medical friends drill a hole in my skull and stick the tracking device into my brain with tweezers you found in your medicine chest? Were the tweezers even sterilized? The inside of that cottage was pretty funky, like an abandoned meth lab. But they gave me an injection right away, and things got vague after that. Did they give me stitches to close the wound? How come I don't have bandages on my head?

It was done with an injection. The thing in your head is organic. It might as well be an amoeba, except that it's also a state-of-the-art computer, devised by a team of rogue technicians, people who worked on the first generation of iPhones back in 2005. It goes beyond anything Apple ever dreamed of. It has more than a million times the processing power of the device that landed a man on the moon back in 1969. It takes whatever shape it needs to take to obey our commands. But once it's gone there won't be any sign that it was ever there. Invasive? Sure. Unethical? Maybe. But I'm satisfied that the ends will justify the means.

I never trust anyone who says things like that.

Me neither.

I'm feeling guilty, so I tell him to drive to the best restaurant in the city, where I'll buy him a nice dinner. It's the whole top floor of a tall building, revolving slowly. The food is great, but the panoramic view is even better, extending thousands of miles in every direction, eastward all the way to the Gateway Arch on the Mississippi, north to the silhouette of Mount Saint Helens, westward all the way to the huge stone heads on Easter Island, south to the ritual stones in the public squares of Machu Pichu. I rave about how wonderful it is to see so much, naming all the distant places. Stu Vortex nods and smiles but says he can somehow see a lot more, possibly a side effect of the tracking device in his head, going past the gleaming arch on the Mississippi, past the Washington Monument, all the way into the Devil's

Triangle, which turns the mid-Atlantic mist into something that looks like the inside of a chambered nautilus, and going past the plume of smoke rising out of Mount Saint Helens, past the radioactive smokestacks on the northern shore of the Great Bear Lake, straight into the magnetic turbulence of the North Pole, which turns the fierce edges of Arctic air into something that looks like a Portugese Man of War, and going past the heads on Easter Island, past the shadowy spires of Angkor Vat rising over the jungle, all the way to the face of the Sphinx, which makes the desert air look like a flatworm under a microscope, and going past the sacrificial stones of Machu Pichu, past the fleets of reed boats moored on the shores of Lake Titicaca, setting down on the coast of Tierra del Fuego, a labyrinth of prismatic mist, which looks like a gigantic scheming octopus, camouflaging itself by changing colors.

Stu Vortex tells me that the view is so expansive that he wants to eat more than he's ever eaten before. I buy him whatever he wants as a token of my appreciation. He orders five different meals and wolfs them down like he's having oral sex. Then he tells me that he's still horny, so we go to an upscale sex club and I buy him a lap dance from a woman who's got hundreds of five-star Internet reviews. Just the customer descriptions of her performances would be enough to mess up anyone's pants. She's even better than the descriptions. She does things that I would have thought were physically impossible. She's a gymnast of erotic pleasure, an acrobat of the obscene. I buy Stu Vortex extra time, since he's been such a good sport about everything else. Then the three of us sit down for drinks. There's nothing seedy about the club. It's filled with enchanting music, something like Tangerine Dream on Orange Sunshine. Shadows glide on the walls and it feels like a cave in a mountain wall, looking out over a valley filled with unforeseen constellations.

He laughs and tells her: Honey, you know who's buying your drinks right now? None other than Rip Van Winkle.

She giggles: Like the guy in the story? The one who slept for twenty years?

I nod and smile, though I'm annoyed that Stu Vortex told her my name. It makes me feel too exposed. But he probably figured that since she knows nothing about the Doomsday Project, there's no harm in revealing something so harmless, especially since it has comic value, making it seem like we're all just drinking buddies.

She says: That was my favorite story back in high

school. Rip Van Winkle was such a sweet guy. His best friend was his dog, who liked to sleep a lot. Rip's wife thought the dog was a bad influence on her husband, leading him to be lazy instead of working hard and supporting his family.

I shake my head and say: Rip wasn't really lazy. He did lots of work around his village, helping out his neighbors. But he just couldn't bring himself to do things for money. He didn't want to show up for a regular job. It drove his wife crazy. They had a family to support. She pestered Rip into a state of desperation. Sleep was the only escape.

She says: I love how Rip decided that he'd rather sleep than work. If I didn't like my job, I'd want to sleep too.

Stu Vortex says: No kidding! It's an ongoing struggle to wake up and do stupid work.

I laugh: I always thought of it as a tale for children, the kind of thing you read in fifth grade English. But when I re-read the story, I saw more in it than I expected to. Rip wasn't a man-of-the-house kind of guy. He finally had to escape from a situation he wasn't suited for, the tensions of making the kind of living sanctioned by society, so he went to the top of a mountain, took a psychedelic trip, met Henry Hudson at a bowling alley in the wilderness, and woke up in the future.

Stu Vortex laughs: You make him sound like a hippie.

I shrug: Sure. Why not? Re-read the story. It's stranger than most people think. I remember being in a college English class, we had to write an essay in response to a question: Did Rip Van Winkle do the right thing? We'd been studying the story for the past few days, and the teacher wanted a full discussion. I gave him a one-word answer: Yes. He made me do the assignment again, this time with detail from the story. I objected that my answer was perfect, the kind of response Rip himself might have given, assuming he'd been willing to show up in a classroom and take a test. Some of my classmates were amused, strongly agreed with me, and started calling me Rip Van Winkle. So when I needed a fake name later, Rip Van Winkle seemed right, absurdly right, the kind of name that throws people off track, since it sounds like a joke.

She looks at me with a skeptical expression: So Rip Van Winkle isn't your real name, right? It's just a nickname based on a goofy classroom situation.

It's become my real name. I guess you could say that

it's not who I was, but who I've become. I've grown into the name.

She's nodding along, but I can tell she's not convinced.

I smile and say: I'm guessing you've got a real name too?

Same as in all the reviews: Cassie Troy.

That's a real name?

I don't let anyone call me anything else. Even Vince Butter.

Vince Butter? The multi-trillionaire? The guy who bought the Everglades last week? You know him?

I don't just know him. I own him. I can do things for him no one else can do. He dreams about me night and day, like in that song.

Stu Vortex laughs: How often do you see him?

Whenever he wants to buy what I do best.

Stu Vortex says: Lap dances?

Not exactly.

There's something else you can do that's even better?

Ask Vince Butter. But actually, you can't. He's out of town for the next three months. He's in Nepal. He's buying Mount Everest.

Stu Vortex puts on a look of mock disgust and says: Just Mount Everest? Why not the whole fucking range, a package deal for the Himalayas? Why settle for one mountain when you've got enough to buy the Roof of the World?

He's good friends with the Prime Minister of Nepal, and he's too nice to take away everything that the Prime Minister holds sacred. After all, without the Himalayas, Nepal's economy would collapse, no tourist money.

I look out the front window of the club, the lights on the other side of the bay, and for a few seconds I tell myself it's beautifiul, even though I know that rich people live there, and some of them no doubt have doomsday bunkers I'll need to be destroy. I look at the people here in the club, enchanted by the music, the view and the sexy dancing. They look just like the people back in the restaurant, like they have a lot more money than they need. They might have doomsdsay bunkers. I wonder how long it will take to rid the world of doomsday bunkers.

When I catch myself thinking this way, I'm surprised. I sound like a dangerous person trapped in a violent obsession, yet I've taken the name of one of the most lovable characters in American literature. As Cassie Troy just said, Rip's best friend was his dog, and there was a time when this was true for me too. I'd rescued an old beagle from an animal shelter because I felt sorry that so many old dogs never get adopted. I went out of my way to make the last few years of his life as pleasant as possible, and it was fun to watch him sleep on the couch for hours. It created a peaceful feeling in my apartment. One time, he fell asleep for a week. I thought he was dying. But he woke up on the eighth day fully refreshed, ready for action. I was amazed. It was like sleep had made him younger. I started sleeping more, sometimes staying in bed for days on end, with my dog asleep at the foot of my bed, snoring deeply. I became convinced that the dog was teaching me how to sleep like a dog, and that sleep for a dog was like traveling in a torchlit gallery, a cave of musical images, like the ones I'd seen in the subterranean chamber near the Great Bear Lake.

I woke one day and there it was on the tip of my tongue—the Doomsday Bunker Project, as if I'd somehow created it while sleeping. At first I thought the idea was extreme, the kind of thought that sounds good for a day or two, then sounds idiotic, misguided, unrealistic. But as I began to enjoy sleep more and more, the project began to take shape. I told friends about it, and they were eager to make it happen. They made a detailed plan, based on their expertise in the fields of medicine, neurochemistry, computers, and political theory. They were all convinced that the one-percenters needed to get their asses kicked. Somehow they weren't surprised that the Doomsday Project came from a sleeping dog. They all agreed with me that Rip Van Winkle did the right thing. They liked my *nom de guerre*. They said it was the kind of name you might give yourself on acid. But our project goes beyond hallucinations.

I look at Stu and Cassie talking, like they're old friends discussing old friends. I'm wondering if I should tell them that Mount Everest is in both Tibet and Nepal, that the Prime Minister of Nepal can't legally sell Mount Everest, unless the Chinese agree to the deal. But I don't want to spoil the chemistry Stu and Cassandra are developing, so I keep my mouth shut. I've got bigger fish to fry.

Stu Vortex asks: Why is Vince Butter staying away for so long? How long does it take to buy Mount Everest? Wouldn't it be a simple matter of writing a check and walking away with the deed of ownership?

Cassie Troy says: I've never bought a mountain, so I'm not sure. But I think that while he's over there, he's also planning to visit the Great Wall of China. He might want to buy it, so he wants to check it out first.

Why would he want to buy the Great Wall of China? What good would it do him?

It's a long story. But the short version is that he and the U.S. president hate each other. The president is obsessed with building a wall, so Vince Butter wants a better one. Plus, the president prides himself on his Chinese foreign policy. Vince Butter figures that if he owns the Great Wall of China, he can get control of the Chinese economy, and replace the president as China's favorite American big shot.

I shrug: But the Great Wall of China has nothing to do with China's economy.

Yeah, but Vince Butter doesn't know that. And neither does the President. They both figure that China has a tourist economy, with the Great Wall as a major attraction, when in fact China has a manufacturing economy. They actually make things.

Stu Vortex puts his hand on her hand and says: Honey, it sounds like you've got more business sense than the two most powerful men in the world.

I have to work for the money I make. They don't.

I say: I admire your work ethic. And judging from your reviews, a lot of other people do too. But if you want to make some extra money while Vince Butter is buying the roof of the world, I've got plans you might want to hear about. When can we meet?

I'm booked solid for the next few days, but I'm free most of Sunday.

Can you stop by at 5 on Sunday? I've got some friends I'm sure you'll want to meet.

She smiles and I hand her my card. Under my embossed *nom de guerre* are the words *Enhanced Financing*, which I'm pretty sure means nothing, though it sounds like something someone with power and influence would do. She looks at the card like it might have magic powers, when in fact she's the one who's got the magic powers, and the role she plays in Vince Butter's life could help my partners and me take a big step forward in our project. He's probably got several bunkers himself, and all his rich friends must have them too. It's amusing to think that a sex worker has such power, especially since in some ways Cassie Troy reminds me of Nancy, my anthropologist ex-lover. She's got the same hair and nose and lips and cheekbones, the same laugh, and looking at my fake business card with such obvious pleasure, Cassie's eyes are Nancy's eyes, her smile is Nancy's smile. Nancy would have thought it was beneath her to enjoy turning one of the world's most powerful men into an erotic slave, though it wasn't beneath her to sleep with a guy who could help her increase her status in the academic world.

I don't know what Nancy is doing right now and I don't care. But now that I've connected her with the top lap dancer in the world, I feel strangely close to someone I didn't know two hours ago, and it's hard to imagine planting a tracking device in Cassie Troy's head. It's not my style at all to treat people as pawns in a game I'm playing. But sometimes you have to do things that don't match up with your deepest convictions, and maybe after you've done these things you'll regret it, or maybe you'll see that you were never the good person you always told yourself you were. Or maybe the dubious things you've done will change you forever, warp your conscience, and you'll spend the rest of your life doing similar things, without hesitation or remorse. Or maybe you'll just block everything out, or remember what you did in modified form, so it doesn't sound so bad. Or maybe you'll tell your friends what you've done, and they'll tell you that it's no big deal, taking your words and rearranging them, emphasizing certain things, de-emphasizing others, and the story will sound quite different when they're done with it. Or maybe or maybe or maybe or maybe or maybe. So many maybes.

But history will show that Rip Van Winkle did the right thing.

SACRED PLACES

Three years ago, my family disappeared. It was at a place called Hidden Beach in northern California, just a few miles west of the largest redwood forest in the world. We got there by following an overgrown cliffside trail, then inching our way down steep switchbacks. We were there for hours by ourselves. It wasn't the kind of place that would attract the usual tourist crowd. Getting there was too difficult. It wasn't even mentioned in regional guide books. I learned about it from a friend back home, who told me it was a well-kept local secret, the kind of sacred place you have to search for, assuming that you even know it exists. I'm not religious. I don't believe that anything is sacred. But the silence at Hidden Beach felt like more than the absence of sound.

I fell asleep for an hour beneath a crude lean-to made of driftwood. It might have been constructed by someone who'd been there recently, but there weren't any nails or fasteners of any kind. It could have just been the random result of the tides. It would have given me shade from the sun had there been any sun. But instead there was that same deep mist we'd found in the redwood forest a few days ago. The sound of the ocean made the silence deeper, more expansive, but the fog was so thick that I could barely make out the waves, even though they were breaking only a hundred feet away, and some of them ran up on the smooth sand to within a few feet of my feet.

But then the kids wanted food. We hadn't packed anything, so we had to find a place to eat. We had to give up our quiet existence. We had to drive into a town filled with traffic and billboards. We had to enter the TV system, the all-encompassing network of picture tubes in public space—in supermarkets, restaurants, clubs, bars, waiting rooms, game arcades, laundramats, amusement parks, bus depots, fast food places, motel and hotel lobbies, shopping malls, airports, gift shops, barber shops, train stations, garages, repair shops, nail salons, department stores, convenience stores. You can't escape them. No matter where you look, you see commercials, media faces doing silly things, dramatic things, offensive things, self-righteous things, impossible things. There's always music, not something to really listen to, just noise, mixing with the noise of voices talking, messages on messages on messages, juxtaposed and superimposed, interrupting and talking over and changing into each other. If a referendum was held, how many people would vote to maintain the TV system? Who really wants it? Who thinks it serves any good purpose? I'd hate to meet the person that did.

We got out of town as quickly as possible. We took back roads to avoid strip malls, even though our GPS told us the trip would take twice as long. We soon got lost and found ourselves on a dirt road surrounded by redwoods. I started figuring out how to get back on track, but Marianne, my partner, was fascinated by something she saw in the dark of the forest. She insisted on getting out and walking a few hundred feet on an overgrown trail, leading to a small stone hut. We went inside. It was obvious that the place had been abandoned long ago. There were moldy beds in two of the rooms, a decaying circular table in the main room, which had also been the kitchen, where a white cermaic stove and oven combination looked like it hadn't been used in a hundred years. Marianne wanted to buy the place right away, turn it into a yoga retreat center.

Marianne was a compelling woman, so clever and articulate that within a few minutes she had me believing in her plan. She wanted to form a yoga collective centered on an enlarged and renovated version of the hut. She reminded me that a close friend of hers taught meditation at the nearby state university, and could refer students to our center, so that we could quickly get a good number of people involved, sharing our belief in a quiet existence. There was no stopping Marianne once she got an idea, and she stayed up half the night in our motel room, doing online research, designing the yoga center in her head and on screen, adding rooms for various purposes, a full second floor, and a possible third floor later, with an observation tower.

She was still talking about it non-stop the next day, when we packed our own food and went back to Hidden Beach. I wanted another nap under the lean-to. Marianne and the kids went down to the water, eager to play in the place where the mist and sea became interchangeable. At first I couldn't sleep. I kept trying to imagine the new yoga center, Marianne's version of a sacred place. I wanted to be in that observation tower, surrounded by the silence of redwoods. I tried to form a clear picture I could dream about. But I was too stuck in my rage at the TV system to fully concentrate. I couldn't accept that something so worthless and invasive, something that no one really wanted, had somehow become a permanent part of society. Who set up this hideous network? Who decided that public space should be filled with noise and distraction? Was it part of a plan, like the border wall the president wanted to build? Or did it just happen, with no design or agenda, like tree roots growing under someone's house and finally destroying the foundation? Was it the consequence of consumer economics, the unplanned but still unavoidable result of a sell-at-all-costs social system? Would it some day reach Mount Everest, greeting groups of climbers with commercials when they reached the top? I couldn't stop the rant in my head. The words were mine, I wanted them to shut up, but they just kept going. I needed Marianne's stone hut, where I knew there would never be media noise. Someone once told her that she looked and talked just like a well-known TV journalist, Beth Barton, but in many ways, Marianne was the opposite of Beth Barton, captivating in ways that had nothing to do with media glamor.

Finally I fell asleep, dreaming that dolphins were leaping and splashing in the wake of an ocean liner, maybe the Titanic, Strauss and Mozart on a sinking ship. I woke up three hours later. I looked for Marianne and the kids but didn't see them. The fog was even thicker than before. I looked up and down Hidden Beach for hours, until it got dark. No sign of my family. I called the police and with heavy duty flashlights and megaphones, they helped me continue the search. Nothing. I drove back to our motel room half-expecting them to be there somehow, having played a misguided joke on me. They weren't there.

I stayed up all night. I saw an ACLU report on my computer. The President's border atrocities were becoming even more predatory, with more than 2000 families torn apart in the last few months, victims of policies that served no constructive purpose and weren't even legal. I'd seen the pictures of children in cages, faces pressed against rusty chain-link fences, banging on bars of cells, or pressing handwritten notes against dirty windows begging for help, juxtaposed on the news with bruising footage of the President's face, his obnoxious voice declaring that foreigners needed to be kept out, for reasons of national security, as if that meant anything. Normally, I would have sent out tweets, texts, and emails, calling on the legislative branch to impeach the racist buffoon as soon as possible. But I couldn't concentrate long enough to send out anything.

I went back to the beach the next morning. Again the fog was thick and again I found nothing. This went on for a week. I started resenting the fog, which never left, not even for a second. I'd always loved foggy days and felt that there weren't enough of them. In the past, when the morning light burned off the mist, I'd hated the sun. I didn't want things heating up. I wanted the chill, the phantom zone. Now these things were more than inconvenient. They seemed deadly.

At one point I found a cave behind a heap of driftwood. I took a quick look inside and saw that the space got smaller the farther I went. If I'd continued, I would have had to go down on all fours, and then down on my belly, sliding my way forward into darkness. I remembered reading that in paleolithic times, people crawled through long tunnels in total darkness to reach subterranean chambers, where walls were covered with pictures. I never understood why the art was so inaccessible, but some expert said that facing the darkness was probably a Stone Age rite of passage, that only people willing to snake down into the earth, struggling along in dirt and stone through claustrophobic tunnels, could earn the right to contemplate the images, which came to psychedelic life in flickering torchlight. Were the caves regarded as sacred places, meditation chambers, sources of secret knowledge? Back in my late twenties, I'd seen the caves in southern France, and I'd been impressed by the images. But I knew that I had no way of knowing what a Stone Age person's reaction might have been when he looked at them for the first time. In his daily life above ground, he wouldn't have been surrounded by constant visual stimulation, like we are today. Wherever we go, bright images are waiting for us. They're forced on us all the time. They're nothing special. We see them without having traveled through absolute darkness on our bellies. But 40,000 years ago, a person gazing at cave paintings in torchlight might have been have stunned, transported by an unforeseen experience, knowing he'd seen something most other people would never see.

I thought of Marianne's plan to build a yoga center in the middle of nowhere. Maybe it was her version of a Stone Age cave. I tried over the next few days to find the stone hut again. Even though I knew my family couldn't have gone there without our car, I still thought that somehow they might be there, with Marianne explaining the plan, telling the kids that they would soon be off the grid, beyond their phones and computers. But I wasn't sure where the hut was. I tried all the dirt roads I could find, driving as slowly as possible, but saw nothing but trees and mist. Maybe only Maryanne knew how to locate the hut. Maybe she was like a Stone Age magician, and she alone could find the secret entrance to the sacred cave. I felt silly thinking this, but in my desperate state of mind, lots of weird things seemed possible.

Finally, I gave up and went back to Hidden Beach. Helicopters were summoned and searched for three days. Coast Guard Cutters with powerful searchlights went up and down the coastline. They found nothing. At some point it occurred to me that maybe they weren't lost at all, that Marianne had decided to leave, taking the kids, going in secret to start a new life without me. Maybe she didn't want me or anyone else to know where they'd gone. I dismissed this possibility. It would have been unlike Marianne to sneak off while I was sleeping. She would have told me to my face that she wanted her freedom. She never backed away from confrontations. Still, I wanted to think that my family was still alive, even if they wanted nothing to do with me.

Finally I had to go home. I couldn't stand our motel room any longer. But the day before I left, I was walking up and down the beach, trying to relax as the frothing tide ran over my feet, when I came across a man who looked like my father, not the man who raised me in his thirties and forties, but a version of him in his early twenties, someone I'd only seen in pictures. I told him what my problem was.

He creased his brow and said: A woman in her late thirties, tall and slim with long blonde hair, and two kids who might have been ten or so, both blond?

Yeah.

Kids named Kirk and Betsy or Betty? Both kind of skinny?

Right.

They were wading in the surf. They kept going farther out. There were fins sticking up from the water.

Sharks?

Dolphins. A whole pod of them.

You can tell the difference? Even in the fog?

Absolutely. When you live in a place like this, you learn the difference.

So?

So the woman seemed to know they weren't sharks, and she kept going further. The kids were afraid at first, but then they went with her, further and further. Soon the dolphins were all around them. And then the woman and the kids were on the dolphins' backs, riding out into the ocean.

You're messing with me, right?

He shook his head: Not messing with you.

So then?

Like I just told you: They disappeared into the fog on the dolphins' backs.

So where are they?

The man looked at me strangely, then smiled and shrugged and said: What happens to people who ride on the backs of dolphins into the sea?

I was thinking at first that he was prompting me to say something hopeful. But I couldn't come up with anything. I knew there were stories about people being saved in the sea by friendly dolphins. In Classical times, people believed that virtuous souls were carried after death by dolphins to sacred islands. But I'd always assumed that dolphins were just aquatic mammals with no special place in the human condition.

I looked toward the waves in the mist. I looked back at him and shrugged.

He finally said: Sorry, man. I hope things work out.

Then he walked off into the fog.

I should have followed him right away and gotten more details. But I was stuck in his question, wondering what he might have meant, other than that he was telling me to accept the obvious: my family must have fallen into the sea, and the dolphins couldn't save them, assuming that they felt even the slightest desire to. My wife and kids hadn't run off to start a new life without me. They were floating somewhere face down, rising and falling with the waves.

Finally, I rushed after him, but he wasn't where

he should have been, maybe two hundred feet away. For the next hour, I searched the beach for him, but couldn't even find footprints.

I was still unsettled by it, three years later. The police decided that somehow my family must have been abducted, but all their investigations came to nothing. I hired a Private Eye, supposedly one of the best. He too found nothing. I finally gave up and dismissed him. I knew I would never stop missing my family, but I resigned myself to being alone. Before I got married and became a father, I used to enjoy being single. I even wrote a book on the pleasures of being unmarried. It sold so well that I'll probably never have to look for a job, especially since I don't mind living on almost nothing. Now that I was on my own again, I remembered what I used to like about it. I sold our house and moved into a small apartment. I fixed it up with stuff I found in thrift shops, battered rugs and chairs and lamps and bookshelves, a bed that was also a sofa. It was strange at first just living in a single room, but before too long it began to feel like home. I enjoyed waking up in it, coming home to it. If I really believed in sacred places, my apartment might have been one of them. Not that it was perfect. It was old and things didn't always work. The landlord was lazy, unreliable. He kept promising to paint the place but he never did. You could always hear big city noise through the windows, even when they were closed. But I had a good view of the city. I had music, books, and friends. And there was something nice about doing whatever I wanted, not having to figure things out with Maryanne all the time.

She wasn't an easy partner. She had strong opinions on everything, and didn't hesitate to fight for what she believed. She often made me feel like an idiot. When she wanted something, she insisted on getting it, even if was awkward or inconvenient for me. I didn't miss the difficulties we created for each other. But she was a funny, brilliant, beautiful woman, and there was no way not to feel terribly empty at times, especially when I thought about our kids. They filled my life in ways I couldn't anticipate before I became a father. They were often cute and funny. But taking care of them was challenging. Marianne and I had very different ways of being parents, and this led to bitter fights. The kids themselves were difficult, not like the kids on TV shows or Hallmark cards. But their absence left a huge gap that couldn't be filled by anything else. On some nights I felt like I might go crazy, and I had to go out and walk for hours and hours, through neighborhoods I didn't recognize, down streets of old brick factories with broken doors and windows.

On one of those nights I reached a turning point. I was on a street where most of the streetlights were broken. I passed by empty shopfront windows, watching my face in a series of cracked reflections. My features weren't the same as they were three years ago. Everything about my face looked different. I'd lost most of my hair and grown a double chin, something I tried to conceal with a long white beard. I now wore thick tortoiseshell glasses, though I hated the way the frames felt on my face. I walked for blocks, down side streets back to main streets back to side streets, without seeing anyone. I didn't know where I was. I told myself I didn't need to.

Then I came to a place that didn't seem abandoned. I went inside. About fifty people were seated on folding chairs in front of an empty stage. There was silence, then laughter, silence, then laughter, silence, then laughter. I watched for fifteen minutes. No one was making jokes on the stage, yet everyone was laughing. I wondered about the audience. Were they just a random collection of comedy lovers, somehow amused by the absence of a comedian? Were they members of a secret society practicing an absurd ritual of some kind? I liked the second possibility, a group of people actively seeking or staging nonsensical situations, convinced that they were transforming themselves in important ways. But after a while, I got tired of what I didn't understand. I was just about to leave and forget about it, but a tall blonde woman from the audience was leaving too, so I stopped her outside the door. She looked startled, like someone who wasn't there was in her way.

Sorry to interrupt you. But I need to know: What was going on in there?

What was going on in there? What do you mean?

You were all just sitting there laughing at nothing.

So?

So why were you all just sitting there laughing at nothing?

We enjoy it.

Even with no one on stage entertaining you?

We don't need anyone else to entertain us.

You entertain yourselves?

Sure, why not?

Can't you just do that at home, by yourselves.

Sure. Everyone does that. But sometimes it's fun to meet somewhere and do it together. Now, if you'll excuse me, I've got somewhere else I need to be.

She shouldered past me, walking briskly away. The

sound of her shoes on the pavement made the darkness even darker. I knew if I didn't follow her, the dark would get even worse. I caught up with her.

Sorry I disturbed you.

Yeah, no kidding.

I mean, I'm out here by myself because there are nights when I can't be at home. I lost my wife and kids about three years ago, and I'm still not over it.

You lost them? They died in a plane crash or something?

They disappeared. No one can find them, probably an abduction of some kind.

That's horrible.

So I thought I saw something strange back there. But maybe it was just dark, and something completely normal was going on, and my imagination—

Look, it's okay. You've had a horrible loss. I don't have kids myself, but I can imagine how devastating it must be to lose them and not know where they are.

We were standing outside what looked like an old café. She looked sympathetic, feeling my sadness, then looked puzzled, like she was reading through my forehead, confused by vanishing patterns of words and phrases. She nodded and smiled slightly, as if she'd come to a decision, suddenly knew who I was, not just a perfect stranger. She touched my arm and said: Why don't we go inside and get some coffee.

Inside, the place was dark. There were only three small circular tables, two of them occupied, people having quiet conversations. A young man was playing guitar on a small stage. Or rather, he was pretending to play guitar, moving his hands expertly up and down the fret board, gracefully plucking the strings, face animated with playful concentration, without producing any sound, filling the room instead with something like water, except that it wasn't wet and didn't interfere with our breathing.

We sat at one of the tables. A guy came and took our order. The woman took off her sweater, showing off her supple arms and shoulders. Suddenly I knew who she was, a Cable News anchor widely admired for being beautiful, though not for being brilliant, even though she'd won awards.

Beth Barton?

Okay, so you finally recognized me. Now what?

I'm nervous about being with someone I've seen a thousand times on the TV screen.

So you like the way I present the news?

You make disaster seem sexy. You make the stupid and vicious things the president says and does seem sexy. But I hate TV.

You hate TV? It sounds like you watch it.

I hate how it's everywhere. Don't get me wrong: I like seeing your face all over the place. But I don't like the way it's impossible to escape it.

It's not impossible. There's no TV in here.

I looked around. The walls were covered with pictures of tropical fish, painted with photo realist precision, so it looked at first like the place was a huge aquarium.

Yeah. There's no TV. It's incredible. And you don't look like you do on the picture tube. You look more intelligent.

I look stupid on TV?

That's not what I meant.

What *did* you mean?

Your face on TV is so perfect that it looks like you're just there to get attention. Every facial expression, every move you make, looks planned, carefully staged to make you look stunning, irresistable. But here you just look like a person.

That's why I like this place, this neighborhood. It's almost off the grid. No TV. No Internet. The people here don't want to be media clones. It's almost like a sacred place.

You believe in sacred places? You're religious?

I didn't mean it in a religious sense. I just meant—

I'm glad you didn't mean it in a religious sense, because the last time I was at a so-called sacred place, my family disappeared.

Where was this?

Hidden Beach in northern California.

Is Hidden Beach an official sacred place?

Not exactly. But it's a beautiful place where you can be by yourself, without the usual tourist bullshit—at least it was like that three years ago, when no one knew about it.

Has it been discovered?

I don't think so, but it probably will be. Nothing will ever stop the human race from trashing the world. Even Mount Everest, once considered inaccessible, has become a tourist trap. People with enough money can buy guided tours to the top of the world, and it's so crowded at this point that it's become dangerous. When Tenzing and Hillary first got to the top, the mother goddess of the mountains was dangerous in a very different way.

The mother goddess of the mountains?

That's what it's called in Tibet and Nepal, *chomolungma*, the name of a sacred place, or it used to be, before the British came and changed the name. Now it's just another photo op. People go there just to take pictures of themselves.

She looked at me with affection, took my hand across the table. I smiled and imagined that she might be attracted to me, though I'm not sure why. She could have any man, the richest and best-looking guys in the world. Why would she settle for someone like me? But there was no doubt that she was looking at me with interest.

She rippled her shoulder muscles, something Marianne used to do when she wanted me to want her. Suddenly I could see why people used to say that Beth and Marianne could have been doubles. She let the moment grow by remaining silent, then said: Anyway, this neighborhood has been forgotten by everyone. It's almost a ghost town at this point. It's becoming special, a place that won't ever be gentrified, or rediscovered by hipsters.

It's strange. I'm not even sure how I got here. All I know is that one street led to another. I'm not sure how to get back.

The guitarist on stage was moving his hands up and down the fret board, not strumming or plucking the strings at this point, but moving his hands like he was petting a dog or cat, making his instrument sound like a barely audible symphony ten blocks away. The music was making the paintings move. The fish were quick and graceful, darting in and out of underwater vegetation. They weren't just on the walls anymore. They were swimming through the air, over the tables, over the stage.

Do you live around here?

Right around the corner.

Even though you make a million dollars a year?

I like it. I've got a whole building. I had it renovated before I moved in.

So now it's a fancy place, with that generic designer look? Something I can expect to find in *Architectural Digest*?

Not at all. It's a place where I feel at home, not the kind of space you can only see in glossy magazine pictures. Believe it or not, I'm more of a slob than a snob. I like battered sofas and unmade beds.

Is that an invitation?

Only if you say yes.

She took my hand more firmly. Her hand was Marianne's hand.

I laughed slightly: Your husband's not around?

I divorced him two months ago.

Why?

He wasn't good enough.

Good enough?

He didn't like tropical fish.

I wasn't sure what to say. I'm a big fan of tropical fish. I think the world would be greatly improved if everyone traded their TVs for aquariums. I think our tax dollars should fund this project, with money redirected from the obscenely bloated defense budget. But it was hard for me to imagine Beth Barton supporting such a project, since TV had made her wealthy enough to buy and fix up a whole building.

She was looking at me closely, like someone finding ways to enjoy a painting they'd never liked before. She narrowed her eyes and tilted her head and said: Kiss me. Kiss me right now and die.

I laughed: Sure, whatever you say.

I'm serious. You need to release me.

By kissing you? Like you're that girl in the fairy tale? Sleeping Beauty?

You need to release me. I'm stuck in the picture tube, like a genie in a bottle. Only you can release me.

This might be the strangest thing I've ever heard.

Strange or not, just do it.

Not without an explanation. Kiss you and die and release you from the picture tube? I mean, what the fuck?

Okay, here's how it works. TV has made me who I am, to the point that most of my soul is no longer mine. I've become an image, part of a system of images. I had a dream that someone who's lost everything could release me. But he had to kiss me knowing that he would die, and he had to do it in a place with no name. This place used to be called The Green Dolphin, but now it doesn't have a name, and I've heard that the owner won't name it again because he thinks names are bad luck.

Names are bad luck? Look, this whole thing is getting too weird. I mean, obviously I'd love to kiss you. You're one of the world's most beautiful women. How often do regular guys like me get a chance to kiss women like you? But the other part of it sounds fucked up. Sure, you could say I've lost everything. But it's really not so bad. I still like my life. In fact, in some ways I like it better now that I don't have anything left. What you want is just too weird.

I'm sure it is. But sometimes you just have to do something crazy. You don't do it because it makes sense. You do it because it doesn't make sense.

I like the way that sounds. It's like something a hippie philosopher might have said, back when people were turning on, tuning in, and dropping out.

So what are you waiting for?

Beth Barton stood, looking impossibly beautiful in the gliding aquarium light. I walked around the table, eager to kiss a woman everyone in the world would love to kiss. But once I kissed her I'd die? It couldn't be true but what if it was? What if she had something deadly on her lips and teeth and tongue? I wanted to live in the moment before the kiss, a prelude to a kiss, like in that Duke Ellington song. I thought of Tenzing and Hillary, seconds before they reached the highest place in the world, knowing that they were just about become famous, living legends, but savoring the moment right before the highest moment. Would something be lost forever once they reached the top and looked down?

I tried to make the moment last, noticing something strange in the look Beth Barton was giving me, as if she'd been looked at so many times that now she was poisoned, loaded with a radioactive charge, and touching her was dangerous. Then it wasn't Beth Barton standing there smiling. She was starting to change into someone who looked like she might be the woman I lost, emerging from the aquatic light of a place that had no name.

She said: Recognize me now?

Where have you been?

The place where everyone finally goes. Your permanent home.

I'm not dead yet.

You might as well be.

I won't be dead until I kiss you, right? That was the deal.

She laughed softly and said: The dead don't make deals.

They don't?

They don't have to.

So what happens now?

Put your lips on mine and find out. Kiss me the way you've kissed me a thousand times before—only better, much better.

I tried not to. I didn't want the kiss of death, even if Beth Barton was really Marianne, even if she'd traveled with a pod of dolphins to a sacred place, and now she was inviting me to join her there, a place that was forever outside the TV zone, a place that would never appear on a billboard, a place beyond all human interference. I was tempted to think it was time to make the big move, the final transition. But I didn't believe in life after death, especially if it was a place of rewards and punishments. Besides, there was something unpleasant about her voice, the way she was forming words. She sounded like she'd been trained to sound persuasive, to sound like she knew what was going on, confident that everyone would believe her. And then there were questions: Why had she treated me at first like a perfect stranger? Had I changed so much that in the dark she'd only recognized me after we'd spent some time together? How could she be Marianne and also Beth Barton? Were such transformations possible in other dimensions? Did such dimensions even exist? I'd always thought people who talked about other dimensions were kidding themselves. Why would I start to believe in such things now? Why would I make decisions based on shadowy perceptions, formed in a place that had no name and might be underwater. There was no way I could trust the situation.

I did what I've learned to do when things get strange. I slowed my breathing down, letting my body settle back into itself, as if I were sinking into an old familiar chair facing a window.

I gave Beth Barton the softest kiss in the history of passion. Her eyes were closed. She might have smiled. I left without a word.

JUST ANOTHER EMERGENCY

When Tom was growing up, he didn't like having his picture taken. He didn't like the smile he was expected to show the camera. This feeling got even stronger as he got older. He saw with increasing clarity how the world was trapped in pictures. He hated the famous people, the glamorous people. He hated the way they seemed to live from one photo op to the next. Why didn't they think it was stupid to flash so many fake smiles? Why were their faces always on magazine covers? Why were politicians always smiling? Why were they showing their teeth and why were their teeth always getting sharper?

These questions are still on Tom's mind each and every day. But not right now. Right now his long-time lover Destiny Stump has her head in his crotch. She's had him right on the edge for thirty minutes. He's about to explode. Then his pager beeps from the hospital scrubs beside him on the sofa. He tells her not to stop but the pager beeps again. Again and again, each time louder and longer, like they need him right away. It's got to be a life-or-death situation, something only a world class neuro-surgeon like Tom can address. Again he begs Destiny not to stop but he knows that they probably should.

The wall-mounted TV set on the other side of the room pops on. Tom doesn't know what's going on. The TV has never done this before. It's not the kind of set you can schedule to turn itself on in advance. Destiny gets up and grabs the remote, shutting the TV off but it pops back on. She shuts it off again but it pops back on. She shuts it off again but it pops back on, again and again, as if it were somehow connected to the pager, as if it were calling attention to a life-or-death situation.

There's an all-too-familiar face on the screen. U.S. President Barry Trap is standing in front of a church. He's holding a Bible upside down in his right hand, as if he were planning to read it standing on his head. He tries to look firm and serious, but instead he looks like he just lost all his money at a Blackjack table. Cameras flash, making his head and body expand like an orange balloon, each new flash inflating him further, pushing him to the point where he might explode. The TV screen expands to contain the inflating president's body. It bulges until it can't get any larger. But the screen doesn't pop. The President pops. He's not there anymore. There's a pale orange glow where the President was, a heap of orange dust on the pavement.

The screen goes blank, pops back on much louder with a commercial. A giant octopus crawls up onto a beach, crushing bathers with its huge tentacles. People run and scream but the creature is quick and only a few escape. The rest are like tubes of toothpaste getting squeezed. Cars and buses and trucks get crushed like beercans. A voice-over says: With global warming changing the way we live, mythical sea monsters become an ever-present danger! Now they can live on land, with arms that reach to the distant corners of the globe! Nothing is safe, unless you protect yourself with Liberty Mutual! Liberty Mutual customizes global warming so that you only pay for what you need. Liberty—

Finally Destiny pulls the plug, rips the TV out of the wall, lifts it above her head and smashes it down on the hardwood floor. It shatters into a thousand pieces, thrashing like dying fish on the deck of a ship. It takes at least three minutes for things to calm down.

Tom shakes his blue-balled head, puts on his pale green hospital scrubs and staggers toward the door. He looks at Destiny Stump and shrugs and says: Sorry I can't stay and help you clean things up, but—

She says: No problem. It's all my mess. Sometimes I think I have anger management problems. But I wish more people smashed their TVs. It felt so good to put the damn thing in its place! Anyway, you better get going. That pager sounds like it really means it!

Tom goes out the front door and calls an Uber. The pager finally stops, as if it doesn't like being outside. Two minutes later, a blue Mirage appears. When Tom gets in, the driver is already talking, apparently making a daily speech that begins first thing each morning, ending only when he falls asleep late at night, insisting that the pandemic is a hoax, a global psychotic episode, a playground for the crisis queens of worldwide mass information, that the dreaded coronavirus is nothing more than a common cold, and there's no need to wear a mask, which in any case is no more effective against a microbiotic invasion than a chain link fence would be against a swarm of ants, but the New York traffic is so loud that Tom can only make out a few isolated phrases, while the driver gestures wildly with both hands off the wheel, and the radio pops on, breaking news about riots all over the nation, reactions to the latest racist episode, a Minneapolis black man murdered by a cop, who crushed the guy's throat for nine minutes while he pleaded for his life, and three other cops stood a few feet away and did nothing, the story abruptly cut off by a beer commercial, happy jingles and lame slogans, then a car commercial, happy jingles and lame slogans. The driver stops and gets out, still talking non-stop, and someone else gets in and starts driving. She turns and looks at Tom like he's a picture of himself. She turns off the news and turns on jazz, something that might be "Pharaoh's Dance", an improvisation from *Bitches Brew*, but it's riddled by frequent bursts of static interference, overdubbed with traffic noise. She looks in the rear view mirror, meeting his eyes, looking like she thinks she's seen him before, like he might be a long-lost friend or a movie star. She's wearing a handkerchief mask, which prevents him from clearly reading her face, but her eyes are filled with amusement. Tom thinks he's supposed to fill his eyes with amusement too, like they're sharing a joke or devious plan or they're in the same sinister cult, but he isn't sure what's going on and starts to feel stupid. Then he gets it. He isn't wearing a mask. He must have left it at home. The driver must think it's funny to see a doctor in scrubs not wearing a mask, especially since they're in a car together, less than six feet apart. Now he feels like a kid in a classroom corner wearing a dunce cap. He remembers that he had to do that once, when he got freaked out by a flatworm under a microscope, the paranoid cross-eyed glare on both of its heads, which told him that it didn't want to be studied, magnified on a slide, written about in textbooks and scientific papers, and when he wrote this on a test the teacher thought he was making fun of her, turning science into fiction, so she made him wear the pointed hat and face the wall and repeat the phrase, "I'm a dunce and that ain't good," something Tom is remembering now for the first time in decades. The driver stops at a traffic light, gets out, and someone else gets in and starts driving. He's wearing a Cleveland Indians baseball hat and a cowboy face bandana, and Tom remembers reading that Lakota Sioux activists wanted the Indian's smiling face removed from the hat, since it made it seem that Indians were demons, fiendishly happy, always planning mischief. But the President rejected the objection, claiming that the smile could just as easily mean that Indians were proud to be the first inhabitants of the Western Hemisphere. Tom thinks back to the President popping out of existence ten minutes ago, but of course it might have been a trick, or a picture tube glitch of some kind. He wants to ask the driver about it, but the guy is cursing loudly at the midtown traffic, flipping off other drivers and pedestrians, running three consecutive red lights, making a U-turn, racing the wrong way down a one-way street, slamming on the brakes. He winks at Tom in the rear-view mirror, a move so theatrically perfect that Tom assumes the guy must have been practicing. Maybe the driver can also do ballet on stilts or whistle complete symphonies. But now he's getting out of the cab and someone else is getting in. She's dressed like a farmer's wife in a porno movie, tight blue overalls with nothing underneath. She asks him if he's seen the new movie everyone's talking about. She hasn't seen it yet but she really wants to. She can't remember the title, then remembers that it doesn't have one. It's focused on people waiting in line to see a movie. The film is based on the things they say while waiting, except that suddenly in the background there's thunder and lightning, and a huge woman, maybe a hundred feet tall, comes storming up to the White House, reaches into the Oval Office, yanks the President out and holds him up into the storm, watches him thrashing and squirming, clearly enjoying it. Then she bites his head off. The driver sounds excited, still caught up in cinematic imagery, as if she were doomed to be stuck in a theater seat for the rest of her life. Finally she checks Tom out in the rear view mirror, looks puzzled behind her mask, pulls out a brush from her handbag, running it through her long red curly hair, steering with her knees, removing the mask to blow a gigantic bubble of gum, popping it loudly, sucking the gum back into her mouth and replacing the mask. She turns and offers Tom a pack of Bazooka Joe bubble gum. Tom remembers that his older brother used to collect the Bazooka Joe comics that came inside each pack, used to memorize the Bazooka Joe jokes and tell them at parties, and everyone thought he was a really cool guy, until he vanished in a plane that got sucked into the Bermuda Triangle. The driver looks at him in the mirror with a sympathetic face, as if she can tell that he feels like a fool, a doctor without a mask. She turns on the washing fluid to clean the windshield. The wipers smear the glass and she can't see clearly. She sprays more washing fluid, but the wipers make the grime on the glass even worse. She stops at a red light, gets out and someone else gets in and starts driving, running the light. Behind his Spiderman covid mask in profile, he looks like Grover Cleveland on a thousand dollar bill. He plays with the radio dial to get better reception for "Pharaoh's Dance", finally gives up, declaring that you can always get good reception for bad top-40 stations but not for progressive jazz stations. Tom thinks that it's all about money, even with a musician like Miles Davis, who owned a brownstone on the Upper West Side, where a one-bedroom apartment now sells for half a million, less than ten blocks from the site of a rundown farmhouse in which a penniless Edgar Allan Poe became famous for writing a poem he didn't even like. The poem became so popular that people all over the nation were reciting it on the streets, and Tom thinks Poe must have felt like a rock star. He wonders if Grover Cleveland felt like a rock star after becoming the only U.S. president to serve two non-consecutive terms. But he remembers that Grover Cleveland was obese, and who ever heard of an overweight lead guitarist? But then, how many people have ever spent a thousand dollar bill? Or even seen one? Or even know that such a thing exists? Tom thinks of how pleasant Poe's life might have been if he'd had even one Grover Cleveland thousand dollar bill, how many great poems and stories Poe could have written if he hadn't been worrying constantly about money. But of course Grover Cleveland was only a twelve-year-old boy in 1849, the year Poe died, wearing someone else's clothes outside a Baltimore tavern. The driver pulls over so fiercely that he nearly destroys the one remaining mailbox in the neighborhood, gets out and someone else gets in and starts driving. She's wearing a mermaid face mask, a mermaid bikini, and when Tom compliments her on her costume, she says that she's going trick or treating after work, that she was born twenty thousand leagues under the sea and her father was Captain Nemo, which leads Tom to think of Columbus mistaking manatees for mermaids, and he wonders how the driver can drive with only a fin where feet should be. When she checks him out in the rear view mirror, giving him a puzzled look, he wonders if she thinks he's just wearing scrubs because it's Halloween, since after all an authentic doctor would know enough to wear a mask, but then Tom remembers that Halloween is five months away, and he wonders how the driver can be so confused, wonders if maybe she trick or treats whenever she's in the mood, regardless of the date, just to get free candy. She stops and tumbles out and someone else gets in and starts driving. The new driver has big mirror shades reflecting and reflected in the rear view mirror. He's wearing a navy blue blazer over a slender bare torso, dirty white cargo shorts and a horseshoe lip ring. No mask. He smiles when he sees that Tom isn't wearing a mask, apparently pleased to see that even doctors don't always cover their faces, even when they're less than six feet away. He pulls out a small paperback from his inner coat pocket, puts the book on his lap, glances at it quickly, looks back at the noisy, congested street, looks back at the book then back at the street then back at the book then back at the street, mouthing a phrase he's apparently trying to memorize. His mirror shades in the rear view mirror multiply a billion times, advancing and receding, reflecting only reflection itself, depth and surface becoming interchangeable, then nothing, eyes quickly moving back to the page of unfamiliar language. Tom listens and tries to figure out what the driver is trying to memorize. At first it sounds like *how are you* or *have a nice day*, but then it sounds like *nothing is ever missing* or *something is always missing*, or maybe *all you need is love* or *all you need is food*, or maybe *the quick red fox was in a bad mood*, or maybe *I'm a dunce and that ain't good*. The more Tom tries to figure it out, the more it sounds like something else. The driver pulls over and stops and puts his book away and gets out. Someone else gets in, inching back out into traffic, wearing what Tom can see is an authentic surgical mask, made carefully to stop invading microbes dead in their tracks. A piano passage from "Pharaoh's Dance" breaks forcefully through the static. The new driver does a double take when he sees that Tom is wearing scrubs but has no mask, then says that a month ago he was a well-known Washington DC immunologist, an expert on the coronavirus who said the wrong things to the President, who refused to take the dangers of the pandemic seriously, insisting that there was no need for serious action, making sure that people who told him otherwise lost their jobs. Tom asks him what the cure for covid is, and the guy meets his eyes in the rear view mirror, nodding his head to the twists and turns of the "Pharaoh's Dance" piano, the turbulent rhythm, upright bass combined with bass guitar. He says something about a biochemical decoy, but the phrase gets lost in honking horns and radio static, which drown out "Pharaoh's Dance", cutting off the best bass clarinet solo of all time, just as the Mirage pulls up in front of the hospital.

The driver says: Here's a once in a lifetime offer. Answer this riddle and the ride will be free. When is a doctor most annoyed?

Tom stares at himself in the rear view mirror, knowing he's never known the answers to even the simplest riddles. He tries to relax but he feels like he's in a corner wearing a pointed hat and all the other kids in the class know the answer. They're giggling and smirking and even the teacher is failing to keep a straight face. Tom's never felt more desperate for a moment to be over. He finally shrugs.

The driver says: A doctor is most annoyed when he runs out of patients. Get it? Patience: p-a-t-i-e-n-c-e.

Tom smirks and shakes his head and says: That's got to be one of the lamest puns I've ever heard! You've got to be kidding me!

The driver smiles: Lame or not, it stumped you. You could have had a free ride.

Tom pulls out his phone and looks puzzled: How much do I owe you? It's not clear on my phone.

The driver says: It's $40, but you need to give me eight $5 bills.

Why?

I get $5, and each of the other drivers gets $5. Eight times five is forty.

Tom gives the driver a puzzled look in the rear-view mirror. The driver says: Times are tough. Eight of us are splitting one Uber job.

So you collect the money and split it with the others later?

Right. That's the way lots of us do it now. Even Uber jobs are hard to find. People are staying inside because of the quarantine. No one goes anywhere anymore. By the way, I've got an extra mask in the glove compartment. I know you can get a mask inside, but you're going to look like a fool if you show up without a mask of your own, and the extra mask I've got is the real thing, not just a wash cloth. It's yours if you give me an extra five.

Tom takes it eagerly, gives the guy a high five, gives the guy nine fives instead of eight, and rushes into the Emergency Room. There's nobody in the reception area. It's the only time he's ever seen it empty, but it still feels crowded, since TV noise bombards him from all four directions, ads for cars and beer, ads for shampoo and insurance, interspersed with the face of Beth Barton, the glamorous TV journalist, asking various experts about the President's disappearance. They're all just as confused as everyone else. All of them talk about quantum decoherence, but they can't explain exactly what it is, and the more they talk the more confused they become, and soon they can't even make the facial expressions of TV experts. Tom doesn't like the quantum interpretation. He wants to think that somewhere, maybe thousands of light years away, a decision was made to eliminate the President, who was judged by a panel of intergalactic experts to be a threat to the sanity of the universe. After all, just two hours ago, he ordered police to use tear gas, flash-bangs and rubber bullets to assault peaceful protesters near the White House, even though they were exercising a consitutional right. He did this for the sole purpose of setting up a photo op, posing with a Bible he'd never read in front of a church he'd never attended. The photo op was all about making sure rightwing Christians voted for him again in the upcoming election, but it was supposed to be his way of condemning the violence that led to the death of Jeff Toy in Minneapolis, though the Rose Garden speech he'd given fifteen minutes before only mentioned the murder in passing, and instead of vowing to take action against the ongoing racist violence of the police, he warned that if the protesters didn't shut up, he would force them out of the way by calling in federal troops.

The photo itself has gone viral, and Tom is surrounded by it in the ER reception room. The President stands with the Bible raised in his right hand, trying to look like the soul of integrity, but instead he looks overstuffed and belligerent. In back of him, a sign in front of the church says All are Welcome. Tom tells himself that secretly some are a lot more welcome than others.

Tom can't stand the sight of the Orange Cheeto, who's bound to show up everywhere, now more than ever, since he doesn't exist anymore. And now Tom sees another face that he doesn't want to see, a very tall middle-aged guy who carries himself like he wants to be shorter. It's the Senior Clinician, Samuel Pump, flashing what looks like a mischievous smile behind his surgical mask.

Sam! So sorry I was delayed. The traffic—

Not a problem, Tom.

So, what was it?

What was what?

My pager was beeping non-stop half an hour ago.

Dr. Pump shrugs: There was a guy here who claimed to be the mayor of the northernmost town in the world, yet his driver's license said he lived in Toledo.

Ohio or Spain?

I don't remember. His license said his name was Rex Torpedo, but he called himself Lex Luthor.

From Superman comics?

Apparently. And get this: he claimed that he would soon become the next U.S. President, that nothing would be more appropriate than if Barry Trap, a cartoon president, got taken out by a cartoon villain, though in this case the villain would be a hero, and a flesh-and-blood human being. Anyway, our ER cognitive scientist couldn't make heads or tails out of the guy, and she wanted your opinion. I tried you several times on the phone but you didn't answer. Finally it occurred to me that the best way to quickly get your attention was to give you an emergency call on your pager. But Lex Luthor escaped. He might still be in the hospital, but right now no one knows where he is. We've checked everywhere. Someone saw him dart into a surgical theater, and a janitor on duty there saw him throw himself onto an operating table, then move his right hand clockwise, his left hand counter-clockwide, above his chest and stomach, creating a double vortex of iridescent mist. Then he wasn't there anymore, though a nurse who arrived a few seconds later insisted that she saw him in the background of a painting on one of the walls, which featured a man in a bowler hat riding bareback on a pissed off armadillo, while a jazz band played on a hill in the background, and she swore that the trumpet player was a dead ringer for Lex Luthor, but when we double-checked a few minutes later, the trumpet player looked to me like Miles Davis, though another surgeon claimed it was Freddie Hubbard, not Miles Davis. Frankly, I'll take Freddie over Miles any day.

I think Freddie was more consistently good, though he never did ground-breaking work like *Kind of Blue* or *Bitches Brew.*

Yeah, but Freddie was a good guy. Miles was a jerk.

He wasn't always a jerk. He did some cool things for a lot of the great young jazz musicians.

Okay, maybe. But right now we have no idea where Lex Luthor went. And something else has come up.

You've heard that the President vanished, right? Not shot by a cartoon assassin—just gone.

I saw it on the tube. At the time I was otherwise engaged, so I didn't see everything, but it looked to me like the flashing of the photo op cameras was inflating him like a balloon, and he got so big that he popped and—

You haven't seen the latest footage? One of the protesters asked him a weird question. Something like: *What part of this sentence am I leaving out?*

I didn't hear that.

Nobody did at first. But then when the footage was carefully studied, it was obvious. A guy at the protest was asking that question, and the President said in response: *The second part comes before the first. But the second part doesn't exist yet.* And then he was gone.

He got through two logically connected sentences?

Depends on what you mean by logically connected.

But why would those sentences make him disappear?

No idea. Experts are trying to figure it out, but so far everyone's baffled. They've studied the footage closely in slow motion, frame by frame, and all they can say is that right after the President said "the second part doesn't exist yet," he seemed to become an organic balloon getting popped by the sounds of the words, though they can't explain why those particular words did what they did. They consulted a linguist, who confirmed that there was nothing about the phonetic design of the President's final phrase that should have had the power to make him pop out of existence.

Okay, but now that we're talking about it, Sam, I'm thinking about the word "yet," the President's final unit of meaning. It suggests that something is likely to happen soon, but it doesn't say when. It's like the second-by-second process of reality unfolding is trapped in a pause, an uncertainty.

Sure. Yet you and I say the word *yet* all the time, and we don't disappear.

Right. But we're trained to investigate uncertainties. We see them as opportunities for unforeseen understandings. As you know, for people like us, for scientists of all kinds, knowledge is what happens when we move from question mark to question mark, like planting our feet on the planks of a swaying footbridge over a chasm. Whereas an authoritarian schmuck like the President can't stand any uncertainty, since it makes him look weak and indecisive, like he doesn't have all the answers, at least not yet.

Yet billions of people have trouble with uncertainty.

It's not a problem unique to the President. Yet they don't disappear if they say the word yet.

Right. And yet is only one letter away from yes, a word that signifies affirmation, agreement, connection.

Sometimes one letter can make all the difference in the world.

What about the guy who asked the question? Who was he? Has he been questioned?

He was just some guy. He doesn't know anything.

But he asked a weird question, didn't he? What part of this sentence am I leaving out? Why would a protester pose a question like that?

He said he was planning to say something else, but forgot what it was.

So the words he was planning to say disappeared?

Right. And right after that the President disappeared.

You think there's a connection?

I don't know. And no one else does either. Not yet.

Tom laughs: Yet in the sentence that just came out of your mouth, not yet means yet. Yet means the same thing as its negation: Not yet.

Sam nods like a zen master and says: When is not not not?

Tom knots his brow and looks at his watch, which looks like an eye winking back at him.

He quickly looks back up, hoping Sam Pump didn't see him checking the time, which might suggest impatience, or that he wasn't paying attention. Tom thinks about how difficult it can be to pay attention at times, even though he's made his reputation paying attention, surgically making his way through damaged brains like a rat in a maze. Tom knows that he's supposed to respond within a second or two, according to the expectations of normal conversation, so he says the first word that might fit the situation: Why?

Sam looks alarmed and says: Why what?

Why what?

Yeah, why what. You asked me why. I was wasn't sure what the why referred to.

I wasn't sure what the why what referred to either.

Tom forgets the time again, has to look back down and look back up again quickly, hoping Sam Pump didn't see him looking down, which might suggest that he can't remember what he saw just a second before, that he's a victim of Brain Fog, a lapse in short-term memory, a possible covid symptom.

Tom forgets the time again, looks back down, tries to look back up, but he's caught in the circular motion of the second hand, gets caught in the slower motion of the minute hand, gets caught in the much slower motion of the hour hand, gets caught in all three motions at once, all three speeds, moving in a circle, no stopping point, unless the watch gets broken, yet even then the circular motions will continue, billions of hands on watches all over the world will just keep turning, seconds and minutes and hours, driving the sun to keep rising and setting, making sure that one thing leads to another, making sure that not even a microsecond forgets to show up for duty, while an octopus appears on the four Emergency Room TV screens, eight enormous tentacles crushing pedestrians, each tentacle with a brain of its own, eight separate speeds of perception, coming together in eyes that have no blind spot, unlike all the other eyes on the planet.

Tom tries to meet the eyes of the Liberty octopus, giving them time to meet his eyes and penetrate the depth of his soul, even though Tom is too scientific to use a word like soul. He smiles at Sam and says: Liberty Octopus would be a great name for a prostitute or stripper, wouldn't it?

Sam looks puzzled at first, then smiles: It really would be. I'm surprised that no one has thought of it yet.

There's the magic word again: yet.

There's a pause while they stare at Liberty Octopus crushing picture tube people. Then Tom says: Wait! I just got it!

Got what?

The word yet. It's the mark of the beast. No wonder the president isn't here anymore!

Sam pauses, not quite smiling: The mark of the beast? Maybe you better explain.

You don't get it? Really?

Really.

The word yet is really a number. Think of what it's made of: three letters, right? Y-E-T. Two consonants and a vowel, though of course at times Y can be a vowel, so it's like a joker in a deck of cards.

Really?

Yeah, sort of. Anyway, think of the alphabet in numerical terms. Y is the 25th lettter; T is the 20th. Add the two consonants up and you get 45, right? Then look at the vowel, E, the 5th letter in the alphabet, right?

I'm with you so far.

So divide the sum of the consonants by the vowel. 45 divided by 5 is 9, right? And 9 is really the number 6 upside down, right? And the word yet has 3 letters, right? So take the number 6 and repeat it 3 times. That's 666, the mark of the beast.

Sam says: So…

So the president ended his cryptic remark with the mark of the beast, which had the power to make him disappear, like in the Book of Revelation.

Sam laughs: Which was written by a guy who lived in a cave and suffered from migraine headaches.

That makes it invalid? Lots of brilliant people have neurochemical issues, but that doesn't mean that what they produce is worthless.

No, but seriously Tom, we're trying to come up with a rational account of an unprecedented political event. The art we practice is founded on scientific inquiry. I don't think we can include crackpot numerology in that category, can we?

You got a better idea?

Not yet.

Yet? Which means the same thing as its own negation? As you yourself asked a few minutes ago: When is not not not?

Liberty Octopus disappears, replaced on screen by the *Jeopardy* theme song. Sam doesn't seem to hear it, but Tom feels like he might vomit. He puts his fingers in his ears and starts counting down from one hundred by sevens. When he reaches the number 9, it flips and looks like the number 6. He tells himself not to let it repeat 3 times. He pulls his fingers out of his ears and the sound from the TV stops.

Sam looks at Tom with concern: Tom? Are you okay?

I think so, yeah. That *Jeopardy* theme song really gets to me. I haven't heard it in decades, but it brings back hideous memories. Let's not go there.

Sam nods: Right. No need for PTSD issues right now, especially when they're triggered by a prime time theme song.

Tom looks at his watch again, this time without caring if Sam Pump notices. He remembers a riddle he couldn't solve at a party of nerds in high school, a contest he badly wanted to win to impress the smartest girl in the school: What time is it when you can't read a watch? He still doesn't know the answer, and now it occurs to him that this is why he always looks at his watch in tense situations. He wishes he could talk to Sam about it, but he knows Sam's interest in emotional health is focused on finding the right medication, with no concern for traumas from the past.

Tom finally looks at Sam and says: Well, anyway. No matter what really happened, the main thing is that Barry Trap is gone.

Sort of.

Sort of?

Yeah, sort of. I mean, you're going to keep seeing pictures of him for years, everywhere you look. The final footage will be endlessly replayed and discussed, like the footage for 9/11 or JFK getting shot in Dallas. Think of all the conspiracy theories we'll be dealing with, all the books and movies that are bound to come out in the next few years. Barry Trap will have a very rich life after death.

I'm going to ignore all of it.

Good luck. You have to be disciplined to put the media out of your mind. I suggest a trip to Mount Everest.

I've already been there. It's become a tourist trap. But a friend of mine suggested a place called Hidden Beach.

Where's that?

Somewhere in northern California. I'm not sure where exactly. Apparently, it's a well kept secret. And I've heard spooky stories about it. People who go there don't return without a profound sense of loss, like the place has some kind of sinister power, giving you something important, solitude and silence deeper than anywhere else in the world, while taking something important away. You're not the same when you come back from Hidden Beach.

So why did your friend recommend it?

He thought I might be ready for the transaction that happens there.

The gain and the loss?

Something like that.

But when you come back, you'll just be dealing with the same old media shit.

Who says I'll be coming back?

You can't just stay there, can you?

Why not?

Can you get food at Hidden Beach? Is there lodging nearby? It doesn't sound like it. And what about your career? You're an important part of our team here. You're the best brain surgeon north of Tierra del Fuego.

Tom recalls the bass clarinet from "Pharaoh's Dance", its motion through improvised bursts of electric piano. It starts to take him somewhere, away from his dread of the President's resurrected picture tube face.

He nods and smiles and says: Yeah, okay. I'll be back. But I'll still need a paid leave of absence, a few months off, until most of the media bullshit goes away.

Normally, I'd say no. But you're a special case. I'll tell you what: I can't really give you more than a few weeks off, but I'll have the hospital pay for a media therapist.

What's that?

A person trained to make you immune to media noise.

I've already taken a step in that direction. My lover Destiny smashed our TV set right before I left to come down here.

That's great. But it's not enough to just kill your TV. The picture tube is only one source of toxic nonsense. Media noise is pervasive at this point, coterminous with nature itself. Until recently, no one ever recovered from Information Sickness. But after a few good sessions of media therapy, you can be just a few feet from a noisy TV and tune it out entirely, like I did with the *Jeopardy* theme song just now.

It really works?

I had a few sessions last year, and they made me feel like a brand new person. Normally, as you know, I would laugh at someone who claimed that they'd been so thoroughly transformed. But it really worked!

What happened? Did you spend hours talking about your childhood, carefully figuring out how your parents failed you so miserably that you got hooked on billboard slogans and big-hit music?

Nothing like that. It's more primal. It's all about growling. During the first few meetings, they showed me magazine ads, TV shows, Hollywood movies, network news. We picked apart their lame persuasion techniques and growled at them fiercely. By the fifth session, I was growling as soon as I was exposed to even a few seconds of media poison. They told me this was a clear sign that I was ready for my culminating experience. We celebrated by growling fiercely for hours.

They? Who were they? Serious people with diplomas?

I'm sure they had diplomas of some kind. But they weren't serious in the customary sense of the word. They were lively, hilarious beings who talked in riddles. What has a neck but no head? What has a ring but no finger? What breaks when you speak its name? What word becomes shorter when you add letters to it?

Riddles always baffle me completely. You had answers?

I just said the first thing that came into my head, and each time I was right.

What were the answers?

I don't remember. But the fun came at the moment when I circled the question with enough spontaneous precision that the answer had to reveal itself.

Tom looks puzzled: And what was the culminating experience? It sounds ominous.

It sounded scary when they told me about it. But

it turned out to be rather pleasant. They showed me a film of it later. They took my brain out and put it on a table. Then they flattened it with a rolling pin, turned it into a neurochemical pancake, seasoned it with cinnamon, tumeric, thyme, and garlic, baked it until it was bubbling and moist, massaged it for several days in a room of strange aromas, which might have been jasmine and lavender, sandalwood and frankincense, rosemary and myrrh, or all of them or none of them at once. Then one of the doctors clapped his hands and the other four doctors threw all the windows open. The blue silk drapes were filled with bursts of arctic wind, having traveled south for thousands of miles, making the walls and ceiling move like aurora borealis. Then they gathered my brain back up and shaped it into a ball of Silly Putty, kneading it carefully, smoothing out the surface over and over again, until they had a perfect sphere. Then they put it back in my head.

Tom looks doubtful: Was it expensive? Is it something only rich people can afford?

Normally it would cost a lot. But remember: since you're a special case, we'll pick up the tab. Neurosurgeons like you aren't a dime a dozen. It's not like we could replace you by putting an ad in the paper.

But is the procedure painful, the part where they

remove your brain and then reinsert it? I'm assuming they have to make holes in your head?

Yeah, but they use nanobots and give you the most delightful anaesthetic on the planet. And they play celestial music while they're performing the operation. I would give anything to hear it again. It was better than Mozart.

Better than Beethoven? Better than Bach?

Yeah.

Better than Brahms? Better than Mahler?

Way better!

Better than Debussy? Better than Ravel?

No comparison.

Tom nods eagerly and says: Cool! Sign me up!

He and Sam shake hands and smile at each other, holding the pose as if they were waiting for someone to take their picture, even though Tom hates having his picture taken, even though he feels contempt when people smile for cameras.

Over the past five minutes, the waiting room has filled with people. They're turning in circles, all with the exactly the same blank facial expression. Tom has seen them before. They arrive each afternoon at the same time, and as soon as they arrive the clocks in the waiting room all stop, and don't start again until the people are gone. He remembers discussing the situation with Sam, who smiled as if he understood completely.

No doubt they've all got TEST.

TEST? Like a test you take?

No. Test like Terminally Stale Entertainment Trauma.

That's TEST? Shoudn't it be TSET—T,S,E,T?

Sure. But the people in the Acronym Department made a mistake, and they liked the mistake so much that they made it stick. Now TEST is firmly entrenched in medical discourse. I'm surprised you're not familiar with the term. It works much better as an acronym than TSET, which isn't a word in itself like TEST.

How can we know for sure that they've all got TEST?

We can give them a test.

We can test them for TEST?

That's right, and the test itself is a cure for TEST if they pass it. Sounds simple, right? But the problem is that no one ever passes. And the people who re-take the test get even lower scores.

The test teaches you to fail it?

More or less.

What does a case of TEST do to you? I can see that all the victims here right now look dead behind the eyes. They're spiraling in circles. What's going on, neurochemically?

They're convinced that life is a movie they can't stop watching.

Can't they just kill their TVs and stop going to theaters?

They can. But they won't. They're convinced that since life is a movie, if you stop watching you stop living. And they don't want to kill themselves. So they tell themselves that they don't really want to stop watching, even if it makes their condition worse. If you tell them that the situation is hopeless unless they stop, they get pissed off. They think you're telling them to commit suicide.

Can't we just refer them to a media therapist.

They can't afford it.

That sucks. But I've got a cousin who's formed what he calls a post-political party. Members of the party kill their TVs and fill their homes with aquariums. If the party ever gets power, they'll cut the defense budget by ninety percent, and everyone will get fish tank benefits. They'll give people a strong alternative to stale entertainment: the grace and color of tropical fish, a fully funded condition of relaxation.

Tom can't remember what Sam said next, but apparently TEST is still a significant issue. The people crowding into the waiting room all have the same look, as if they've been drugged by stale entertainment for decades. Their circles resemble the motion of ceiling fans in obsolete sports bars, even though they're in the best medical center in New York City. There couldn't be a better place for people who need to get tested for TEST.

But Tom and Sam aren't available, though they're only a few feet away. They're trapped in a smile that's more than a smile, a facial expression that's come a long way to look like what it looks like now. They keep shaking hands as if there were something stopping them from stopping, a riddle without a solution, a watch whose hands keep turning. The longer they keep shaking hands the more alarming the situation becomes. They don't have time to waste. They're serious men in a serious world. So many people expect them to keep things going, make things better. But they just keep shaking hands, and no one comes to take their picture.

A BIG DIFFERENCE

Ben Bowman got home early from work. Noise was coming down from the second-floor bedroom. Was his wife in bed with one of her many lovers? He tip-toed up the stairs, hoping to surprise them. He'd done it before with amusing results. He'd even found some clever put-downs on the Internet, things to say when you catch your spouse red-handed. He stopped and listened. Something was different. He tried to tell himself what it was, but he wasn't sure. He opened the door slowly, hoping they wouldn't notice, and he could step quietly into the darkness of closed venetian blinds, creep up to the bed and switch the light on the nightstand on and off, laughing at their embarrassment, just as he'd done a few months before, and a few months before that, and a few months before that.

But this time was different. The blinds had been left open, the room was filled with light, his wife Elaine was in bed with a woman, and the woman was someone he knew. He'd seen her on TV hundreds of times, a tall blond thirty something with a low smooth voice: none other than Beth Barton, the glamor face of Cable News, looking great with nothing on. Many times, he'd fantasized about meeting her, and one time, a few months ago, the dream had come true.

He'd been at a comedy club on the Upper West Side of Manhattan. He didn't like comedy clubs, the canned routines, the performers on stage desperate to make people laugh, often failing, looking stupid, pathetic. He liked spontaneous humor. He didn't need a script, stage lights, a mic and an audience. He was only there because a comedian friend had asked him to come, then hadn't shown up. But Ben Bowman had already paid, and he thought it might be rude to leave during someone's performance, weaving awkwardly between people at other tables on his way out, so he decided to stay until intermission, resigning himself to an hour of mediocre amusement. He was pleasantly surprised when Beth Barton was introduced. He didn't know she fancied herself as a stand-up comic.

She stumbled onto the stage in a loose trench coat, her hair a dirty mess, and awkwardly hugged the much shorter male emcee. She began: If you really want to punish yourself, think of two words: Whole Foods! Whole Foods is like nothing I've experienced anywhere else in my life. Beth Barton then made a big deal about how righteous the shoppers at Whole Foods are, solemnly paying big bucks for foods designed to make them live forever, only to reach the cashier and discover that they might have healthy meals in their carts, but now they couldn't pay the rent. There was scattered laughter and hooting. She looked distressed. But Ben couldn't sympathize with her obvious embarrassment. There was something fake about her joke. He knew Beth Barton had no trouble paying her rent. She made at least a million dollars a year.

Then she did a routine about how you know you're a New Yorker when your favorite take-out place is right across the street. Scattered laughter, tension, another C+ joke at best. Something was wrong. She didn't have her TV face and voice. She looked overweight and tired and now pathetic, like she was trying too hard, desperate for attention, even though she got mass attention every day on the picture tube. She tried five more jokes, all C+ at best. Then she stumbled off the stage, trying to act like she hadn't made a fool of herself. She sat at a corner table with another woman, who made an excited face, apparently praising the performance. Beth Barton shrugged and shook her head and faked a big smile, then tried and failed to get a server's attention. Soon, the friend got up to go to the bathroom, leaving Beth Barton alone. She pulled out her phone, pushing buttons.

Ben Bowman wasn't the type of guy to sit down uninvited with a woman he didn't know. But he felt he did know Beth Barton. Millions of people no doubt felt that they knew Beth Barton. They watched her on the news every day. They shared the illusion of eye contact with her as she talked smoothly at the camera, delivering her scripted lines. So many times, he'd had imaginary conversations with her. Now he could have a real one. Plus, they had the same initials: BB, like B.B. King, the greatest blues guitarist that ever lived. How wrong could things really go?

Ben walked over and sat down. She was too busy playing with her phone to notice at first.

He said: I hope you don't mind some company. I thought your set was awesome. That joke about the takeout place was killer.

She looked up confused, annoyed: Have we met?

No. Not in person.

Then why are you sitting here?

You're gorgeous.

She sighed: Gorgeous?

Yeah. I've fantasized about you hundreds of times. I watch you every day on Cable News. You're the only reason I watch. I don't watch for the news. I don't like news.

How can you not like news? It's not something you can like or dislike. It's a fact of life. It tells you what you need to know.

It's a way of presenting life. It's not life itself. I prefer life itself. But you're so beautiful I'm willing to set aside what I believe.

You know how many tweets I get each day telling me I'm the world's most beautiful woman? I'm discussing serious topics, and you guys all have your hands in your pants.

We don't watch because we like serious topics. We watch because—

Look, I'm glad you liked my routine. Now, if you don't mind, I'd like some privacy.

She picked up her phone from the table, pushed a few buttons and said: Hi Victor, it's Beth. Yeah, it's been way too long. Listen, I might need some help. I'm at the Comic Spot, and there's this creepy guy at my table who won't leave me alone. What? Yeah, he might be dangerous. Can you get here right away? Okay, great.

Ben Bowman nodded quickly and got up and left. Now he was watching Beth Barton fuck his wife. He had no idea Beth Barton went to bed with women. He didn't know his wife did either. But now he remembered that his wife always said Beth Barton was stunning. He thought it was just admiration. Apparently, it was more than that. But how had Elaine met Beth Barton? Had she found out that Beth Barton would be appearing at a comedy club and managed to meet her there and seduce her? Possibly. But he was surprised Beth Barton would be attracted to Elaine, a short, slight Vietnamese woman in her late forties. Then he remembered: Beth Barton was married to a Japanese guy. Maybe she had a thing for Asians. She wouldn't be the first. So many people had ethnic sexual obsessions. He'd always thought it was racist in some way, even though it might outwardly look like a sign of respect.

They were fucking so fiercely that they didn't seem to know he was there. He stood for thirty seconds enjoying the view. No doubt about it: Beth Barton was hot in bed, and she made Elaine look hotter than usual, giving her so much pleasure that she glowed with an uncharacteristic intensity, the kind he could remember from the early days of their sex life. It made him feel hot, like he wanted Elaine more than he had in years. He wanted to say something, but then he thought it might be fun to leave unnoticed, let Elaine think she could keep her cheating secret. He liked the idea of watching her lie, especially since Elaine normally made a big show of being honest. He hated it when people proudly announced how honest they always were, as if it were a sign of moral integrity.

He closed the door quietly, went downstairs and turned on the TV. There was Beth Barton, in a yellow sleeveless dress on the four o'clock news. Or rather, there was an image of Beth Barton in a yellow sleeveless dress on the four o'clock news. He knew the real Beth Barton was upstairs fucking his wife. The picture tube Beth Barton had to be part of a video segment shot a few hours before, now presented as if it were breaking news. Repeatedly, she flashed her picture tube smile, knowing she was driving millions of men crazy all over the nation. And women too, apparently.

He heard footsteps on the stairs. Elaine was coming down, still wearing nothing, but acting like nothing was wrong.

He said: Look who's on TV!

She looked puzzled and said: Is that Beth Barton?

Yeah. And she's really hot in that skin-tight outfit, don't you think?

Wow, yeah!

You're not jealous that I think she's hot?

No, she's just an image on a screen. She doesn't look like that in real life.

How would you know? Have you ever seen her off-screen?

No. But I've read articles about how the screen images are manufactured appearances, created through staging techniques.

Ben pointed to the screen: So she doesn't really look like this?

Elaine looked puzzled: Of course not! I'm surprised that I have to explain this to you. It's really basic.

Have you ever fantasized about going to bed with her?

I'm straight.

I know. But sometimes straight people fantasize about same-sex encounters. And you told me once you thought Beth Barton was hot. You've really never imagined being in bed with her?

She's not my type.

Really? She's not your type? Of course she's your type. She's everybody's type. Just look at her! If they couldn't make her look like someone everyone wanted to fuck, she wouldn't be there. She has a shopping guru out there 24/7 selecting her outfits. She has make-up gurus choosing her cosmetics. Trust me: She's everyone's fantasy.

Elaine paused. Ben could see she was still glowing with the excitement of being in bed with the world's hottest news anchor. She finally said: Yeah, you're right. She's everybody's type.

And I bet in bed she'd still look good, even without the staging techniques.

Elaine shrugged and smirked: Yeah, she'd still look pretty damn good.

Do you think she's actually good in bed. Lots of beautiful women admit that they don't really like sex.

Does Beth Barton look like she doesn't like sex? Every move she makes in front of the camera suggests that she likes to fuck. Her body's used to being desired. Every inch of her skin, every muscle and bone, knows what it's like to feel wanted.

Ben laughed: Right. But still, how do you know it's not just an act? She gets paid to make the news seem sexy.

Yeah, and she's so good at it that millions of people somehow think that the news is sexy.

Ben pretended to stroke his chin: How can all the horrible things the President does seem sexy? How can separating children from their parents at the border seem sexy?

OK, but her version of a tragedy story will be the sexiest one, even if there's no way to make it really sexy. And it'll be surrounded by other stories that aren't so grim, so guys will still finish her program with their hands in their pants.

Ben paused and smiled and said: Just guys?

Elaine looked away.

He laughed: Just guys? You don't think she makes women horny? I know she makes *you* horny. You've said so many times, though not in so many words. I wonder what would happen if you ever met her. Would you want to seduce her?

She tried not to look like she'd gotten caught with her hand in the cookie jar. She finally said: Yeah, I'd want to seduce her.

And you'd succeed?

I'd succeed.

Footsteps came from upstairs, Beth Barton approaching. Elaine looked embarrassed at first, then she was laughing hysterically. Beth Barton was laughing too, swinging her high heels by the strap, wearing nothing. She looked at Ben fiercely. She crossed the room and slapped him hard in the face.

She said: Your wife is better in bed with me than she is with you. Any other questions?

Ben Bowman was angry and embarrassed, but he kept his cool. He tried to take control of the situation, to move it in a more dignified direction. He nodded slowly and said: Yeah, as a matter of fact I do. I've got lots of questions. Let's start with this: Since you're the sexy face of world events, tell me who I should vote for in the election next month.

Not the President.

Not the President? So you're not a Republican?

What's that got to do with anything?

You've got enough money to shop at Whole Foods, don't you? That makes you a Republican. Or wait: I guess rich pseudo-liberals shop there too!

Whole Foods?

Yeah, like in your lame comedy routine.

She studied Ben more carefully, a look of slow recognition.

Yeah, Ben said, that was me that night. Remember? You pretended I was harassing you and called your bodyguard. But anyway, I don't like holding grudges. Just tell me why I should vote for anyone ever again. And please: no talk about my first ammendment rights. In 2020, you're just choosing between one corporate tool and another.

I've heard that oversimplification a million times.

Right. And it was true every time.

She turned to Elaine and said: How do you put up with this creep?

It's not easy. That's why I got in touch with you, remember?

Ben tried to look betrayed. He said to his wife: *You* got in touch with her?

Not exactly. I saw her OkCupid posting: Beth likes middle-aged Asian women.

Ben smirked at Beth Barton: So you're a cultural fetishist, not the luke-warm feminist you pretend to be on the tube.

Luke-warm? Try ambivalent. And I make no apologies for that. I like having equal rights, but I also like getting attention for my looks. It makes me feel powerful, like people can't control themselves when they look at me. Like Elaine here. She never thought about going to bed with a woman until she met me.

A ring tone came from a yellow dress on the floor beside the staircase. Beth Barton got the phone, pushed a few buttons and stared at the screen.

Elaine said: What is it?

A weird link. It says: http:/something is.always/missing.com.

Beth Barton clicked the link and stared at the screen in disgust. She said: It's a clip of a guy jerking off in bed.

She looked at Ben then back at the screen then back at Ben then back at the screen, then held the phone up so that Ben could see the screen and said: This is you, isn't it?

Ben squinted at the screen and shook his head and said: It looks like me but it's not. Why would I send you a picture like that?

Because you're a creep.

But I don't know your phone number. And the picture

was sent a few seconds ago. How could I have sent it? I was standing right here.

You probably had a friend send it. You might know someone who knows me and has my number. You men are all such creeps. Expect to hear from my lawyers!

Your lawyers? You have a team of lawyers?

You better believe it! And they know how to get things done.

Lawyers are a bunch of nasty parasites. I can't be around people who threaten me with lawyers.

Soon Ben Bowman was rushing down the street looking over his shoulder, half-expecting to see two naked women chasing him shouting insults. But instead he walked for hours without interference, finally reaching streets he'd never seen before, ending up in an old industrial neighborhood, vacant lots filled with garbage, factory smokestacks rising in silhouette in a dark red sunset, brick warehouses probably built before World War I, cobwebbed broken windows, broken doors, and a gathering wind.

There was light in one of the factories. Ben stepped inside and walked down several dark corridors. Soon he found what seemed to be the source of the light he'd been following, a banker's lamp on a desk, where a guy in a green uniform told him to stop. Another guy in a green uniform was snoring loudly with his face in his arms. The first guy shook him awake.

The other guy looked baffled: Dude! Why the fuck did you wake me up?

The first guy said: This guy just showed up. We're supposed to question him.

We are?

Yeah, don't you remember?

Not really. I mean, why do we have to question him?

That's what we're getting paid for. We sit here and wait for someone to show up. Then we ask questions.

Why? Why do we have to ask this guy questions? Did he do anything wrong?

Everyone has done something wrong.

What questions do we ask?

The first guy went blank. He checked all his pockets. He said: Shit! I had them all written down on a piece of paper. But now I can't find it. Let me check the bathroom.

The bathroom?

Yeah. Maybe it fell out of my pocket when I was taking a shit. I'll be right back.

The first guy got up and walked down the hall to the bathroom.

The other guy looked at Ben Bowman and shrugged and said: My friend will be back in a minute. I guess. I mean—

Ben Bowman said: Look, I'm not here for any reason you need to ask me about. I just walked in here because I'm lost.

You need directions? Where are you trying to go?

I don't know. I came home to find my wife in bed with the hottest anchorwoman on the planet. And they weren't embarrassed about it. They were really mean to me.

The other guy nodded: Sounds rough, buddy.

The other guy's cell phone rang. He pulled it out of his pocket and stared at the screen. He looked baffled and glanced at Ben Bowman and said: Hold on a second. I've got to take this.

He pushed several buttons on his keypad, then muted the phone and held it up to his ear. He listened for fifteen seconds and said: The Sahara Desert? Really? You can't be serious! The fucking Sahara Desert? No way! You've got to be kidding me. The Sahara Desert? Fuck you!

Ben Bowman said: Dude, it looks like you're busy. You can ask the questions later. Just tell me how to get out of here.

The other guy shrugged: Same way you came in.

Ben Bowman couldn't remember how he came in, not exactly. He turned and walked down three unlit corridors, then passed through glass doors into a large room, exposed brick walls and TV studio lighting. A microphone descended thirty feet from an old tin ceiling. In front of the mic, on a tall wooden stool, Beth Barton read from a teleprompter, wearing nothing but her six-inch heels.

She said: Language is a battlefield. It's a fundamental human technology, a crucial part of our evolutionary toolkit, one of the primary factors that's made our species what it is today, not just bipedal hominids, but apex predators, indeed the greatest apex predators our world has ever known. Yet millions of people all over this great nation of ours want portions of language banned from public use. For such people, the word fuck should never be said, yet copulate is fine; the word shit should never be said, yet excrement is fine; the word cunt should never be said, yet vagina is fine; the word dick should never be said, yet penis is fine. In each case, the unacceptable word means the same thing as the acceptable word. Yet somehow words like fuck and shit and cunt and dick disturb millions of people greatly. In fact, it goes beyond disturbance. Such people are convinced that these words are evil, and can do great damage if they're used in public space. Right now, as I speak to the nation, much of what I'm saying is being deleted, obscured by an infantile noise, a beep or blip that tells people that an evil word has been suppressed, that Cable News, like all other commercial news networks, is protecting the world from

Satanic language. Yet nothing protects anyone from the truly dangerous language. Public space is filled with ads and political speeches, sound bites and top-forty lyrics, deceptive and invasive images and messages, generating stupidity and confusion. No one questions this. No one thinks of protecting us from bullshit. I myself contribute to this bullshit. I'm an image that sells carefully edited versions of the world. It's made me rich enough to buy almost anything I want. I can even shop at Whole Foods without going broke. But I'm here today to announce that from this point on—

Her voice cut out and everything went dark. He stood there expecting the lights to come back on, but the dark got even darker, more opaque, flattening out as if it were trying to turn itself into a blackboard. He heard Beth Barton's high heeled footsteps moving away, turning down several corridors, fading into silence. Minutes passed. He backed up until he felt a brick wall behind him. He lowered himself to the hardwood floor and waited. He pulled out his phone but it didn't work, then pushed the button that lit his digital watch but it didn't work. He sat for what felt like ten or fifteen minutes. The darkness felt like more than the absence of light. Then he shouted: Is anyone here? What the fuck is going on? No answer. He shouted: What am I doing here? How do I get out? No answer, though there might have been soft laughter coming from the floor above, the sound of people moving bulky furniture two floors above, the sound of a TV football game three floors above, the sound of a vacuum cleaner four floors above, the sound of a dentist drilling five floors above, the sound of a beagle howling six floors above, the sound of a doomsday sermon seven floors above, the sound of fruit in a blender eight floors above, the sound of canned applause nine floors above, the sound of a toilet flushing ten floors above. A few minutes later a small door opened in the distance, a rectangle of dim blue light. It closed quickly. He sat for another ten minutes, then got up and walked toward the door. He stretched out his arms in front of him, like a cartoon character walking in his sleep, trying not to slam face-first into one of the walls. Soon he could feel the door against his fingertips. It opened again, and he stepped inside.

At first there was only dim blue light. He moved like he might be on the moon or the ocean floor. He heard a faint sound. He turned a corner and walked and turned another corner and walked and turned another corner and stopped, sat on a crude wooden bench behind a small table, facing a stage where two musicians were playing, shining with perspiration, gracefully swaying back and forth. One was on her knees, beating a small drum with her bare hands. The other was playing a flute in the lotus position. Both were focused on something directly behind him, as if they were carefully reading a score of darkness.

He studied the place more carefully, beyond the dim blue light. It appeared to be a small club with a low ceiling, but he saw no bar, no drinks or food being served. A door on the opposite side of the room was open, but beyond it was nothing but intergalactic space, making him think that if he stepped outside, he'd have nothing to stand on. He would just be falling forever with nothing to breathe. People at other tables were caught in the music, swaying back and forth, and soon Ben Bowman was swaying back and forth, closing his eyes and slowly relaxing, sinking into the sound as if he were drifting down through a dark pool, thousands of miles away in a desert oasis.

He heard a voice and opened his eyes. The woman who'd been playing the flute was taking his hands in hers across the table. She held his eyes firmly and said: Remember me now?

Should I?

You've been gone a long time. Where have you been?

Her voice was familiar. He remembered a one-room house with sky-blue walls, the heat of a Sahara Desert night. He remembered the passion they'd shared, and pleasure rippled up and down his body, as if they were still in bed, kissing fiercely.

He said: I'm not sure where I've been.

Then you need to pay close attention, follow the music, all the way to the border of silence, but don't stop there. Keep going. You need to get rid of him.

Who?

The man in charge. The big bad spoiled rich boy. The one who makes all the noise. The one who wants to keep everyone out. The one who wants to keep the world safe for the people who have all the money. You need to get rid of him. He's dangerous. He doesn't care about anyone but himself.

You want *me* to get rid of him?

That's what I said.

How?

That's up to you. Make language go backwards. Make the story untell itself. Narrate in reverse until he doesn't exist yet.

Then what?

End the story before it starts all over again.

Tamper with the details?

She nodded slowly: It's always a matter of tampering

with details, choosing the ones you need and trying to put them where they belong.

Ben Bowman closed his eyes. He felt like he was the dumbest kid in the class, and the teacher was putting numbers on a blackboard, trying patiently to explain what all the other students understood.

Then she was back on stage, playing her flute in the lotus position, swaying back and forth, looking past him. The sound was getting softer and farther away with every second. Soon it was like he was seeing the stage through the wrong end of a telescope. He got up to leave, but instead of a door behind him there was a blackboard, and a teacher was writing numbers, trying patiently to explain. The students were swaying back and forth, caught in the music the numbers were making. Ben Bowman began to sway too. It felt so good, like the right thing to do. Soon he wasn't sure why anyone anywhere would do anything else. It all began to make sense, to make a big difference. Now he knew how to penetrate the blackboard, how to practice a different kind of math, his own kind of math.

He raised his hand and smiled at the teacher, who told him to come to the front of the class. He went to the board and erased all the numbers, picked up a piece of chalk, drew a door and pushed it open, stepping through to the other side. He was back in the abandoned factory neighborhood, standing beside a mailbox. At first he was surprised. He hadn't seen a mailbox in years. He might as well have been standing next to a phone booth, or gazing into a vinyl record store through dusty shopfront glass. He thought of himself as a letter he could address to himself and drop in the box. He felt folded up and thin as a page, as if he'd been tucked inside a paper enclosure sealed by giant hands. Things were happening outside, but he couldn't see them, though he might have heard gulls and foghorns on a misty harbor night, voices cursing their way through a stupid argument, honking horns in a traffic jam, a plane shooting through the sky like an opening zipper. Then the sound of bed-sized envelope getting ripped open, huge hands dumping him out onto a sidewalk wet with rain, and he was at the concrete stoop leading up to the door of his house.

When he walked in, Elaine asked him where he'd been.

He shrugged and said: I've been given instructions.

Instructions?

Yes. Now I know what to do.

Elaine looked at him strangely: You know what to do? What's that mean? What are you supposed to do?

What has to be done.

Elaine wasn't sure what to say, so she made a funny face and changed the subject, telling him that Beth Barton had stormed out five minutes ago, enraged by a fight they'd been having.

Ben laughed: Why were you fighting? I thought you were falling in love.

Elaine said: You must have heard about the way she displayed herself two hours ago in front of a nation of Cable News watchers. I told her she was being an exhibitionist, showing off her nude body to make her ideas seem sexy, when she should have let the ideas speak for themselves. But she kept insisting that by appearing in the nude she was shocking viewers, jolting them out of their customary habits of perception, the only way to get people to really hear what she was saying, and not just what they thought she might have been saying.

Ben Bowman looked puzzled: Did Cable News broadcast an uncensored version?

Elaine said: No, but I found it on youtube. And I even found a video that showed the Cable News version and the uncensored version side by side. It was so fucking funny! But something weird happened. I'm amazed you haven't heard about this. Right when Beth Barton was about to make a decisive point, someone pulled the plug. Everything went blank. She said it was the strangest thing, like she wasn't there anymore. I heard her high heels on a hardwood floor, then a colossal noise coming down from the sky, like the Milky Way getting ripped in half by a giant. Then she was standing on our doorstep, like she'd never left. But she felt so proud for having made her obscenity proclamation. I'm glad the uncensored version is going viral. Billions of people have seen it by now.

Ben Bowman said: Great, but still, the uncensored version is one step removed from the real thing. It's not the same as what she did in the studio.

What do you mean?

In the studio, she was there in three dimensions.

You're talking as if you were really there, in three dimensions. But does it make any difference? The youtube version was still uncensored, right?

I think it makes a big difference. If you'd been in the studio, you could have touched what you were looking at, not just Beth Barton, but the brick walls and the polished hard wood floors, a microphone coming down from an old tin celing. On youtube, the only thing you could have touched was a glowing screen.

I didn't need to touch her on the screen. I was touching her all afternoon. Remember?

Yeah.

Did it bother you?

Yeah.

You'll have to get used to it. We're planning to do it

again, probably on a regular basis, even though when she left a few minutes ago, she was really pissed off. She's doesn't like it when people disagree with her.

I've noticed.

So you don't mind if she and I become lovers?

I do mind, but you have my permission, so long as I get to watch.

We'll be making videos. You can watch them any time.

No videos. I want the real thing. It makes a big difference.

WHERE THE REVOLUTION BEGINS

Several weeks ago, the president got impeached. The Democrats finally took decisive action against the worst thug in White House history. But was it really decisive? The Senate still has to throw him out, and they won't. The Senate is Republican. They don't care if the president is a crook. They want their side to win. Randi Castle, my partner for the past ten years, tells me she'd like to kidnap the Senate Majority Leader and put him under a spell, make fundamental changes in the way his thinking works. It's useless to work through the system when it's run by people like him. It's time for aggressive interventions.

When I go online I see his face all the time. He looks like boiled cabbage. He smiles like he's trying to hide his teeth. He's not a great speaker. He lacks charm and intelligence. He thinks the rich deserve to be rich and the poor deserve to be poor. He's opposed to universal health care, abortion rights, and free education. He stonewalls all progressive legislation, blocks all non-Republican Supreme Court nominations. By humane standards of any kind, the man is a monster. So how could people have been dumb enough to vote him into office? Why does he keep getting re-elected?

I'm different from Randi Castle in that I'm angrier at voters than I am at the politicians themselves. It's not that I don't see how contemptible our so-called leaders are. It's just that in some ways I can understand their bullshit. I know I would have serious problems if I tried to function in our current political system. I'm too indecisive, and I get confused when things get difficult. But recently I came up with a plan that would change the way things work.

Five years ago, I got a large aquarium, filled it with tropical fish, and I liked it so much that I've gotten four more tanks. I've surrounded myself with beauty. I strongly advise everyone to do this, to kill their TVs and replace them with aquariums. The U.S. government should guarantee all citizens enough money to buy at least one aquarium and fill it with as many fish as they want. If I were going to run for public office, I would form an Aquarium Party. A popular song in the sixties celebrated the Age of Aquarius. I think they really meant the Age of Aquariums. Think of it: If everyone had an aquarium instead of a TV, the nation would be more enlightened than it is now. Instead of the noisy bombardment of ads and prime time nonsense, we'd have the grace and color of tropical fish, swimming peacefully through lavishly designed environments, fully financed by federal programs. Instead of the disgust and frustration many people feel when they know their tax dollars are funding the U.S. war machine, they'd have the satisfaction of knowing that their money was being distributed through the Department of Aquarium Management into the homes of their fellow Americans, helping them to enjoy the comfort and beauty fish tanks can provide. It would make us all better people, more peaceful and intelligent. It's true that aquariums take work. It's a daily struggle to maintain a healthy environment for the fish. But it's worth the effort. Why not spend your time creating something beautiful and relaxing?

I look at the six aquariums in our living room. They take up four entire walls, the floor and the ceiling. There are hundreds of fish in the room with me right now—angel fish, neon tetras, flame tails, rainbow fish, clown loaches, trigger fish, bumble bees, midnight peacocks, blue dolphins, red swordtails, discus fish and fantail guppies—swimming beside and above and beneath me. I'm drifting in and out of sleep, a state of mind that feels like it might last forever. There's no TV and there never will be. Yes, I pay a lot for the set-up

I've got, but the absence of a cable TV bill helps cover my aquarium expenses, and since I live in New York City I don't need a car, so I don't have to pay for gas or insurance. If I were President, a lower middle class person like me wouldn't have to budget so carefully to pay for a fish tank environment. Everyone could enjoy what I've got here now, without paying anything.

Resting on my couch this morning, I feel like an aquarium myself. The fish are swimming through my body, weaving between the words floating through my head, making the things I tell myself more graceful and exact. It's like meditation, a mental bath I take every day. The gradual result has been an increase in self-awareness, which led me to quit a high paying job a few years ago and start working in a pet store, one of the best in New York City. It has an impressive range of tropical fish and designer fishtanks. The pay is surprisingly good because the owner likes my political plan. She wants to see it work, and she's got a friend who's building our website free of charge. Because my old job paid so well, people thought I was crazy to quit, but things are working out. Between my pet store wage and Randi Castle's cutting edge work as a hypnotist, we can still afford our Upper West Side apartment, especially since it's rent-controlled.

I look at my watch and see that I'm due at work in less than an hour. I always leave early, giving myself time to wander and enjoy the neighborhood, its tree-lined streets and nineteenth-century houses. But today is different. As I look down the block toward Central Park, I'm not sure what to think. The park is burning. People are rushing away from it. Others are rushing toward it. Everyone looks terrified and confused. The block is filled with screaming and shouting, honking horns and sirens. I quickly assume I'm confronting disaster on a grand scale, an apocalyptic situation of some kind. Then it all stops and I realize that the block is being used to make a scene from a disaster movie. The street has been roped off. It's filled with lights and cameras and other filming devices. There's a goateed guy with mirror shades and a beret in a director's chair, waving his arms and shouting through a megaphone. Beside him a slender woman with a shaved and tattooed head seems to be jotting down what he says, as if his abusive commands were worth preserving. Then she closes her pad and power walks in my direction.

She gives me a somber look: You'll have to leave.

I have to leave?

We're shooting a film here. Can't you see that?

Yeah, but that doesn't mean you own the street.

We've paid to control this block for the next three hours.

Just so you can shoot another stupid action movie?

Action movies make billions of dollars.

That doesn't make them good movies.

People enjoy them. Now, if you don't mind—

I do mind.

Then I'll have to get nasty.

I'm used to it. My partner gets nasty with me all the time.

I'm not your partner. I won't just call you names. I'll call the police.

She pulls out her phone and starts thumbing the keypad. Within seconds, I hear sirens, and not just the ones from the movie. I think of clever things I could say. In movies, people always have witty comebacks. But something tells me to leave before I get accused of something and taken somewhere. I rush toward Central Park, which is no longer burning. I'm not sure how they put out the fires so quickly, especially since there aren't any firetrucks. But as I get closer, I see that hundreds of people wearing identical yellow outfits are folding up a gigantic trompe l'oeil painting of Central Park in flames. For a second I think that if I joined them in their work, the police wouldn't know that I was the one they were called to apprehend. But I'm not wearing a yellow uniform. The cops would recognize me right away. So I try to look like nothing is wrong, walking calmly into the park down a gravel pathway, which leads to three more pathways, then a clearing where people are playing miniature golf. This looks like the perfect place to conceal myself, to act like I'm just another guy with a golf ball and a club.

This isn't just another miniature golf course. Each hole includes a huge emoji, a smiley face or a crying face or crazy winking face, a thumb's up sign or a victory sign or a sign that used to mean everything's cool, though it's now become a neo-nazi symbol. The President makes this sign at all of his rallies. It's a way of reminding his fans that he's a white supremacist.

I stop at a wooden kiosk and pay for my golf ball and club. I can hear police sirens back on Central Park West, voices in megaphones shouting incomprehensible things. I put my ball on the putting green and try to look normal. I tap the ball toward the smiley face emoji fifty feet away. It ends up three feet from the hole. I'll have a simple second shot. It occurs to me that they've made the first hole easy, encouraging players to like the course, to smile like the emoji. I walk toward my ball with a broad emoji smile.

My ring tone interrupts me. It's Randi Castle on the phone, wondering where I am. She'd called me at the pet store, and I wasn't there.

I'm playing miniature golf to escape the police.

You suck at miniature golf.

Not anymore. I've been practicing. I almost got a hole in one.

Are you at that emoji place in Central Park?

Yeah, it's pretty cool.

I've heard great things about it.

The eighteenth hole is the pile of poop emoji.

Perfect! When you finish, you'll feel like you're the shit or a piece of shit, depending on your score! So clever! But you know what? That place cost the city ten billion dollars.

That much?

Yeah. They had to pay big bucks to get the emoji rights.

Emojis are copyrighted?

You better believe it. The guy who owns the emojis also owns the Taj Mahal, the Kremlin, the Pyramids, and the White House.

The same guy who owns Google, Apple, Amazon, and the New York Times?

Yeah. That guy. Right now he's making a deal to buy the Everglades.

He likes alligators and humidity?

No. He's buying it so he can get rid of it. He wants to build a designer golf course there, with holes featuring patriotic portraits of U.S. presidents.

How can he do that? A golf course is only 18 holes, and we've had 44 presidents.

He's going to leave out the Presidents he doesn't like.

If I were him, I'd leave out almost all of them.

Be careful what you say. This call may be recorded for quality and training purposes.

Let me talk to your supervisor.

I'm *your* supervisor. Remember? So why are the cops after you?

I annoyed a film crew person.

Oh fuck no! Really? You're such a dumbass! The last people you want to annoy are the film crew people. They can really fuck with you.

Waterboarding?

For starters.

There's a pause and then she says: Guess what? I just got a request on my website, a guy who's read Yelp reviews of my state-of-the art hypnotic techniques. And

I checked out his Facebook page. He's a dead ringer for Mitch McDonald.

The Senate Majority Leader?

Yeah. He calls himself Rip Hindenburg, but I'm pretty sure he's really that guy we're always complaining about. Rip Hindenburg is probably a fake name.

You think you can bring yourself to work with someone who's either Mitch McDonald or looks just like him? I mean, even if he's really Rip Hindenburg, you'll have to work hard to remember that he only looks like one of the most viciously self-serving politicians in Western history. Won't it be too distracting? A conflict of interest?

I think I can manage it. I'll have to be extra careful, but I know what I'm doing. Don't forget: I have twenty years of experience. I've worked with my share of creepy people.

What does he want?

He wants me to put him under a spell, then make him think he's good in bed.

Can you do that? Does hypnosis have that kind of power?

Sure, why not? He didn't ask me to make him good in bed. He asked me to make him *think* he's good in bed. And changing his self-image won't be a problem.

You know that new technique I've been talking about for the past few weeks? It's perfect for psychological alterations and transformations, just what Rip Hindenburg is looking for. No matter how small he thinks he is right now, he'll think he's a really big man between the sheets by the time I'm done with him! Anyway, he'll be stopping by later today. The timing is perfect. I haven't had enough work lately and my bank account is running a bit low. I was going to have to ask you for a loan. And get this: once he's under my spell, I'm going to call him Bitch McDonald's. My post-hypnotic suggestion is going to be based on that name.

He'll start calling himself Bitch McDonald's?

Yeah. I'll tell him he needs a *nom de guerre* to maintain his new sexual confidence. He'll walk away from our session convinced that Bitch McDonald's knows how to give women what they really want in bed.

Will he call himself Bitch McDonald's on Capitol Hill?

No. Only when he's in sexual situations and needs to think that he knows what he's doing, knows how to play precisely the role he's suited for, to play it so well that women can't resist him, the kind of guy who makes them think he wants to be their bitch, exactly the kind of bitch they've always wanted.

That's hilarious! The Senate Majority Whip getting whipped in bed!

Not exactly. The Whip is the number two guy. Mitch the Bitch is the Senate Majority *leader.* He tells the Whip what's what.

Then why not call the number two guy the Senate Majority Wimp?

Because he gets to whip everyone else into shape. He's anything but a wimp, though of course that's only his public image. He might be a wimp in bed. Lots of dominant political types are wimps in bed.

So under your post-hypnotic suggestion, Mitch McDonald will think that he's been waiting all his life to become a little bitch for the woman he loves.

Right. That's the plan. I read in the *Times* that his wife is driven by an inexhaustible desire to be on top. I assumed they were talking about her political ambitions. But maybe they also meant her life in bed. Anyway, I'm hearing sirens in the background. Are the cops still hot on your trail?

Maybe. I better get off the phone and try to look like I'm not being chased.

I hang up and look around. People are getting arrested up and down Central Park West. It seems random. The police cars stop, cops jump out, grab whoever they can grab, and shove the person into the car. At first I think it's part of the movie they were filming. Then I think it might be the chaos that developed after I made my escape, a chain reaction of police insanity triggered by whatever I did back on the film set. I walk to the second hole, which ends with the crazy winking face emoji. I place my ball and bend and squint, lining up my shot, but strong hands grab me from behind, force me down face first onto the green turf, tie my hands behind my back, yank me up onto my feet and push me out of the park and onto the street, shove me into a police car screeching violently up to the curb.

I sit there dazed. A woman bursts into the car beside me. She's wearing denim shorts and a light blue t-shirt that says, "I'm Just Here for the Food," with a picture of a hot dog smeared with mustard and relish above it.

I say: Cool shirt! Just looking at you makes me hungry.

She pulls a badge out of her pocket and looks at me like an evil dentist.

I say: You're an undercover cop?

She says: Looks like it, doesn't it?

I notice her plump seductive lips. Her eyes are like blue tigers. Her long red hair looks too expensive for a cop, like her number one priority is looking good on Facebook.

I start to smile, stop, put a crease in my brow, stop, cover my mouth with my hand and pretend to cough, stop, meet her eyes with bedroom eyes, stop, start to flinch when she looks like she might want to slap me. I finally say: What's going on? Why am I here? Where are we going?

She shrugs and says: You're under arrest.

Why?

Because you pissed off the wrong person.

That's a crime?

You better believe it.

Why? What did I do wrong?

She shrugs again: Does it make any difference? If you pissed off the wrong person, we don't owe you an explanation.

I look toward the front seat, where two other cops are silently facing the windshield. I'm trying to see if they're at all disturbed by Lazy Girl's ideas. But now that I'm looking carefully, the guys in the front seem weird, like they're mannequins, or maybe made of cardboard. I check their faces in the rear view mirror. There's a cardboard version of Mickey Mouse at the wheel. A cardboard Donald Duck is riding shotgun.

I start to ask Lazy Girl for an explanation, but I'm worried that I might get accused of something else, like showing disrespect for cartoon characters. So instead I ask: Where are we going?

The station.

What happens there?

What always happens there.

Can you be more specific?

You get booked. We take all your information. The information gets sold to people who want it. They use it against you in ways you won't understand until it's too late. When they're done with you, you won't have any money. You won't be who you are anymore, and you'll feel like you never were.

Identity theft?

Call it whatever the fuck you want. You signed up for it when you pissed off the wrong person. Any fifth grader knows that it's dumb to piss off the wrong person. But you don't seem to get it. It's time for you to learn.

She sits quietly for ten minutes. Above the midtown buildings, on advertising blimps, pictures of the President flash on and off. He smiles and winks and burps and licks his lips. He pulls boogers out of his nose and licks his finger.

I finally make myself ask a scary question: What happens after they steal and sell my identity?

Your credit rating is fucked up forever. Good luck ever getting good interest rates again. And that's just the beginning. You—

But what happens at the station after they've stolen and sold my identity?

They slap you around, ask the same bizarre questions over and over again, slap you around again, ask more insane questions, until you're so confused and mentally worn out that you confess to what someone somewhere thinks you did or might have done or might as well have done. Then they put you in a cell where a crew of tattooed guys built like sumo wrestlers glare at you for a while, then force you to lie face down on floor while they take you up the ass, one by one.

Will it hurt?

Fuck yeah.

How long does it take?

Way too long.

Then what?

Then they put the octopus in the jar and you watch until it's over.

They put the octopus in the jar? Is that a metaphor

of some kind, designer slang only cool people understand?

Not a metaphor. Not slang.

By the way, what should I call you?

Lazy Girl.

She points to her badge, which has a smiling Siberian husky with a long series of numbers arching over its head. Below its head I see the name Lazy Girl.

Really? You're Lazy Girl?

Yeah. It's supposed to be ironic.

I didn't know cops were capable of irony, or at least not intentional irony.

Don't get smart. You're in enough trouble already.

The police car slams to a halt and the door beside me opens all by itself. Lazy Girl yanks me out onto the street. Pedestrians rush by in both directions. It takes me thirty seconds to realize that they're not extras on a film set. Some of them point at me and laugh. Others shake their heads and talk on smart phones. Lazy Girl points to a nearby hot dog stand, which is flying a black white supremacy flag, a smiling neon green frog that will probably glow in the dark when the sun goes down. The frog says "Ask Me If I Care!" and sticks his tongue out.

Lazy Girl says: They make awesome hot dogs!

White supremacy hot dogs?

Is there any other kind? Wait right here.

She goes over and buys one. I stand there watching people pushing buttons on their phones. One of them shouts: Fuck fuck shit fuck fuck shit fuck! A speakerphone voice on the other end says: Could you repeat that? He repeats it, though I'm pretty sure the order is different this time around.

Something slams down on the pavement ten feet away. At first I think it's a bomb that didn't go off. Then I see it's a head with lifeless eyes and eight motionless arms, tentacles with suction cups, apparently tossed from a window in the building beside me. I look up and see a man's face looking down from a window ten floors up, probably a guy who threw an octopus out the window, looking now to make sure it's dead. It's dead. It's flat as a pancake. Suddenly I remember getting a C instead of a B on a high school biology final exam because I filled in a blank with octopus instead of amoeba. Biology was my favorite subject at the time. The low grade made me mad. So I looked up information about amoebas, looked at pictures and diagrams, studied them under microscopes. I didn't want to make the same mistake twice.

Coming back to me, Lazy Girl almost steps on the

dead amoeba, or rather octopus. She jumps to the side and says: Gross!

I laugh and say: Lazy Girl, weren't you worried that I might get away?

We always do it this way. When I go to buy an awesome white supremacy hot dog, some people dart off into the crowd and disappear. They're free. Others are like you. They don't know what to do. They just stand there.

So there's only two kinds of people, those who run and those who wait?

You catch on fast.

She swallows the dog in one big gulp like a hungry boa constrictor, then reaches into her fanny pack and pulls out a spiked dog collar. She puts it around my neck in one quick motion, tightens it until it's puncturing my skin, locks it with a small key. She says: Okay, dog face, get down on all fours.

I go down on all fours. She jerks the leash and I follow her through an old steel door, down a dim hallway and into a smelly room with old steel desks and computers where keyboards are clicking but no one is typing. Words appear on all the screens. She ties the leash to a leg of one of the desks, then sits and studies the screen, reading aloud. I read along with her, making my voice sound just like hers: "Peering down through electron microscopes, we can almost view an amoeba from an amoeba's point of view. But even with the most powerful magnification money can buy, when we ask ourselves what it's like to be an amoeba, we're still really wondering what it might be like for a person to be an amoeba, with no way of knowing what it's like for an amoeba to be an amoeba. And when we turn away from the microscope to write things down, describing the amoeba, we're thinking of it in a human context, especially at the end of the day when we leave the lab and observe millions of macroscopic things and events amoebas can't possibly understand, a world amoebas nonetheless inhabit, a world that would be fundamentally different without them. They can cause mental and physical diseases if they're in the wrong place at the wrong time. Sometimes even our best medications are powerless to stop them. Even so, the human race wouldn't exist in its current form without amoebas. If they weren't feeding on our brains, we couldn't think."

She looks at me and points to the screen and says: This is you, right?

That's me?

Yeah. These are your thoughts, right?

They might have been.

Might have been?

Yeah. I don't always remember what I'm thinking, even while I'm thinking it.

She points to the screen: You were thinking this. Exactly this. A few minutes ago on the street. You were thinking about a biology test you failed. You—

I didn't fail. I got a C.

A C is an F in Century 21. Unless you've got above a 4.0, you're cold meat in the postmodern world.

But I—

Don't try to deny it. Let's go.

She yanks my leash and leads me down a long filthy corridor. It's filled with broken light from broken lightbulbs. She opens a door to a room of benches, people sitting and staring at the floor, talking into their hands as if they were smartphones. A guy who looks like Mr. Clean with tiny wings flapping out of his temples whispers something in Lazy Girl's ear, then hurries to the front of the room.

Lazy Girl turns to me and smiles: You're in luck! There's no one here to slap you around and fuck you up the ass today.

Why not?

They got taken away. They got white supremacy hot dogs on their lunch break from the stand outside. They tried to leave without paying, and now they're paying a different price.

Where are they now?

She gives me a nasty look and says: You haven't learned a thing. If you ask the wrong questions, you get the wrong answers.

She points to the front of the room. There's an empty jar on a small square table. Mr. Clean is now standing there, and I notice a picture of an octopus on his light blue t-shirt, with words that say: It's Time to Put the Octopus in the Jar. The tiny wings on his temples wiggle fiercely.

Lazy Girl rushes to the front of the room, claps her hands three times to get everyone's attention, then says: Repeat after me: It's time to put the octopus in the jar.

Everyone says: It's time to put the octopus in the jar.

Mr. Clean pulls out a large ziploc bag filled with muddy water. Inside there's an octopus, all suction cups and anxious eyeballs. I remember reading somewhere that an octopus has eight brains, one in each arm. When danger approaches the brains combine to make the octopus look like something else. But here the octopus doesn't seem to know how to blend in with its surroundings, how to make itself look like the bag it's trapped in. So it starts glowing. Mr. Clean pours it into the jar, stuffs it down in several places to make it fit, then screws on the lid and turns off the lights. The octopus glows in the dark and looks transparent, like a jellyfish. We sit for half an hour. The octopus flashes off and on. Its eyes look pensive and sad. No one says anything.

Then the tentacles start moving, squeezing their way through a space that's not really big enough, slowly at first, then faster and faster, turning the lid of the jar, filling the room with surges of light. The lid stops, then turns, then stops. Someone says What the Fuck, but he's told to Shut Up. The lid turns, stops, turns, stops for five minutes, then turns with increasing speed until it pops off. Someone says What the Fuck, but he's told to Shut Up. Mr. Clean takes the octopus out of the jar. It squirms in his hand and looks annoyed. For a second I think it might shape-shift out of his grip, slide down his leg and across the floor like a giant amoeba. From there it could shape itself into a transparent thread, gliding under the locked metal door or sliding through the keyhole. Mr. Clean isn't taking any chances. He puts the octopus back in the bag and zips it shut. The tiny wings retract instantly into his temples. He unlocks the door and leaves without saying a word.

Lazy Girl turns on the light, takes out a marker,

draws a door on the wall, opens the door and tells us to get the fuck out and keep our mouths shut. I watch to see if anyone asks her why. No one says anything. We file out onto an empty street and stand there. We look at each other and someone starts to laugh but quickly stops. No one says What the Fuck and no one tells anyone to Shut Up. There's a feeling we all seem to share, that it's not safe to talk, that one of us might be working for Uncle Sam, or Uncle Spam, that anything at all might get us in major trouble and ruin our credit scores. I nod and turn and leave. I don't look back. I'm ten blocks away before I remember the collar around my neck. I don't have the key. I'm thinking that I'll have to call a locksmith, but I'm guessing that if you have the collar removed people come and get you. Besides, Randi Castle will like the collar. We have a sexual game where I pretend that I'm her dog. Maybe Bitch McDonald's will soon learn how to play it.

I decide to walk home, even though it's forty blocks, since I want some time to think about what's just happened. It's the first time I've ever seen a jar opened from the inside. I'm wondering how many humans could do it without the appropriate tools, especially if they were crammed into a jar that was too small for them. I'm left with great respect for the octopus. After all, it's got a brain in each of its tentacles. Its arms are the smartest arms on the planet. And it managed to function skillfully despite the stress of the situation, a disturbance I saw in its eyes once it was squashed into the small container and the lid was screwed on. I start to think I'm a better person because of what I've seen the octopus do. I'm pretty sure this wasn't what the police expected me to feel. I'm proud that I've survived with a good attitude, that they couldn't upset me the way they apparently wanted to. Then I remember the octopus crushed on the pavement, having been thrown out a window. Suddenly I'm convinced that the one I just watched will be thrown out a window. It makes me hate police violence, and the violence of our species. It makes me wish that we never existed at all.

Finally I'm back on my block, opening my front door. Before too long, the house with its tropical fish begins to relax me. The aquariums reassure me that people are still capable of beautiful things. I lie on my couch and watch. I'm floating, surrounded by hundreds of colors and motions. I tell myself that this is where the revolution begins, a society built on a fully-funded condition of relaxation. After the revolution, politics won't exist anymore.

But now I'm aware of a sound I was too relaxed

to notice at first. It's Randi Castle's voice. It's coming down from her upstairs office. It sounds like the incantation she's always used at the end of her sessions. I'm wondering how things went with the guy who might be Mitch McDonald.

The incantations ends. There's a pause, five minutes of silence, followed by a burst of ecstatic laughter. Then it sounds like she's rummaging around, looking for something, and now she's coming downstairs, clearly excited, carrying an aquarium we bought a long time ago, back when we got our very first tropical fish. Inside the tank, there's a little man jumping around, frantically calling for help in a tiny high-pitched voice. Randi Castle looks happier than I've ever seen her before. I ask her what's going on.

She's laughing so hard she can barely speak: Somehow something went wrong at the end of the session. I said the wrong words and ended up making him smaller. At first I was appalled. But now I think it's perfect.

I look closely at the tiny gray-haired man in a three-piece suit. He can't be more than five inches tall, maybe ten pounds at most. Jumping with outstretched arms he's still not even close to the top of the tank.

I smile: That's him all right! That's the Senate majority leader. None other than Mitch McDonald.

Bitch McDonald's! Remember? I told you on the phone when you were playing emoji golf. From now on, he'll be calling himself Bitch McDonald's.

We stare at him for a while. It's really funny. He's jumping and pounding the glass in desperation, begging and screaming. I get a fork and reach inside the tank and knock him over, look at Randi and say: What do you think? Should I impale him? There's something about him that really pisses me off. I'd love to jam this fork into his crotch and cut him in half!

She shakes her head: No, don't! He'll bleed to death! I don't want to end up in jail for the rest of my life.

Okay. But what are we going to do with him? I mean, I'm sure we could have fun with him for a while, but that whining little voice is driving me crazy.

Me too. And he'll still have the same oppressive political viewpoints. Can you imagine if we had to hear them every day, or if we had sit through a fillibuster in that squeaky voice? I think the novelty of keeping a little man as a pet would wear off pretty quickly. We have to get rid of him.

But how?

We sit and stare for a while. Then Randi says: Got it! Let's put him in a jar and screw the lid on tightly. We can leave him outside that abandoned laundramat on the corner, in the alley beside it, so no one sees him. Then we can email his wife, using our secret account so we can't be traced. We'll leave a message telling her where she can find him. I've heard she likes little men. I'm sure she'll be thrilled when she sees him now!

Just leave him there? What if he gets out?

Look at him jumping around like a helpless gerbil! Do you really think Bitch McDonald's could manage to unscrew a lid from the inside?

Earlier today I watched an octopus do it.

You did? Where?

At the police station. They made us watch an octopus escape from a jar with the lid on tight. It was amazing! I think it was supposed to freak us out. But I'm glad I saw it.

And now you're afraid that Bitch McDonald's might do it?

Yeah.

She points at the jar, laughing: There's no fucking way! An octopus has eight brains. This little bitch has less than one.

TWENTYTWENTY

Right after we heard the hurricane warnings on the radio, we got lost. We took several dirt roads, getting more and more confused, coming to places that looked like the places we'd come from, the same trees and streams and fields and hills and ravines, before we finally came to the house with the gravel driveway, the place the Century 21 agent mentioned. It looked more like a tower than a house. It was five stories high, about fifty feet from a cliff looking over the sea. It was in bad shape, on the verge of collapsing. But you couldn't beat the location. Having moved to the East Coast just a month before, we were searching for an old house facing the ocean, and the view from this place was the best in the world.

We knew we didn't have much time. The storm was approaching. The waves were huge and smashing into the cliff like they really meant it. The wind was strangely warm and getting stronger. If we'd known in advance that there might be dangerous weather, we never would have taken the risk. But the storm had come out of nowhere. The weathermen were shocked and confused.

How had they failed to notice Hurricane Ahab, issuing warnings only when the disaster was just thirty minutes away? We should have played it safe and driven back home as fast as we could. But now that we'd finally arrived we felt that we had to take a quick look.

We went eagerly inside, but things felt wrong. It was hard to say why. It went beyond the obvious problems. The wallpaper was peeling. The plaster underneath it was chipped, with holes that revealed moldy planks underneath. The sofas, chairs, and lamps were torn and dirty. The mirrors and rugs were covered with dust. There were cobwebs everywhere. The keyboard of the grand piano was missing at least ten keys. The grandfather clock was somehow still keeping time, but the glass and wood were scuffed and cracked. The dining room table and chairs were probably more than two hundred years old. They weren't antiques anymore. They didn't even belong in thrift shops.

But beyond all that, the place felt stale and deadly, as if decades of abuse had worn it out. It was almost embarrassing. It felt like generations of meth and smack freaks had been living there, though we saw no addiction equipment, no pipes or syringes. When I peed and washed my hands in the grimy bathroom, my face looked ten years older in the mirror, as if my hair and my teeth were about to fall out. I wanted to take a long shower as quickly as possible—somewhere else.

The wind got cold and hard, then much harder. The rain came down in blinding bursts. We knew we had to leave quickly. Somehow we found our way home down dirt roads turning into mud. We almost hydroplaned several times on the highways. Then we spent the next ten hours in the basement of the house we'd been renting week by week, listening to the big wind going crazy. Allison isn't the type to get scared, and when she does she conceals it well behind her sense of humor. But now she kept gripping my arm and saying, Ben are we going to survive this? I nodded and said of course and massaged her back like I wasn't afraid. But I'd never heard wind so loud. Things were crashing and shattering upstairs all night long.

When we finally went upstairs around eight the next morning, the house was a wreck. I was glad it wasn't a place we owned and cared about. Most of the windows were broken. Chairs and tables were smashed and smeared with mud. The floor was covered with pools of dirty water and shattered glass. Still, I was relieved that the place hadn't fully collapsed. I didn't want to move again until we bought our own house.

Now we're going back to see if the house by the sea

was completely destroyed. I like it when Allison drives because she's a better driver than I am, but we've already taken five wrong turns, even though we've got navigation. It's like the storm knocked the world off course and nothing works anymore.

But the radio works well enough to fill the car with disturbance, presidential candidates making their all-too-predictable noise.

Allison finally turns it off and says: This is going to be the worst election ever.

Jack Bison is an embarrassment. Barry Trap is even worse.

Trap is at least fun to hate. Jack Bison is no fun at all.

He can barely finish a sentence.

I used to think it was because he was afraid that his dentures might fall out, but now that he's got designer implants, there's no excuse.

Those implants are way too white. His smile looks like it's made of ice.

I always get nervous when a politician smiles.

They look like they're getting ready to bite somebody.

Allison makes a face and says: Trap's teeth look like he's already bitten someone and chewed them up. In the clips I've seen from last night's speech, he kept flashing his teeth without smiling, as if he were making threats, and the speech itself was actually just a lame collection of fragments. Within a five-minute burst, he bragged about the electoral votes he got in 2016, praised Andrew Jackson for squashing Nat Turner's revolt, claimed he was first in his class at the Wharton School of Economics, said that his response to COVID-19 was really terrific, declared that you can't always get what you want but you get what you need, insisted that his face belonged on Mount Rushmore, bellowed about the virtues of the U.S. penal system, said that his TV ratings were better than those for 9/11, talked about UFOs and the need to fund the Space Wars program, referred to himself as the world's most intelligent man, boasted about the border wall he was building, claimed that voter fraud was likely if ballots were cast by mail.

I shrug: But his gibberish works well for his legions of followers. It's sad to watch them at his rallies, eating up his bullshit. They're suffering from a bad case of Stockholm Syndrome. They're in love with a guy who doesn't care about them, doesn't have what it takes to understand their struggles, since he's never had to pay his own bills or taxes. They're three months behind on their rent, yet they vote for a guy who's famous for putting tenants out on the street.

Allison yawns and says: Can you believe that in the world's most powerful nation, where we get a chance to elect the most powerful man in the world, we're stuck with two embarrassments, a sham and a scam, a mentally deficient nobody and a mentally deficient asshole?

The road is getting rough. It's full of potholes and branches blown down by the storm. We're surrounded by big trees that block out the sun. It's hard to see where we're going.

I look out the window, down into the steep ravine beside the road. It looks dark and overgrown, like a monster might be living there, ready to emerge when it gets hungry. I say: We have this political conversation at least once a day. Can we talk about sex instead?

Sure. Or better yet, let's fuck when we get there.

Yeah. Maybe if we fuck there we can figure out what's wrong with the place. I've heard that you can fuck evil spirits out of a haunted house, drive them away with passion.

Allison shakes her head: I don't think it's haunted. Remember my sister Julie? She used to do paranormal investigations, and I helped her out with a few of them, so I know what haunted houses feel like. Our house is something else. It isn't just that it's falling apart. The problem is in the atmosphere, some kind of lingering disturbance that has nothing to do with tormented spirits.

Right. There's a sense of exhaustion, stale resignation.

I wish that feeling weren't there because in some ways the place is perfect. And we've probably got enough saved up to make it a functional house in a month or two.

Let's hope it's still standing. I guess you've heard that Hurricane Ahab was the most destructive storm in the past one hundred years.

It's weird that no one knew it was on its way until it was almost here. Normally, you get warnings days in advance.

No doubt it's because the environmnent is all messed up.

I saw footage on the news yesterday. Atlantic City got destroyed.

Trap's bankrupt casino must have been leveled.

Allison laughs: His Winter White House got massacred too. The footage on that was awesome. Trap's golf course looks like a garbage dump.

She reaches into my crotch and massages my dick: So let's have sex in that huge main parlor when we get there. I want to sit on your face and look out at the sea.

I close my eyes and say: Me too. We can make as much noise as we want. There aren't any neighbors to complain about it. When we were there a few days ago, I didn't see any houses nearby.

We reach a fork in the road. The GPS on the dashboard shows that both directions are good. She takes a left, trying to move further from the ravine, but the road turns back to the right, and we're beside the ravine again. Soon there's another left, but again it leads us back to the ravine. I catch myself thinking that something is trying to pull us over the edge.

I say: I'm not sure why, but I'm getting weird feelings about this ravine. It's all shadows, and they seem opaque, like they're eating the sunlight, like maybe they're living creatures with skin and a full set of bones and organs. This might be a good place for a monster movie. The Attack of the Shadows!

Actually, the White House is the best place for a monster movie. The Attack of the Cheeto!

I laugh: So now we're back to politics again.

I think I might need to talk myself past the voices I hear in my head. They're telling me that my attitude about the election is a cynical cop-out.

The voices in my head are telling me that I'm an idiot if I forget that elections are travesties, cynical imitations of something that doesn't exist and never did. Remember that youtube documentary we saw a few weeks ago, where it said that most members of Congress are millionaires? Same with Supreme Court justices. And all Presidents since Truman. Millionaires make up less than 3% of the general public, but they control all three branches of the federal government. Working-class people make up about half of the country. But they've never held more than 2% of the seats in any Congress since the nation was founded. We're talking about a plutocracy, not a democracy.

Allison smirks: Wow! You sound informed, tossing off those facts and figures. You're like one of those left-wing Internet commentators we sometimes watch, like you might be auditioning for The Young Turks. Did you really memorize the statistics, or are you just making them up?

I watched the documentary a second time and wrote a few things down.

You're such an A student!

It might seem like it now, but actually back in high school I had trouble getting C's. I couldn't get myself to focus. That's why it's better if you drive instead of me. Once you focus on something, there's no stopping you.

My cousin Wendy was always a better student. Now

she stands outside Walmart and Target with a clipboard and tries to get people to register for the elections.

I blow air out of my mouth and say: I've always liked her. She's funny and her heart's in the right place. But I think what she's doing is wrong. She's encouraging people to act as if the elections were authentic. They're not. No matter who wins, you're going to end up with a corporate stooge in the White House.

Allison nods: I've said things like that to her. Last week I tried to convince her that the only intelligent thing to do at this point is to boycott the election, flood the Internet with messages to convince people that anyone nominated for a mainstream political position got selected only because they're in bed with the one-percenters.

She didn't agree with that?

Hard to say. Her reaction is always the same, that if we don't vote we might have four more years of Trap.

I shrug: Well of course she's right. Another Trap term is hard to imagine.

But there's a good chance of it happening. The Democrats are such sell-outs that they'd rather lose with a moderate than win with a progressive.

The GPS gets weird. It's mapping out routes that

don't exist, lines and arrows that form what looks like a face on the glowing screen.

I say: You better pull over. Something's wrong. I think we're lost.

She pulls over carefully, since the chasm drops off sharply beside the road, and there's no real shoulder. We look at the face on the dashboard.

You're seeing what I'm seeing, right?

Allison nods: Yeah, there's a face, someone smiling and winking. It's really just messed up GPS directions. But it's hard not to see that face.

What's messing with our GPS?

Allison laughs: Google? The CIA? Or maybe some of your creatures down in the chasm.

Maybe they're amoebas magnified a thousand times due to global warming, and in their larger form they're projecting an electro-magnetic charge that's distorting the airwaves.

Or maybe they've escaped from a demented scientist's lab.

Sure, why not? In fact, this whole situation reminds me of a screenplay I wrote for my high school creative writing class about a huge amoeba created in a lab. The biologist claimed it was just an error in calculation, but he really did it on purpose, and he controlled the amoeba's movements and behavior through a remote control device. He set it loose on the world. It was messing everything up. At some point clever detectives broke into the biologist's house and found the device. They slapped him around until he told them how it worked, but he tricked them into making the amoeba sneak into the White House, where it did all sorts of damage and devoured the President. There's a long climactic scene where the President begs for mercy, trapped in the Oval Office with the creature approaching. He delivers an impassioned speech, but what good are speeches when you're facing an amoeba? In graphic detail, the amoeba consumes the President limb by limb, until it finally sucks in his head, still pleading and screaming. The President is gone, but it's curtains for the amoeba too, since the President is so toxic his carcass poisons the amoeba. It dries up within a few hours, turning hard as stone, which creates problems for the White House maintenance people, since the corpse is too large and won't fit through the doors and windows. At the end, there's a huge stone sitting in the Oval Office, and the new President and his staff are forced to work around a massive obstruction. No one knows how to remove it.

Allison is laughing. That's how it ends?

Yeah. I turned it in for my class, and the teacher

rejected it, claiming it was disgusting and politically offensive. But I showed it to my biology teacher, who thought it was great, and gave me extra credit for it.

She liked it that much?

She had a thing about amoebas. She was always telling us that amoebas are the most underrated creatures on earth. She insisted that the stuff they're made of isn't just raw material. It's alive and conscious. I remember she used the term cytoplasmic streaming. She claimed it was a form of intelligent behavior and said it moved in self-organizing patterns our science is too primitive to grasp. So maybe it's giving off an electrical charge that's fucking up our GPS.

Allison laughs: Your teacher sounds pretty crazy, but I'll bet it was fun to be in her class.

Totally. You never knew what she was going to say next. She had all sorts of theories about the Bermuda Triangle, though she always called it the Devil's Triangle.

Really? The Bermuda Triangle in a biology class?

She claimed it was a biochemical entity.

What's that mean?

I'm not sure. I don't remember. She had an elaborate explanation. But let's get away from the chasm. It's making me nervous.

Allison laughs: You really think there might be giant amoebas?

Probably not, but let's not take a chance. Remember the Rip Van Winkle story? He's on a mountain top, and sees something rustling and thrashing in a ravine. That's when the trouble begins. When he goes down into the chasm, things get funny.

Funny?

He meets Henry Hudson, and Henry's crew is getting drunk at a bowling alley, even though Henry and his crew had been dead for more than two hundred years.

That's really in the story? I don't remember it being so weird.

It's totally weird. And when he drinks with Henry Hudson's men, he ends up going to sleep for twenty years. Apparently, it wasn't normal booze. Anyway, let's get out of here.

Allison speeds up as much as she can, but it's a bumpy road and we don't know where we're going. The smiling face on the GPS doesn't change, except now it looks like it's eating something. Then I see a dirt road to the left, leading up and away from the chasm. I point and she turns, and five minutes later we're up in a sunlit meadow, a sky with big white clouds and cold wind, perfect East Coast mid-October weather. In the distance, I see the house. It towers above the countryside. Though it's too far away now to see clearly, it's still there. The hurricane didn't knock it over.

The face isn't on the GPS any longer. Instead, there's a clear path from road to road, ending near the house.

I look at Allison, who looks confused. I say: Wow! That was fucking weird!

Yeah, I'm not sure what just happened. It was like we were in a pocket of disturbance, a local eco-system with a sinister life of its own. I'm sure your biology teacher would have loved it.

She was always talking in class about monster movies.

Movies with monsters don't scare me that much. Zombies and vampires are boring. The real monster movie is taking place in Washington, and it's not even a good horror flick. When you get to the climactic scene, the monster is just a fat guy with a big mouth eating Oreos in the White House.

You sound like you're ready to become the first female in history to assassinate a world leader.

But think of how stupid it would look, taking out a guy wolfing down junk food, Oreo crumbs falling out of his bleeding mouth! Besides, if I did that, I'd spend the rest of my life in jail. Or actually, since I can pass for a first-world middle class woman, I'd probably just end up with community service.

I laugh: So you're saying that Lee Harvey Oswald and John Wilkes Booth would just be doing community service if they were alive today?

Booth for sure. He was a famous actor, remember? And celebrities never do serious time. But Oswald was different. Everyone thought he was a communist.

Was he really? Or was that just paranoid COINTELPRO bullshit? I've heard he was secretly in the CIA, a double agent.

I saw a documentary recently where they were quoting from Oswald's diary right after he moved to the Soviet Union in 1959 and applied for citizenship. And he wrote something like "I want citizenship because I'm a communist and a worker. I've lived in a decadent capitalist society where the workers are slaves." So yeah, either he was the real thing, or he knew how to sound like it. He had a subscription to *The Worker*, the official communist party newspaper. Before he shot JFK, he tried to kill an ultra right wing U.S. general. He didn't really hate Kennedy. He didn't know Kennedy. But he hated the beaming media smile of the all-American boy.

Most of us are probably closer to Oswald than to

Kennedy. We're not ruling class leaders with photo op smiles; we're workers who don't want to be treated like slaves.

Allison laughs: Except you and I aren't really Marxist workers of the world. We've always worked hard to avoid hard work. I'm amazed that we've got enough money for a down payment on a house with an ocean view.

If it weren't for that exercise book you sold, we'd be much more limited. How much did you make on that again?

The money's still coming in. With all the DVDs people bought and keep buying, in addition to the book, we've still got a fairly good income.

It's funny that you don't exercise anymore.

It got too boring.

But you were the poster child for the active, healthy woman—tan, athletic, strong, glowing with muscle tone.

Sure, and the image sold pretty well. But being an image gets exhausting. It's no fun moving from one photo shoot to another, beaming the media smile of the all-American girl.

I'm glad you don't have to do that anymore; otherwise, we might have to install gym equipment in our house.

I can't imagine it. One of the reasons I liked the place enough to come back for a second look was that it didn't seem like the right place for exercise machines, like it got built before there was any such thing as fitness.

But it's definitely large enough to give both of us personal space, which I'm sure we'll need. I haven't lived with anyone in fifteen years, and I think it's been ten years for you, right? So we'll both want private time.

Totally. I've never understood how people can want to be close to each other all the time. With a five-story house, each of us can have two floors all to ourselves, with one shared floor.

I squint and say: It's perfect. But right now, I'm wondering what's going on. The house doesn't look like it's getting any closer, even though we've been moving toward it for the past ten minutes, and the GPS says we're on the right road. The house is more like a picture of itself.

And we're in a picture of a car driving on a picture of a road?

Something like that. At first I wasn't sure if it's the same house. But it's got to be. How many five-story prewar houses do they have in this county? The realtor said there was only one place like that anywhere near here, within a two hundred mile radius.

What was his name again? Ike Beer?

Yeah, Ike Beer. That's either a great name or a terrible name.

He thought it was great, the secret to his success. Remember?

We both start laughing, recalling our meeting with Ike Beer a few days ago. The sign said Century 21, Beer Properties. Looking through the window from the parking lot, we saw what looked like an empty office, except for an unshaven guy sitting at a desk in a corner, wearing only boxer shorts and a dirty wife beater, looking depressed. But when we came in, he perked right up, flashed his teeth, excused himself politely, ducked into the bathroom, and came back a minute later dressed like a film noir tough guy, a white blazer with black silk shirt, a white necktie with what looked like a diamond stickpin, a gangster fedora cocked at a rakish angle, a big Havana cigar and rings like skulls on his hairy fingers.

I wasn't sure what was going on, but I managed to say: Hi! We just moved here from southern California, and we want to buy a house.

He spoke with what used to be called a Brooklyn accent: Of COURSE you want to buy a house, but not just ANY house, you want to buy YOUR house, the house you were born to buy! Well I'm here to help you do just that! My name's Isaac, Isaac Beer, but you can just call me Ike. All my friends do. Ike Beer!

And just like that, we were close friends with Ike Beer.

We expected him to start tapping on a keyboard. But there was no computer. Instead, he pulled a stack of listings out of his desk drawer, flipped through them quickly, then shrugged and threw them over his shoulder into a trash can. He smiled: I don't need listings to sell you guys a house. I can tell what you want just by looking at you.

Allison laughed: You can?

I sure can. Let me let you in on a simple truth. If you to want to succeed in this game, you gotta have a slogan that sells. When I started out, I realized that I couldn't use "I like Ike," since I might get sued by a former president, who was still alive at the time. Could I use it now that he's dead? Does anyone really remember Dwight David Eisenhower? Maybe five percent of the people who walk through the door here can even remember his name. But they remember his warning against the military-industrial complex. And they remember the slogan that got him into the White House: "I Like Ike." So I came up with something better, still using my name: "I Like Beer!" Pretty cool, right? I've got a stash of "I Like Beer" lapel buttons, and when people sign up to work with me, they get a button I ask them to wear when we're out there searching. It works like a charm! Beer makes everyone think about baseball, our national pastime. Whenever I show people houses, they picture themselves at the stadium, drinking ice cold beer on a hot summer day, eating hot dogs smothered with mustard and relish, or stuffing their faces with peanuts, cracker jacks and cotton candy, or pretzels and coke and nachos dripping with cheese. How can you turn away from all that? When people buy houses from me they think they're eating all their favorite foods, and getting so drunk they don't give a flying fuck who wins the game.

But Ike Beer got annoyed when we told him what we wanted, that we wouldn't even look at a ranch house in a subdivision, that we wanted something that looked like a haunted mansion, exactly like the place we're approaching now, a stark silhouette on a cliff, facing the ocean. Ike Beer gave us the address on a scrap of legal pad paper he found in his pocket, more as an afterthought than a recommendation. I remember his parting words: Feel free to drive by on your own to see if it's still standing. Must have been built around the time that General Abner Doubleday invented baseball, right before the Civil War. Never seen the place myself. No reason to. To get there you've got to take at least five dirt roads. It's easy to get lost and it takes forever. The weather gets weird over there. And there's strange stuff happening, cult activity, leftwing hippie shit. Why would I want to go there, just to sell a house that's probably falling apart, even as we speak? I'm doing alright with the kinds of houses you guys won't even look at. And they're all only minutes away, easy to get to.

Allison shakes her head: The guy seemed to think that nothing was more American than a ranch house! If we lived in a subdivision, we'd be surrounded by soccer moms and briefcase dads. They'd single us out as the weirdos in the neighborhood.

No doubt. We're better off in a place that's not in a neighborhood. But I still can't put my finger on the problem with the house. It felt like a victim of abuse, a place hollowed out by tenants who didn't give a shit.

Something is approaching in the sky. I'm thinking at first it might be a giant bird or a small plane, but as it gets closer I see that it's an observation balloon, painted like a map of the earth, with continents and oceans and polar ice caps. It comes toward us until it's maybe a hundred feet away, fifty feet above the ground. Then it hovers, apparently watching us. I can see little men in a square basket, focusing on us with telescopes and binoculars, gesturing to each other, writing things down, brandishing clipboards. There's anger and disturbance in their voices, though their words are indistinct from this distance.

Allison says: Are they observing us?

Apparently. Either that or their telescopes and binoculars are fake.

Are we doing something wrong?

They're acting like we're enemies or intruders.

Or maybe we're specimens, and they're making observations, gathering information.

So they're scientists of some kind, conducting a study?

Possibly.

What could they possibly learn by studying us? Is it because we're from a mythical faraway land—Southern California?

How would they know we're from Southern California?

Maybe they have detection devices.

What function would such a study serve?

No idea.

But they look so disturbed. They don't have that calm, rational demeanor I associate with scientific people.

I make myself sound nasal: Maybe we're not what they were hoping for. Maybe our presence here goes against a prediction they made, and now their conclusions are no longer valid.

Allison laughs: Let's wave and see what happens.

We lean out of the car, smile and wave.

They get even madder. They're jumping up and down in sheer frustration.

Allison leans out again and gives them the finger.

Now they're shouting what sound like obscenities, hurling rocks, but their aim is so bad that we're not in serious danger.

I say: What the fuck! Why do they have rocks?

Maybe to keep the balloon from drifting too far up? I'm not sure how it works, but there has to be a way for a balloon pilot to keep the thing from rising over the clouds and into oblivion.But now that they're throwing rocks, they'll lose their ballast.

Allison laughs: Maybe they don't know what they're doing. Maybe they're just a bunch of idiots who stole a balloon.

Right. And now they can't remember how it works, so they're getting freaked out.

They're signaling to us, as if we could tell them what to do, or find someone who can.

And they're mad because we don't understand what they need and we're not taking action. But if that's really what's going on, why are they throwing rocks?

If they're dumb enough to steal a device they don't understand, then they're dumb enough to ask for help by attacking the people they're asking.

The balloon starts drifting north. The guys in the basket keep yelling at each other, pointing in our direction, but soon they're the size of a tennis ball in the sky, then a golf ball, then a marble, then a dot, then nothing at all.

I say: Okay, so now what?

The GPS is messed up again. Maybe the balloon guys had an electromagnetic device of some kind, and it threw our gadgets off.

Let's try the radio.

There's only static, voices popping through with random words and phrases, bits of music, then static again. There's a whispered phrase that might be "something is always missing," but the words are quickly sucked into a burst of noise.

Allison laughs: So they came all this way in a balloon just to fuck up our devices? Or to let us know that "Nothing is ever missing"?

I thought it was "Something is always missing."

Whatever. The result is the same either way. Our devices are messed up again.

Fuck them, fuck their devices, fuck our devices, fuck all devices! Let's find our own way. We're old enough to remember how to use maps, right?

Right. But we don't have any maps.

But we've got the pre-Internet state of mind that allows us to figure things out without needing a machine to do it for us.

I switch off the GPS. It looks like it's making a face, doesn't like being sent away. When it finally fades out, it makes a faint growling sound, like a dog not getting scraps at the dinner table.

A car appears from the forest, coming toward us. It's on our side of the two lane road. Allison hits the horn but the car stays on our side, as if the driver were trying to stage a head-on collision. Allison swerves to the left. The other car swerves to the left. Allison hits the brakes and pulls off the road. The other driver hits the brakes and pulls off the road. We stop and the other car stops. It's exactly the same as the car as we're driving, a blue

2002 Mirage. Allison looks at me in shock which turns to rage. We jump out of the car prepared for a confrontation. The people in the other car do the same thing. I shout, "What the fuck were you trying to do!?" The other guy shouts the same thing. Then it's clear. They look just like us. They might as well be imitations, and they're no doubt assuming that Allison and I are the imitations. We keep walking toward each other, saying nothing.

Allison stops and says: Who are you?

Allison's double stops and says: Who are you?

We say we're Ben and Allison. They say they're Ben and Allison.

I'm not sure what to do. I'm starting to panic. But I manage to control myself and consider the situation. There's no way to sort things out with any confidence. There's no prescribed course of action for something like this. There are no clever things to say, no established understandings to fall back on. I suppose we could all start laughing, sharing the absurdity. I look at the other couple for signs of laughter. They look like they're watching us for signs of laughter. But it never quite comes, and instead I'm watching the trees in back of them catching the wind, tossing with a sound we're not close enough to hear. The upper half of the house looms over the trees, and I'm wondering if Ben and Allison were there a few minutes ago, and now they're driving back to see Ike Beer and make a down payment. I can picture him smiling robustly, shaking hands like they're just about to have their pictures taken, as if the transaction would soon become front page news in the local papers, and he's cracking jokes he's made a hundred times before, looking into their eyes like he really means it, like they've just made the wisest move they could have made, and their lives will be different now, much better, more authentic. I don't know how long we've been standing here saying nothing, but it's starting to feel like a long time. Clouds in cold wind scatter the sunlight, turning the meadow into a pattern of shadows. I feel like if I don't say something we might get stuck here forever, so I finally say, as calmly as I can: Nothing is ever missing.

The other Ben quickly replies: Something is always missing.

Suddenly they don't exist. They're gone and their car is gone.

I'm staring at the forest below the silhouette of the tower. As if someone has thrown a switch, there's sudden background sound, wind in the trees, waves crashing up against rocks. Then silence again.

I turn to Allison and say: Did that just happen?

She turns to me and says: I was just about to ask you the same thing.

What would have happened if I hadn't said what I said, if one of them had said it first?

We'd be gone and and our car would be gone, and they'd be here asking the questions we're asking now.

I shrug: Then I guess it's a damn good thing I said what I said.

Yeah, no kidding. So what happens now?

We just get back in the car and keep driving.

As if nothing happened?

As if nothing happened.

We get in the car and start driving. The house looks like a slide show version of itself, a sequence of pictures with gaps in between, as if it weren't quite there all the time, though the breaks are too brief to create a full interruption. It's clear to me that nothing is ever missing. The clouds are moving through each other, above and below and beside each other. It's clear to me that something is always missing. The clouds aren't moving at all, as if they were trapped in a giant postcard. We're silent for maybe five minutes, approaching the outskirts of the forest.

I start to feel dizzy. There are too many things to

consider, too many gaps and moving parts. I remember feelings like this from decades before, in high school, when I had to take tests and write essays and couldn't stay focused. I always gave up. I drew funny pictures instead, though I had no artistic talent, pyramids and blimps and faces with idiotic disguises. My teachers repeatedly called me an under-achiever. My parents weren't thrilled when they had to show up for disciplinary meetings. They punished me and got tutors and sent me to summer school, but nothing worked. I wanted to improve, if only to make them less alarmed, let them know that the boy they'd raised would survive in the big bad world. They'd both been outstanding students themselves, had advanced degrees and impressive jobs. They expected me to be smart and do well, and when I got bad grades they tried to be patient. But whenever I tried to study, I lost interest and got confused.

I'm amazed that when I grew up I found a good way to support myself, writing pamphlets and online publicity for an environmental activist organization. But a year ago, the job disappeared, undermined by the CIA, who claimed that the group had antifa connections, ties to Al-Qaeda, which was obvious nonsense. I loved working for the organization, and felt enraged by the

CIA's interference. But even at my best, doing work that my employers consistently praised and paid me well for, I often felt overwhelmed, like I wasn't smart enough to get things done. That's what I'm feeling now. I want to focus but I can't.

I'm thinking back a few weeks, a cognitive test the president took. I remember I'd always done badly on standardized tests, but when I saw the questions Trap was given, I felt better. It wasn't an IQ test. It was given to make sure he was still mentally competent, that he wasn't becoming senile or demented, or a victim of Information Sickness, overwhelmed by drivel, much of which he'd produced himself. The test had him identify pictures of three animals: an elephant, a camel, and a lion. Another question asked what month it was. Then he got a sequence of words: man, woman, child, camera, stupid. Five minutes later, he had to repeat the words from memory in the same order: man, woman, child, camera, stupid.

He was later interviewed by Cable News anchor Beth Barton, reportedly a closet neo-conservative, though others called her a closet neo-liberal, and others were convinced that there wasn't much difference. Trap told her that the start of the test was simple, but claimed that questions 30-35 were a serious challenge. Beth

Barton laughed and said that the test had only thirty questions, the last of which asked the President to list within a minute all the words he knew that began with F. To get a passing score he needed to list at least eleven. This was apparently one of the challenging questions.

Once I saw what the leader of the so-called civilized world needs to know, I was pleased with myself. I was glad I knew what an elephant was, glad I knew what month it was, glad I remembered the words in the proper sequence: man, woman, child, camera, stupid, glad I could list eleven words that start with F: fly, fool, form, flop, fill, from, fry, fish, flank, flip, fail, and that took only fifteen seconds, only using one-syllable words. Trap couldn't do that many in sixty seconds. When Beth Barton made a joke of it, Trap got mad, claiming that Jack Bison would have done even worse. She said she found that hard to believe. She had her assistants text Jack Bison and ask him to take the test. He said no. They asked again. He said no, nothing more than no. They got the hint. He really meant no. He could have said nothing, made no response at all, or sent a thumbs down emoji. But saying no means more than saying nothing. It means you mean it, no room for negotiation. It means that you don't have time for embarrassing bullshit. It means you've got enough money to make annoying people suck your dick. It means that you won't even let them suck your dick.

I'm not quite here right now, but Allison doesn't seem concerned. She's seen me like this before and she doesn't ask why I've gotten so quiet. She finally says: We've got to find a restaurant, or even just a convenience store. I'm craving junk food. What I want more than anything else is a pack of double stuff golden Oreos.

I laugh: That's what Barry Trap is addicted to. There are White House aides whose only job is to make sure double stuff golden Oreos are available throughout the presidential mansion. Trap is the only one who gets to eat them. If anyone else gets caught with an Oreo, they get dumped.

So why don't they just make sure that they don't hire aides with an Oreo fetish?

It's supposed to be a loyalty test. If you truly believe in Trap's plan to make America great again, then you won't touch a single double stuff golden Oreo, even if it's your favorite food, even if you're starving.

I would flunk that test right away.

Most of Trap's aides don't even last a week.

Just imagine: those aides have graduate degrees from prestigious schools, and the best job they can get is buying Oreos and serving them up to a semi-literate junk food addict.

Or imagine showing up for work with your favorite food available everywhere on full display, and you can't even touch it. That's probably what it's like to be in hell, like one of those Classical tortures.

I've heard that one reason Trap gave such a pathetic speech back in June, right after the Jeff Toy murder, is that his aides were so distracted by all the protests that they forgot to go shopping, and Trap couldn't find his Oreos when he needed them.

I nod: So when he couldn't eat, he did the next best thing, and staged what might be the most offensive photo op in photographic history.

It's funny that he's got an Oreo thing. Oreos used to be racial symbols, referring to people who were black on the outside but white on the inside. Obama got accused of being an Oreo. But that's only the original chocolate Oreos. Trap won't touch them. He's a golden Oreo man all the way.

What does that mean? A rejection of Obama?

It's known that Trap's racist buttons got seriously pushed by Obama's achievements. He couldn't stand the sight of a black man doing as well as Obama was doing. So he hired a black guy, a Faux-bama, to impersonate

Obama, and the guy had to sit in Trap's office and nod and smile pleasantly in response to insults Trap directed at him. This was captured on video, and at the end of the video Trap fired him. I've heard that Trap still watches the video when he's having a bad day—or even a good one.

Allison laughs: Normally, I would assume that this is just some nasty joke you're making. But with Trap, the jokes are real.

Like that cognitive test he took. No one could figure out if it really happened. Many people assumed it was just a bad joke.

I heard they made him him take the test for TEST.

TEST?

Yeah, TEST. You've heard of that, haven't you? Terminal Stale Entertainment Trauma.

Wouldn't that be TSET?

Yeah, but TEST works better as an acronym, and in the twenty-first century, acronyms rule, even botched acronyms. Anyway, when Trap took the test for TEST, he got a low score. When he retook the test, he got an even lower score. They were thinking of taking away his TV set. But a famous doctor pointed out that everyone fails the test and they get lower scores every time they retake it. So Trap's low score was considered normal. He was just as traumatized as everyone else.

I hold up my hand like an umpire calling a strike and say: But there's a major difference. The other TEST victims don't insist on becoming the president. They don't make their traumas everyone else's problem.

I've got a friend who's a triage nurse at a New York City hospital, and she tells me that people with TEST show up in the Emergency Room every day, staring at the ceiling and turning in circles.

At least Barry Trap hasn't reached that point.

No, but the things he does are a lot more damaging. Those people turning in circles aren't a direct threat to our national security.

I nod and point ahead: See that sign? There's a crossroads coming up. Judging by where the house appears to be now, I think we should take a right.

Yeah, it's a dirt road, probably the same one we were on a few days ago, right before we got there.

But ten minutes later, it's clear that it's not the same road. It keeps twisting and turning, going up and down, doubling back on itself, so it feels like we're getting nowhere, and at least ten turns and thirty minutes later, we're farther away than we were before. We're on the other side of the house, which clearly isn't the same as the side we were on half an hour ago. The other side is all magnificent porticos and gables, grand stone balconies, and a huge white belvedere with a swell-bodied weathervane, while this side has a mansard roof with dormer windows, a large wrap-around porch that reaches almost to the edge of the cliff. I'm thinking of how relaxing it must be to sleep there, the sound of wind and waves all night. I feel like I want to buy the place without further hesitation.

But something changes. The house now looks like a distant silhouette with bright clouds behind it. The weathervane looks like a neuron giving and taking information.

I grab Allison's wrist and say: What's happening? Where are we? We were right beside the house and now it looks like it's miles away.

She slowly nods and tries to sound like she knows what she's talking about: We need to turn left up here. That should bring us around to the other side.

We drive through a patch of dense fog that wasn't here two minutes ago. It feels like it might have come out of a package delivered when we weren't looking. We have to slow down, moving in and out of deep ruts that might break the car in half.

Allison stops and says: Ben, you need to take the

wheel. I'm getting messed up. I can't tell which side of the house we're on, if it's this side or the other side. What I'm looking at always seems to be this side, but when we get to the other side it's become this side, and the other side is the one I called this side, but now it's the other side, and vice versa.

Next time we should ask Ike Beer to find us a house with only one side.

It was weird, wasn't it, that he didn't want to come with us?

There was something about him that didn't add up.

She nods eagerly: His Brooklyn accent made him seem non-threatening, like your favorite neighborhood guy. But he seemed like he might get mean if you didn't know how to tie your shoes, or if you forgot to shave, or if your shirt was buttoned up wrong, or if you said that you didn't like reading junkmail, the kind of guy who would claim to be tall in Milwaukee and short in Miami, fat in Albuquerque and sleek in Topeka.

I take the wheel, moving slowly up and down bumps and gullies, watching everything carefully, peering into the slowly vanishing fog. I keep thinking it's here to hide something that needs to be concealed. I don't know what it is, but I can't help feeling that it's obvious, something anyone else would be aware of, know how to avoid, something that will make me feel like a fool when the fog is gone.

Then we're near the house again, but not on the other side, where I thought we'd be. We're on the same side as we were before, as if we've gone in a circle. I stare at the dormers lost in the mansard roof, stop the car and stare at the house and scratch my head and say: We're where we were ten minutes ago. We need to turn left.

Not right?

Right. Not right.

I pause and make a face like I'm thinking carefully, as if making the face were a way to make sure my thinking was careful enough. It feels like I'm having trouble reading the bottom line of an eye chart. I finally say: I'm pretty sure we need to turn left up ahead. That should bring us to that huge lawn and the gravel driveway where we parked a few days ago.

Something appears in the sky again, but not a balloon this time. It's a huge amoeboid storm cloud that looks like it might surround the house and slowly absorb it, dissolving it with cytoplasmic acids. I can almost hear it growling and licking its lips. But then it splits and I see that it's not a cloud and not an amoeba. It's a giant flatworm making the sky look like it's on a slide in a lab, magnified under a microscope that's slightly out of focus, a cross-eyed two-dimensional creature with a head on either end. The eyes look cold and angry, annoyed that they're being studied. It's clear that they don't appreciate the procedures they've had to endure, violence that's revealed the tricks they can play. You can cut them into small pieces and each piece becomes a full new flatworm, exactly like the original. You can cut off both flatworm heads and the body grows two new heads, and the severed heads grow two new bodies. How do they do it? Not even the smartest people can figure it out, let alone do it themselves. You can peel a flatworm off a petrie dish like a postage stamp. You can even use it as a postage stamp, and the post office goes along with it. The flatworm looks so scary that no one dares to raise an objection. There's something spooky about the cross-eyed stare. It doesn't have time to put up with any nonsense.

It moves like a giant slinky through the sky in two directions. It stretches out and recoils, stretches out and recoils. A sound like a gigantic window breaking fills the sky, and the flatworm curls up into itself and changes into a volvox, a form of blue-green algae that normally lives in ponds and ditches. It's a slowly revolving transparent sphere, filled with reproductive spheres growing into and out of each other, every sphere comprised of smaller versions of itself, as if it were modeling infinite self-replication. It's an animal that behaves like a plant and a plant that behaves like an animal, though the creature itself doesn't know that there's any difference. It moves and reproduces by turning inside out then outside in, over and over again, a series of echoes. Now it's turning inside out releasing bolts of lightning. They hit the weathervane which makes the sound of rippling aluminum foil. Then the creature is swallowed up into the clouds with the sound of a closing zipper.

The house remains intact, like nothing happened. Even a mega-protozoan attack hasn't made any difference. Even Hurricane Ahab hasn't made any difference. I'm pleased. After all, if the house can defend itself against lightning and hurricanes, we should get good insurance rates, even if the house is almost two hundred years old.

Allison licks her lips in the rear view mirror. She says: The house seems to come with incredible special effects. I wonder if it's a regular occurrence, or if you have to pay more if you want psychedelic displays in the sky. But on a more mundane level: Do you know where we are?

I think we've gotten closer.

I was just about to say we're farther away.

There's another fork in the road up ahead. Should we keep turning left?

Allison squints again in the rear view mirror: I think if you're trying to solve a maze you're always supposed to turn right.

I slow down as we approach the fork in the road. I yawn and say: It's a shame that we don't have a compass.

Do you know how to use a compass?

Not really.

I don't either.

I laugh: So much for that. But I've heard that a compass won't work in the Devil's Triangle. Apparently north is west and south is more than south and less than south and east is north in the summertime and south in fall and winter.

Allison shrugs: But we're not in the Devil's Triangle.

We might as well be. I mean, look at the GPS now. It's turned itself back on, and the roads on the screen are an observation balloon.

Allison laughs: First it shows up in the sky; then it shows up on the phone. It's because of what's in the sky that the phone is possible. But it's not what's in the phone that makes the sky possible.

My teacher told me that in the Devil's Triangle everything happens twice, but at the same time.

There's also the theory that Kennedy was tough with Khrushchev during the Cuban Missile Crisis because he knew that the Russian ships would be sailing through the Triangle, and if he blew them up he could deny it by saying that the ships got swallowed up by mysterious forces and weren't destroyed by U.S. weapons. I guess JFK assumed that Khrushchev was familiar with Bermuda Triangle stories and hadn't just dismissed them as paranormal nonsense. Otherwise, Khrushchev never would have believed him, and an all-out nuclear war would have started.

It's funny how so much complexity gets filtered out of conventional history books. I had no idea that JFK was planning to use the Triangle as an excuse. Then again, he was good at making excuses. He had to crank out a lot of them to cover up his trips through subterranean tunnels to meet the women he was fucking. And Jackie must have been good at pretending to believe him.

Allison puts her chin on my shoulder: How close are we to the so-called real Bermuda Triangle?

I'm not sure, maybe a thousand miles away. I've heard it changes position. I heard a story about the captain of a ship who sailed into it, and for hours he had the overwhelming feeling that he was just about to get used in a sandwich. And there was a story about a pilot who started panicking as he reached the edge of the triangle. He said something like "Wait a minute! What's that? Things are getting strange. Everything is wrong! What's happening? What's happening? Stendex! Stendex!"

Stendex?

No one has any idea what he meant.

Stendex sounds like a cleaning product.

Speaking of which, we're going to need lots of cleaning products once we move into the house.

Allison looks disgusted and says: You know how much I hate cleaning. Don't ever use that word around me again. People who enjoy cleaning are like the people who come to your door and give you pamphlets about the end of the world. Back when I was in my early twenties, when I had a better body than I do now, I would answer the door in the nude when the Bible guys came around.

Too bad there weren't any smart phones back then. It would have been funny to make a film collage using all the embarrassed reactions.

Most of them said excuse me and giggled and backed away saying have a nice day. But some of them got an instant stiffy, so they put a Bible in front of it, as if I didn't know what they were hiding. I loved it. It gave me a feeling of power.

They didn't just get to spew their Bible shit at you.

No. But think about it. Mainstream politicians assault us with a steady stream of self-serving bullshit. And no one stops them. No one even questions their right to spend huge sums of money on self-promotional gibberish. It should be classified as noise pollution.

I nod: Trap recently claimed that one of Jack Bison's chief supporters is Osama bin Laden.

Even though he's dead? Or supposedly dead?

Doesn't matter. If you say a word or phrase that triggers strong feelings, people remember it, no matter how crazy it is. So maybe Jack Bison gets falsely connected to 9/11 and Al-Qaida. Then people who go to the polls undecided, not sure who to vote for, make a barely conscious connection between Jack Bison and bin Laden, and they vote against him, against al-Qaida. They're not really voting for Trap; they're voting against bin Laden.

Allison shrugs and says: Intelligent people won't buy it. Idiots will. And Trap's base is loaded with idiots.

That's harsh! Don't you feel bad calling them idiots?

No.

But a lot of them are just poor people getting stabbed in the back.

Allison nods: Yeah, and they've had four years to figure out who was holding the knife.

We turn left, ignoring the rule for solving mazes. We can see the house above the trees, getting larger and closer.

Allison tilts her head and says: There's this odd pressure in my ears, like I'm on a plane and we're going up or down and my ears are popping. I hate that feeling. It always make me feel like an armadillo.

Not a manatee?

No, an armadillo.

Not a dugong?

What's the difference between a dugong and a manatee?

One of them is more wrinkled. I forget which one. But wait, here's the next road. Let's turn.

The trees form a dense canopy, blocking out the sky, so the road looks like a tunnel, maybe not all that different from the tunnels the Vietcong used in resisting the U.S. invasion, or the tunnels in caves that led to Stone Age chambers filled with images painted on walls. For fifteen minutes talking seems impossible, like anything we might say would be inane or insane, offensive or explosive, syllables collapsing, like icebergs losing themselves in climate change, drifting into graves of warming water. Slowly refracted sunlight seeps through the clouds, spreading through the treetops, which bend in the breeze and make shadows move. The house looks like it's only a hundred yards away.

I say: It's funny how we can't stop talking politics. Of course it makes sense because it's an election year. But it's not about issues anymore; it's about personalities. Jack Bison is playing it smart by not campaigning. We don't get to see who he is. We don't get to see that he's not all there. We don't get to hate him. He might get elected simply because we don't know much about him. Back in the 1850s, the alternative to the Democratic Party was called the Know Nothing Party. When you asked them what they stood for, they were supposed to say: I Know Nothing!

No way!

It's true. Look it up on your phone.

There's no reception here. Oh wait, now there is. It keeps going in and out.

Allison presses buttons on her phone, reads the screen for a minute or two, then starts laughing: It says here they were convinced that a papist conspiracy had been launched with the goal of depriving Americans of their civil and religious liberty. Does that mean that they thought Catholics were out to get them?

More or less. They also called themselves the Native American Party. But none of them were Indians. They were against immigration, even though most of them were the sons and daughters of immigrants.

They sound almost as warped as our two main parties today.

I wouldn't go that far! Party members today don't even know that they know nothing. They might not think that Catholics are out to get them, but they think that Terrorists are. And a generation ago, they thought that Communists were.

She gives me the look she always gives me right before sex. It's hard to describe it exactly. It's not the sexy look you see in movies. I don't know if anyone else would think it was hot. But it makes me horny. I stop the car, run around to the other side, coax her out of the car, and we lie down on a smooth patch of grass that looks like it's there to make sex better, like grass on a golf green. Did the people who designed this road make sure to provide smooth patches of grass at regular intervals, so if drivers got horny, they'd have nice places to stop and fuck? Do local drivers have special maps that indicate where these nice places are, so sexual pit stops can be scheduled in advance? Sometimes people can be insanely clever, but there's no time to think about it now because Allison is on top of me. She sits on my face then I sit on her face and we drive each other crazy.

We rest for a while in post-orgasmic splendor. I'm drifting in and out of sleep. Then I look to my left and see what looks like a large gray wolf about thirty feet away, calmly watching us, barely visible in dense foliage. Allison looks and whispers: Is that a dog?

I don't think so.

Too big to be a coyote, right? So it's probably a wolf?

Yeah.

She looks really cool. And she doesn't look dangerous.

Not right now, anyway. I'm sure if she was starving or protecting her pups, she could do some damage.

She doesn't look like she's starving.

I guess there's plenty to eat around here.

The wolf sniffs the air, then turns and disappears into the woods.

We stare for a minute or two at the empty space she's left behind. We get up and get back into the car and start driving. Allison says: Do you think that wolf was watching the whole time we were doing it?

Probably. She got there at a good time, that's for sure! But I didn't know there were any wolves left in this part of the country. I thought they'd all been killed or driven away.

Maybe wolves have survived undetected around here. We should ask Ike Beer.

He doesn't seem like the kind of guy who would care. I'm guessing he thinks it's cool to hunt and kill animals. He's probably got a moose head mounted over his mantelpiece, right next to the gun rack and the flat-screen TV in his wood-paneled family room. I used to write nasty articles about people like that.

I remember. And Ike Beer had an NRA sticker on his car. That tells you a lot.

About ten years ago, one of my friends was hiking in the mountains of northern Alaska, and she was suddenly surrounded by wolves. They had her trapped, and one by one they attacked and bit her, and she was bleeding all over. If other hikers hadn't approached and scared off the wolves, they would have killed her bite by bite and had her for dinner. She was an animal rights person up until then. But not anymore.

The wolves were probably starving.

Sure. But when you're getting attacked like that, you don't care why they're doing it.

How many people have been killed by wolves over the years?

I read somewhere that in the lower 48 states, no people have been killed by wolves in more than a century. Far more people have been killed in hunting accidents.

She shakes her head and stares outside for a while, then says: That sex was awesome, wasn't it?

Sex is always better when it's unplanned.

So is laughter.

So is music.

So is driving.

I clear my throat: Maybe that's why it's taking so long to get to the house. We keep trying to follow a plan generated by a mechanical device, when we should have been improvising right from the start.

It's amazing how much we trust mechanical devices.

Ike Beer doesn't. In fact, he doesn't even need paper documents. He just plays it by ear, which rhymes with Beer. Except in our case, he was tone deaf.

Allison narrows her eyes and says: But wasn't it weird how he suddenly remembered the note in his pocket? I didn't get a good look at it. Can I see it?

I reach into my shirt pocket and hand it to her. She unfolds it and starts laughing and says: Listen to this! "People have been told to wear masks to protect other people from getting the virus. Millions are refusing to cooperate. But if they'd been told that by wearing masks they'd be protecting themselves—underlined—everyone would have complied."

That's on the note? All I remember was the address and a brief comment. Where did that thing about masks and the virus come from?

It's on the other side. Look!

She hands me the note but I can't take time to read it, since I'm driving and I need to pay close attention. The road keeps changing directions, and it's full of deep holes we need to avoid.

I say: We're lucky that we're in a place where no one seems to have gotten the virus. That was a pretty thorough inspection we had to pass before they let us enter the county.

So whoever wrote that note must have been thinking about the rest of the nation. No one here sees any need for masks.

We've moved to what seems to be the one safe place in the world—or at least in America.

Barry Trap won't wear a mask. He thinks it makes him look weak.

I laugh: Trap should see it as an opportunity to keep his trap shut.

But a mask wouldn't stop him from tweeting. The guy never stops.

He never starts either. He's got a guy on staff who writes his tweets for him. The guy who used to be Coke's PR Director.

Allison smirks: Imagine: a president who can't even write his own tweets. And he might get re-elected because the Democrats refuse to nominate anyone with balls. Jack Bison? Jack Normal Jack Nothing Jack Jackass. Plus he's probably a pedophile. He likes to sniff little girls' hair. And to top it off, he's half senile.

Only half?

But that's better than Trap, who should be a registered sociopath. In a saner country than this one, both of them would have mandated tracking devices in their foreheads. They wouldn't be out there making asinine speeches and posing for pictures.

I nod and make a disgusted face and say: Speaking of tracking devices, my brother knew someone who had to wear one, a rogue biologist who got killed several years ago because he knew too much. Or someone thought he did. He was working with the Air Force, stationed at Groom Lake, otherwise known as Area 51.

Is that the place where people think they see UFOs,

but they're really seeing state of the art airborne military devices, things that look like flying jellyfish?

Yeah. You get there from Vegas by going north on the Extraterrestrial Highway. Back when I was in college my girlfriend and I took a trip to Area 51 in a Corvair I bought for fifty dollars. Did I ever tell you about this?

Allison shakes her head.

We drove through an empty desert for several hours. Today, Area 51 is full of tacky extra-terrestrial amenities, an Alien Center where you can buy UFO paperweights, keychains, T-shirts, and stuffed aliens, but back then there wasn't much more than a WARNING/KEEP OUT sign and miles of barbed wire fencing and scrub vegetation. Right before we arrived, the car broke down. There was steam pouring out of the hood, and we knew nothing about how to fix cars. There were no cell phones back then, so we couldn't call for roadside assistance. We couldn't find a call box. There was nothing to do but hope that a very kind person would stop and help us. So we found an old shed and hung out in the shade and waited. No one came, which wasn't surprising. No one knew about Area 51 back then. Extra-terrestrials hadn't yet become a tabloid attraction. The heat and silence and emptiness made it hard to talk, like we couldn't remember how to do it, like our teeth were in the way. At some point we fell asleep, and woke at midnight. The stars were bright, huge, and throbbing, more intense than in that famous Van Gogh painting. The whole sky seemed to be tilting and revolving, advancing and receding. We waited for an hour but there still weren't any cars. By then it was twenty degrees cooler, so we started making love. Then right at the peak of our passion, a guy walked quietly into the shed. He was nine feet tall, had huge iridescent wings, and a lava lamp instead of a chest. Or no, his chest was more like one of those radios people had back in the 1930s, one of those vacuum tube sets with wooden frames and glowing circular dials.

Allison laughs: Not like a lava lamp?

No. I mean, yeah, like a lava lamp.

Not like an old radio?

Yeah, more like an old radio. I'm not sure. Both at once maybe. Anyway, his legs were like writhing boa constrictors, and his tail was made of lightning bolts. We were scared at first, but he put us at ease by talking to us in clear and elegant English. He said he was lost and—

Allison grabs my arm and says: Wait, you didn't say what his face was like.

Like a multi-colored catcher's mitt which opened

and closed when he talked. Or no, it was more like a sea anemone, or a cross between a squid and a gila monster. Or like—never mind. To tell you the truth, it was too dark to see clearly. I can't remember his face. I think it kept changing.

Okay, so he was lost—

Right. He said that he'd ended up on earth by mistake, and he wanted to get back home. We asked him where he was from. He said it was hard to explain in simple English. We shrugged and said we didn't know much about astronomy, or how to build flying saucers, then nodded towards our car, explaining that we too were unsure about how to get home. He looked at the car for a minute, then turned and lightning darted from his tail, bathing the car in crackling iridescence. Then he said that the car was good as new. We looked at him like he was crazy, but we checked it out anyway, and saw that he wasn't joking. It wasn't just that it started right up. It looked like a whole new car, like a GTO or a Thunderbird from the late sixties. We were obviously pleased, but also felt foolish, since he'd solved our problem, but we knew that we couldn't solve his. We told him we felt sad that we couldn't help him, since his difficulties were beyond us. He looked disappointed, but he handled the situation with quiet dignity, thanked us for our time, excused himself, and wandered off into the night.

You're not serious, right?

I'm serious.

Did you tell anyone about this?

You're the first one I've told.

Okay. But what about your brother's friend?

Who?

Your brother's friend. The guy who got killed because he knew too much.

Oh yeah, the rogue biologist, Ken Pencil. He had a regular security clearance because he worked there, but he got caught snooping around in a zone of Area 51 where you needed an *extra special* security clearance, and some psycho Technical Sergeant accused him of seeing things he wasn't supposed to see. Ken Pencil told him he hadn't seen much of anything, but the Sergeant insisted on making a report, accusing him of having discovered that a virus had escaped from an alien spacecraft, which was in a carefully guarded cell a mile below the Extraterrestrial Highway. From what Ken Pencil told my brother, the spacecraft looked like a DNA molecule, a spiral helix, and nothing like a flying saucer.

Is this for real?

I wish it wasn't. But according to the Sergeant's official report, Ken Pencil had figured out that the virus was here on a mission, sent by enlightened beings millions of light years away to destroy the U.S. political system.

Allison laughs: Why would anyone millions of light years from here give a shit about our political system.

They're apparently an intergalactic police force, and their job is to detect and destroy dangerous and dysfunctional forms of life.

In that case, they came to the right place. Sounds like *The Day the Earth Stood Still*. So what happened?

They locked him up and inserted a tracking device in the nape of his neck. They let him go, planning to monitor every move he made. But instead of allowing people to track him, the device picked up random TV commercials, and his brain was filled with promotional gibberish. He shot himself a few weeks later. It was ruled a suicide, but my brother went to court and tried to get it re-classified as a homicide, since the airforce was responsible for the tracking device and the overdose of bullshit. After years of litigation, the case was thrown out on a technicality.

What the fuck does that mean? You hear it all the time—a "technicality." Like the process of making sure that justice is served becomes unimportant because someone hasn't followed courtroom rules and procedures exactly? It's always sounded asinine to me, but recently it worked in my aunt's favor. She was facing a malpractice suit. She's a hypnotist and accidentally shrank one of her customers.

Shrank? She made him smaller?

Yeah. Suddenly the guy was six inches tall and weighed about ten pounds. She's still not sure how it happened, maybe a glitch in her incantation, the influence of monsters from the id. But the customer turned out to be the Senate Majority leader.

Mitch McDonald?

Yeah. But after he got shrunk he started calling himself Bitch McDonald's. Anyway, his wife filed a malpractice suit, but the case got thrown out because Bitch McDonald's had signed a release form prior to the session.

So the wife was stuck with a six-inch guy?

Allison laughs: Right. But from what I've heard, she kind of likes it, now that she's gotten used to it. She can do all sorts of funny things with him. And when he makes her mad, she just puts him in a jar, screws the lid on tight, puts him in a closet and closes the door.

Wasn't she a Barry Trap cabinet member?

That's right. The Secretary of Transmutation.

I think you mean Transmigration.

Whatever. She resigned when Trap got mean to her, threw a party-size pack of double stuff golden Oreos at her in the Oval Office, just because she refused to join his entourage for that photo op he staged at the Church of the Presidents.

I shake my head: He threw a party-size pack of Oreos at her? I find that hard to believe. Oreos are his favorite food, and if he threw a pack of them across the Oval Office, they would have shattered on impact, ended up on the floor, and he would lost out on his favorite snack.

Clearly the guy has anger management issues. He's thrown food at people several times in the Oval Office. Recently Bill Barf learned that you don't make Barry Trap mad when he's eating a pizza.

Does Jack Bison throw food at people?

No. So that might be a good reason to vote for him.

I laugh: You know damn well it's a mistake to vote at all.

I take a right, and we're on a paved road that becomes the main street of a town that looks like it's still in the 1920s, craftsman and clapboard houses, American foursquares and shingle style homes, Cape Cods and Saltboxes, even a few Eastlake Victorians, with wraparound porches and people in rocking chairs smoking pipes, white picket fences and tree-lined streets, elms that don't have the Dutch Elm Disease. The cars are all Hudsons, Nashes, Packards, and Model A Fords, with headlights that look like the eyes of a Praying Mantis.

There's an old wooden phone booth outside a Five & Dime store. It's the kind of booth Clark Kent used when he ripped off his business clothes and changed into Superman. It's never been clear to me how he got away with it, since it wasn't exactly a private space. People on the streets could have seen him doing it, day after day. And when he'd ripped off his business suit, revealing his superman costume underneath, did he just leave the discarded suit in a heap on the floor? Surely the next person in the booth found the pile of clothes. Did they just ignore it? Or did they inspect it, turn the pockets inside out, discovering Clark Kent's wallet, maybe stealing his credit cards, his social security number, his secret identity, ruining him through identity theft before the term even existed? And why were there no episodes with Superman returning to the booth to change back into civilian clothes, his ace reporter outfit? He must have done it thousands of times. I'm about to ask Allison what she thinks, since I know she used to be a big Superman fan. In fact, back in her teens she used to write letters to the DC Comics editors, pointing out gaps in their narrative logic, and some of the letters were published, along with the editors' clever responses. I picture the editors poring through heaps of letters, skimming them to decide which ones to respond to, reading them out loud to each other, laughing at most of them, but getting stumped by a few of them, like the ones that Allison sent. I'm picturing her as a younger version of herself, pulling a carefully worded letter out of a manual typewriter, carefully sealing it in an envelope, walking ten blocks and dropping it in a mailbox, and then I notice, a block away, that there's a green cast iron mailbox, the words "U.S. Mail" and "Letters" engraved in white below the mail slot. I've never seen one like that before, except in old black and white pictures. Back in 1920, it was normal for people to write letters. I try to remember the last time I wrote a full letter, actually using a pen to put words on paper, forced to cross out mistakes instead of deleting them. Just the thought of it feels overwhelming. But Allison used to do it all the time, writing out rough drafts and revising them with ball-point pens, then making final typewritten copies, pounding away on her black Smith-Corona keyboard, refusing to suspend disbelief and let the DC writers make aesthetic mistakes.

We come to a traffic light. On one side there's a Starbucks; on the other side, a McDonald's. I don't see how we could be in a 1920s town and have fast food places, but it's almost as if the town is here for the sole purpose of saying that the wrong things can exist at the wrong times in the wrong places, and if you don't like it then fuck you.

The light looks like a stoplight in a museum. It's mounted on a cast iron pole with only two colors: red and green, with stop and go in white letters imprinted on the lamps. The men are wearing bowler hats, fedoras, homburgs, derbys, and newsboy hats. The women have cloche and flapper hats that look like they're from *The Great Gatsby*. No one seems to notice the fast food places. People walk past and through them as if they're not there. But for us, they're not illusions. They're signs of the corporate junk food culture we want to escape. We can't stop glaring at the logos, the siren and the golden arches. They're like uninvited guests at a birthday party.

I look at Allison's angry face. She says exactly what I'm thinking, word for word: Ike Beer didn't say anything about shit like this!

He probably assumed we would see it as a positive sign, just like he assumed we would want a ranch house.

She sounds panicky: Let's get out of here fast.

The light's red. I can't go now.

She grabs my wrist and says: Just run the light.

I run the light. The town slowly disappears in the rear-view mirror. Soon we turn off the paved road and we're on a dirt road again, so we have to slow down. The wind gets even more intense, and the trees on either side of us are filled with sound and motion, briefly lighting up as the sun breaks through, then shadowed with clouds. The foliage is so dense that I can't see the house now.

Allison is taking deep breaths, so I ask: Are you ok? Having an anxiety attack?

No, I think I'm okay. For a second there, I thought we might be near a TV zone. You know how I always feel sick when we're near a TV zone.

You didn't really see TVs, did you?

No, but once you see fast food places, you know you're in a TV zone. You know that most of the public places will have at least one TV.

I shrug: Even though it looked like the 1920s back there?

It felt like if I held a conch shell to my ear, there would have been a laugh track instead of the ocean. It was like two different times had been connected, maybe through a gap in the fabric of spacetime, an accidental passageway, an open door that should have been closed, keeping 1920 in the past and 2020 in the present.

Sure. Except that there aren't any doors that keep the past in the past and the present in the present. Call it a passageway, call it a gap or door—you're talking in metaphors.

Actually, I'm concerned about something more definite: if the fast food places aren't really there, and the house is really outside all TV zones, can it be rigged up for Internet access, if we decide we really can't live off the grid?

I laugh: I'm sure it can be arranged if we're willing to pay.

But what if it's one of those houses that can't be modernized? I've heard that people freak out when they find out that the house they've just bought can't be brought up to date, so they tear the place down and build something new, even if a big part of their initial interest in the place was that it was built a long time ago.

But if the house can't support an Internet connection, we're prepared to go off the grid, right? I think we more or less agreed on that, didn't we?

She slowly nods: More or less. I mean, It's scary. But

it's probably worth it. Yeah, for sure. Like you said before, fuck all devices! But why did those fast food places appear back there at the light?

For the sole purpose of showing that the future is always part of the past.

She does a double-take: Is it? I was going to say it might be a centennial thing. It's been a hundred years since women got the right to vote, so the town is acting like it's 1920, but not the rich guys that own Starbucks and McDonald's. Every day they make billions. They can't afford to take a day off in 1920.

How would a voting centennial work? Would the women there celebrate by voting all day long? I didn't see any ballot boxes.

Just think: one hundred years after we women got the right to vote, there's nothing worth voting for any longer.

Any longer? You think there were things worth voting for in the past? In 1920? You think that Warren G. Harding was worth voting for?

Allison is laughing: Believe it or not, as an undergraduate I dated a guy who was totally obsessed with Warren G. Harding.

History major?

A 1920s expert. And yes, back then people thought

Warren G. Harding was worth voting for. He ran against Eugene Debs in the presidential election, and won by a landslide. Then Debs got thrown in jail for speaking out against the war, and Harding went on to become a popular president, even though he was a total slob, almost as bad as Barry Trap, according to some of his friends. But then he got connected with scandals after he died, and people today think he was the worst president ever. And now Barry Trap might get an even lower ranking, and still get re-elected.

I nod: It's all too possible. But when we first got there, I was thinking the town might be a theme park or simulation of some kind, except that there was no admission fee, no visitors information center, no amusement park stuff, and no staff people in uniforms making sure that visitors didn't fuck things up. Besides, the people seemed real. They looked like they were living their lives and not just pretending to.

Do people who work in simulation towns have to act like part of the simulation all day long? For me, that would get exhausting, not to mention boring.

I think at Tombstone, Arizona they have re-enactments of the famous gun fight every three hours, so the workers get breaks. But here there's no famous event being re-enacted. It's just a town that's in the twenties. The people must work in shifts. Maybe three different groups of people work four-hour shifts.

The place is only open twelve hours a day? Then the workers punch a time clock and go home and the town is empty? Or do they get to stay in the town after they're off the clock, without pretending anymore that it's 1920? Do they go to Starbucks or McDonalds late at night, after it's no longer 1920?

Allison looks puzzled: I saw people passing through the fast food places like they weren't really there, like they were holograms. I doubt there was real junk food inside—or any inside at all, for that matter. Or maybe they had plastic models of Big Macs and Frappuccinos. Or no, wait: they couldn't have had models of things that didn't exist yet.

So it might not have been a real simulation town. I'm leaning toward that interpretation, that it was just a place that got stuck in 1920.

But how does a whole place get stuck in 1920? Do the people all have to agree to it?

I rub my jaw like I might have a beard: Maybe we should investigate further, find out if that stop light is a gateway to a time warp. You hear about time warps in sci-fi movies and books, but what if we've really found one? Shouldn't we find out what it's like to be in a time warp? We might be paving the way for profound scientific advances. Shouldn't we go back and park and go outside and find out what's going on?

Allison shakes her head: No way. Once we're out of the car, we'll be back in 1920. We won't exist yet. Or we'll bring the place up to the present, a hundred years into the future, and none of the people there will exist anymore.

By the way, did you notice that the light was just red and green, stop and go.

Right. There was nothing in between.

And what did you think of that green cast-iron mailbox? Was it really green or was it just the color of oxidation? I love that color!

I've seen them in movies. I think they used to be black. But everything seems to lead back to sleazy politics. I can't see a mailbox anymore without thinking of Barry Trap's latest bullshit.

Right. I can't either. What a scumbag!

If he can't get re-elected he can sabotage the election, preventing people from voting him out of office, removing mailboxes throughout the nation.

I guess I don't see why he assumes that covid mail-in votes will go against him.

I don't get that either. Maybe he's figuring that the people observing the quarantine most carefully, probably liberals, are the ones most likely to stay inside and vote by mail?

It's funny how he's afraid of liberals. Most of them are all talk and no action. They're closet capitalists, progressives only so long as their bank accounts aren't in danger. Remember that in our supposedly liberal home state, sunny California, people voted against increasing the minimum wage. These are the people Trap is afraid of?

Apparently. And he's not even being subtle about it. There are pictures all over the Internet of tractor trailers filled with uprooted mailboxes being taken away, apparently to a garbage dump, a mailbox graveyard.

Allison smirks: I want to feel sorry for Trap. He's like a pathetic little boy who's never been taught to lose gracefully. He doesn't have the dignity card in his hand, and his crass behavior should embarrass him. But it doesn't. That's what makes him so disgusting. He feels justified in tampering with the election, in plain view of the people who will soon be deciding his fate. Does he assume that voters will approve of what he's doing? Does he think they'll quietly accept the destruction of an essential service?

I nod: The mailbox is an icon, a democratic symbol. Now it's being destroyed, all because a guy is afraid to lose.

For most of us losing is normal; for Trap it's unacceptable. He was brought up to think he's above it. But in just a few months, he might lose. It's a definite possibility. Imagine him refusing to leave the Oval Office, sitting behind his desk and refusing to budge. I'm picturing people talking to him, nicely at first, then more abrasively, telling him it's time to go. They don't want to drag him out physically. They want to be polite. They want to give him a chance to leave with dignity. But finally it's clear that they'll have to use force. Big guys with mirror shades are summoned. They knock him down and pull him out by his feet. Or maybe they give him an injection, and when he passes out they move him out on a hospital gurney. He wakes up somewhere else, a recovery room in a medical facility, and before he can figure out that he isn't in the White House any longer, he's offered Oreos and pornography. Before too long he's happy again, no longer forced to do a job he isn't qualified for.

I'd pay to see it.

It'll no doubt be the greatest youtube clip in viral history. But I'm guessing that if he loses, he'll claim it was a fraudulent election. I can easily imagine him inciting his followers to riot, storm the Capitol building, bursting inside and breaking things and getting drunk and posting pictures online, a social media bonanza.

What's the name of that messianic cult? Qanon? The people who think Trap was commissioned by God to save the nation from liberals?

Allison laughs: Right. They're starting to get more media time. Even though their basic assumptions are ludicrous, they're still a force to be reckoned with. They're a mob that can be summoned if Trap feels desperate. They're a bunch of clowns until they bring out their guns. Ultimately, it's always about guns. I hate guns!

I'm not sure what to say so I don't say anything. There's a point in most conversations where both people need to shut up. If they don't, things go downhill fast. I think we've reached that point. We may have reached it a long time ago without knowing it.

Ten minutes of silence later, I see a barely visible dirt road branching off to the left. It leads to what looks like a park about three hundred feet away, a bandshell and a dark stone statue of a giant on a throne.

I stop. Allison wants to know why, so I say: Look

to your left, down that old dirt road. There's a park of some kind.

She squints and slowly nods: Yeah. There's a huge guy with antlers on a throne beside a bandshell.

Right, and there seem to be rows of people in folding chairs, facing the statue, like an audience waiting for a performance, a speech or maybe a concert. Let's take a look.

I move the car down the road but it's overgrown and bumpy. It takes us five minutes to go a hundred feet. Then the statue stands and begins what sounds like an incantation. He's over a hundred feet tall and he's got a voice deep enough to break boulders. His listeners sway back and forth to the rhythm his words are making. From the arm of his throne, he picks up a silver bowl and holds it up to the sky. A lightning bolt shoots down and fills the bowl. He tilts it and drinks what appears to be liquid lightning. His body glows and trembles. The tips of his antlers pop and send off sparks. He flashes up into the sky and disappears in the gathering storm clouds. His people rise from their chairs and shout, one long transforming syllable. Then they all drop at once and start writhing on the ground and laughing wildly.

Allison gives me a let's get out of here look.

I back the car out the way we came in. It's even

harder in reverse and takes three times as long. When we're back on the gravel path we look at each other, stunned and silent. Finally Allison says: That was way too weird!

It sure was. Who the fuck was that huge guy?

Except for the antlers, he looked like Zeus in a famous painting, I forget who the artist was, a neo-classical French guy, maybe Ingres or David, I get them mixed up.

But instead of hurling thunderbolts down from the clouds, the statue guy became a thunderbolt and shot up into the clouds.

Zeus in reverse.

I rub my eyes and shake my head. Then I'm laughing: Is this what Ike Beer meant by "leftwing hippie shit"?

That's right. That's the phrase he used: "Leftwing hippie shit." But whatever you want to call it, don't you think we better get out of here?

I'm still laughing: Get out of here? Why? Nothing horrible really happened.

Allison pauses and strokes her chin. She often does it ironically, to pretend she's in deep thought. But now she's not pretending. She finally says: I guess not. Those people writhing on the ground weren't really in pain. In fact, they seemed to be ecstatic.

Right. And Zeus didn't do anything horrible. It looked like he had awesome powers, but no one got hurt.

So, as far as I'm concerned, we can just live our lives and let those people live theirs. Different strokes for different folks. Like Muhammed Ali once said. Or Sly and the Family Stone.

I'm nodding eagerly: Absolutely. Nothing wrong with leftwing hippie shit, as far as I'm concerned. And they had a bandshell. Maybe they have concerts.

So they might be good neighbors, providing free music.

But what if they're using the house? What if it's home base for cult activities?

There was definitely something fucked up about the atmosphere of the house. But I didn't get Zeus cult vibes.

I didn't either, and of course we don't really know if what we saw back there was a cult ritual, or if it had anything to do with Zeus. Who knows what those people were doing?

But it's possible that they're using the house in some way, so we need to take a closer look. All the more reason to get there as soon as we can. Let's keep moving.

Allison takes a quick look down the road to the park, apparently still disturbed. I decide it might be wise to change the subject. I laugh and say: Maybe stuff like this happens in the Devil's Triangle. I remember a book by a guy who'd gotten sucked into it and somehow lived to tell about it. He said that none of the devices in his airplane worked once the Triangle sucked him in.

Did he say what it was like inside the Triangle?

He said it was like being inside a crumpled piece of paper.

While it was being crumpled?

Yeah.

I can see why most people never get out.

No kidding. But how do you like this gravel road? Driving on it sounds pretty cool, if you're going slow enough. Like hamburgers frying in a skillet.

I'd like to see that line used as a campaign slogan: Vote for Jack Bison! He's like the sound of hamburgers frying in a skillet!

If only we had the right kind of people coming up with campaign language, maybe the elections wouldn't be so boring.

And still, thousands of decent people like my cousin are out in shopping malls with clipboards and sign-up tables telling us to register to vote, reminding us that in lots of countries, people don't get to vote, not mentioning that in lots of countries, people have something worth voting for.

They do? Where? Give me an example.

Allison thinks for a few seconds, wrinkles her brow, then shrugs: Okay. Scratch that.

I feel sorry for your cousin. She's such a conscientious person. My nephew is pretty much the same. He's too young to be disillusioned by mainstream politics. He goes to rallies and protests and really believes that there are decent politicians out there, people with alternatives. A few months ago in Minneapolis, when the Jeff Toy protests got going, he and some of his friends set a police car on fire. A few seconds later, the cops brought out a Long Range Acoustic Device and a horrible, nauseating pain shot through his body. He didn't understand at first that he'd been assaulted by sound. His body went into panic mode. He told me it was like the sonic equivalent of looking too long at the sun. He later found out that others there had lost their hearing, just because they were challenging the police force and its homicidal violence.

Don't they call that the LRAD? It's chilling to think of the nasty technologies our tax dollars are financing.

That's why it's our moral duty to cheat on our taxes. If we had choices about what our tax dollars paid for—if we could check boxes on our 1040s to show that we wanted our money to fund universal healthcare, environmental projects, free education—then I wouldn't mind paying. But I have no intention of helping them pay for an LRAD.

The house comes back into view, and it's surrounded by trees of all kinds—poplars, evergreens, maples, oaks, hickories, elms, birches, aspens, yews, and willows—so many that the first three floors are almost invisible. Millions of leaves take the wind and make a lovely sound, surrounding the house with tranquility and color. Even if the house were collapsing, I'd want to live here. I'm surprised that the hurricane didn't do more damage, as it did almost everywhere else along the coast.

Allison, isn't it weird that there's almost no sign of destruction here, no windows destroyed or trees blown down?

Very weird. I'm wondering if there's some kind of force field that offered protection. I wonder if it's included in the sale price, or if they make you pay extra. I don't recall Ike Beer mentioning a force field. I wonder why. It would have been a huge selling point.

You really think so? You think people would have been pleased if Ike Beer mentioned a force field? Sure, a few people like us might have liked it. But most people would have thought he was crazy and stayed away. It would have been bad for business.

Right, but I'm not sure Ike Beer knows what's good or bad for business. Remember how he talked about our house. First he compares it to the White House, since both places have six floors if you count the basements. Then he laughs at his own comparison and says: "But don't get me wrong: this place ain't exactly the White House." What kind of salesman trashes his own merchandise? Especially after he tells you that he's never seen it.

Allison says: I'd take our house over the White House any day. The White House always looks so clean and tidy that you'd feel weird just hanging out, relaxing and being a slob. It's like one of those museums where they don't let you touch anything. In fact, I heard that Trap himself doesn't like it there, because they won't let him watch his porn. And they give him weird looks when he chomps down into his Oreos and leaves crumbs all over the carpeting. But I don't think we'll worry too much about trashing our place. Who cares if it's a mess? It's not like anyone can enforce regulations and punish us.

So it sounds like we're pretty sure we're going to buy it?

Yeah, but let's check it out really carefully this time, since we won't have to rush away to avoid a hurricane. I mean, sure, these trees are amazing. But let's not forget how hard it's been to get here, and there aren't any stores for miles around, and maybe no Internet or cell phone reception.

Is your phone working now?

She pushes buttons, lifts the phone up and moves it side to side, then says: Nothing! It was fine half an hour ago. Now there's no signal.

Fuck it! Let's just try to be here now, like that hippie philosopher said.

I keep moving slowly along the gravel, savoring the sound. We seem to be moving along a very wide arc, so after fifteen minutes we don't seem much closer. But the wind in the trees and crunching gravel combine to create a meditative effect. I'm glad I'm here with Allison. We've always liked doing strange things together, not consciously trying to find them, but keenly aware of the bizarre situations that seem to come out of nowhere.

Some of these situations are more than bizarre. Our meeting with the duplicate versions of ourselves an hour ago was a good example. I'm thinking now that they really weren't our doubles, not independent beings. They were us a few hours later, rushing back to find Ike Beer and buy our house, but since we haven't gotten there yet, they were out of synch and hadn't quite reached the point of full existence. They'd gotten ahead of themselves. When we finally decide to buy the house or not, we'll be doing what they were doing, but we'll be doing it on time, not ahead of time. When I saw them at first, I thought we were meeting our doubles. But doubles don't always have the same name or home or personality. I learned this when I first met Allison fifteen years ago.

We were at a party. Before I even knew her name, I was talking with her seductively, finding out that we had a lot in common, hoping that the night would end with sex. She excused herself for a trip to the john. I watched her cross the room and enter the bathroom. Just as the door closed behind her, I turned and found her standing right behind me. She looked at me with no recognition, as if we hadn't just been having a lively interaction. I picked up the conversation right where I thought we'd left off, and though she seemed confused at first, not following what I was saying, when the subject of life on other planets came up, she was eager to talk. It turned out she was a big fan of Area 51 conspiracy theories, more than just a fan, more like a believer, embracing UFOs with the zeal of a religious fanatic. Someone called out to her, using the name Maureen, then pointed to the back door, toward the backyard veranda. She took my arm and guided me outside, where people were watching the sky. The night was full of shooting stars. Maureen and I watched with amazement, inching closer to each other. She smelled like booze, though I couldn't tell what kind. Soon she was pulling me toward a bedroom, where we had sloppy mediocre sex and then made awkward conversation. The party's host came into the room and asked us what we were doing. Maureen got up and left without a word, clearly embarrassed. But the host, an old college friend of mine named Zach Fillmore, thought it was funny. He said two other couples had used his room that night for the same thing. He was thinking of posting a sign-up sheet.

About an hour later I saw her again, and I made a joke out of what had happened before. She looked confused. She said her name was Allison, not Maureen. I apologized for the mix-up. But I knew her name was Maureen an hour ago. We hit it off again, connecting just like before she'd gone to the john. But the sex with Maureen had been so awkward that I carefully kept my distance, even though the more we talked the more I suspected that she wasn't Maureen. I got her number before I left to go home.

Two nights later I gave her a call. I figured it was worth another try, that she might be better in bed when she wasn't so drunk. She was glad I called and invited me over.

Her place was a converted water mill, all brick and hard wood floors and large French windows, with a porch extending above a turbulent river. She bought it after she got a big royalty check for a book she'd written, an exercise manual teaching women how to flatten their bellies. The surging sound of the water made her bedroom seem to be floating.

Your name really isn't Maureen?

No. It's Allison. Why would I lie about my name?

When we met at the party, I could have sworn you said your name was Maureen. I called you Maureen several times on the veranda, watching the shooting stars, and later—

Shooting stars?

Yeah. On the backyard veranda. It was amazing. Were you too drunk to remember?

I wasn't drunk, and I wasn't on the veranda. I don't drink. It gives me headaches. I've always thought meteor showers are over-rated.

That wasn't you? You weren't with me in Zach's bed?

What? No way. You must have been with another woman. You must have been so drunk you thought it was me.

I don't drink.

It gives you headaches?

No. I just don't like the feeling. I get sluggish, stupid.

So you were sober? And you had sex in Zach's bed with someone—

I had sex in Zach's bed with you.

No. It didn't happen. I didn't have sex with you. But I'd like to now. You're cute when you're confused.

When we made love it wasn't anything like sex with Maureen. Allison was lithe and strong and forceful, while Maureen had expected me to do all the work.

Over the years, I've gotten so attuned to being with Allison that it's hard to believe I ever thought she was someone else. But now she's remarkably quiet, apparently entranced by the motions of all the trees we're surrounded by. I squeeze her hand and say: You remember that night we first met?

Sure. At Zachary Fillmore's party. What's he doing now?

I haven't been in touch with him in years. He became a Republican. But remember what happened that night?

Kind of. I remember we were hitting if off big time, and then I went to the bathroom, and you disappeared, and when I ran into you later, you seemed different. I was so glad when you got my number and called me a few days later, and the sex was just as good as I knew it would be. I remember thinking that as soon as we started talking, I wanted you to fuck me.

I wanted you to fuck me.

I'm not sure now if I should mention Maureen, since Allison hasn't mentioned it, maybe because she doesn't want to remember that part of the story. I decide to avoid it, since I know that sometimes Allison gets mad if I talk about other women, even if I'm clearly not interested in them. But now that I'm back in the memory, I'm convinced that Maureen was Allison's double. They were wearing the exact same outfit that night, a blue crop top that exposed a lot of midriff, revealing that both had nicely chiseled abs. I'm wondering if Maureen went on to sell fitness books and DVDs, the way Allison did. Or does Maureen feel strange when she sees copies of Allison's book in stores? It's possible that she doesn't spend time in bookstores, but it's likely that someone has pointed out that her double is on the cover of a popular book. It might be fun to get in touch with her at some point. Actually, it probably wouldn't. If Allison found out she'd get pissed off.

She has an anger problem. It doesn't take much to get her pissed off, and she takes it to extremes and seems to enjoy it. She's funny and articulate when she's mad, and she doesn't know when to stop. Five years ago, she was at my place when I got a call from a former girlfriend, who sounded and looked like a much younger version of Hillary Clinton. I recognized her number and didn't answer, but later when I was in the bathroom, Allison got my phone, played the message back and listened to my ex girlfriend saying she was horny and wanted sex.

As soon as I came out of the bathroom, Allison sneered: Was Meagan good in bed? Was she better than I am?

Meagan?

Allison held up my phone: Yeah, Meagan. She said she's horny. She wants your dick.

You played back my messages? That's kind of creepy.

Not as creepy as having an ex who calls you for sex.

How often does she call you? When was the last time she sat on your face?

She didn't like sitting on my face. That's one of the reasons we broke up.

Was she hot? Let me see a picture.

I don't—

Never mind, I'll find her on the Internet. What's her last name?

Mustang.

Meagan Mustang? Sounds like a stripper name.

Allison did a quick Internet search and found a picture, Meagan Mustang making a valedictorian speech at Yale University.

She looks like a younger version of Hillary Clinton.

Everyone always said so. But she hated Hillary Clinton.

You must have had sex with her thinking you were fucking Hillary Clinton.

No way! Not even once. Don't make me sick. I—

If she was good enough for Bill, she would have been good enough for you.

Not necessarily.

Necessarily.

Allison pushed me against the wall and I knew I should shut up and let her yell. But I thought she was being ridiculous and told her so, and things escalated quickly. She started throwing and breaking things, so I grabbed my phone called the police. But before they answered she ripped the phone out of my hand and ended the call.

You idiot! Don't ever call the police.

You're out of control—

So what? When you call the cops and they come to investigate, they always take someone down to the station. And guess which one of us they'll take? Hint: not me. It's always the guy.

About thirty seconds later, there was a knock at the door. A young cop walked in. I told him I'd called by mistake, but he looked around anyway. The place was trashed. The guy had to be thinking that something extreme had just happened. Allison looked at him with bedroom eyes and told him we'd been cleaning and some things had gotten broken.

He looked at Allison strangely. Then he said: Wait! Aren't you that famous exercise expert?

Allison smiled: That's me!

My wife has your book and two of your DVDs.

Really? How cool! How's she doing?

Great. She was overweight six months ago, but now she wears bikinis at the beach!

Wow! You'll have to send me a picture.

Sure will.

Then he winked at me and said: You're a lucky guy.

He apologized for interrupting our "housework," took down Allison's address and promised to send a picture, then left. We waited until we were sure he was gone. Then we burst out laughing. We couldn't stop, not until we had each other's clothes off. We haven't had a fight like that in years. I've learned how to practice damage control when I sense that a fight might start. I don't like being the one who always has to back down. But Allison is worth it. She's smart, funny, and good in bed.

Now she looks like she's getting pleasantly lost in the sound of wind and gravel. She says: We just have to keep following the gravel path. We'll get there at some point. And there's no reason to hurry, is there? It's really beautiful here!

It sure is. I wish I didn't have that rushed feeling in my body.

I think that's part of being alive in Century 21.

Maybe that's why no one buys this house. Driving here drives them crazy. It goes against the speedy feeling their bodies have learned to crave.

The trees keep sifting the wind, relaxing every cell

in my body. I put my hand on Allison's thigh and say: I can't wait to see what it's like to go to sleep here.

All that beautiful sound all night!

I mean, it's perfect for people like us. There's so much great stuff you can't include in a real estate listing, or else you'll freak out potential buyers. So without the weird things, the house just sounds like it's falling apart in a remote location, with no smart phone service. No one wants that, so the price goes down. Then people like us come along and we've got a great deal. Ike Beer makes a commision, even if it's less than what he gets when he sells a subdivision house. So everybody wins. Wouldn't that be a great campaign slogan? Jack Bison for President! Everybody wins!

Allison shakes her head fiercely: The competitive types would hate it. They're not okay unless they're beating someone, unless somebody's losing. If everybody wins, it goes against the economic logic people like Trap depend on, Jack Bison too. The U.S. economy runs on feeding the war machine. This country can't be number one unless bombs are dropping on countries that can't fight back.

Remember that rally in Tulsa back in June, with all the empty seats driving Trap crazy? He can't stand empty seats. It makes him think that people don't love him. He blamed the TikTok people for trashing him online, then tried to ban TikTok. Meanwhile, the rally takes place on Juneteenth, which celebrates the official end of slavery, and in the rally speech he doesn't even mention it. He ignores the fact that everyone in the nation is horrified by the racist violence of the police, the death of Jeff Toy in Minneapolis, yet he refers to the protest movement as a mob of left-wing terrorists, never mentions that the largest racist massacre in U.S. history took place just a few neighborhoods away from the site of the rally, and talks instead about the importance of supporting the Military Industrial Complex, concluding that the defense industry can't sell bombs unless we're dropping them on people. No need for supply without the demand. No demand? No problem: we'll create one.

Translation: Money equals murder.

Jack Bison won't be any different.

If you don't want to bomb other countries, the job of U.S. President isn't for you. After all, when you sit at the Oval Office desk, you smile like a nice guy when your picture gets taken, but you're still the bomber in chief. You're killing people all over the world.

Allison takes a deep breath and says: The last time I was drunk, maybe two years before we met at Zach's party, I went to bed with two guys who had jobs in the Pentagon. And they kept raving about gadgets of mass destruction, tiny machines that could blow up whole nations in less than a second, how we needed things like that if we wanted to stay on top, if we wanted to preserve our democratric freedoms, or some shit like that.

I look at her in disbelief: I know you can't stand military types. Why were you going to bed with them?

I was really drunk. After that night, I swore off booze. I've been sober ever since.

So you did them both at the same time? A threesome? You were part of a Devil's Triangle? It's supposed to be bad luck.

I know. Like I said, I was really drunk. And they both kept insisting that everything was cool, since Devil's Triangle threesomes were pefectly okay if the two guys never made sustained eye contact.

Eye contact was a problem?

I think eye contact would have meant that the guys had a gay connection.

So you were there to make it seem that they weren't really gay?

I guess.

Who cares if they were gay?

The Pentagon, for starters.

This doesn't sound like you at all. You must have been *really* drunk.

It gets worse. The guys were identical twins. I couldn't tell them apart.

Devil's Triangle incest?

More or less. I'd rather be in the actual Devil's Triangle, even if I never came back, than spend another night like that.

She takes a deep breath and I know it's time to stop talking again, time to let silence do its job, give her time to sweep the Pentagon's underbelly back under the rug. It's another good reason to separate ourselves from the coming election.

The arc of the gravel driveway goes on and on. It's an exercise in patience and humility. You can't rush to get home here. You can't plan to be home by a scheduled time. Speed won't help you get there any sooner. Late and soon become dated concepts, relics of an obsolete way of life. You can't shape your future with intentions and ambitions. You just have to let things happen. If you try to sort things out you make a mess.

Finally we're pulling up in front of a huge wraparound porch and an old wooden staircase. We leave the car and go inside, hoping it feels better than it did before. It doesn't. Something about the place still feels wrong. It's obvious right away, though again it's not obvious what the problem is. There are people who cleanse or purify haunted houses, like Allison's sister. You can even buy a book and do it yourself. But I don't think the problem has much to do with ghosts or ancient curses. I see no signs of cult or drug activity. I sit on the dusty piano bench and put my hands on the keyboard. I bang out a few notes, but the keys turn to powder under my fingers. I jerk my hands back and jam them in my pockets.

I catch my blurred reflection in the glass of the grandfather clock. I notice something I didn't see the first time we were here. There's a face carved into the clockface, a woman whose eyes are looking right through my head, apparently troubled by something she can see in the mullion window behind me. I turn but at first there's nothing to see, just bending trees in the wind. But then there's a blue car in the distance. It's too far to know for sure, but it looks like it might be our Mirage, moving slowly down a dirt road, trying to find our future home. The car stops near the park where we saw the huge guy on the throne. Then it backs up and turns and disappears into the mass of trees.

I'm thinking it's us in the car, but the thought collapses, unable to sustain its own absurdity, as if I were slipping into Brain Fog, a mental blur that doesn't resolve itself, sometimes seen as a Covid-19 symptom, sometimes seen as the result of over-exposure to media bullshit. Both possibilities are disturbing. But with Covid, vaccines will no doubt soon be available. The same thing can't be said about the information sickness everyone suffers from. It's a metastatic condition, but thinking about it leads me to something else, an idea which makes a grand appearance, accompanied by a silent flourish of trumpets. Suddenly I'm convinced that the people who lived here before filled the house with noise—ads and TV shows and big-hit radio. It's what everyone does these days. It's what everyone has been doing for decades, and can't stop doing, eagerly subjecting themselves to Media Poisoning. I've never heard that exact term before, but I'm sure if I looked on the Internet I'd find it more than once. At some point, the name for it was Terminal Stale Entertainment Trauma, or TEST. Then someone pointed out that the acronym was wrong. It should been TSET, which wouldn't have sounded nearly as cool as TEST, since it wasn't a pun. I'm not sure if people still say TEST when they mean Information Sickness. Either way, it might begin to explain what's wrong with the house.

But the view out the back toward the sea explodes with power. The French windows take up the entire back wall. I remember Ike Beer saying that a realtor friend who'd actually seen the house raved about the huge French windows on every floor. They're dusty and cracked and probably just as old as the rest of the house, but they're strong enough to have faced Hurricane Ahab without shattering. The waves crashing into the cliffs burst upward hundreds of feet before dropping back, refracting the fading light seeping through dense layers of cumulonimbus clouds. The cold wind makes a wild but comforting noise in the trees all around us. We lie down on a large couch that has to be more than a hundred years old. But somehow it's in good shape. The pillows are soft but firm and supportive, as if they were specially made for people who fuck five times a day.

I say: There's still something wrong here.

It's like it's still someone else's house, even though it's empty.

We need to fuck the bad out, whatever it is.

Let's do it.

Things heat up fast and soon we're driving each other crazy, pleasuring each other in ways we've developed over the years, games that we didn't learn from x-rated movies and magazines. Our passion is lifting us out of the room, over the waves, toward the place where the eye of the hurricane was, an eye that's learned to see, so well in fact that now it has spherical vision. We can see the sun going down behind the Golden Gate Bridge. We can see the moon at midnight pressing down on the Great Wall of China. We can see emperor penguins waddling toward the coast of Antarctica. We can see bears catching fish in waterfalls on Kodiak Island. We come together perfectly, then hold each other as if there were nothing else in the world.

Allison finally says: That was the best sex we've ever had.

No question about it. And we did it under pressure, which made it more difficult. The stakes were high. If we failed, the ghosts of TEST would have filled the house with deadly noise. We wouldn't have had the normal ghost noises. In the middle of the night, we would have heard laugh tracks and jingles and football announcers.

Our words fade into something like sleep, but slightly more conscious. We can feel each other's flesh, warm and moist and familiar, shadows and sunshine gliding over the floorboards. The sounds of the sea are woven into the sounds of wind in the trees. It feels like years are passing, though it's really no more than an hour. Then Allison's lips are on mine and we're wide awake, deeply refreshed.

We get up and wander from room to room with no clothes on. The rooms feel like they've been fiercely fucked and now they're all relaxing, exactly the way a home should feel if you're serious about buying it. The stale and creepy feeling isn't entirely gone, but it's fading, replaced by the sound of the trees and waves. If the problem was media poisoning, it's been driven back by our passion. We'll no doubt have to make love several times each day to complete the process. But it's great to think of fucking as a way of saving the house. If I had any doubts about buying this place before, I don't anymore.

I say: I think we should fuck in every room.

How many rooms are there?

I don't remember.

Ike Beer didn't say in the listing?

No. Remember? The only description was: "House for Sale. Great Location! Needs lots of TLC."

TLC? I don't think so. TLC sounds like work. Why buy a house when it makes you work?

I scratch my head: Some people like working on a house.

I'd rather live in it. If you can't, you should buy something else.

It doesn't matter. The main thing to consider when buying a house is the feeling it gives you. We both knew something was wrong before. But now things feel much better. I'll take RGS over TLC any day.

RGS?

Really Good Sex. We're living in the Age of Acronyms.

Allision grips my arm and says: Let's be exact: How many more acronyms are in circulation today than there were twenty years ago.

We can just ask Siri.

We can't, remember? There's no cell phone reception, no Internet. I think when we had reception about an hour ago, it came from that Starbucks that might or might not exist. I wouldn't want to go near that place again, except in a life or death situation.

Cool, no problem. If we never ask Siri again, we won't be missing anything. I hate the way everyone Googles everything all the time, like nothing matters more than to know as many things as you can that you don't really care about. I mean, do you really care that Scriabin died because he cut himself while shaving?

She laughs: I love his music. I don't care about the details of his life. Or death.

I don't either. But now that we're on the subject, his music sounds like it could only have been composed in a place like this.

Right: the way it is now. Not the way it was before we fucked. Can you believe it? You've got a house that would normally be filled with the most beautiful sounds that nature can make, but you block them out with media noise.

Has anyone ever had good sex in the same room with TV commercials? No way. The two things can't exist in the same space.

It's true. Scriabin's music sounds like it was composed by someone who was never exposed to a TV ad. American mass advertising was pretty much the idiot child of the roaring twenties. How much great classical music was composed after that?

When John Cage tried to do it he ended up composing four minutes of silence. Milton Babbitt ended up writing an essay called "Who Cares If You Listen?"

Allison grips my arm again: Wait! I just thought of something. Does this place have plumbing? Electricity?

I peed when we were here a few days ago, and the toilet worked. I washed my hands in a sink. It was in bad shape but it had those old porcelain faucet handles, and when I turned them water came out. It was brown at first but when I let it run for ten seconds it looked okay.

Allison nods: Just looking around the room, I don't see lamps or outlets. But the people who lived here before must have had electricity. Otherwise, they wouldn't have been able to watch TV and play bad music. Maybe some rogue electrician came after the people were gone and removed all the outlets, then sold them online. In fact, I can see places above the floorboards that look plastered over, like someone covered something up.

I shrug: So maybe we'll just have to get used to living without electricity. Or pay a non-rogue electrician to make things work.

That might get expensive. We might be better off getting lots of candles.

Either that, or we can go to sleep when the sun goes down and wake up when the sun comes up. We can readjust ourselves to natural cycles.

But in the Winter we'll be going to bed in the late afternoon.

I laugh: No problem, right? We'll have more time for sex.

Yeah, that's true. Okay then!

No electricity, no media poisoning. Just nature and long nights of sex in a place that feels like Scriabin's music. Sounds perfect! Let's call Ike Beer and sign on the dotted line.

We can't. Remember? There's no phone reception. Besides, what's the hurry?

I say: I'm just nervous that he might sell the place to someone else before we make a deposit. That happened to my brother. He found a great house he liked, told the realtor that he wanted it, then played a round of golf because he'd been invited by his boss, so he couldn't afford to offend him by cancelling, and by the time he reached the 18th hole, his dream house had been sold to someone else, who ended up tearing the place down and using the land to build a miniature golf course.

Ike Beer won't sell it. Remember? He doesn't have the listing. The house exists only on the folded piece of paper, and it's not in his shirt pocket anymore; it's in mine, or rather in yours.

I look around the room and smile: It's like we've got our own territory now. We can set up a micronation.

My favorite micronation is Elgaland-Vargaland, the one that exists between all borders.

Between all borders? How does that work?

Between nations, between people, between waking and sleeping, between good moods and bad moods, between the number one and the number two and the number three, all the way to infinity, between all states of mind. Whenever you cross a border, you're in Elgaland-Vargaland. Whenever you change your mind, you're in Elgaland-Vargaland. It's almost as if you're never not there.

Maybe we can stipulate that our nation exists everywhere that you can't go online.

We could call it Offline.

We can take turns being the Offline President every other day.

Allison tries to sound authoritarian: Our consistution will only have one sentence, a sentence that changes every day, a consitution that never gets old and has no stable content.

Great. But before we set up a conceptual framework, shouldn't we look at the rest of the house? We've got four more floors, plus the basement.

Maybe we only need one room, this room. Dealing with all the other ones would only complicate things.

But both of us enjoy privacy, so we should see what's above us.

Allison shrugs: We already know.

We do?

Yeah. We know that all five floors have huge French windows facing the sea.

I nod, slightly confused: Right. But that's only on one side of the house. What will we see from the other side?

Everything else.

What if we don't like it? What if the view is just endless subdivisions and shopping malls, a gigantic TV zone?

Allison shudders: Good question. I guess we better check.

We walk across the room to the old wooden staircase. We start to go upstairs but stop, confronted by a wolf on the staircase landing, watching us so calmly that she almost isn't there, not moving even slightly, ice-blue silence in her eyes. Her stillness prevents us from moving or speaking, like we're flat as a page with incomprehensible pictures, taken from the kind of book you might find in a small town thrift shop.

The wolf yawns and sniffs the air and goes upstairs. I can hear her graceful feet on the second floor, moving down a corridor, then up another set of stairs, moving down another corridor. The whole house seems to relax. We look at each other stunned.

Allison says: Well, I guess that answers our question.

What question?

About the rooms upstairs. It looks like at least one of them is already occupied. I wonder if Ike Beer has any idea.

I doubt it. Didn't he tell us that he's never been here?

Yeah. But his realtor friend might have told him.

Whatever.

Allison smiles: I think it's pretty cool. What a beautiful creature!

You're okay buying a house that we'll have to share with at least one wolf?

She gives me the sexy look and says: Why not? Even if the upper floors are already occupied and we've only got one floor, the place is still a great buy. And besides, can you think of a better roommate?

LIKE PANTS

It sounded like the sky was being ripped open. I woke and stared out the window, expecting disaster, pillars of fire descending from the heavens, buildings knocked flat by the sonic blast, rubble and garbage everywhere, like in a Ground Zero picture of Hiroshima. But everything looked normal, a cloudless afternoon in late December. People were shopping and walking their dogs and sitting and talking in small cafes. I told myself there was nothing to worry about. I could just fall back to sleep.

Instead I turned on my computer. There was news. A hundred feet off the northern coast of Ellesmere Island, only five hundred miles due south of the North Pole, a new rock formation stood like an old pair of pants, towering two hundred feet above an icy beach. A guy in a kayak had seen it first. He'd lived in the region all his life, knew the northern coast of Ellesmere Island better than his own name, yet he'd never seen the huge rock before. He'd paddled home to the town of Awake and told the police, then guided them back to the spot. The pictures they took were now showing up on the Internet.

At first people thought it had to be a joke, a photoshopped image. But the people who took the pictures, the police in the northernmost town in the world, weren't big on trick photography. They weren't part of the social media scene and had no reason to send fake images. The sandstone rock formation had to be real, even though its resemblance to a pair of upright pants was enough to make anyone laugh. It was hard to believe that something so huge could be so ridiculous, hard to believe that no one in the world had seen it before.

But everyone in the world had heard the violent sound in the sky. Some said it was like a page the size of a soccer field getting torn, or a zipper the length of a mountain range closing and opening, a window as large as New Mexico getting smashed, or a perfect strike in a bowling alley for giants. No one could explain it. Why had such a massive sound come out of the sky? Why was reality still so apparently normal, unaffected? Could things of great magnitude happen without changing anything?

The Awake police chief thought the giant pants might be the answer. Maybe the sound had been made by a new geological form popping into existence. The effort of something that wasn't there to make itself into something that was, taking up space that a second before had been empty, had made a colossal noise that stunned the world, but somehow left it mostly the same as it was.

Experts were quick to make fun of this idea, pointing out that rock formations took shape over milennia, created by shifts in the earth's crust, by the motions of glaciers, sculpted by water and wind, by erosion and sedimentation. Such things didn't just pop into existence. The towering rock had probably been there for millions of years, but hadn't been seen before because there was no one there to see it, and also because it had always been surrounded by mountains of snow and towering icebergs, which had recently melted because of rising temperatures, exposing the largest pants in the world. Yes, the shape was odd, but this didn't mean it was incomprehensible, supernatural, or part of some sinister process or plan.

But many people still wanted to think that the sound and the rocks were connected. Speculation continued for weeks, taking attention away from everything else. Everyone was talking about the Qarlinngua, an Inuit word that meant "like pants." In Arctic City, the nearest place with a population of more than 500, local companies were planning guided tours, Arctic Ocean adventures, journeys to the last mysterious place on the planet. Virtual brochures were being designed, online videos, the Qarlinngua juxtaposed with polar bears and the northern lights.

The lame duck U.S. president was furious. He'd just lost the 2020 election, and he was loudly claiming that the results were fraudulent. He didn't want a huge pair of pants near the North Pole stealing the spotlight. So he acted like he was mad that yet another wonder of the world would soon be reduced to a tourist attraction. He claimed to be indignant that a monstrous noise in the sky had not been identified and addressed, since after all it might pose a grave threat to national security, a sign of dangerous plans by a foreign government. He wanted the Space Wars program to mobilize, even though at this point it only existed on paper. He wanted to start bombing terrorist countries, even though they were all being bombed already. He wanted all Russian hackers sent to Siberia, even though they'd supposedly made him the president four years before. He wanted to send troops to the Chinese border, keeping new forms of the "Chinese Virus" from spreading, even though guns were useless against microcellular creatures, even though vaccines were becoming available, and the dangers of Covid-19 would soon be reduced. Most of all he wanted as much attention as he could get. He wanted everyone to think that millions of fake votes had been cast. His followers were preparing to make things difficult. They were painting their faces and getting tattoos and wearing Viking helmets. He was urging them to get violent.

I'd just gotten over a bout with Covid myself. I'd spent days in bed, scared that I might be dying. I'd always been a healthy person—never had any smoking or drinking or blood pressure problems—so I figured I'd survive, but even for survivors Covid-19 can be a traumatic event. I was disgusted by the lame duck president's talk of the "Chinese virus," his use of recent events to make sure people were focused on him. Now that he'd lost the election but seemed prepared to make serious trouble, I wanted him gone—before he could do more damage.

I thought of my former girlfriend Becky Burger. I hadn't talked to her in two years, but she came to mind right then for three reasons. First, she was one of North America's foremost cognitive scientists. Second, she knew a guy who knew a guy who knew a guy, the last guy being the White House Chief of Staff. Third, her current boyfriend, the weirdo she'd hooked up with right after we split, was a full-time computer whiz and part-time cybercriminal. It all came together in my head on New Year's Eve, a day I can't stand. I hate all the noise people make, the scripted celebrations, as if a new year of the human race was worth all the loud excitement. So I spent the night in my private room, my sound-proofed meditation chamber, which was filled with tropical fishtanks and MC Escher posters. A few hours into a very peaceful night, protected from the nonsense going on outside, I made a plan, and I called Becky up the next day.

Becky Burger knew all about the brain, and her boyfriend, who called himself Haiku Style, was like a cybertage encyclopedia. I told Becky that I wanted the lame duck president gone, dead or at the very least kept off stage.

She laughed: Really? Why now? He lost the election. He'll be gone in less than three weeks.

I said: He won't really be gone. You can see that he can't accept defeat. He'll try to incite riots, waste people's time with election audits in the swing states that went against him. Millions of people will do what he tells them to do. There's no telling how much damage he's capable of. It'd be one thing if he was a principled revolutionary. But we all know that he's just a silver-spoon asshole, an overgrown toddler who throws a fit if he doesn't get what he wants.

She laughed: So get a gun and put a bullet through his head.

I laughed: I don't want to spend the rest of my life behind bars.

OK. But why tell *me* about it?

You remember that Beatles Song, "All You Need Is Love"? Well, it should have been "All You Need Is Food." I just figured it out last night in the meditation chamber. Food is a basic necessity; love isn't. Food will get you through times without love a lot better than love will get you through times without food.

There was a long pause, then Becky started laughing: Yeah, you're right. "All You Need Is Food" would have sounded absurd as a popular song refrain, and it wouldn't have sold as well, but it would have been true, not just another top-40 sweet-nothing.

So what would happen if we installed a modified version of the song in the lame duck president's brain and had it play over and over again?

So he just kept hearing "All You Need Is Food" non-stop?

Yeah.

He'd have what's called an Earworm, which would

burrow into his brain and slowly consume it—no pun intended—becoming an essential component of his mental processes, indistinguishable from his own thoughts, and soon replacing them. He'd remember the original version, "All You Need Is Love," a song his brain was conditioned to enjoy back in the late sixties, so he'd be receptive when he first heard the familiar melody. Then the slight but significant change in the lyrics would make him wonder, might even make him mad. But he'd hear the new message repeating itself throughout his waking hours, and even in his sleep. Slowly "all you need is food" would become an important ingredient in the neurochemical soup that tells him who he is and what he should do.

Would it change his behavior?

Becky paused: He's a hard case. But yes, in theory at least.

So here's part two of my plan. Get Haiku Style to make a device or write a program, something to invade the lame duck president's brain. I have no idea how it would work, but Haiku Style is good at that kind of stuff, isn't he?

The best. No question about it. So good that he's dangerous. But I'm just about to break up with him. I made a New Year's resolution.

Break up with him? I thought you thought he was a really cool guy.

He's not in love with me; he's in love with my boobs.

Isn't everyone?

Sure. But with you I could tell that you knew I was more than just a good set of tits. You seemed to like my intelligence, even if it made you feel stupid. You supported my scientific ambitions. You enjoyed my success. But Haiku Style is so obsessed with my chest that he doesn't care about my professional life. In his mind, all you need is boobs. I'm totally sick of him.

Totally? Or do you still think he's weirdly sexy, the phrase you used when you started going out with him, right after we broke up.

It's hard to be in love with anyone who's got such rigid communication rules. I never told you about this? According to Haiku Style, any sentence longer than ten words is self-indulgent. He's always insisting that if you can't say something in ten words or less, you haven't thought about it long enough to make it worth saying.

So that's how he got the name Haiku Style?

Yeah. It's a *nom de guerre.*

What's his real name?

Pete Moth.

Pete Moth? Not Pete Moss?

It used to be Pete Moss, but everyone joked about it, so he came up with Pete Moth, which almost sounds like the same name, but has different connotations, moonlit flight instead of soil enrichment. He thought it would make a big difference, but people kept making the same joke, so he started avoiding social interactions. A few years before he met me, he stopped having person-to-person contact with everyone. He became a Nevermeet. All communication was virtual. He met lots of women online and had virtual sex with them. He made himself look amazing on his website, knowing what he knows about photoshopping. He wrote what he called "The Nevermeet Manifesto," claiming that the elimination of face-to-face interaction was a way to neutralize one of the world's most unfair situations, the advantage glamorous people have over people who aren't conventionally attractive, since after all on the Internet you can make yourself look perfect. It was badly written, but "The Nevermeet Manifesto" got millions of likes. People all over the world felt free in ways they'd never felt before. More and more people became Nervermeets, avoiding physical sex. There was more and more virtual sex taking place and a lot of it was insanely inventive. All sorts of erotic scenarios got created, vividly enhanced by cybertechniques, and Haiku Style was everyone's online sex guru.

So how did you manage to coax him offline?

A friend of mine told me about him, and I was missing you at the time, so I went to his website, forced myself to read the Nevermeet Manifesto, then issued a challenge. I claimed that if he met me offline, the sex would be better than anything he could find online.

That was bold! How could real sex measure up to fantasy sex? They're not the same thing. It's an apples and oranges comparison.

I was figuring that he'd still have some residual interest in the physical feeling of skin, the pleasure of fondling breasts like mine. The brain is hardwired to want and respond to organic three-dimensional flesh, and virtual sex can't provide that, not yet at least. I knew that when Haiku Style started feeling me up, he'd be over the moon.

And was he? Was the sex uncontrollably exciting? More exciting than his Nevermeet extravaganzas?

He admitted it freely. He said my breasts drove him crazy.

I know you liked him at first. But if he'd been doing sex exclusively online before he met you, wasn't he awkward at first with physical sex? Could he really perform?

He was flabby and inept. But that left me in charge. I ran the show. I've always liked being on top, as you already know, and with him I was on top all the time, playing with him like a sex toy. I didn't care if he was a wimp. He was perfect for me, and he could tell that he was doing something right by doing nothing, which helped him relax, since he didn't have to force himself to perform like a superstud in bed, with a great body, designer techniques, and loads of physical confidence.

But it sounds like you've had problems right from the start. Those problems weren't in the sack?

Right. Not in the sack.

So...

So when we met offline he was already Haiku Style, an established Nevermeet celebrity, and he'd developed his rigid rules for verbal communication. Millions of Nevermeet followers adhered to his procedures.

And you assumed he would be loose about his word-limit rule when he talked offline with you?

I took it as a joke. It's not. I figured I could change him. I couldn't.

What happens if you string together a long sequence

of short sentences? You'll get to talk a lot, but you won't be going beyond the ten-word restriction.

You only get one sentence at a time. Then you have to pause and let him speak.

So if I were talking to him, he wouldn't allow me to say "It's windy and cold outside. It's also dark and raining hard," eleven words. I'd have to say "It's windy and cold outside," pause to let him respond, then say "It's also dark and raining hard"?

Yeah.

Are there punishments for long sentences?

Online, he blocks your account. Offline, he pretends to fall asleep when you're under the sheets with him.

So you're fed up. It's time to break up with him. But you can wait until he's done the job I want him to do, can't you?

Sure, but why don't you just talk with him directly? That way I can finish things off right now and I won't have to put up with his weird conversation rules again.

He hates my guts, remember? You made the mistake of telling him that you liked me better in bed. Besides, at this point you've had lots of experience with ten-word sentences. You know how to handle yourself in Haiku Style's communication bubble. I know you can't stand it any longer, but I'm sure you can do it just one more time. And anyway, you're the one who can get us into the Oval Office. You know a guy who knows a guy who knows a guy, don't you? The White House chief of staff, or whatever they call him?

Yeah.

And when you actually meet the lame duck president, you'll take him by surprise. Based on your credentials, he'll be expecting a scientific type, a severe woman with short hair and wire-rimmed glasses, too tense and abstracted for sensual pleasures of any kind. But instead he'll get a sexy woman whose boobs will drive him crazy. He'll assume he can have his way with you. He won't suspect that we're having our way with him.

This all sounds really sleazy.

It's a meaningful action. We're doing it to restore the health of the nation.

Restore? Was our nation ever healthy, except in patriotic fantasies?

Of course not. But you know what I mean. Slightly healthier than it is now. More or less.

Okay, I'll do it. But under one condition: You have to have sex with me for a week if I get the job done. You have to do all the kinky stuff with me that we used to do.

Sounds good.

It did sound good. The sex with Becky Burger had always been great. Our problems weren't in the bedroom. They were everywhere else. Like so many people in so-called committed relationships, we had the same nasty arguments over and over again, even though we could see them coming a mile away, and knew in advance that nothing would be resolved. Besides, I was too much of a slob, and it drove her crazy. She finally said we should live in different places. That's when Haiku Style showed up, more than neat enough for Becky Burger or anyone else. He spit-shined the hardwood floors in his place every day without using a buffer, working on his hands and knees with a rag and a tin of floor wax. Back in the days when he still saw people in person, no one could walk on his floors without seeing themselves beneath their own feet.

I couldn't come close to that and I didn't want to. But now I would have the guy who replaced me working for me without knowing it. I got off the phone with Becky Burger feeling triumphant. We had a plan that sounded flawless. We'd be getting away with murder!

But things weren't quite that simple. A few days later, a lightning bolt fell from a clear sky, not a cloud in sight. It hit a guy in the foot, made his body glow like a neon sign, filled his brain with the sound of hamburgers frying in a skillet. He collapsed on the street, convulsing, and five days later he woke in a hospital bed feeling like a new person, remembering things he'd never done, places he'd never been. When he looked at himself in the mirror, he saw someone else, the mayor of a town on the Arctic Ocean. The doctors were baffled. The guy correctly mentioned all sorts of details about a hamlet called Awake, though people who knew him said he'd never been anywhere near the Arctic Circle. The doctors decided they needed advice from an expert, so they contacted Becky Burger, and after a long interview with the man, she came away bewildered, despite her exhaustive knowledge of how the brain works. For the next few days she got in touch with colleagues, exchanging long emails about the baffling case. They were just as confused as she was. She finally got in touch with me.

She sounded shocked on the phone: You know me. I like to think I understand the brain as well as it can be understood. But this guy is beyond everything I know. His name is Rex Torpedo, but he calls himself Lex Luthor, the mayor of Awake, the northernmost town in the world.

Lex Luthor? From Superman comics? The guy who

lost his hair when Superman saved him from burning alive?

I've never read Superman comics, but—

Lex Luthor was Superman's arch nemesis, a brilliant but evil scientist. He was furious that Superman made him bald for the rest of his life, even though Lex Luthor would have been fried if the Man of Steel hadn't saved him.

I didn't know that. But when I asked him about his intellectual interests, he said that DC comics were the only thing worth reading. Anyway, Rex Torpedo claimed he'd led an expedition out of Awake a few years ago, before he became the mayor. Apparently they got lost in a brutal snowstorm and had to pitch tents in a cave that provided partial shelter. When he and his team woke the next morning, the storm was gone, the skies were clear, and it turned out they were only about a hundred feet from a rocky beach on the Arctic Ocean. And right there in front of them was a sandstone rock formation that looked like a huge pair of pants. They could tell right away that it had to be hundreds of feet tall.

Maybe Rex Torpedo heard about the Qarlinngua on the news and worked it into an Arctic fantasy after he got hit by lightning. His mind was scrambled, so he tried to piece things together with memories and things in the news and—

That's what I thought at first. But he also said that words were inscribed on the rock, a new detail about the Qarlinngua, something that hasn't appeared on TV or the Internet yet, a phrase that his Inuit guides were able to translate: "Something is always missing." But Rex Torpedo was skeptical, knowing that his guides were uncertain, since the phrase was in an archaic dialect no one speaks anymore.

I tried not to laugh, but I couldn't help saying: I'm always annoyed when experts insist that nothing translated from an archaic language is ever more than a rough approximation. Then why bother at all? Approximations are dangerous, since they end up being taken as the truth. Nothing is more deceptive than the truth, as someone I can't remember used to say.

Becky Burger sounded annoyed: You're too quick to dismiss the rough approximations we're forced to work with. The mind is a translation machine, and any version of reality we produce will have the limitations of a translation. Our modern descriptions of the world are always approximations, no matter how carefully they're developed and tested.

Sure, but if you're starting with an archaic dialect,

you're at least one step further into uncertainty than if you're working with modern words and phrases. Right? I mean—

You haven't changed, Becky said. You've always known how to sound a lot more intelligent than you really are.

Fuck you.

Fuck you.

We both started laughing. I knew that the week of sex we were planning would be incredible, and I also knew that a week was all we could stand. Once we'd been around each other for a few days, we always started getting on each other's nerves, and we couldn't get away from each other too soon.

The Rex Torpedo story soon went viral. Everyone was talking about it, learning as much as they could about people hit by lightning. There were hundreds of examples. One guy who got hit woke up the next day with a new tattoo, a lightning bolt in a fractal pattern running from his neck all the way to his crotch. It looked like it might be a calligraphic symbol, but linguists who studied pictures of it quickly got too dizzy to say what it meant, or might have meant.

Another guy was fishing in northern Maine when a lightning bolt hit him. A minute later a bear showed up and stole the fish he'd caught. But later, when the man was attacked by wolves, the bear showed up and protected him, then led him to the safety of a ranger station. The same thing happened at exactly the same time to someone who lived in the Yukon, almost four thousand miles away. Both men were sure that the bear who stole their fish was the same bear that saved their lives, since in both cases the bear was missing an ear, a rare condition among black bears.

Two twenty year olds were making love in a forest when they got hit. Their sexual prowess increased a great deal after that. Before too long they were doing only threesomes, designing a website made to attract third partners. They called themselves the Twins of Sudden Lightning, and even though some wise guy tweeted that all lightning is sudden, that the adjective was redundant, they were getting lots of likes and glowing reviews all over the Internet. People started calling them TwentyTwenty.

Lightning struck a minor league shortstop in the seventh inning of a game they were losing 3-0. He was dazed but stayed in the game and he hit a grand slam in the last of the ninth, the first home run of his career. After that, he retired and started reading *Finnegans Wake*, one page a day, one phrase a day, one word or syllable a day, developing new interpetive models that made the book more accessible to the so-called common reader. More than eighty years after it first came out, it became a best seller, though it took much longer to read than the average novel.

An out of work reference librarian in Dover, Delaware got split in half by lightning and became twin versions of herself. One of them opened a yoga studio; the other became a crack dealer in Casper, Wyoming. They saw no reason to stay in touch with each other.

And now Rex Torpedo was becoming famous, a name coming up in millions of conversations all over the world. Everyone knew his face, the electrified smile and gleaming teeth, more charismatic than Che on the famous poster, more diabolic than the Charles Manson photo from *Life* magazine. Tabloid pictures and articles made him a superstar, but even the mainstream media followed him carefully.

The lame duck president hated it. Again, he wasn't getting enough attention. No one was even mentioning fake mail-in votes anymore. His attorney general, Bill Barf, had resigned in disgust, calling the president's tweets about election fraud a bunch of bullshit. Trap responded by throwing a plate of food against an Oval Office wall, covering Gilbert Stuart's iconic portrait of

George Washington with sausage pizza. He waited for someone else to clean things up, but everyone acted like nothing was wrong, probably because they were all sick and tired of his self-indulgent rages. The pizza remained for several days, pissing him off even more. In deep frustration, he came up with a plan, telling his aides to do research on people hit by lightning, finding out the best ways to make it happen. He figured it was the only way to compete with Rex Torpedo, come up with a better story, better photo ops and sound bites, maybe a magazine cover showing him getting hit by a bolt from the blue. I was surprised. In the past when the lame duck president wanted something, he just made things up. He generated fake news. Why wouldn't he do the same thing now? Why was he now insisting on the real thing? Had his loss in the recent election made his lies sound less authentic? Or was the public hungry for a new sensation, someone like Rex Torpedo, a total unknown a few weeks before?

I was in my favorite dive bar when I saw him in action for the first time, on an afternoon talk show. Aside from the manic smile and sizzling teeth, he looked like a panda with glasses, nothing at all like a weapon fired by a submarine.

The host of the show, a woman who'd become famous because she always wore a zoot suit and a fedora, asked Rex what life was like in Awake, the northernmost town in the world.

He said: It's all dive bars in quonset huts, polar bears and icebergs. We get the northern lights eight months out of the year. We spend most of our time outside on our backs, warm in sleeping bags we've made ourselves, watching the best light show on the planet. Once in a while a polar bear comes and someone gets devoured, but other than that the aurora borealis is more than amazing. The other four months, when the sun is out all the time, we stay inside, get drunk, and watch the Film Noir Channel. It's the only station you can get from the North Pole. Of course, we used to feel stupid watching noir in a tacky modular bar with linoleum floors and fluorescent lighting. So I raised local taxes and used the extra money to make the bar look totally different, just like the bars you see in film noir movies. The Noir Bar. Great name, right?

The host giggled: So your favorite bar in Awake looks just like a bar on a Hollywood film set? A simulation of a simulation?

I guess you could say that.

The studio audience laughed.

Why did you decide to become the Mayor? Did you have to campaign?

No one else wanted the job. I got it by default. The previous Mayor knocked on my door one day and told me that I was the Mayor. I didn't say no.

The studio audience laughed and laughed.

What things do you have to do as the Mayor?

Not much of anything. You sharpen lots of pencils and answer occasional phone calls, most of them from people who've got the wrong number. I get calls from Savannah, calls from Texarkana. I get calls from Missoula, calls from Chattanooga.

The studio audience laughed and laughed and laughed.

What was it like to wake up and see the Qarlinngua?

No one could believe it. We all thought we were losing our minds. But twenty people don't lose their minds all at once, in exactly the same way. We just stared at the thing for a while. Someone said it was like a huge pair of pants and we all agreed. Like a giant saw something weird and got so freaked out he jumped out of his pants, and some day the guy will drop back down, fit into them perfectly, and walk away as if nothing has happened. But just to confirm that the big rock formation was really there, we threw rocks at it. They hit the sandstone surface and bounced off into the water. They made the same sound that all stones make when they hit something. Actually, that's not true. Stones make different sounds when they hit different things. But I don't want to make myself sound like an expert on rocks, or on throwing rocks at solid objects. I'd never thrown a rock before in my life. I'd never thrown anything.

Really? You've never played baseball?

You don't play baseball in a place where the average yearly temperature is five degrees below zero. I've never seen a baseball game. I've heard it's boring.

The studio audience laughed and laughed and laughed and laughed.

So tell us about yourself. You were born in Toledo?

That's right. I was born in Toledo and many other places since then.

Toledo like in Ohio, or Toledo like in Spain?

Toledo like in that famous El Greco painting, with a sky like aluminum foil.

I suppose you've heard that the words you said you saw on the stone have been confirmed by other people, but their guides have come up with different translations.

Nope. Haven't heard a thing.

Rex Torpedo smiled, and when he wiggled his ears, he looked like Casey Stengel, the legendary coach of the best and worst teams in baseball history.

The studio audience laughed and laughed and laughed and laughed and laughed.

It's true. The Inuit guides you relied on said the words meant "Something is always missing."

Right.

But another Inuit guide said the words meant "Nothing is ever missing." And another one said that the words meant ""Nothing is something else" or maybe "Nothing is anything else" or maybe "Nothing is everything else." And another one said that the words meant "Far from here" or "Far from nowhere."

He shrugged and yawned: So?

So?

Yeah. I mean, why so much emphasis on ancient inscriptions? Do you really think people knew more back then than they do now?

No, but—

People have always been full of shit. Far from here? Far from now? Who cares?

Okay. Let's change the subject: As a politician yourself, what do you think—

I'm not a politician. I hate politicians.

Okay. But as the mayor of the northernmost town in the world, what do you think of the current lame duck president, Barry Trap? What do you think of his claims that the election results were fake?

I think Barry Trap should bury himself. Just once, I think he should get caught in a real bear trap, and find out what it's like to chew off your own leg just to escape.

The studio audience laughed and then stopped.

Rex Torpedo stared at them and said: Not so funny this time, is it?

The host of the show looked embarrassed, then finally said: I've heard that in your official Arctic duties, you call yourself Lex Luthor, a comic book villain. Is that supposed to be a joke, the kind that no one gets? Are you for real?

I'm as real as anything else.

That's not saying much.

It's as much as I can say, as much as anyone can say.

The host got the word on her headset to make room for a commercial. A Liberty Mutual ad began, a guy with a blurred out face claiming that he was nothing like your typical consumer, since he was in a witness protection program, and his former self had become obsolete.

I closed my eyes and covered my ears. I'd sworn off TV ads three decades ago. I was having so much fun watching Rex Torpedo, I was caught off guard. I felt stupid. Why had I let myself get anywhere near a TV? I'd always seen them as sources of mainstream poison. I put a crumpled twenty-dollar bill on the table and rushed outside.

Over the next few days, I avoided the Internet. If the lame duck president had succeeded, learning how to put himself in the way of a lightning bolt, I didn't want to know anything about it. I might have had to abandon my plan if he'd gone through serious changes. Then Becky texted me to say that Haiku Style was almost ready. Three days after that, she had the computer chips and knew how to install them. She used her connections to get a White House appointment. I wasn't there, of course, but she told me later exactly what happened.

She walked into the Oval Office knowing that her breasts would make two strong first impressions. She also brought three party-size packages of Oreos, the double-stuff golden kind, the lame duck president's favorite food.

He said: Wow! You brought Oreos! I was going to compliment you on your boobs, but first I need a snack.

Becky said: No problem.

She put the Oreos on the lame duck president's desk. He sprayed a package with disinfectant before he opened it. Then he started stuffing his face, grunting frantically.

Becky said: While you're eating, can I use your phone? I forgot mine, and I need to call my neighbor to get him to walk my Saint Bernard. Or no, it's a New-foundland. Or no, it's a Great Dane. Or no, it's Mastiff. Yeah, I need to get my friend to walk my Mastiff. That sounds kind of sexual, doesn't it? Hey baby, walk my Mastiff!

The lame duck president pointed to his phone on the floor beside his desk, unwilling to interrupt his meal by talking.

Becky got the phone and pried it open. She pulled out several chips, took the new chips out of her purse and clicked them into the lame duck president's phone. Then she snapped the phone back together and put it back on the floor.

The lame duck president didn't notice a thing. He was too busy stuffing himself and his mouth was full, but he managed to say: These golden Oreos are way way better than the black ones! They're fucking awesome!

Becky said: They really are. I always get two packs of them on my way home. My Saint Bernard loves them!

The lame duck president said: It's a Mastiff. And don't interrupt me when I'm eating!

Sorry. I better be going now.

The lame duck president's mouth and hands were full of Oreos. He tried to be polite and say Nice meeting you. But partly-chewed cookies sprayed out of his mouth when he tried to speak.

As Becky walked out of the White House, she sent a text to the lame duck president's phone, a link that would appear on his screen as a full-color ad for double stuff Golden Oreos, an image that she knew he would study with pleasure before he clicked the link. The face penetration program she'd just installed would record the lame duck president's eager face, and when he clicked on the link "All You Need Is Food" would plant itself behind his eyes, filling his mind with a song that wouldn't stop playing. He would soon forget his own greedy thoughts, unable to avoid the revised big hit from the Summer of Love.

But the change took longer than Haiku Style predicted. For the next few days, nothing changed. The lame duck president was still enraged. Now there were hundreds of others who eagerly claimed they'd been hit by lightning, all of them with detailed, vivid accounts. Some of them talked about weird sounds making the sky seem thin as paper, as if a huge pen were preparing to write an incomprehensible sentence. These people were sure that nothing was ever missing, and equally sure that something was always missing. They talked as if lightning bolts were nothing more than parts of speech.

Rex Torpedo's Che-plus-Manson face was showing up everywhere, on posters taped on walls and telephone poles, as an online meme, on daytime soaps, in grad school seminar rooms, in horror films and left-wing documentaries, on advertising blimps and counterfeit money. Everyone now called him Rex the Lex or Lex the Rex or Luthor Lightning, and soon he was being touted as a presidential prospect, even though or perhaps because he hated politicians. The only problem was that no one could figure out if he was a Republican or a Democrat, especially since he repeatedly turned down social invitations by saying that he wasn't a party person.

There were also new translations of the Qarlinngua message, which apparently dated back to the early paleolithic period, when tribal magicians were making mysterious art on the walls of caves. Some of the new translations sounded like failed profundities, inept riddles, incompetent prophecies. Some of them made the inscription sound like advice or a cryptic warning; others made it sound like a salutation, or like a vicious insult aimed at the future, sneering at anyone dumb enough to think they could make a translation. Debates about which translation was right were raging all over the Internet, bitter conflicts between virtual scholars, and also talk show appearances by leaders of the psycholinguistic community, as if the future of language were at stake.

Everyone had forgotten about the election, even the lame duck president's closest allies, even the ones who tried to lynch Tim Pitchfork, the vice president, who refused to follow the president's orders and overturn the election results, even the ones who'd been inspired by Dick Bone and Mickey Finn, the president's most dangerous and patriotic henchmen, the same Dick Bone who had Richard Nixon's head tattooed on his back, the same Mickey Finn who'd been accused of treason, terribly clever people with ties to white supremacist networks, the Proud Pricks and the Shit Kickers, who led the fierce charge through police lines and barricades into the Capitol, howling and barfing their way through the Rotunda, slashing the paintings with knives and axes, ripping Trumbull's *Declaration of Independence* out of its frame, covering Franklin and Jefferson with shit and spilled domestic beer, pissing all over the inlaid patterns of tiles built into the hardwood floors, smashing doors and banisters and chandeliers and statues, throwing laptops through the line of arched windows facing the National Mall, setting piles of important papers on fire, posing for pictures that made them Internet superstars for a week or two, especially those who painted their faces and bodies red, white, and blue, wearing buffalo hides and viking helmets.

Now they barely remembered their violent fun. They didn't care about Qanon or Pizzagate any longer. Everyone now was focused on other things, deeply concerned with what might happen next, the sounds that might come out of the sky—not the sounds themselves, but all the things those sounds might be compared to.

But the song in the lame duck president's mind was inescapable, recomposing the stories he'd always told himself about himself. Within a few months, he'd joined the Green Party and was seeking their nomination for the next presidential election. He'd publicly distanced himself from right-wing agendas. The Republican party was a thing of the past. His platform called for raising taxes on the rich, switching trillions of dollars from the defense budget to world hunger foundations, creating hundreds of thousands of high-paying jobs in the environmental sector, dissolving all student loan debt, and imposing luxury taxes on Fortune 500 corporations to raise money for a universal health care system. He'd declared the northern coast of Ellesmere Island a national refuge, preventing tourist companies from invading the Qarlinngua zone, which would soon become a world heritage site.

Everyone wondered how he'd suddenly become such a thoughtful politician. He said he owed it all to a song in his head. People weren't sure what he meant, and when he sang the "All You Need is Food" refrain on Cable News, there were serious questions about copyright violations, not to mention his sanity. Everyone wondered why a mentally sound person would turn a great upbeat song into a blunt reminder that billions of people all over the world were starving.

A few months later he was dead, a bullet from his own pistol in his head, ten seconds after his final tweet, which said that he'd been driven mad by a song that wouldn't stop playing.

Stephen-Paul Martin has published many books of fiction, poetry, and non-fiction. His most recent collections of fiction are *The Ace of Lightning* (FC2, 2017) and *Changing the Subject* (Ellipsis Press, 2010). His 1992 book of stories, *The Gothic Twilight*, was nominated for the National Critics Circle Book Award. From 1980-1996 he edited *Central Park* magazine, a journal of the arts & social theory. He is the co-director of San Diego State University's MFA program.

Made in the USA
Las Vegas, NV
23 August 2023

76525908R00270